Hibiscus
Strong

Karen Hodges Miller

Open Door Publications

Hibiscus Strong
Copyright © 2024 by Karen Hodges Miller

ISBN: 978-1-7328202-9-6
Printed in the United States of America

This work is part memoir, part fiction. All the stories are as true as I can make them. While I obviously was not present for many of the events I relate, they are all based on stories told to me by my family.

I have researched as thoroughly as possible not only my family history, but what was happening in Miami at the time. Sometimes the dates and facts I found did not line up with exactly how the stories have been told to me. I tried to make adjustments to be as accurate as possible while still using Mark Twain's advice, "Never let the truth get in the way of a good story," as my guiding principle.

Published by

Open Door Publications

Willow Spring, NC

Cover design: SweetnSpicyDesigns.com

For my family—past, present, and future

About the Cover Photo

The photo of the woman on the cover was adapted from a black and white photo taken of my grandmother, Agnes Sawieja Rogers, sometime in 1922 or 1923. The original photo that my grandmother kept in one of her many boxes of family memorabilia was cropped so that the fisherman's fork was cut off in an awkward way. I want to give special thanks to my friend Steve Procko for working his photographic magic on the original and completing it in a seamless way for the graphic artist, Jaycee DeLorenzo of Sweet N Spicy Designs, to use. You can find more about the history of this photo and the original photographer as you read *Hibiscus Strong*. I don't want to give all the secrets away here, in hopes that you will enjoy the treasure hunt to learn more about its origins as you read the book.

Contents

Introduction
On the Porch

All families have stories they tell at every gathering, from Sunday dinners to funerals to afternoon picnics until everyone knows them so well that they are boiled down to a punchline. "Do you remember the time Uncle Bill drove the car into the lake?" Or "You know, Aunt Harriet could never cook. Remember when she left the Christmas turkey in the oven overnight?"

That's all that needs to be said before everyone laughs. They already know that Uncle Bill never drank but his younger brother had slipped bourbon in his Coca-Cola. They know that Aunt Harriet's dog began barking when smoke began to pour from the stove, waking everybody up so no one was injured, the firemen put out the fire quickly, and Aunt Harriet got the brand-new beautiful kitchen she had always wanted.

Sometimes, however, the details of the story that are lost over time are the most important parts of all. And then there are the tales that aren't told, only whispered. They are too tragic or they just make us too uncomfortable because they tell a truth about ourselves or our families we don't want to hear.

My family was no different than any other; we had stories we told and those we did not. And as time marches on, and we get farther and farther from the people and events in each anecdote, this collective wisdom is lost and forgotten. But the personalities involved are more important than just the funny or happy or scary story. These are the fabric of a family, part of what makes each of us unique and makes us who we are, even if we no longer know why. They are the shape of a hand, an expression on a face, a way of walking—the little things that make each one of us individual and at the same time connect us to our ancestors, even when we no longer realize it.

I come from a family of immigrants. By that I don't mean that we came from a foreign land, although if you go back far enough, all of us did. I mean that in the early part of the 20th century, each of my family members came from Missouri or Ohio or Georgia and ended up in Miami, Florida—the last frontier on the East Coast of the United States.

They came for different reasons: a new opportunity, a job, escape from a controlling family, or just for the wonderful weather. They brought stories of their own childhoods, of the reasons why they came to Miami. Many of the settlers who came to Florida in the late 1800s took one look at the endless miles of sawgrass and scrub pine, the swarms of mosquitoes so large in number they could kill a herd of cattle in one night, the sudden torrential downpours, and of course, the hurricanes, and they turned right around.

But there were others, like my family, who stayed.

Florida history is fascinating, and I've always been proud my family played a part in it, no matter how tiny. My family drove the trains, strung the electrical wires, and ran the plumbing pipes. And because the town was so small, some of my family bumped elbows with many of the famous and infamous.

My great-grandfather, Herbert Spencer Roberts, worked for Henry Flagler, who built the Florida East Coast Railway. When his children were born, they were delivered by Dr. James Jackson, the first doctor in Miami for whom the world-renowned Jackson Memorial Hospital was named. My grandparents knew Marjorie Stoneman Douglas, who wrote *The Everglades, River of Grass*, a quintessential book about the environment that changed the way people thought about learning to live with this unique land rather than trying to conquer it.

On a slightly less savory note, Herb's son, my grandfather Bert, was Al Capone's plumber when the gangster lived on Palm Island in the 1930s and '40s. He never actually saw Capone, but Mrs. Capone "was very polite and always paid in cash," he told us. Slightly closer to home, we were related by marriage—for a short time, anyway—to "one of the biggest bootleggers in south Florida." That's how my grandmother described him. She hadn't liked that particular brother-in-law very much, but she seemed to respect his family's ability to make good liquor.

Yes, Florida, and Miami in particular, seems to have always attracted a certain number of eccentrics. And no matter who they are or why they come, they are changed by the land.

I call the matriarchs in my family "Hibiscus Strong," the

South Florida version of the Steel Magnolia. Magnolias are fragile flowers, a bland pale white. Hibiscuses come in vibrant colors—orange, yellow, red, hot pink—just like the women in my family. They were, and are, sassy, strong, self-reliant, and with an extra dose of the Florida quirkiness that comes from knowing every time you take your garbage out—whether it is real or metaphorical—you just might encounter an alligator in your backyard.

These are the tales I want to tell. The tales of my family, the women and the men, the good and the bad. Some are heroes, others are not. There is an old Southern truism, "In the South, we don't hide our crazy relatives in the attic; we put them on the front porch and hand them a cocktail." Some of the people in this book are just those characters we put on the porch and hand a cocktail—or a Coca-Cola. Both beverages were very important in my family—even more important than sweet tea.

If you could ask my grandparents or parents, they would shrug their shoulders and say, "I never did anything important. Why are you writing about me?" But everyone's story is important. And if some of my family members would have been embarrassed to find themselves in a book, at the very least they will not be forgotten.

Chapter 1
Heat—and Snow

Heat isn't just something you feel. Heat needs all your senses to really experience it—touch, sight, taste, smell. You can even hear heat.

Heat is itchy, scratchy, prickly. Stiff blades of St. Augustine grass tickle sweaty legs and arms as you lie in the sun, panting after a swift game of tag.

Heat is the sun's glaring light reflected on rows of white tile roofs, sparkling so brightly you have to squint to look at them, or the waving reflections drifting up from the sand as you run tiptoe across the beach to sooth scorched toes in the ocean.

Heat is the taste of a Coca-Cola, chugged straight out of a sweating glass bottle you pull from the ice chest at the 7-Eleven.

Heat is the sweet smell of night-blooming jasmine, the moldy smell of cut grass in piles, the odd potato-like odor of melaleuca trees, all mixed with that hint of salt that blows in from the ocean and pervades the air night and day.

Heat is the noise of a lawn mower breaking the silence of a quiet afternoon, the high whine of crickets in the night, the soft shooshing of palm fronds moving slowly in the breeze.

Heat. All of my earliest memories begin with heat.

~~~

"Mama, when will it snow?"

That was my sister, Cheryl Anne. It was a hot December evening, and we'd just finished watching *Frosty the Snowman*. Only the family called my sister by both of her names. Everyone else just called her Cheryl. I called her Chera-lanne, hitting a high note on the second syllable and dragging "lanne" out as long as I could in my best Southern drawl. It always irritated her. You just can't drag out "Karen Lee" the way you can Cheryl Anne.

"Never," Mama replied to her question. "We wouldn't have a Miami if it snowed here."

"But Mama, it must snow sometimes."

"I've seen snow, you wouldn't like it, Cheryl Anne," Grandma Rogers said in her gravelly cigarette voice. Grandma

Rogers was the only one in the family who could make that claim.

"But I want it to snow. If I pray hard enough, will God make it snow?"

My sister was stubborn. She always thought if she fought hard enough, whined hard enough, prayed hard enough, everyone would eventually come around to her way of thinking and do what she wanted them to do.

It usually worked. But not this time. Even my sister couldn't make it snow in Miami.

Well, all right, the National Weather Service did record a few flakes in 1977, and Cheryl did get to see them, but that was long after this story takes place, and not my tale to tell. So let me repeat what I just said:

It never snows in Miami.

It was the same in every household in Miami after the children watched one of those sentimental Christmas movies that end with beautiful, fluffy white stuff floating down and covering the landscape.

Just like my sister, the children don't believe it at first. They are sure their parents are wrong. It takes many years for them to believe that not only is there no Santa Claus, they really will never see snow if they don't travel outside Miami—far outside Miami. All the way to the North, like maybe Georgia or the Carolinas.

Cheryl Anne and I wanted to see snow. We wanted it desperately. For years we prayed at night for snow. Just a little bit. On Christmas Eve. And God, if we couldn't have snow, could we at least have cold weather? You know, cold enough that we could wear the crocheted shawls Grandma Hodges made for us to Midnight Mass without sweating to death?

Snow is an endlessly fascinating topic to Miami children. The ones who have lived in the North or visited there during the winter are constantly questioned. What does it look like? How cold is it? (And we don't believe them when they tell us. We can't imagine anything *that* cold.) We are sure it all comes down in a big white lump at the beginning of October and just stays that way, a fluffy, pristine white carpet, covering the ground until May. After all, in those Christmas movies the snow seems to pile up a foot high in just a few minutes, and they never talk about it leaving. You never see the gray slushy mess or the black ice. And Christmas movies make shoveling snow look like fun. Ha!

A few days after that conversation with Mama and Grandma Rogers, we went to buy our Christmas tree in a big, vacant lot on Biscayne Boulevard. Mama had picked us up right after she finished teaching. She wore my favorite green dress with the wide skirt, stockings, and pointy-toed pumps. Not the perfect outfit for standing in the heat and sand, but she only had so much time after school and lots to do. Luckily, we'd had time to change out of our gray and white school uniforms and wore shorts, t-shirts, and sneakers as we stood sweating in the 90-degree heat, unrelieved by even the tiny shade of a palm tree.

"A new shipment is just coming in, ma'am," the Christmas tree guy said. "You'll get a better selection if you wait a few minutes."

"Oh Mama, do we have to?" I whined. Even at seven or eight years old I wasn't into waiting around for things like the perfect tree. Cheryl was.

And so we waited, along with several other families who happened up in the next few minutes. Finally, a big tractor-trailer came rumbling down the boulevard and into the lot. The driver swung out and smiled at all the children waiting for a Christmas tree. It must have made him feel like Santa Claus to see all these kids waiting anxiously for him to arrive.

"Come with me, kids," he said as he walked to the back of the truck. "When I open the doors, you'll see snow on the Christmas trees."

He opened the truck, and we all crowded around. He was right! White, icy stuff lay on the stacks of pines and spruces. I wonder now if the bits of white stuff clinging here and there to the branches were really snow or if just frost from the refrigerated air piped inside to keep those cold-blooded Northern evergreens alive. At the time it didn't matter, of course. We were thrilled. We'd seen snow!

~~~

I was sixteen when I saw my first real snowfall—not just frost in a truck. We were visiting friends in Boone, North

Carolina, for Thanksgiving, and when we got up one morning we saw about a half an inch of snow on the grass and on the hoods of the cars. I carefully collected as much as I could, saved it in a paper cup, and put it in the cooler we kept in the car. I babied that cup of flakes for the rest of the trip, checking on it so often that it probably helped it to melt more quickly.

I cherished it throughout the trip and, even though it was just a cup of water by the time we reached home, on Monday morning I took it to school as if I were six years old again, and this was my show-and-tell exhibit.

"This was snow! It was really snow! I saw snow!"

I had proven the myth. I'd seen it with my own eyes and brought some home as a trophy. Everyone gathered around and oohed and ahhed over that little cup of water. And remember, we were high schoolers.

That is the mystique of snow in Miami.

~~~

In fact, the only reason Miami exists is because it didn't snow there one year. After learning it will never be cold enough for frozen precipitation of any kind in Miami, the next thing children learn is the story of Julia Tuttle and Her Oranges.

You've never heard of Julia Tuttle? She is famous. In South Florida, at least. Julia Tuttle is the Mother of Miami, and the story goes like this.

Back in the 1890s, the Tuttle family owned a lot of land in South Florida, and not much else. They grew oranges, but that didn't really make them a lot of money.

Then the rumors started. Henry Flagler was going to bring his railroad all the way down the east coast of Florida, bringing hotels and tourists and MONEY along with it.

Julia was excited. She couldn't wait. Since most of her land was in the northern half of what was to become the City of Miami, she knew she was going to be rich. But Mr. Flagler stopped his railroad in the town of Fort Pierce, 129 miles north of Miami. It might as well have stopped at the North Pole for all the good that was going to do Julia.

She went back to her orange grove, but her dream never died.

Then came the Great Freeze of 1895/96. It was a disaster. The tourists shivered on the north Florida beaches, then packed their suitcases and headed back home. Worse still for the state's economy, oranges froze on their branches, and many of the trees were damaged or died.

Except in the very southern tip of mainland Florida.

Julia had an idea. She packed some beautiful, healthy, frost-free oranges in a box and sent them to Mr. Flagler. He got the message. He expanded his railroad the rest of the way down the coast.

The town had a little less than five hundred souls when that first train, which happened to have been driven by my great-grandfather Herbert Spencer Rogers, pulled into the station.

Chapter 2
A Christmas Fire

1896

It was supposed to be a tropical paradise. That was what Mr. Flagler said when he told Herb he was moving him from the Jacksonville/Fort Pierce route to the new Miami run of the Florida East Coast Railway. It was an honor, Mr. Flagler said, to be the engineer on the first run. An expression of how much he valued him as an employee. If the run was successful, Herb would have the position permanently, and he should think about relocating his family there. But Herb's wife, Mary, wanted to be sure this newfangled idea of a daily train south to the wilderness was going to work before she made another move. She wasn't on this first train. She and their two boys, Leo and Eddie, were waiting back in Fort Pierce.

It was too dark in the town for Herb to see much of anything as the fifteen-inch wood-burning Schenectady engine pulled five cars into the station at nine p.m. on the night of April 22, 1896. *Well, 'station' is a pretty highfalutin word for a wooden platform with just a tiny telegraph office at one end,* he thought.

As soon as the train had fully stopped, Mr. Flagler, dressed in a frock coat and top hat, hopped off and greeted the few people who had come out to meet them. The infamous Mrs. Tuttle was there, Herb noted. She was the one who had pushed and pushed to get the track run all the way down to Miami. Half of Florida knew Mrs. Tuttle. Of course, there were so few people living on the southeast coast that it was more like one long, skinny small town than a large portion of a state.

"We'd planned some speeches," she heard the woman say, "but with the train so late, most everybody already headed home."

Herb jumped down from the engine and headed back to the caboose to get his bag, wondering where he could get a room for the night. He could see a few wooden buildings lined up along the street so he and his conductor, Ed Steinhauser, headed that way.

"It's a pretty hard-looking hole, ain't it?" commented Ed.

"Sure is. I can't see asking Mary to bring the boys down here to live, at least not yet," Herb replied.

"Maybe it will look better in the daylight."

"When did you get to be such an optimist?" Herb laughed.

They had asked a few people at the station where to get a room. The Hotel Miami, one man said, was their best bet. It wasn't finished, but they could probably snag a blanket and a spot on the floor. Someone else suggested they try Captain Vail's, an old river steamship that had been turned into a hotel. It was moored at the mouth of the Miami River, down near the bay. Other than that, there were some tents in the woods outside town, and maybe someone would be kind enough to let them stay, but the man didn't recommend it. You never knew who was living out there at any given moment. Could be a mite dangerous.

Herb and Ed headed east, toward where they knew the water was, even though they couldn't see it.

"Looks like they've got big plans around here," Herb said as they walked.

The streets had already been laid out, even though almost no buildings had been built. Trees had been grubbed up, and rocks lined the dirt paths, showing the layout for the eventual "Magic City," as the town's movers and shakers were calling it. The debris was piled so high you couldn't see anything over it, not even Biscayne Bay; they knew must be just up ahead because they could hear the water lapping softly again the shore.

The April night was sultry, but after a day spent next to the firebox of a steam engine, the light breeze was refreshing. It was warmer than it had been a hundred miles north in Fort Pierce. The crickets were chirping, and the scent of the night-blooming jasmine and gardenias, already in flower here, was in the air.

Another noise assaulted their ears as they neared the edge of town. Two saloons stood side by side; they could hear a piano playing and the shouts of men who had obviously had a few too many. One of the buildings had a sign, "Woods' Saloon," over the door, and two men came bursting out taking jabs at each other. One of the men fell at their feet, scrambled up, then turned to continue the fight. The two trainmen stepped around them and kept on their way.

As they reached the water they could see where an old side-wheeler steamboat was moored. "Captain Vail's Floating Hotel," proclaimed a large sign hung from poles at the foot of the dock. Another nearby sign advertised "Fresh Fish and Oysters."

"I hope to God he's got a room," said Ed as they walked down the planks. "I don't fancy sleeping on a floor tonight."

"I hear you."

They knocked politely on the cabin door. An older man of about sixty opened it, still pulling on a navy coat over a white dress shirt with the collar off.

"Captain Vail? We heard you might have a room or two available," Ed said.

"I've got a few open tonight. You come from the train?"

"Yes, we just drove it into the station, and we don't head back until the day after tomorrow. We sure could use a couple of beds."

"Yep, got two rooms, $2.50 each per night."

"That's awful high, ain't it?" put in Herb.

"You see any other hotels with beds around here?" the captain asked.

"He's right, Herb."

Herb sighed and dug into his pocket.

~~~

The town didn't improve much the next morning when they saw it in the light of day. Oh, the weather was beautiful. The sky was a clear, deep blue mottled with huge, white, puffy clouds, and a slight breeze always cooled things as it blew in from the bay.

It was hard to believe anyone was going to want to live here, though. If you crawled over the downed trees and huge rock piles. If you ignored the tents lining the shore of the bay and the wet laundry hanging from lines around each tent. If you disregarded the dozens of empty barrels and other trash strewn around the shore, you could see the beautiful view of the barrier islands and glimpse the ocean beyond. Yes, if they could just clean it up and build it up, this town was going to be magic, just like everyone here claimed.

~~~

Herb drove his engine into the city every few days for months, and each time it seemed as if it had grown a little more. In July the town fathers incorporated it as The City of Miami, the "Magic City," with 444 residents, the new local newspaper proudly declared. A few months later the first Catholic church opened. Herb was happy to tell Mary about that, especially since it seemed he was spending more nights at Captain Vail's Floating Hotel each week than he was at home. Knowing there was a church would make it easier for her to move.

Herb had gotten to be good friends with Captain Edward Vail, one of the many characters who had heard the siren call of Miami and moved down to make his fortune. He was "a rough-talking old buzzard," Herb and Ed agreed. A born storyteller, he never passed up an opportunity to sit down with his guests, share a beer, and talk about all he had seen and done.

Captain Vail was born in Massachusetts and became a sailor with a steamship company at the beginning of the Civil War. He'd been given command of his own vessel during the last couple of years of the war, patrolling the blockade and making sure that supplies did not reach the Confederates.

After the war he opened a hotel in St. Augustine, but when it burned, he purchased an old steamship, the Rockledge, and converted it into a floating hotel, complete with kitchen to serve his guests. The ship could easily move up and down the coast to wherever the need for a hotel was greatest. And in 1896, that was Miami, which was attracting people faster than they could construct buildings to house them.

In typical Miami fashion, where records for "biggest," "fastest," and "newest," were broken daily, the floating hotel only remained the town's largest for a few more months until the Royal Palm and the Hotel Miami were completed the following year.

~~~

On Christmas evening of 1896, Herb's train pulled into the station filled with Northerners ready to spend a few days of their Christmas holiday in the warmth of sunny Miami.

The town had grown considerably in the nine months that Herb had been on the route. The Hotel Miami now had furnished rooms and beds to offer customers. The Royal Palm Hotel, which had been built by Mr. Flagler himself as a smaller sister to his Royal Poinciana Hotel in Palm Beach, was scheduled to be finished in a few more months.

"I'm glad I got to spend Christmas morning with Leo and Eddie," he told Steinheiser, referring to his two sons. "I feel like I'm missing so much."

"Mary still not ready to move down here to 'the wilderness?'"

"I'm getting closer to convincing her. I think she's starting to see that I'll be home more nights with the family if she's down here than if she stays in Fort Pierce."

They were walking to the Floating Hotel where Captain Vail kept two rooms ready for them on the nights they were in town. There was always a little something waiting in the dining room for them, too, even if the train was delayed.

"Merry Christmas! I've got a couple of Florida lobsters waiting for you boys," Captain Vail called out as they reached the dock.

"You've got a heart bigger than that Royal Palm Hotel is going to be," Herb told him, slapping him on the back.

"Yeah, and that's the problem. When that place opens up, I'm thinking there won't be any more need for a floating hotel here. I don't know where I'm going to go next. This was pretty much the last undeveloped town on the coast."

"We'll miss you, that's for sure," said Ed. "But I understand your point. Even Herb and I won't be needing hotel rooms much longer. Some of the railroaders have already moved their families down here, and Herb's angling to get his family down, too. If they come my wife will follow. Those big hotels are for the tourists; the people who are going to build this town are going to want houses, not just rooms."

"Well, that sounds like a solid plan. What this town needs is more families and fewer single men looking to get rich quick— and those are the kind that come to me. The people here need to start thinking like the city they want to be, not just a collection of buildings. Look at this article the *Metropolis* put out this week."

Vail handed over a copy of the weekly newspaper. Owned by Mr. Flagler (*Wasn't everything?* Herb thought), it had printed its first edition just a few months before.

Herb read out loud. "'Miami has been very fortunate so far, not having a fire alarm. We tremble when we contemplate our exposed condition and how inadequate we would be to handle a fire if one should be started.' They're right," he added. "Everything down here is built of wood. All it would take is one spark and everything could go up. This town is growing; most places this size have a fire department and some kind of equipment."

"That's why we need more families like yours here," Vail said. "Single men don't think ahead. They just think about how much money they can make today. It takes women who want to protect their children to think about the future."

The men chatted on amiably as Christmas fireworks rose over the town, then headed off to their rooms for the night.

~~~

The noise of shouting and running feet woke Herb at about two a.m. He groggily rose and looked out the window.

Fire! The sight cleared his head of sleepiness immediately. He could see smoke and flames rising from the buildings down in town.

"Vail! Wake up! The whole town's on fire!" he called out as he hastily pulled on his clothes. He pounded on the doors of Ed's and Captain Vail's rooms, then on the other rooms he ran past, all the while yelling, "Fire! Fire!"

He headed down the gangplank and quickly joined a bucket brigade that was already working to put out the blaze that had started at E.L. Brady's grocery store. Men and women lined up to pass buckets of water, but they were no match for the brisk wind blowing in from the bay.

Herb saw Julia Tuttle organizing everything, sending some men to find more buckets, others to check the nearby buildings and make sure everyone was awake and out of any structures in danger of burning. Many of the buildings were two-stories, with businesses on the lower floors and apartments opening onto long porches on the second floor. People could easily be trapped upstairs. He knew one of the other engineers with the FEC, Ed Davies, had rented an apartment for his family in one of those buildings. He was glad to see the man already in the line passing buckets of water.

"Good to see you made it out," Herb said.

"Yeah, I came out the door to head to the station, and I saw everything burning. I roused Dr. Jackson—he lives a few doors down, you know, and we sounded the alarm," Davies told him, referring to the town's first, and so far only, doctor.

"Your wife and kids okay?"

"Shaken up, but nobody's hurt. We're going to lose everything, but as long as we're all together we'll just start again."

Herb passed buckets as he watched the fire quickly spread to the neighboring bank building, a pool hall, and beyond. Even though the conflagration was out in two hours, almost half the buildings in town had been destroyed.

Exhausted men and women sat on the streets wondering what they would do next. Herb felt sorry for them. Only one man had died, but so many of these people had lost everything. What would they do now? Would the little town at the southern end of the mainland be able to survive this disaster?

As Herb was heading toward the station to make sure there was no damage to his engine, he heard a new commotion. A group of men were lined up on the tracks drinking.

"Where'd you men get all that liquor?" Herb called out.

"It's from Mr. Lossly and Mr. Reneke's store," one man responded. He held out a bottle toward Herb. "You want some? There's plenty."

"Of course, I don't want some. You men are stealing," he said indignantly.

"No, we aren't," another man said, swaying and burping. "We're rescuing it. It was locked up 'cuz there's an ordinance against selling liquor. It was going to burn up. We had to rescue it."

"Well, you men get off the tracks. The trains still need to run today. You're holding up progress."

Herb impatiently waved them off and walked on to the station. The trains and the tracks were fine; the fire had not spread this far. He would be driving back to Fort Pierce this afternoon.

After catching a few hours' sleep back at the floating hotel, he and Ed returned to the station several hours later. The town already had a different feel. Instead of the exhausted men and women sitting in despair, now it was filled with people busily cleaning up debris and bringing in lumber and bricks from the storage yard behind the hardware store to reframe and rebuild what had been lost over night.

"Well, it looks like I was wrong," Herb said to Ed.

"Wrong about what?"

"I thought that fire was the end of Miami. I figured the town would just dry up and people would move on somewhere else. But not these people. They're determined to make something of this place, even if it is the back of the beyond. *They're pretty good about making something out of nothing here,* Herb thought. *It's the kind of place I want my kids to grow up.*

"We've still got a little time before we fire up the engine. I saw a 'for rent' sign on a house over on Second Street," he told Ed. "I'm going to stop in and put some money down. There's a lot of people going to need new homes. I better get one while I can."

Chapter 3
The Gold Coast Railroad

Miami is a city of color. Vibrant, tropical colors assault the eyes wherever you look. The cool turquoise of the ocean, the green palms framed by deep blue sky, and huge, white clouds. The deep reds and vivid yellows of hibiscus and ixora, the watermelon-colored bougainvillea and orange poinciana trees. And all are punctuated by row after row of pink and yellow and purple and green and blue houses topped with red and white tile roofs. Vibrant. Hot. Tropical. Sultry. Everywhere you look.

But the old Blimp Base was gray. The gray concrete skeletons of the three blimp hangars stood sixteen and half stories tall, towering over the dull green sawgrass and scrub pines that were all that would grow in the fine gray-white sand covering the area.

The Blimp Base was in the wastelands—so far south that it wasn't really Miami, so far west that it wasn't the city of Homestead, either. Cheryl and I thought of it as the wilderness, and we used to pretend we were pioneers traveling in a covered wagon whenever we went there since it seemed to take at least an hour. At that time the Palmetto Bypass wasn't finished, and the Turnpike Extension was barely a dream. If you had asked my grandparents if they thought the city would ever grow far enough west that people would build houses out there, they would have laughed. If you told my city-loving sister, Cheryl, that one day she would live that far from the center of Miami, she would have cried.

We could see the concrete towers for several miles before we ever got to the base. The hangars had been built in World War II to house the blimps that scoured the ocean looking for Nazi ships. Yes, there really were Nazi ships off the coast of Miami in World War II. Every time we went down to the Blimp Base, Mama would tell us how in high school she and her friends would drive to the beach to look for German ships hovering just offshore.

But the Blimp Base had burned in 1945, thanks to the

wooden structures that were attached to those giant concrete skeletons. They caught fire in a hurricane and, as the war ended just a few months later, the base was never rebuilt. The two thousand acres of dusty gray land was considered pretty useless and were donated to the University of Miami.

And there it sat empty for years and years until the university allowed a portion of the land to be used by the Gold Coast Railroad Museum. That was the fancy name a group of old railroad buffs had given to their collection of steam engines, railroad cars, and other memorabilia of the Florida East Coast Railway, most of which was way too big to be housed anywhere other than the wilderness.

The group laid a circular track of about five miles, and four or five times a year they opened the museum to visitors who would come to learn about Florida's history and ride in circles around the scrub pine and sawgrass. No fake Indian attacks or train robberies or anything kitschy and touristy here. In the land that had made its reputation on attracting snowbirds with mermaid shows, gator wrestling, and trained dolphins, the Gold Coast Railroad was different. It had trains. Just trains.

Almost every weekend the museum was open, Mama and Granddad and Grandma Rogers took us down. I loved it. Granddad loved it, too. You see, our family had a special connection to the Gold Coast Railroad because the star of the museum, the engine that was used to pull everyone around those few miles of track, was the Old 153. And the 153 had been my great-grandfather Herbert Spencer Roger's last engine.

Herb had driven several engines during his more than thirty years at the Florida East Coast Railway, but the Old 153 was special. He pulled the train carrying Calvin Coolidge to Miami in 1928 with that locomotive. And he ran it daily from Miami to Key West on the Overseas Railroad until most of the bridges on the 300-mile track known as "Flagler's Folly" was destroyed in the Hurricane of 1932. In fact, it was the last engine to reach Miami before the hurricane struck that day.

My granddad, Herb's son Bert, knew all the old railroaders who now volunteered their time at the museum just for the love of steam engines. While all the other kids' parents had to pay fifty cents to ride the train maybe once around the track, my sister and I usually got to ride more. If it was crowded we would ride in the passenger car or the dining car first. Then the second trip was for the caboose, our very favorite car, with its ladder up to a wooden platform where the trainmen had once rested.

But best of all was when one of Granddad's friends was driving the 153 and we were allowed to ride in the engine. It was hot and crowded and uncomfortable and noisy and dirty. The fireman would shovel wood into the burner as the train pulled out. The 153 would puff a cloud of steam back at us, coating us in wet, sweaty dust, then the engineer would pull a cord, and the whistle would blast so loudly that we had to cover our ears.

It was heaven.

Yes, the 153 was special, and not just to me. In fact, it still is. The engine is listed on the National Register of Historic Places. Although it hasn't actually run in many years and the museum has moved from the Old Blimp Base to a new location a few counties up the coast, it is still the pride and joy of the Gold Coast Railroad Museum. It is a Pacific-type passenger steam locomotive that ran on the Florida East Coast Railway from 1922 until 1939.

But even though the Hurricane of 1932 is the one everyone in Florida always talked about, at least until Hurricane Andrew in the 1990s, that wasn't the hurricane that my great-grandfather remembered. It wasn't the hurricane my family talked about over and over again. The hurricane my great-grandfather talked about was the Hurricane of 1919.

Chapter 4
The Hurricane

1919

"I don't like it. You know the Weather Bureau says there's a hurricane coming."

"Mary, the Weather Bureau is about as reliable as a chocolate teapot," Herbert scoffed.

His reaction didn't sit well with his wife. Mary sniffed loudly, trying to make the sound scornful, but he knew very well she was trying to hide her tears. After almost thirty years of marriage, she couldn't fool him. Mary didn't like his job. Well, that wasn't strictly true. She used to like it. She had liked it until five years ago. That was when he'd switched from the Miami-to-St. Augustine run to the Key West run.

It paid more and was only a half-day trip, which theoretically meant he was home most nights. He only had to stay over in the Keys if there was a problem. However, there were a lot of those. Even five years after its inaugural run, Mr. Flagler's Overseas Railroad was still called "Flagler's Folly" by most Miamians. And that was Mary's issue. The daily trip to Key West was dangerous.

Thunderstorms popped up unexpectedly, and lightning was wildly attracted to the one-hundred-and-sixty-four miles of iron track that snaked through the islands from Miami to Key West. Bridges seemed to go down at any and every moment—and with several dozen bridges ranging from tiny spans of a few yards to the wonderous Seven Mile Bridge, something was always going wrong.

"I'll be home tonight with nothing more exciting than a little rain to tell you about," Herb said, trying to reassure her. He got up from the kitchen table and gave her a long kiss. "Don't you worry about me—and don't worry about what those people at the Weather Bureau say. They get it right less than half the time."

He headed to the back door, but then stopped and turned.

"Come on, Bert. You don't want to be late."

His son, Bert, ran out behind him, the screen door slamming as he jumped the five steps that raised their bungalow higher than flood level. At sixteen he was 5'11", a hair taller than Herb, with sandy brown hair and deep blue eyes that looked just like Mary's. Bert tried so hard to be a man, but now, swinging his lunch pail wildly as he walked next to his father, Herb could still very much see the boy he used to be.

They headed down Fifth Street to the train station at First and First, the intersection of Northeast First Street and Northeast First Avenue. The street names were a testimony to the optimism of the town fathers who had laid out the City of Miami in four quadrants back when they founded the town in the 1890s. Herb thought about his first trip into Miami. It had been twenty-three years this past April since Mr. Flagler had entrusted him with driving the first train into the city. He snorted and shook his head. Bert looked at him questioningly.

"I was just thinking about when we first got here," Herb told him. "I'm surprised your mom didn't put your two big brothers on her hip and jump on the first train back to Ohio."

"Why would she have wanted to do that?" Bert asked. "She always says Miami is so much better than it was up North."

"Well, back then it wasn't the big town it is now. Do you know I read in the *Gazette* that there are almost 40,000 people here now? Back when your mom and I got here there were only about 400. Actually, she wouldn't move down here from Fort Pierce until Gesu Church opened up, a few months after I started on this run."

Bert nodded in understanding. His mom attended Mass every single Sunday—missing one was impossible to fathom.

"So why did she stay?"

"Well, truthfully, we didn't have any place else to go. There wasn't enough work up North, and so when I heard about Mr. Flagler's new railroad, I jumped on the chance. But it's been hard on your mom, you know. Leaving all her family behind."

"Well, there's enough of us now," said Bert. "She can't miss family when there's seven of us—eight if you count Sadie."

The disdain for his oldest brother Leo's wife was evident in his voice. Bert might only be sixteen, and one of the youngest of the Rogers brood, but more and more he was the one his siblings turned to when they had a problem. He had quit school after eighth grade and gone to work as a baggage handler at the railroad station, bringing his salary home to his mom like the good boy he was. Herb hoped to get him an apprenticeship on an engine someday soon.

Yes, times had gotten a lot better for the Rogers family since they had moved to Miami, some of the first of a long stream of Northerners searching for a better life in paradise. The two oldest boys had been born in Ohio, but the rest of them were true Miamians. Their third child, Stella, was even the second baby born in the entire City of Miami.

She and her sister Anna Mae made things easier for Mary now by helping around the house, although he'd bet it wouldn't be long before Stella married her beau, Stanley. The boy wasn't a railroad man, but he had a good steady job as a painter, and he treated Stella well.

As they turned a corner, the wooden train station came into view. Herb took his bandana out of his pocket and wiped his forehead. The air was sticky and heavy today, and it was only eight a.m.

"Sure is a hot one today, isn't it?" his son said. "It feels like hurricane weather."

"Now don't you start. You've been listening to your mom too much," he grumbled as they reached the station.

Bert laughed and, with a quick wave, headed off to join his fellow baggage handlers as Herb headed into the yard to check over the train before the run.

"Hey, Herb! Have you heard about the storm?" Charley, his conductor, asked.

"Come on, Charley, you know you can't believe anything the Weather Bureau says. Those 'forecasters' have as much luck telling us what the weather will be as a fortune teller with a crystal ball."

"Well, they predicted that bad rainstorm last week," Charley countered.

"And we're supposed to be impressed?" Herb scoffed. "It rains almost every day in Miami this time of year."

"Yeah, but it's just got that feel to it today, ya know? I've lived in Florida all my life, and I know hurricane weather when I see it."

Charley was an old-timer; he'd been born in Florida, and he never let anyone forget it. His parents had come here when the Everglades stretched almost to the Atlantic Ocean and the Seminole Indians were known to raid the small, isolated settlements. That is until Julie Tuttle had sent oranges to Mr. Flagler. That was when the yearly trickle of settlers to South Florida had become a flood. Charley loved to remind Herb that he was a "true" Floridian while Herb had spent the first twenty-five years of his life as a Northerner.

"Well, let's just get those passengers on the train so we can leave on time, old man," Herb told Charley.

"Since when have you ever had to worry about me making the train late?" Charley asked, feigning offense.

But he turned and walked away, calling "All aboard! All aboard for Homestead and Key West."

In no time the last of the luggage was loaded, the freight cars as well as the tanker cars filled with fresh water for the people of Key West were checked, and the passengers were ushered aboard. As the train headed out, Herb let off steam and blew his whistle as he passed Bert moving bags and boxes off *The Havana Special,* which had just arrived from New York.

Bert waved, and a moment later the station was out of sight as he was headed through the sawgrass to the town of Homestead, the last town on the Florida mainland.

~~~

It was a beautiful day for the trip to Key West. Herb never got tired of the view. Some people might think it was the same every day, just mile after mile of ocean dotted with mangrove islands linked together by bridge after bridge, but Herb had learned the nuances of the Keys.

The smaller islands were just mangrove swamps and birds. Sometimes it seemed as if there weren't enough tree branches for all of them. Herb had learned their names and enjoyed teaching them to his kids whenever he had the time. The great white herons stalked slowly and majestically, always alone.

The double-tailed black frigate birds glided silently, high in the sky. The noisy pelicans and seagulls swooped and played, ducking into the water to catch fish.

Crossing the larger islands, he saw the occasional tiny key deer hiding in the bushes. And, of course, there were the homesteads where families of fishermen lived, sometimes only one or two houses, sometimes as many as twelve or fourteen making a settlement together. He'd often see fishing boats out on either the ocean side or the gulf side, but as they drew closer and closer to Key West, Herb noticed that today they were all tied up at their docks.

Still, as they crossed the final bridge into Key West, Herb forgot to worry about the fishing boats. It was an old town, almost as old as Toledo, and its grand Victorian houses reminded Herb of his old home—if you dipped Toledo in a bucket of rainbow paint, that is. Toledo's houses were painted in shades of gray and green while the homes in Key West were painted pink and yellow and blue, with wide verandahs and sleeping porches decked in fanciful gingerbread trim.

He pulled the train into the station at twelve thirty p.m., right on time. With two hours to go before they pulled out again, Herb headed to Duval Street to stretch his legs, walking toward the Atlantic side of the island where most of the stores were located. The sky was a deeper blue than you ever saw in Toledo, and the sun was shining. Yes, there were some darker clouds hanging out over the ocean, but really, why should he worry? So they'd have rain on the way home, which was nothing new this time of year. Mary was just being a worrywart. They'd laugh about it when he got home. He felt bad that she worried so much about him.

He passed the jewelry store. A lot of wealthy Northerners wintered in Key West, and the dangling diamond earrings and fancy cameo brooches shown in the window reflected that fact. That day a young clerk was rearranging the display as Herb walked by. The man added a tray of rings to the window, then stepped outside to look at the effect.

"Nice day," he said to Herb.

"You must be the only one who thinks so," Herb said.

"Everyone else I've seen today can talk about nothing but this hurricane that's supposed to be coming."

"Well, maybe it will and maybe it won't. All I know is that my boss wants me to set up a new display. If it all gets blown away tonight, that's his problem, not mine. What do you think?" He nodded to the window. "Does this catch your eye? Make you think about taking something home to the missus?"

"I don't think I have the money for the trinkets in your store," Herb told him. "I'm just a railroad man."

"That's not true. We've got baubles in every price range," the clerk said. "Look at this ring here." He pointed to a wide gold band decorated with a curlicue pattern engraved around two hearts. One heart held a diamond chip, the other a tiny ruby chip.

"That's real pretty. That's my wife's and my birthstones—April and July," Herb said.

"Come on in the store. I'll show it to you."

The clerk had drawn Herb in. *The man is a good salesman*, he thought. He really didn't want to go into the store but somehow couldn't resist. The salesman took the tray from the window and held out the ring to Herb, who stared at it, hands behind his back.

"Come on, you can hold it. It's not that expensive either," the clerk said, placing the ring in Herb's hand. "They're only chips, of course, but they are real stones. I guarantee it. Only $8.57, and you can make your lady's day."

"I don't know," Herb said. But then he stopped. He had enough money on him that day. And they were doing better financially than they ever had before, now that most of the kids were grown.

"What time's the train leave? I can have it engraved with your wife's initials in less than an hour."

Herb thought about the tears in Mary's eyes as he had left this morning. "All right. I'll do it." He pulled out his money clip and handed the man several bills.

"You won't regret it. Your lady is going to be thanking you tonight. Now just wait right here for a few minutes. What initials should I engrave?"

"M. A. R.," Herb said. "It's Mary Agnes Rogers."

A short time later he headed back to the station, the precious ring enclosed in a tiny box in his pocket.

When Herb walked out of the shop, he immediately noticed the change in the weather. *Maybe those forecasters do know something after all.* The sun was now hiding behind a very large cloud, and the wind had picked up. It must be blowing ten or fifteen miles an hour. He hurried back down Caroline Street to the station where Charley was waiting.

"We've got an hour until we can leave," Charley said. "Or we can cancel now. It's going to be quite a blow."

"If it's as bad as you think it will be, the bridges will go out and we'll be stuck down here for days. I want to get home to my family. Besides, what will Mr. Flagler say if his engine is stuck down here at the end of the line? I don't want to chance losing my job."

"And if we end up in the drink instead?"

Herb shrugged. "Well, that's the chance we signed up for."

"All right. Let's get her ready so we can leave at two p.m. on the dot." Charley turned on his heel and began calling out orders to the station personnel.

Herb looked at the sky, then put his hand in his pocket to touch the little box nestled there. It was going to be an interesting ride back, but he had a reward waiting at the end—a woman who loved him and seven beautiful children.

~~~

There weren't too many people on the northbound train when they left Key West. Most of the passengers had canceled, deciding they would rather chance riding out the storm on land, even if it was a small island, than in a railroad car hanging over the ocean.

The winds were even higher now. As they crossed over Lower Sugarloaf the fronds were being torn from the palms. Herb instinctively ducked when one flew past the window. Then he laughed at himself. Even a six-foot palm frond couldn't hurt his engine. He patted her side lovingly. She'd get him home.

Yet the train moved more and more slowly as they fought against the wind; the rain was blowing sideways past his windows, and the big, 200-ton locomotive swayed. It was going to be more than the usual four-hour trip to get back home tonight. He rubbed the box in his pocket again. It had become his talisman, a sure sign that he would bring this train and everyone on it back home safely.

The settlements they passed were all buttoned up tight. No children raced the train or waved as he went by. *Even the birds know better than to be out in this weather*, he thought, shaking his head and wondering at his own lack of good sense. By the time they reached Bahia Honda the wind seemed to whip around them in circles. Only two and half miles to the Seven Mile Bridge.

"If we just make it over the bridge," he repeated over and over. "If we just make it over the bridge."

It was almost full dark now. They were usually home by six o'clock, but it was already seven o'clock. He slowed the train to a crawl as he headed out over one of the longest bridges in the world. On the shorter bridges there was a chance that if something happened, they'd still make it out alive. But if anything happened while they were on this stretch of water, they were all dead. His hand snuck into his pocket and rubbed the little box one last time.

He could see nothing outside the windows except the rain whipping past as he fought the storm for control. And then it happened. The rain was pushing past his window from north to south, not south to north. Was his train going backward?

He put on as much power as he could. Inch by inch, then foot by foot, the train slowly crawled forward again until he could just make out the beginnings of land ahead. When the engine entered the southernmost tip of Marathon, he began to relax just a little bit. As he made it north of Marathon, one of the larger keys in the chain, the wind seemed to diminish, and the rain let up slightly. It still wasn't going to be an easy ride back, but the worst was behind him. Herb took his first full breath since heading onto the Seven Mile Bridge.

~~~

It was another two hours before they finally pulled into the Miami station. It was raining, and there was a good, stiff wind, but it was nothing like he'd seen crossing the lower keys. He called goodbye to Charley as he stepped off the train. And stopped.

There, standing on the platform, barely sheltered by the small overhang, was Mary.

"What are you doing out in the rain?" he asked, taking her in his arms.

"I couldn't wait at home. I was just so worried. And I didn't like the way we'd left things. I didn't even tell you a proper goodbye."

"I know you worry, but it's what I have to do to make a good life for our family. Still, I've been thinking about you all day. Maybe that's why when I saw this I wanted to bring it back to you as a reminder that I'll always come home." He took the box out of his pocket and opened it.

"Herb! You shouldn't have done something this extravagant. We can't afford—"

"Yes, we can. And yes, I should have done it. You deserve it. You put up with me every day," he said as he took the ring out of the box. Taking her right hand, the one that did not have a wedding band on it, he slipped it on her finger.

She held up her hand. "It's beautiful, Herb. I'll treasure it always." Then she leaned into him and kissed him passionately. "Come on, let's get home and get out of the rain," she said.

She slipped her hand into his as together they walked home.

Chapter 5
A Tale of Two Rings

What is fact, and what is fiction? My grandfather, Bert, always talked about the hurricane where the wind blew so hard that his daddy, an engineer on the Florida East Coast Railway, swore his train was pushed backward on the Seven Mile Bridge. But could a train really be blown backward and stay on the track? Particularly while hanging precariously over the ocean on the Seven Mile Bridge?

It always seemed impossible to me. Wouldn't the train fall off the track and into the ocean? I questioned it every time the story was told, but everyone in the family swore it was true: The wind blew so hard it pushed the 465,000-pound locomotive and all of its cars straight backward. I began to research the subject.

I'm sure you've experienced the illusion in which you feel as if you are moving backward when you are either standing still or going forward. The illusion is known as "The Wagon Wheel Effect." Our brains process the images we see at a "frame rate" of about two hundred frames per second when processing light, but only thirteen frames per second when processing motion. In other words, our eyes can see faster than our brains can make sense of it. And that, for me, explains why my great-grandfather thought his engine was being pushed backwards.

Then there is the ring. Yes, there really is a ring. I don't know exactly when Herb gave it to Mary. I was always told the stones represented their birth months, and the initials inside, "M.A.R.," stand for her married name so he must have given it to her sometime after they were married.

So when did my great-grandfather give the ring to his wife? I don't really know. But as I was writing about my great-grandparents, I looked down at my right hand, saw Mary's ring, and decided to make it a part of the story.

Why I wear my great-grandmother's ring is a story in itself.

When we got engaged, I informed Sam, my future

husband, I didn't want a diamond. Everyone wants a diamond when they get engaged, right? Not me. First, diamonds are the most expensive gemstone, and I am always worried about spending money—even when it was my future husband's and not yet mine.

Next, as the assistant women's editor at the *Butler Eagle,* I'd recently read an article about the history of engagement rings.

Diamonds are not rare. They haven't been rare since the 1870s when the huge African diamond mines were discovered. It took very little time for the mines' British financiers to realize the market would soon be saturated if they didn't do something so they created De Beers Consolidated Mines, Ltd., to control the diamond trade, stockpiling and selling diamonds strategically to control the price.

They commissioned research to find out just what people thought about diamonds—and learned the average person didn't think about diamonds at all. They were considered something only a very, very rich person wore. To continue to make money, De Beers needed to change that perception so in 1930 hired a Philadelphia advertising agency to make diamonds valued by the average person. The campaign focused on the importance of the diamond as an emotional symbol of love.

It was a huge success. By 1981, when I was getting engaged, every girl I knew wanted a diamond engagement ring—which meant, of course, I didn't want one. If everyone was doing it, I always wanted to do the opposite.

I suggested a ruby. Sam would say it was an order, not a suggestion, and that's what he chose for me—red for love and his birthstone, too.

Fast-forward twenty-five years. My engagement and wedding rings were falling apart. The wedding band had thinned to almost nothing, and one of the prongs on the engagement ring had worn away. Afraid I'd lose the stone or break the band, I quit wearing them.

"Why aren't you wearing your rings?" Sam asked one day. "You look like you are unclaimed."

My feminist side was offended. "Unclaimed!" it roared. "Am I a piece of luggage lost at the station? How dare he!" My romantic side melted a little. "After twenty-five years he still worries that someone else might want me," it cooed.

And then there was that cheap—er, frugal—side. It didn't want to spend any money. But our anniversary was coming up and, since Sam's original wedding ring was also looking worn, we decided to celebrate by buying each other new rings.

Luckily, the husband who had accepted that I didn't want a typical ring the first time around understood when the setting I picked out for my ruby didn't look like a wedding ring.

But when I began to wear it, Sam still didn't feel as if I looked like I'd been "claimed," and it was too thick to comfortably wear with a second, plain wedding band on the same finger.

That was when I remembered my great-grandmother's ring, which had been sitting in my jewelry box for a number of years. I took it out and put it on my right hand, where it's been ever since.

When I first began wearing it, I could still see Mary's initials inside. After almost twenty more years of additional wear, the initials have faded away to nothing, and the back of the band has gotten thin. But I like to think that my great-grandmother and great-grandfather would appreciate that a ring special to them is still special to someone in their family.

Chapter 6
Grandma Rogers

The most important person in my life until I went to kindergarten was Grandma Rogers. She took care of me every day while Cheryl was in school and Mama and Granddad were at work. Grandma Rogers—her first name was Agnes—was not your typical grandmother of the 1950s and '60s. She got her hair and nails done weekly at the beauty parlor and wore Revlon "Love That Red" nail polish on fingernails that were the envy of all the women in the family. She could grow them over an inch long decades before false nails came into style. Granddad loved her nails and washed the dishes every night so she wouldn't have to get them wet and ruin them.

She almost never wore a dress, and when she did it certainly wasn't one of those long, black "old lady" dresses my friends' grandmothers wore. Grandma Rogers didn't wear typical old lady orthopedic shoes either. On days when we were staying at home she wore Bermuda shorts, a short-sleeved, printed cotton shirt, and slip-on Keds. If she was going out someplace with friends, or over to dinner with the Aunts and Uncles, she put on dress slacks, low-heeled dress shoes, and a dressier cotton print blouse. I think she invented the pantsuit decades before it was invented. On the rare occasions she entered a church she did have one or two dresses that she could put on. They weren't old lady dresses either. They were fashionable. I particularly loved her blue lace dress, which was saved for weddings and other really important occasions.

Grandma didn't like to cook. She had been a working woman. She'd never had what you could call a career but, other than a few years when my mother was very young, she had helped to support the family with various jobs, from cashiering and gift wrapping packages at the dime store to working as a secretary for the Navy offices in Miami during World War II. I grew up thinking that "homemade" pie meant the Sara Lee variety that you picked up in the freezer section of the grocery store and heated at home, rather than buying one from the bakery.

It never occurred to me until I got married that one could actually make a pie from scratch—even the pie crust. While other kids were getting homemade cookies from their grandmas, mine was buying me Oreos—still my favorite cookie. I still think of her any time I eat them. I have to admit that, contrary to most Southern stereotypes, I learned to cook from my Yankee mother-in-law, not the many Southern women in my family.

But Agnes was the best grandma ever when it came to loving and playing with her two grandchildren. I decided one day to make an Indian village out of construction paper for my tiny plastic Indian figurines. She helped me cut out and glue together a half dozen six-inch teepees. She fashioned a paper stream that ran through the village and helped me figure out how to make the paper trees stand up and not just lie flat. And she let me keep my village up on a card table in the living room to play with for over a week. For a woman who was incredibly house proud, that was quite an act of love.

As I grew older our relationship changed. I've always said we worked so well together because we based everything on mutual blackmail. I wouldn't tell Granddad about the weeks she needed to buy an extra carton of cigarettes to make it through, and she wouldn't tell Mama about the times I was late to school or forgot to do my homework.

Grandma, unlike the rest of us who were born in Florida, had been born in Missouri and spent her childhood in a little town called Advance. (That's ADD-vance with the accent on the first syllable; she would remind anyone who pronounced it wrong.)

Grandma did things her way. She didn't care what other people thought. She was the first of the many strong Southern women who were my role models. She had learned to be strong from her mother, Mollie, and she passed that trait on to her daughter and granddaughters.

Chapter 7
Buried Treasure

1909

"Hurry, Sigmund, they'll be here soon," Mollie called to her husband, who had just come home from his work at the barbershop late on a Saturday afternoon in early April.

"Give me a few moments, Mollie," he called back from their bedroom. "I need to change into a clean shirt. You told me you wanted me to look my best."

"Agnes, wait!" she called, as their six-year-old daughter wiggled out of her grasp and headed into the bedroom.

"Daddy, Daddy, you're home!" she heard Agnes call. "Pick me up!"

"Agnes, let Daddy get ready, and you come back in here with your sister and get your hair combed. Aunt Ella and Aunt Jenny will be here soon. We want to all look our best."

Just as Mollie corralled Agnes in the doorway of the bedroom, baby Leon began to cry.

"I'll get him, Mollie. You take care of Agnes and Helen," Sigmund said as he headed to the crib in the corner and picked up his son. "How is my big, strong boy today?" he asked.

His Polish accent always made Mollie smile. It was one of the things she'd found romantic about him when they first met.

"Have you been good for your Mama?" he continued. "I see you are wet."

Mollie headed back to get Helen just as there was a knock at the door of the row house they were renting on Lafayette Street in St. Louis.

"The girls and I will get the door," Mollie called. "Sigmund, can you bring Leon as soon as he is changed?"

Mollie hurried down the stairs, stopping for a minute in front of the mirror by the hall tree to check her hair. She quickly unwound the bun at the top, gathered and fluffed the rest of her hair below it into the popular Gibson Girl style, and pinned it back up. She smoothed down her navy skirt and white blouse and threw open the door to her two younger sisters.

"I'm so glad you are here. I can't believe it's been so long. I can't wait for you to meet the baby," she cried.

Jenny and Ella hugged their sister, then exclaimed over how much Agnes and Helen had grown. Four-year-old Helen, who usually talked all the time, grew suddenly shy and hid behind her mother's long skirt, thumb in her mouth.

"Helen, take your thumb out of your mouth. You haven't sucked your thumb in over a year. What's come over you? You can't have forgotten Aunt Ella and Aunt Jenny!"

The commotion of removing coats and hats continued as Sigmund came down the stairs with baby Leon.

"Let me take your suitcases upstairs," he said after greeting his sisters-in-law. "I'm afraid you'll have to sleep with the girls. We only have the two bedrooms."

"We don't mind," said Jenny, "we're just happy to see all of you."

The sisters made a fuss over the baby, then happily joined Mollie in the kitchen to put the dinner of corned beef, cabbage, and potatoes on the table. After dinner the bedtime ritual of stories and tuck-ins for the three children took up the rest of the evening so it was well after seven p.m. before Mollie had a chance to sit down with her sisters at the kitchen table and catch up. It was chilly for April, and the wood-fired oven still radiated a pleasant warmth.

"Now tell me why you've really come," she said, pouring cups of tea as Sigmund went to the cupboard and pulled out the whiskey.

He poured a shot for himself and added some to everyone else's tea.

"It's just good to see you all so happy here, even though the place is small," said Jenny. "I know you've always wanted land, Mollie."

Mollie and Sigmund exchanged glances. They must be coming to the meat of this visit, although they weren't yet sure what that "meat" was. Since Ella and Jenny lived in Cape Girardeau, it was a several-hour train ride to get together, which meant it wasn't something any of them did often—particularly when it was early spring so the weather might change at any moment and it was not a holiday.

"Yes, I've always wanted a bit of land, but Sigmund is doing well here in St. Louis. He's busy six days a week," Mollie said.

"People need barbers everywhere, though," put in Ella. "Even in small towns."

"What are you two girls going on about?" asked Sigmund. He pulled out his pipe, added tobacco, and tamped it down before taking a few puffs to see if it was drawing, then lighted it. "I know you have something on your minds so just spit it out."

Jenny took a deep breath. "Mollie, you know that property of Mama's? The piece in Advance?"

"Yes," Mollie said slowly. "You mean the property where Uncle Will lives?"

"Yes, that's the one," Jenny said. "Well, wouldn't it be a great place to raise your children? Think of fresh country air and the space there is in that big old house. And Sigmund, I know they need a barber in Advance. The man who had a shop there died last year. Everyone has to go over to Brownville now for a haircut."

"And I'm sure you could do a great business with your hats, Mollie," added Ella. "At Christmas you said you wanted to get back into your millinery business, and it could be the perfect place."

"This is all very nice except for one small problem," Mollie said. "Uncle Will lives there."

Jenny and Ella looked at each other. "Uncle Will died last year."

"What! No one ever let us know. What happened?"

"Well, he lived alone, you know, and no one found him for several days. And I guess it took a while for anyone to think to look for his relatives, even though Cape Girardeau isn't that far away," Jenny explained. "And now the problem is he hadn't paid the taxes in years. The property is going to go to the county if they aren't paid soon."

"And whoever pays them owns the property," said Ella.

"And people are sniffing around the place. You know there were always rumors about it," added Jenny.

"So what are you saying?" Sigmund asked, taking a long draw on his pipe.

"The property was always in Mama's name. It came from her first husband, you know. She just let her brother live there, and he was supposed to pay the property taxes. But he never did. Now that he's died, the county wants to claim the property. I guess someone wants to buy it, and if the county claims it, then they can sell it and get the money," explained Jenny.

"And how much are the taxes?" Mollie asked.

"Fifty dollars," said Ella.

"And how much are the two of you planning to put into this wonderful opportunity?" Sigmund asked, the sarcasm evident.

Jenny and Ella looked at each other as Ella fidgeted with her teacup. "Well, neither of us have much saved. We thought the two of you might have something," Ella said, not looking her sister or brother-in-law in the eyes.

"So you want us to pay the taxes on the property in Advance, and then what will happen?" Mollie asked.

"Well then it's yours," Jenny said. "You can do what you want with it. We just don't want the county taking it and then selling it without anyone in the family getting the profit from it."

"And you don't want any part of it?" asked Sigmund.

"No, really we don't," said Ella. "Jenny's getting married soon, anyway. We just don't want the county to take it."

"You could live there." Jenny jumped in again. "It would be wonderful for you—well, actually, you might *need* to live there for a little while until you sell it—"

"What do you mean?" Mollie asked suspiciously. "Why would we need to live there?"

"You've always liked the country, and you've always said you wanted to do some farming, Mollie. There's an orchard on the property. I'm sure you could make some money from the apple harvest in the fall."

Jenny finally fell silent.

"I grew up on a farm in Poland," said Sigmund. "It's

damn hard work, and I already make a good living here as a barber. It's a lot easier than farming, believe me."

"Let's get back to the part where we might have to live there for a while until the property is sold," said Mollie, putting her hand on her husband's arm. To be perfectly truthful she rather liked the idea of living in a small town and maybe growing apples or some other crop. Jenny was right; she'd always wanted some land of her own. Their father had always said if you had land, you would never be broke. That was one reason he had always insisted their mother keep the bit she had inherited from her first husband.

"It's the rumors. You know. About the treasure."

"What's this?" Sigmund asked, his eyebrows heading for his hairline.

"It's just silly," Mollie told her husband. "Near the end of the war someone said they saw a Rebel soldier near our mother's property, carrying a heavy canvas bag, late at night. The person— no one seems to know who it was—went up and asked him if he needed help, but he wouldn't take any, even though he was obviously starving and freezing. It was late winter, just a few weeks before Lee surrendered at Appomattox. The next day someone else saw the soldier walking out of the woods toward the railroad tracks, and he had no canvas sack. Of course, everyone decided that the sack must have been filled with lost Rebel gold and that he had buried the sack on Mama's land. For the last forty years or so, people keep trying to sneak onto the land to find it."

"They've made a mess of the fields, digging holes all over," put in Ella. "That's why Mama let Uncle Will live there. He was supposed to keep the treasure hunters away."

Sigmund had begun chuckling about halfway through Mollie's story. Now he let out a great guffaw. "That's the worst treasure story I've ever heard!" he exclaimed. "How can anyone believe something that lame? Two different people saw a soldier. Did anyone think they might have been two different soldiers? One saw a man with a bag. One saw a man without a bag. I could make up a better story than that! And Rebel gold? From what I have heard of the war, the Rebels had no money at the end. Why would this soldier have buried gold on a farm in Missouri when the soldiers needed it to fight?" Sigmund had immigrated to America about ten years after the Civil War had ended.

"Well, I never said we believed it," Mollie said defensively. "Just that everyone else around those parts believes it. We even heard it talked about in Cape Girardeau when I lived there."

"And if no one is looking after the property, people will sneak in and tear things up looking for the treasure," said Ella.

"And since there's really no treasure, they just keep sneaking in and tearing things up more," added Jenny.

Sigmund stood up and deposited his shot glass in the sink. "This is a lot to think about, ladies. We can't settle anything tonight. Let's talk again tomorrow after church."

Mollie and her sisters straightened the kitchen after Sigmund headed upstairs.

"Well, Mollie, he didn't say no outright," Jenny said.

"It's not like that," Mollie replied. "Sigmund doesn't just make all the decisions for the family. We make them together. We have to think about what's best for all of us—the children and Sigmund and me.

"Well, I expect you can talk him into anything you really want," Jenny said, with a laugh.

"I just don't know if I want this. It would be a huge risk for us."

~~~

The next morning came far too soon. Mollie and Sigmund had stayed up half the night discussing the pros and cons of moving to Advance and taking on a house and farm.

Sigmund was worried about the treasure hunters. "What kind of man digs up his neighbor's property on the chance of finding gold that doesn't belong to him rather than working hard to make his own money?" he asked. "That is no way for a grown man to spend his time. Men who think like that could be dangerous."

Mollie wasn't worried. She was sure the rumors of people sneaking around the property were exaggerated. And wouldn't it be good to have land? A home in a place where the children could grow up knowing everyone in town and where people looked after each other? After all, Sigmund's entire family was in Poland, and she only had her two sisters left.

It seemed they had barely closed their eyes, still undecided about what to do, when baby Leon began to cry. There was no time to talk that morning, what with getting three children ready for Mass and having two houseguests. It was after Sunday dinner before they had a chance to discuss it again—although the decision had obviously been on both of their minds all day.

"You really want to do this, Mollie, don't you?" Sigmund asked.

"Yes, I do. I've always wanted land. I've always wanted to live in a small town. This is our chance."

"But it will take all our savings just to pay the property taxes. I'd need to stay here in St. Louis for several months to save up enough money to open my own shop in Advance. That means you and the children would be there all alone at first."

"I know, Sigmund, but I'm more worried that people will destroy the property or squatters will move into the house if no one is there. This is our chance to really make something for our children."

When they told Jenny and Ella, the sisters were thrilled. They promised to help all they could, although Mollie knew that not much help would come—they lived almost twenty miles away from Advance. And Sigmund would be even farther away. But Mollie knew she could handle it by herself. It would be an adventure. That's what she would tell Agnes and Helen.

The next morning she saw Jenny and Ella off on the train, then went to the bank, withdrew their savings, and wired the money for the taxes to the county clerk. She felt a sense of triumph. She was a landowner!

~~~

Spring had truly arrived by the time Mollie was ready to head down to their new home on the train with the children and just enough luggage to get them through the first days until a wagon with the rest of their things could arrive.

It was early afternoon when the train stopped at the Advance station and Mollie went to the stables to rent a horse and buggy to drive her and the three children to the farm a few miles out of town.

"Where you say you going to?" asked the stableman.

"I need to go to the old Courtney place."

"Nobody living there now."

"I know. I'll be living there." Mollie could tell that if she didn't answer the man's questions to his satisfaction, she might be there all day so she put on her best smile and explained. "The property belonged to my mother. My Uncle Will lived there until he died. I'll be taking it over now."

"Hmph. Lot of work for a woman running a farm and orchard by herself."

"My husband will be joining me in a few months."

"Never heard of old Will having any married nieces."

"Well, he did. My name is Mollie Courtney Sawieja, and these are our children," she said, pointing to each of them. "Agnes, my oldest. Helen. And this is the baby, Leon."

"Hmph," the man said again as if he didn't think much of the children. "Well, let me get you a buggy harnessed. How long you need it for?"

"The rest of my belongings are supposed to arrive the day after tomorrow. I can bring the buggy back to you then," she said.

"That sounds good," he replied as he took her money and headed over to harness one of the horses. "I'll throw in some feed for the horse. You might not find much of anything out there."

Mollie thanked him and herded the children into the buggy for the short drive to the property. Mollie remembered the way from childhood visits, but dusk was already coming on, and she found she wished she'd managed to get in earlier. She didn't like the idea of trying to get everything set up in the dark.

Nothing had been taken care of for quite some time, she noticed as she turned down the lane to the house. Holes had been dug all through the fields on either side of the road. *Must be the treasure hunters. They really have made a mess of things.*

After helping the girls down, she told them to stay near her as she picked up Leon and headed to the house. She cautiously opened the door, took a step inside, and came to a dead stop. In front of her was a gaping hole. Someone had obviously torn up the floorboards.

Her heart pounded at the thought of her near miss. What if it had been darker? She and the baby could have fallen right down into the cellar and been killed. Then what would have happened to Agnes and Helen? No one would come looking for them until the delivery men arrived in two days.

"Helen, Agnes, come over here and sit on the porch and watch Leon for a few minutes, please," she said. The girls, who had been wandering around outside, sat down obediently. "Now I don't want either of you to move a step until Mama checks everything out, you hear?"

"Yes, Mama," the girls both said.

Mollie moved more cautiously this time as she entered the house. Thank goodness there was still enough light coming in through the windows to see where she was stepping.

The front room wasn't the only one that had been torn up. Most of the rooms had holes in the floors and the walls, too. Luckily, one bedroom, which still had a door, also had its floor intact. They could camp here for the night. She went back to the porch and picked up the baby.

"We're going to play a game," she told her daughters. "You have to step exactly where I step or the alligators will get you."

"Oh Mama, that's silly," said Agnes. "Alligators can't live in a house."

"Well, it's just a game, baby. Don't you want to play?"

"Yes, Mama."

When they were all safely inside, Mollie went back for their food and some blankets, and they settled in for the night.

~~~

The next morning Mollie piled everyone back into the buggy and headed to town. They couldn't live in the house right then, which meant she was going to have to find a tent, not to mention a way to cook. She headed for Brown's Hardware Store first. The man behind the counter, Mr. Brown she presumed, looked at her a little oddly when she asked for his largest tent and a camp stove, but he didn't say much. The woman behind the counter at the general store was another matter entirely.

"I haven't seen you in town before," she said as she packaged up the various canned goods.

"We just got here last night. We are going to be moving into the old Courtney place."

"Really! I didn't know it had sold. I heard that some relative of Will's had paid the taxes."

"That's right. I'm Mollie Sawieja. Will was my uncle, and my mother owned the property."

"You've come a long way for a piece of land that people have been digging holes on," the woman replied.

"Once my husband gets here, I'm sure we'll be able to get things in shape. I wasn't prepared for the house, though," she said candidly. "There are holes in all the floors. It's not safe to stay in until we can get them fixed."

"So you're going back where you came from?" The woman's tone had become decidedly less friendly after she found out where Mollie planned to live.

"No, I've ordered a tent, and the children and I will camp out until my husband can join us."

"And where did you say he is?"

"St. Louis. He is a barber. He'll be opening a shop here when he arrives."

"Well, we do need a barber," the woman reluctantly acknowledged.

"That's what we've heard. Now if my packages are ready, I need to get going. We have a lot to set up today, and it's going to be hard to get the children into any kind of schedule."

Shortly after they got back to the house a wagon pulled up with the tent, and Mr. Brown and another man set it up. It was large enough to stand in, and once her furniture arrived the next day they could even fit the bed and crib inside. She would place some chairs and a table outside near the camp stove, which ran on alcohol. Mr. Brown had brought a supply that would last several days.

"Mama, can we explore?" asked Agnes.

"Don't go any farther than I can see you, and don't go into any of the buildings until I've checked them."

"Yes, Mama."

ﾠ

Agnes grabbed her sister's hand, and they skipped off to have a look at their new home. They headed to where the woods met the field, disappearing for a bit. Mollie was not surprised when they quickly came running back, out of breath.

"Mama, there's ghosts in the trees," Agnes said. Helen nodded solemnly, her thumb in her mouth.

"Agnes, you know there is no such thing as ghosts," her mother replied.

"I heard it. I heard a noise and there was nothing there, so it must have been a ghost," said Agnes.

"It might have been an animal; there are deer in these woods, and rabbits and squirrels. None of them will hurt you."

"You promise, Mama?"

"Yes, I promise. I'll keep you safe."

"I miss Daddy," Helen said, finally taking her thumb out of her mouth.

"I miss him too, baby. He'll join us as soon as he has made enough money to set up a barbershop here."

Mollie sat the girls down for a dinner of tinned meat and bread, thinking about what they had told her. Had the noises they heard really been an animal? Or something larger watching them? If any men wanted to chase them off this piece of land, they would find it wasn't as easy as they thought. Mollie had a few surprises up her sleeve just in case.

~~~

The furniture arrived, and Mollie spent the next several days sorting out what was needed to last the next few weeks and what could be stored in the barn. She opened and arranged the trunks and boxes, moving things around until their tent was as homey as she could make it. She and the girls shared the bed, which was placed in one corner, while Leon's crib was in the other. A rug covered the grass "floor," and an oil lamp stood on a small table next to the bed. Outside the kitchen table and chairs were placed near the camp stove, and the dishes were in a trunk next to it.

When she was done she was pleased with the homeyness of the place and couldn't wait until the following weekend when Sigmund had promised to take the train down to visit them.

~~~

Spring had turned to summer, and they were still living in the tent.

The four of them had waited anxiously at the station the Friday afternoon that Sigmund was to arrive. They swarmed him like bees catching the scent of honey when they saw his tall, slim figure step down from the train.

"I've missed you all so much," he told them, hugging the girls and Leon and then finally taking Mollie in his arms for a long kiss, despite the fact that they were in public.

He had admired the way Mollie had arranged their camp and taken a long walk in the woods with the girls. Sunday had come too soon, and she had to hide her tears when Sigmund got back on the train for St. Louis. Mollie had told Sigmund she would rather save all their money for him to open a shop as soon as possible instead of hiring someone to fix the house. By now they had established a routine, walking into town a couple of times a week, Mollie pushing Leon in the baby carriage and the girls walking beside her. Agnes and Helen loved the outings. She let them walk as slowly as they wanted, exploring every tree, flower, and blade of grass since it kept them uncomplaining.

Her reception in town was mixed. Some people were friendly, others not, and many just seemed suspicious. She mentioned that she would soon be making hats to sell so tried to wear a different one each time she went in to show off her talents. The general store's owner seemed interested in giving her a space to display her wares. His wife, however, turned up her nose. Mollie understood why. Once Sigmund was there for good, she would be a respectable married woman. Until then, she was just a stranger.

She missed Sigmund the most at night, and for someone used to the lights of a city, the total darkness of the farm was difficult to get used to. Every noise she heard was intimidating. Was it a coyote? A bobcat? Or a man seeking treasure and willing to go to any lengths to find it?

They'd been lucky with the weather, only seeing a few spring showers. Mollie had cautioned the girls not to touch the fabric of the tent when it rained because touching it would break the seal and cause the tent to leak.

"Why, Mama?" Agnes asked.

"I don't know, honey. I just know if you touch the canvas tent walls when it rains, they will spring a leak so don't touch them, please."

She dashed out into the rain and brought in cold leftovers for breakfast. Then, wanting to keep them occupied, she got out some paper and books and worked on teaching Agnes her letters. She'd be going to school in the fall.

Leon cried so she went to change him. And, of course, that's when Agnes decided to stand on her chair and see if she could reach the tent's roof.

"Look, Mama, the water's coming in just like you said it would!" the child called out excitedly as if she had just proved a great science experiment.

"Oh Agnes! No!" Mollie ran outside to find a bucket. "Now you understand why I told you not to touch the canvas. Don't do it again. Please!"

By the end of the day they were all damp, tired, and grumpy. A second cold meal didn't help. *At least*, Mollie thought as they went to bed, *I won't have to worry about treasure hunters tonight*. No one was going to come out to dig holes in this weather.

The next morning the weather had improved. It was still gray and cloudy, but it wasn't raining. The girls put on rain gear and went out to play in the puddles since Molly figured it would be difficult for them to get any damper than they were already. She would heat some water, then they could have warm baths. And she could start the day with a hot cup of coffee.

~~~

The weather grew better every day, and Mollie began to see more people. Some of the people she had met in town stopped by for a neighborly visit, bringing bread or vegetables. One time the sheriff stopped by. He was polite but suspicious.

"I've heard there was someone camping out here," he said as he got out of his wagon. He was a tall man and tried to intimidate Mollie by standing closer than necessary, towering over her.

"Yes, we've been here for a few weeks now," Mollie said politely. "Would you like a cup of coffee? I've just made some." She gestured to the camp stove where the pot was simmering.

"No thanks. I don't have time for a social visit," he said. "How do I know you're who you say you are and not some squatters?"

"I have the deed to the property right here," Mollie replied stiffly.

She went to the little dresser that stood in the tent and pulled out the papers. The sheriff looked them over carefully before handing them back.

"Yes, it all looks in order, ma'am," he said as he handed them back to her.

"I am worried about something I hope you can help me with," she said as he got back up in his wagon. "I've heard noises around the property at night, and there have always been rumors about treasure hunters in the area. We're in the tent because of the way the house has been gutted. There are so many holes in the floor, it's just not safe to live in right now."

"Don't you worry about that, ma'am. No one I know would harm a woman and children alone."

As he drove away she noticed he hadn't said that he didn't know anyone who would search for treasure on her property.

From that point forward she was even more nervous at night, although she took great pains the girls would not notice. If Leon picked up on her anxiety and was a little more fussy, well, the only thing she could do was give him lots of attention.

"How are things going out there? You're so far away from the town to be alone with just those three children," Mrs. Brown, the wife of the general store owner, asked her one day when she came in to buy some more canned goods. The woman had become decidedly friendlier over the past few weeks. A steady customer was to be treated with respect.

"I'm taking a 'hands-off' policy for now," she replied. "At least at night. As long as nothing, animal or human, approaches my tent or my children, I won't try to stop them. When Sigmund arrives we can talk about fencing things."

"When will he get here?" Mrs. Brown asked.

"In two more weeks. I can't wait!"

~~~

Finally, the day came. Sigmund would arrive the next morning. She went to the meat market for pork chops—his favorite meal—and the general store for more flour for biscuits, then stopped at a local farm on the way out of town to get fresh butter and milk. She wanted everything to be perfect for his arrival at his new home, even if it was only a tent.

The girls were too excited to sleep, and their restlessness infected Leon, who fussed and wouldn't settle. Finally, everyone quieted and Mollie closed her own eyes. It seemed she had only been asleep for a moment or two when a noise woke her.

Something was stealthily moving near the tent. She lay perfectly still listening to the sound of footsteps. She'd been living here long enough that she could distinguish between a foraging deer, a mischievous raccoon, and a man.

This was no deer or raccoon.

Slowly and quietly, she felt under the bed until her hand touched the shotgun she had stored there the day their furniture had arrived. There had been no need to bring it out until now. No one had come this close to the tent before. It was ironic that after four months these treasure hunters would pick the last night she would be alone to come into the camp. Or maybe not—she'd told everyone when Sigmund was arriving in hopes it would keep them away. Possibly her plan had backfired, and someone was taking advantage of the last night they would be vulnerable.

As quietly as she could, Mollie slipped from the bed and tiptoed over to the tent flap. She pushed it open with the tip of her shotgun. Three men were rummaging through the trunk full of her cooking supplies.

"She wouldn't be keeping it here so close to her camp," one of the men whispered.

"Where else? You think she's going to stash the gold out in the woods when she can keep it right under her nose? No, it's here all right." He discovered the shortbread she had baked for the next day's celebration with Sigmund and ate one. "Hmm, she's a pretty good cook."

That was it! She'd put up with enough. The women who'd

acted like she was lying when she said her husband would soon be arriving. The men who'd condescended to her saying things like "Little lady, you shouldn't be out here all alone. You can't handle all this by yourself." The sheriff who had acted as if she were the troublemaker, not the men who trespassed on her land.

The click as she pulled back the shotgun trigger sounded extraordinarily loud in the still night. The three men became statues, one still bent over the trunk.

"I don't want any trouble," Mollie said. "I just want y'all to leave. Right now."

The man at the trunk slowly stood up. "We don't want any trouble either, ma'am. Just tell us where you've hid the gold. You've been out here long enough, I'm sure you've found it by now."

"Men!" Mollie huffed. "Is that all you can think about, some rumor of gold? Not only have I not found any gold, I haven't bothered to look for any gold. Because there isn't any gold. There never was. I just want to live here in peace with my family. Now you men can just back off right now or I'll have to take matters into my own hands."

"Now you wouldn't want to do that," the man said, taking a step toward her. "You don't want to shoot that gun. It'll wake up those kids. And no mother ever wants that."

At that moment Leon began to cry. Agnes and Helen woke up and, seeing their mother at the entrance to the tent, got out of bed. Helen put her thumb in her mouth while Agnes pulled on her mother's nightgown.

"Who's that, Mama?" she asked. "Are they the ghosts?"

"Yes, honey, I suspect they are the people you thought were ghosts. But see, they're just silly men. There's nothing scary about them at all. And they were just leaving."

"Oh, ma'am, I'm not so sure about that. We haven't looked in your tent for the gold yet." The man who seemed to be the ringleader took another step forward.

"I'm warning you, don't come one step closer."

The man just laughed and took another step.

The blast of the shotgun took everyone by surprise. Leon cried harder, and Helen joined him. The three men turned and took off running.

Mollie sent one more blast after them, just to make sure they continued on their way.

~~~

When Sigmund arrived late the next morning, it wasn't to a cheery camp with a campfire burning and dinner cooking. Mollie, the girls, and even little Leon were sleeping in the one bed.

"Mollie, are you sick?" he asked with concern. "What's wrong? I've never seen you like this."

"Oh Sigmund!" Mollie threw her arms around him. "I'm so glad you're here. Don't ever go away again!"

It took some time to get the story out of her, particularly since Helen wanted to describe the sound of the shotgun firing over and over. But when he finally learned what had happened the night before, his first question was "Are you sure you still want to stay? We can leave. We'll sell the property and go back to St. Louis if that is what you want. Remember, I can make a living anywhere. You said it yourself."

"No! I'm not leaving. I hate to admit it, but now they will probably leave us alone since you're here. I'm not giving up my dream just because of a few stupid men."

"All right. I'll go to town tomorrow and rent the store where the old barbershop was. Anything left over is going for lumber to fix those floors. We are going to get all of you inside four walls as soon as possible."

"That sounds wonderful!" she exclaimed. "We don't need to look for any gold. I've all my treasures right here around me now."

Chapter 8
Trains, Planes, and Automobiles
—and Some Spaceships, Too

I have a memory of running in circles in the backyard, arms out, playing airplane or maybe spaceship. I'm not sure now. But I do know I was obsessed with all things that flew. It was 1961, I was not quite five years old, and I, along with every other American child, was focused on the sky. Alan Shepard was about to be launched into space. I had watched the launch on television until my five-year-old body could no longer stand the inactivity and my grandma had allowed me to go out to the backyard to run off my energy.

I'm not sure if that image of myself, which is so vivid in my memory, is one particular day or if I have conflated several days. Grandma Rogers was obsessed with the space program, and so was I. So the ritual played out several times throughout my childhood, particularly in 1961. We watched all the flights together. First was Alan Shepard's fifteen-minute suborbital flight on May 5. Gus Grissom flew the second Mercury rocket a few months later, then John Glenn, and next Scott Carpenter.

There were many more flights after that, of course, and I watched them all with Grandma Rogers. She and I would stay glued to the television set until either the rocket went up or the flight was scrubbed for the day. We didn't get discouraged if a flight was postponed; men were flying into space for the first time, and there were bound to be problems.

We mourned when Gus Grissom, Edward White, and Roger Chaffee died in a flash fire during a ground test. We spent the day watching their funeral on television. We cheered at each new milestone and discussed each NASA setback in detail at the dinner table. I suspect that Mama, Granddad, and Cheryl were rather bored, but it didn't matter to Grandma and me.

As I got older, I often watched the launches at school since they wheeled televisions into each classroom, but I liked it best when I could watch with Grandma. It was summer when

Neil Armstrong and Buzz Aldrin landed on the moon, and I stayed up all night with her. And when the Challenger exploded on January 28, 1986, I was listening on the radio while working in a newsroom. Grandma was the first person I called when I got home.

~~~

I think Grandma Rogers's fascination with the space program had to do with having seen so many advances in her life. She was born in 1903 and spent most of her childhood in the tiny town of Advance where most people didn't even have a horse. There was the train, of course, that stopped every day if you needed to go to St. Louis. She remembered the first time an automobile had driven through town. Everyone came out of their houses to marvel at the new machine.

When I was younger I never thought to ask Grandma much about her childhood. She was old so not much about her early life interested me. Besides, she had grown up in the "North," which in South Florida had nothing to do with the Mason-Dixon Line. We considered everything above Palm Beach County as "North." If you went to the University of Florida in Gainesville, about a seven-hour drive at that time, you were "heading north." Missouri felt like it must be somewhere close to the North Pole—Grandma had actually seen snow!

We teased her for being the only northerner in the family. She ate her grits with sugar, a barbarous practice, while the rest of us ate the delicacy with butter and salt. She never adjusted to the heat, but luckily, my grandfather treasured her and took care of her. We were the first family on the block to get air-conditioning.

We knew she had come down to Florida with her family when she was about age eighteen, but until I was in college, I never thought to ask her about the journey or why her family had decided to move. Once I heard the story, I was so glad I did.

Chapter 9
An Adventure for Agnes

1920

Agnes stepped down from the trolley car and hurried toward home just as the gaslights were flickering to life in the November twilight. She walked quickly, not because of the cold, she was used to that, but because Dad was coming home today. She couldn't wait to hear all about his adventure. Mama had assured Agnes she wouldn't let him tell anything about his trip until she got home from work, no matter how her younger siblings, Helen, Leon, and Mary, begged.

Dad made good money at the barbershop, but still, with four children, Agnes finally being old enough to work had been a big help to the family, especially since Mama had had to leave her millinery business behind when they moved back to St. Louis. Agnes loved bringing money home, but even more than that she loved her job at the public library. She had plenty of time to sneak peeks at the library's new acquisitions as well as her old favorites as she placed them carefully on their correct shelves. Books were the door to adventure—Mama always told her that. And Agnes wanted adventures. She wanted to see the world, like Dad.

Her dad had been many places. He had come from Poland with his older brother Frank when he was barely a man—just sixteen, even younger than she was now. They had traveled all the way from his small town in Poland to France to take passage on a boat and cross the ocean to New York City. Dad had actually seen the ocean! He'd sailed on the ocean. He had described it to her many times, as often as she asked. He told her about standing on the deck, the waves making it roll under his feet as he clung to the rail and looked and looked to see something besides water—but there was nothing. For days and days there was nothing to see except ocean. Until one day he went outside, and there it was! The Statue of Liberty growing larger and larger in front of his eyes. First, he could just barely make out the torch in the statue's hand, but the beautiful, coppery green woman grew larger and larger until they passed right underneath her as they arrived at the dock in New York City.

Dad and his brother stayed in the city for a few months, but his brother got homesick. Frank got a job on a boat so he could head back home to Poland and the family farm, but Dad had stayed. He wanted to see America. Not just the one corner of New York City, but all of America. Dad had learned to be a barber and worked for over a year until he earned enough money to take a train heading west. He had planned to go all the way to California, but ran out of money in Cape Girardeau, Missouri, and stopped to get a job on an excursion boat that went up and down the Mississippi River.

And that's when he met Mama.

Mollie Courtney and her sisters Ella and Jennie had taken a day trip. "Your mother was so beautiful, I fell in love with her the second I saw her," Dad always said.

"You really just wanted me because I could cook," Mama would put in, and the two of them would laugh. "He could barely boil water and hadn't had a decent meal since he'd left Poland."

Agnes could tell they were still very much in love—even after being married twenty years. She wanted to have that kind of love, too, and wondered if she would ever find a husband.

For now, Agnes hefted the large cloth bag she carried over her shoulder. It contained the six books she had borrowed this week—the maximum anyone was allowed to check out of the library at a time. She was excited because she had finally been able to check out *The Secret Adversary*, the second book by an English mystery writer Agatha Christie. Agnes, her mother, and her sister Helen had all read her first book, and they couldn't wait to read the second. Agnes had had the book on reserve for weeks, and now finally, it was her turn to bring it home. The reviews in the newspaper promised this "second book by Mrs. Christie will not disappoint." She had another mystery, an old favorite, *The Man in Lower Ten* by Mary Roberts Rinehart, in the bag also, in honor of Dad's train trip. She'd read it many times.

"Why do you keep checking out the same books over and over again?" Mama always asked her. "You can't learn anything new if you only read the same things."

Mama was very big on education. That was why she had insisted Agnes finish high school.

Agnes's dad was proud that his children were getting an education, even Agnes, Helen, and Mary, although he didn't really see the need. "They will just get married like my sister did, like you and your sisters. They will have a man to take care of them."

"That was in Poland. Not America. You are American now, and you must raise your girls the same as you raise your son, Sigmund," Mama told him.

That was one of the reasons they had moved back to the big city of St. Louis—the chance for a better education. Sigmund had owned his own barbershop in Advance, even though it was only one chair. Here in St. Louis, he wasn't the owner, but he made more money because there were so many more customers here. Agnes knew he missed being in charge of his time and his work. That was why when Mr. Kowalska, a customer, asked him to be his travel companion on his train trip to the south, her dad had taken ten days off from work.

"He's going to pay me very well, Mollie," he had told their mother. "He will pay even more than I would make in the same time at the barbershop. We can put it toward saving for me to have my own shop again."

"But what if Mr. Adams doesn't want you back when you return?" Mama worried.

"He'll take me back. I'm the only one of his barbers who can speak Polish. I have loyal customers who won't come back if I'm not there."

Mr. Kowalska was one of the men who relied on Sigmund's language skills. He had business in the town of Miami, and his English just wasn't good enough. He had needed Sigmund to act as his translator.

And now Sigmund had had a new adventure. He had been to a tropical land. Agnes had read all about Florida in the library's *Encyclopedia Britannica*. Even if it was part of the United States, and wasn't an island, like Robert Louis Stevenson wrote about in *Treasure Island,* it was still tropical. Maybe her dad had even seen a pirate like Long John Silver.

Agnes shivered with excitement—or maybe it was from the cold, muddy water that the butcher's horse-drawn wagon splashed over her shoes as she waited at the corner. Finally, she was on Compton Avenue with its tiny, narrow row houses.

She hurried up the steps and into the warmth of the little entryway, where she hung her coat on the hook and pulled off her wet boots. Yes! The rest of the family's coats already hung there. Even her dad's. He was home.

Her father embraced her warmly as she walked into the parlor. "Agnes, look at you. I've been gone only a week, and all my girls have gotten more beautiful," her dad said.

"Dad, Dad, now that Agnes is home you can tell us all about your trip," said Mary, her six-year-old little sister, anxiously pulling at their father's coat.

"Yes, Dad, please," added Leon, the only boy in the family.

"Come into the kitchen so everyone can hear while we eat dinner," Mama called.

The four of them crowded around the table along with Mama and fifteen-year-old Helen, who had been helping her. After they bowed their heads to say grace and passed the food around, Dad began his tale.

"Mr. Kowalska and I left St. Louis on Monday morning, and the train began to head south. Mr. Kowalska is a man of business, and he had arranged a sleeping car for us. I've never been to the sleeping car section of a train before. I have only slept in the chairs, and they are not too uncomfortable. But the sleeping cars are real luxury."

"Ooo," said Helen, "if I ever go on a train, I'm going to have a sleeping car. I'm going to have luxury."

"You'll be lucky to ever go on a train at all," said Mama with a touch of exasperation. Helen always wanted more and better than she already had. "Appreciate what you have in life, and don't go pining for more."

"Yes, Mama," Helen said contritely.

"And if you keep interrupting, we'll never hear Dad's tale," put in Agnes. "Ow!" she added as her sister gave her a swift kick under the table.

"Children, that is enough!" said Dad. "Do you want to hear about my trip or not?"

"Yes, Dad," came the murmurs.

"Good, now no more nonsense. Eat your dinner and I will tell you my story. Now where was I? Oh yes, we got to Evansville, Indiana, about lunchtime, and the train stopped for a short time. Mr. Kowalska and I walked around for a bit and got lunch in a diner—yes, Helen, it was cheaper to eat at the diner than to eat in the train's dining car, and we knew we would eat plenty of meals on the train," he said in an obvious attempt to keep his middle daughter from interrupting again.

"So when did you eat in the dining car?" asked Helen.

"Did you see anything interesting in Evansville?" asked Agnes.

Dad answered Agnes first.

"Not really, sweetheart, we didn't have much time. We thought about walking down to the Ohio River, which is only about half a mile from the station, but were told there is a levee because the river often floods in that area. That makes it impossible to see the river or the state of Kentucky, which is right on the other side. Since there was nothing much to see, we just ate and headed back to the train."

He glanced at Helen with a smile. "We were south of Nashville, and it was already dark by the time we went to the dining car. We had steak and potatoes, and it was very good food but nothing particularly fancy," he said before she could interrupt again. "In the dining car you are seated at tables for four so we met different people each time we sat down for a meal."

"Isn't that strange? Eating with people you have never met before?" asked Helen.

"Not at all. I've done it many times. That is how I met your mother, remember. When I worked on the excursion boat I sat down at the table and talked with your mother while she was having her lunch." He smiled at his wife who smiled back. "But back to my trip. We ate with a lovely young couple who were on their wedding trip. They had been all the way to Chicago and were returning to Atlanta."

"Oooo, that sounds romantic," said Agnes.

"When we returned from dinner the porter had opened the beds, and there was no room to do anything but retire for the night. The next morning we woke not long before we reached Atlanta, where we were scheduled to change trains. I noticed immediately it was warmer there so we took off our heavy coats and packed them in our suitcases before we got off the train."

"Can I have more potatoes, Mama?" Leon interrupted and Mollie quickly dished them up, telling her husband to continue his story.

"We had only an hour, and the Atlanta station was quite busy, so we got our bags and hurried across the station to the next track just in time to take our seats. It was a local train with many stops across the state of Georgia so it took all day to get to Jacksonville. We had to switch to a new line there, it's called the Florida East Coast Railway, and we got on just in time to have our beds turned down in our car and go to sleep. And then—" Dad paused dramatically as he looked around at the faces of the children waiting eagerly for the rest of his story. "We woke up the next morning, looked out the window, and what do you think we saw?"

"A pirate?" asked Leon.

"A fairy?" asked Mary.

"The ocean!" said Agnes excitedly.

"No, none of those things. I don't know if there are any fairies in Florida or pirates, but I did not see either during my trip. And we were a little too far inland to see the ocean. What we did see were palm trees. Hundreds and hundreds of palm trees lined the train tracks, and we could see them in the distance, too. The land is so flat you can see for many miles."

"What's a palm tree?" asked Leon.

"It's a very different kind of tree," said Dad. "Its trunk grows straight up almost fifty feet before there are any leaves at all."

"That sounds like a silly kind of tree," said Mary. "Are you making up a story, Dad?"

"No, Mary," said Agnes. "I've seen pictures of palm trees in the encyclopedia. They look just like that. I want to see one someday in real life."

"Well, sweetheart, maybe you can."

"And when is Agnes going to see a palm tree?" asked Mama.

"Well, maybe when we go to Florida," said Dad.

"Go to Florida?"

"When? When? When?"

"Ooo!"

Everyone at the table, from little Mary on up to Mama, began talking at once. Finally, Mama made herself heard over the noise and shushed everyone.

"Be quiet, children. Sigmund, why would you put such ideas in their heads? We would never be able to afford a trip to Florida—all six of us. I can't imagine what the train fare for six would be, even if we did sleep in the chairs," she said indignantly.

"I want to ride in the sleeping car!" said Helen.

"It doesn't matter what you want, Helen, because none of us is going on a train to Florida," said Mama.

"You're right. It would cost far too much for us all to take the train," said Dad, and laughed, but Agnes, watching him, had the feeling that he was really serious about this trip to Florida.

She didn't have a chance to ask him, though, because the noise that erupted in the small kitchen this time was even louder than before. Leon got up from the table and ran in circles around it.

"Chug-a-chug-a woo woo! I'm a train!" he shouted.

Mary, of course, immediately imitated him. "Woo woo!" she said, pounding her fork on the table. "Woo woo!"

"Children, enough! Settle down. Leon, back in your chair, and finish your dinner. Sigmund, what has gotten into you? Did the heat in Miami addle your brains?"

As Leon got back in his seat and Mary quieted down, Dad replied, "No, Mollie, my brains aren't addled, and I'm not talking about a trip to Miami like we are Rockefellers. I think we should move there."

Leon and Mary seemed confused, but Helen slammed her fork down on her plate with a loud crack that made Agnes wince in worry for the poor dish. "Move! Again! No Dad, I'm almost out of high school. I only have a few more months. I don't want to leave my friends."

"That is ridiculous, Sigmund. Where would we live? Where would you work? It's an uncivilized frontier. I hear there are even still Indians there," Mama said.

"Well, yes, I did see a number of Indians in Miami. The tribe is called the Seminoles. And they get haircuts, just like anyone else," he said.

"You're going to cut Indians' hair?" asked Agnes in awe.

"If they come into my shop and have the money," Dad replied.

"This is the silliest conversation I've ever heard," said Mama. "Helen, help Mary and Leon get ready for bed. Agnes, you can help me with the dishes tonight. And Sigmund, we will talk about this later."

Mama's tone was final, and everyone, even Dad, knew it. There would be no more discussion of Miami, Indians, moving, or anything else tonight.

After Mama sent them to bed, Agnes and Helen helped each other roll their hair in rag rollers so it would curl nicely. They both had thick and rather unruly hair; if not curled every night, it never behaved. Helen wanted to cut her hair in a bob, but Mama wouldn't allow it and insisted she wear it long and tied with a ribbon—which always came out because Helen was a tomboy and liked to play ball with the boys at recess. Now that Agnes had a job, she wore her hair pinned around her ears and loved the way she looked with a scarf tied low around her head with a bow on the side; she was sure it gave her a sophisticated air.

Once the two girls had their nightgowns and robes on, they came downstairs to kiss their parents goodnight. Their dad had picked up his pipe and was starting to prepare for his nightly smoke.

"Dad, are we really going to move to Miami?" Agnes whispered quietly in his ear so Mama wouldn't hear. She was busy helping Helen tie a scarf around her head so her curlers wouldn't come out in bed.

"Would you like that?" he asked.

"Yes! I want to go on an adventure to a tropical land."

"It's still part of the United States, you know."

"Yes, but it's so different from here," said Agnes. "Can you tell me more about it tomorrow?"

"Yes, yes. I'll tell you more tomorrow night. But now you and Helen need to go to bed so your Mama and I can talk."

"About moving to Florida?"

"Go to bed, Agnes!" Dad turned her around to face the stairs. "Goodnight, Helen. We will see you both in the morning."

Agnes and Helen dutifully headed to the room they shared. Agnes pulled back the covers, but Helen stopped her.

"You aren't really going to bed, are you?"

"Well, yes," Agnes replied. "That's what I usually do when I'm in the bedroom."

"Come on! You know they are talking about Florida. If we creep down the stairs really quietly, we can hear what they say."

"We'll get in trouble."

"Only if they catch us," replied Helen. "And they'll catch us only if you make noise like the last time."

"I couldn't help that! You sat on my hand."

"Well, keep your hands in your lap. You want to hear more about Florida, don't you?" Helen coaxed.

"All right. But if we get caught, I'm telling them it was your idea."

The girls crept quietly down to the middle of the stairs, then sat in the shadows where they could hear their parents but could not see them. It was obvious Mama and Dad were already discussing Dad's idea.

"It doesn't make sense, Sigmund. You have a perfectly good job here. You have as many customers as you can see in a day, and it's a reliable salary. You get paid the same even on slow weeks. It's not like when you owned your own shop. If no one came in, you didn't make any money."

"I know, I know, Mollie. But that was Advance. It was a tiny town. In Miami it will be different. There are always new people arriving and tourists who need haircuts."

"But it's still a small town. You said so yourself."

"Not as small as Advance, and it's growing every month. I've never seen a place with so much energy."

Agnes could hear the excitement in Dad's voice. And apparently so could their mother.

"I'm already so far from my sisters—it's over a hundred miles to Cape Girardeau. We only see them once or twice a year. I'll never see them again if we move to Miami."

"Come here, Mollie, come here."

Agnes and Helen heard a rustling and knew their mother had shifted to Dad's lap.

"It will be all right," he said.

"And what about education? We moved here so the children could get better schooling."

"There's a brand-new Catholic school in Miami. And there is a new high school, too," Dad said.

"You've made up your mind, haven't you?"

"No, nothing like that. I'm still thinking about it, trying to decide what is best for all of us. We are going to keep thinking and discussing. Maybe Agnes can even do some research for us at the library," said Dad. "She will like that."

~~~

The discussions did continue, and though her parents didn't ask, Agnes continued to look up everything she could find in the library about Florida. Mama and Dad discussed it every night during the rest of November. Agnes and Helen discussed it every night when they went to bed, too, although they were careful not to let their parents hear. Only Leon and Mary were oblivious to the heavy atmosphere that hung over the rest of the family. They were more focused on Christmas than on a move to a place so exotic it might as well have been the Emerald City. That's how Agnes began to think of Miami—a fairy-tale city that was lush and green with palm trees and other tropical plants.

Sometime in December the discussions between her parents changed from "whether" they should move to "how" and "when" they should move. Agnes knew it was a reality the day she came home from work to find the furniture in the parlor gone.

"Mama, where are the chairs?" she asked as she stepped into the bare room.

"Well, your father says that many of the houses there can be rented furnished. Mrs. Baker has always admired the set so I sold them to her today," Mama explained.

"We're really moving! Really! When?"

"Right after Christmas. I want to get the younger children back into school as quickly as I can. We have some more things to sell before we can go. I want to take as little as we can manage. It's a good time to be selling things. People are looking for Christmas presents. On Saturday you and Helen should go through your things and see what you can get rid of. We won't need those winter clothes anymore, I guess."

The next few weeks passed in a flurry of activity until suddenly they were on their way back from Midnight Mass, walking home from church in a light snowfall, bundled in coats, hats, and scarves, with young Mary asleep in her father's arms.

"I guess this will be the last time we go to Christmas Mass in the snow," said Agnes. "Next year we will be walking to church in balmy weather with palm trees all around."

Agnes didn't expect any gifts on Christmas morning. Her mother had made it clear that they couldn't bring much with them, and all the extra money needed to be saved for their move. But as they all sat down for breakfast, Dad walked into the kitchen with a box in his hands.

"What have you done now, Sigmund?" her mother said, voice colored with surprise and amusement.

"It is just a small present—and one for all of us," he said, placing the box on the table and opening it for everyone to see.

"A camera!" shouted Leon. "Wow! A camera. Can I take a photograph?"

Dad carefully pulled the small machine out of the box. It was about the size of a book when folded, but it had metal strips on the side that scissored out and created an accordion-like leather funnel with a round glass lens on the end. "I decided we must have a camera to record our adventure, don't you agree, Agnes?"

The rest of the day was spent taking turns learning how to use the camera, although Mama declared they couldn't put any film into it until they were on their trip. "It is too expensive to waste; we must wait until we have something really new and interesting to photograph."

~~~

The next few days were spent in a flurry of packing.

"You can only take one suitcase each," Mama told Helen and Agnes. "We can't afford to take more."

"Oh Mama, how can I fit everything I need in?" wailed Agnes as she and Helen tried to figure out how to stuff as many of their treasures as possible into their allotted bags.

"It will be easier to manage on the train," Mama said. "We must bring a big basket with food, too. We can't afford to eat every meal in the dining car."

Helen pouted at that. "You mean we're going to eat in our seats out of a basket like peasants?"

Mama had just closed Mary's suitcase and taken it to the door when there was a loud noise outside. A car pulled up and a horn honked loud and long.

"Whoever is making that racket?" Mama asked. "Agnes, are some of your friends coming to say goodbye?"

"I don't know anyone who owns an automobile." Agnes went to the door and looked out. "It's Dad! Mama, look, Dad is getting out of a car!"

Everyone ran to the door, from little Mary to Mama, all talking at once and pushing and shoving to get out to the street, not worrying about coats or hats or the freezing late-December weather.

"Surprise!" Dad shouted as he gestured toward the Buick touring car. "I told you we didn't have to go to Florida by train."

"This is even better than a train," said Helen, running her hands over the shiny black metal.

The vehicle was not new—it had some dings and scratches—but it had obviously been meticulously cleaned and polished. The wide leather seats gleamed, and the canvas roof was a deep black as if the material had been freshly scrubbed. Even the wooden rack designed to hold luggage looked clean, which was a miracle given the slush-covered streets of the city.

"Sigmund! What have you done? You don't even know how to drive," said Mama, her hands at her face in astonishment.

"Well, I do now. The man I bought the car from threw in a driving lesson free!" Dad said proudly.

Leon had already climbed into the front seat and was playing with the steering wheel. Agnes, Mary, and Helen settled in the back.

"You see," said Dad. "There will be plenty of room for all of us. Agnes, Helen, and Leon will sit in the back. You and I will sit in the front with Mary in between us. There is room for our luggage on the rack, and we can store a few things around the children's feet, too," he said.

"You're sure?" Mama said doubtfully.

"I'm sure. It is the best way to get us all to Miami, and once we are there, we can sell the car and have some extra money to buy new furniture if needed. But come on, children, get out of the car. Right now we have to finish packing up to leave first thing in the morning."

~~~

It was just barely light when she got out of bed the next morning, but Agnes didn't care. She'd hardly slept all night. She was finally starting her adventure.

She helped Mama dress Mary and pack the last few items into a suitcase as her father, Helen, and Leon strapped things onto the back and sides of the car. When they were finally loaded, she could barely see the vehicle. The suitcases on the back rack were stacked up to the level of the rear window, leaving just enough room for their father to see what was coming behind him, while others were tied to the running board. Then Helen, Agnes, and Leon had to get in through the driver's door and climb over the front seat to their places in the rear.

"You're too fat!" exclaimed Helen, pushing Agnes as far to the side as she could.

"Don't call me fat, and you're too tall."

"You are pleasingly plump, my beautiful oldest daughter, and you are just the right height, my lovely middle girl," said Dad.

"Helen and Agnes, be nice to each other," said Mama. "We must all work to be pleasant every day. It is a long drive to Miami, and we will be spending a lot of time in close quarters."

After a little more shoving, juggling, and wiggling, the three settled in the back. Mama took Mary on her lap, Dad shouted, "Next stop, Florida!" and they were off.

"Watch out, Sigmund!" yelled Mama as they came to the first intersection. "The trolley is coming!"

"The trolley is half a block away, Mollie," Dad said as he swung the wheel and turned onto the busy street.

Mama screamed and hid her eyes.

"It will be just fine. I know what I'm doing."

But Agnes noticed the car seemed to weave back and forth rather than just go in a straight line like the other cars on the road. She, Helen, and Mama periodically gasped, screamed, and covered their eyes as the car made its way from the residential district into the warehouse area of Laclede's Landing.

"Is this an adventure enough for you, Agnes?" her father called as they took another wide turn.

"Yes, Dad!" she yelled as Helen reached across Leon to grab her hand.

"We are going over the Eads Bridge to East St. Louis and then we will have left Missouri behind," he informed them just as the bridge came into sight. "My mother always said you have to pick up your feet when you cross a bridge or you won't find your true love. So pick up your feet, girls!"

"Well, you already have your true love, Sigmund, so don't you dare pick up your feet. You just drive!" Mama admonished.

Dad laughed, but Agnes and Helen picked their feet up.

"I'm not going to pick my feet up. I don't want a true love," said Leon, who kept his planted solidly on the floor all the way across the bridge.

The girls looked out the window and over the wide expanse of cold water where blocks of ice floated slowly past. It wasn't long before they could see Illinois.

Just as they reached the first street crossing at the end of the bridge, a horse-drawn cart came around the corner. The horse shied when it saw them, rearing up on its hind legs. The driver called "Whoa!" and pulled hard on the reins.

Dad swerved to avoid the horse, and the car ran straight

into a lamppost. The motor shut down, and it was suddenly quiet. There was no noise whatsoever but the sound of steam hissing from the engine.

"Is everyone all right?" asked the wagon driver, running over to check things out. "Is anyone hurt?"

Mama and Dad looked at the children in the back seat. Agnes noticed the fear on her parents' faces, but the three of them nodded; no one was hurt.

"I'm so sorry. This mare just ain't used to automobiles," the driver said. "I'm trying to get her easy with it so I take her out in the early mornings when not many people are around."

"I'm sure it was not the horse's fault," said Mama with a quick glance over at her husband.

Dad said nothing. Once he checked on all the children he got out and walked around the car slowly, running his hands over the sleek, black steel. He stopped at the rear. "Well, this will have to be fixed," he said.

"What's broken, Dad?" asked Leon.

"We have a flat tire. I assume we have a problem with the radiator, too, because of the steam coming out from under the hood. I'll have to find someone to repair it."

"Don't you worry about that," said the wagon driver. "My brother's got a shop just at the end of the block. He's been learning how to fix these newfangled automobiles. Says it's the way of the future. Ma'am, if you and the children will come with me, I'll get you out of the cold while we get my brother to tow this vehicle down the street."

Mama allowed the man to help her out, and the children followed like ducklings. A short time later the Buick was safely ensconced in the shop, getting a new tire and having its radiator repaired.

Dad and Leon watched with rapt attention as the mechanic worked on the car. Mama, Agnes, Helen, and Mary waited in the tiny front office. Helen and Agnes tried to keep Mary entertained while their mother paced.

"This is the most ridiculous thing I've ever heard of," Mama muttered. "Driving all the way to Florida. It will take us a week at least. And your father is so stubborn and won't admit he doesn't know how to drive that thing."

"He'll learn, Mama. He has plenty of time between here and Florida to figure it out," Agnes said, hoping to calm her mother. She could see her adventure ending right here in East St. Louis, barely ten miles from home. "I'm sure he'll be the best driver on the road by the time we get there," she added.

"If he hasn't killed us all first! Well, I will just have to find another way to get this family to Florida!" Mama pulled on her coat and marched out the front door.

"What do you think she is going to do?" asked Mary.

None of the girls had ever seen their mother quite this upset before. Not even when the treasure hunters were digging holes in their property.

"I have no idea," said Helen, shaking her head.

"But she didn't say we weren't going to Florida. She just said we'd have to find another way," put in Agnes.

The girls waited and waited, anxiously moving from the window through which they could watch the progress on the car to the door where they peered out into the street looking for their mother. It was almost noon when Dad came into the room with the mechanic. Leon trailed behind them.

"Where is your mother?" Dad asked, wiping his greasy hands on a rag the mechanic handed him. "We are ready to get back on the road."

"We don't know," said Helen. "She just said there had to be a better way to get to Florida and left."

"She left? Where would she go?" Now it was Dad's turn to pace. He walked back and forth across the small room, stopping to look out the door each time he passed. "There she is!" he called after almost an hour. He practically ran from the room. "Mollie! Where have you been? I've been worried sick!"

Mama sailed into the garage office, her head held high, a young man trailing her carrying a small suitcase.

"Sigmund, this is Dan Severs. He is going to drive us to Florida."

"He is going to do what?" shouted Dad.

"He is going to drive us to Florida." Mama used her patient voice this time as if she was explaining something particularly complicated to one of the children.

Agnes, Helen, Leon, and Mary watched the discussion between their parents, their heads bobbing back and forth. Dan stood nervously in a corner, hat in one hand and suitcase in the other.

"That is the most ridiculous thing I've ever heard! It would cost as much to have someone drive us to Florida as it would for us all to take the train."

"No, he's asked only for food and a room when we stop for the night. You, Leon, and Dan can sleep in one room while the girls and I sleep in the other. We would have needed two rooms anyway," said Mama.

"How do you know he can drive?"

"Well, uh, sir—" stammered Dan. "I drive a truck and make deliveries around town regular like. I've always wanted to see the South so I thought your wife's offer was a good idea."

Dad turned his stern gaze on the young man. "I did not ask you."

"Uh, no, sir. Sorry, sir."

"And we are just going to take him for his word that he can drive?" Dad asked, turning back to his wife.

"No, I drove with him to his boarding house to pick up his suitcase to make sure he knew what he was doing. He didn't hit a lamppost once."

Dad's face grew red, but he didn't say anything. Agnes could tell he knew when he had been beaten. If he wanted to get to Florida, he was going to let this man drive them. He muttered something in Polish under his breath, then turned to the children, who were lined up and watching intently.

"All right. You heard your mother. Mr. Severs here is going to drive us to Florida. Mr. Severs, find a place to put your suitcase. Mollie, you are in the back seat with Mary on your lap. Agnes, Helen, get on in the back seat, too. Leon, you'll ride in the front with me. Everyone in the car. We are wasting daylight."

The family scrambled to obey as quickly as possible. They knew when Dad meant business.

The car that had been designed as a five-passenger vehicle now would hold seven on its 1,200-mile journey—plus their luggage, of course. Once settled, Dan blew the horn, and they were off!

~~~

The trip to Miami took several days, and although after their rocky start things went smoothly. Agnes had to admit that as adventures went this one was pretty tame, but she enjoyed every minute of it nonetheless. At lunchtime they picnicked at the side of the road and took turns taking photographs of each other with the new camera. They sang "St. Louis Blues" and "All the Boys Love Mary," which made Mary laugh and laugh each time. They divided into teams and made up a game of counting cows. Each team had to count all the cows on their own side of the road, and whoever had counted the most cows by the time they came to a stop won—but if a black cow was seen, whosever side of the road it was on lost all their points and had to start again.

There were long stretches of open road between the many small towns, and so by the second day Mama allowed Dad to take driving lessons from Dan whenever the road was empty—but she wouldn't let him drive in the towns.

It seemed to get a little warmer each day; the trees changed from maples and oaks to tall pines, and the landscape changed from fields to swampland.

"Where are the palm trees? I thought you said we would see palm trees," Mary said every few hours.

"Soon, soon," Dad answered each time.

In southern Georgia they saw their first palm tree and stopped the car so everyone could get out and look at it. Finally, they crossed the Florida line, and they all sang "Suwannee River" to celebrate. It took another day's drive to reach Miami.

"We will stop at the train station," Dad declared. "That will be a good place to find someone who knows where we can rent a house."

"Can I go with you, Dad?" asked Agnes when they arrived at the wooden building and all got out to stretch.

"Of course," he replied, and the two of them headed into the tiny station.

As Dad stopped a bellman and began asking questions,

Agnes wandered outside where a train had just pulled in. A young man was transferring boxes and baggage onto a cart, and Agnes stopped to watch.

"Can I help you?" he asked. "Are you looking for any luggage in particular?"

He was tall and thin and had striking dark blue eyes that instantly reminded Agnes of the ocean she had caught her first glimpse of the day before.

"No, my family just arrived in Miami, and we are looking for a house to rent. Dad thought someone here at the station might know where to find one."

"Well, he was right. There is a house just down the street from my family's that's up for rent. If your father can wait about a half hour, I'll be off work and can show you where it is."

"Oh, that's wonderful! I'll go tell him now. My name's Agnes, by the way," she said, holding out her hand.

"Good to meet you," he said. "I'm Bert Rogers."

Chapter 10
Playing Dress-Up

"I get to be the bride this time."

"No, it's my turn."

"You were the bride last time."

"All right, you can be the bride, but next time I get to be Marilyn Monroe."

~~~

There were a lot of girls in our neighborhood: Denise, Mary Beth, two Debbies, and a few more. Since Cheryl and I had the best supply of costumes and cast-offs, not to mention a house with air-conditioning, our home was the favorite place to play dress-up.

Mama, our grandmothers, and all the many Aunts contributed to our stash of finery with broken jewelry, scarves, and dresses. Grandma Hodges sewed so she gave us scraps of lace or rickrack. Since Aunt Helen was always going to parties, she would bring back everything from plastic Hawaiian leis to New Year's hats and paper party horns. One of my favorite pieces in the dress-up chest was a lacy white petticoat that we alternately used as a bridal gown or a very fluffy veil, depending on the chosen bride's mood. Two long rolls of white lace carefully cut from an old dress worked to tie it on so it didn't slip down in the middle of a game.

Some of our favorite scenarios were Movie Stars, Mothers Going Shopping, and Wedding. Of course, in our dress-up games, life was always perfect. And since the men were imaginary, things went a lot more smoothly than they usually do in real life.

In planning our pretend weddings, there were no fights between families over which side got to invite more guests, or whether or not alcohol would be served, or if there would be a musician or a DJ. The groom's family adored the beautiful bride. The bride's family loved the groom, who was handsome and rich. And he never backed out at the last minute.

At one event I went to shortly after graduating college, I

was very aware that the groom had been having doubts. When the minister said, "Do you take this woman to be your lawful wedded wife?" there was a long pause, and I shared looks with the rest of the guests on the groom's side. It was one of those moments when you feel as if you are watching a slow-motion train wreck. You can't stop it, and you can't look away.

Finally, before most of the bride's side of the church noticed there might be a problem, the groom took a deep breath and said, "I do." His friends all took a deep breath with him. That marriage has lasted. I suppose being smart enough to worry whether you are doing the right thing might be one of the signs that you're actually ready to be married.

Then there was the rehearsal dinner where the family dog ate the roast, and the reception where the cake fell off the table. Not to mention the one where the bride's family came up to the groom and said, "Good luck, you'll need it," and "I can't believe you are actually going to marry her." That particular marriage didn't last too long.

Maybe the squabbles we had about who got to be bride were the truest part of our games of dress-up. After years of going to weddings, sometimes as a bridesmaid or other participant, I've seen my share of family drama. It's made me realize just what a fantasy our little girl dreams were. I really shouldn't have been so naïve, though, even at that young age. I'd heard a lot of stories about our own family's weddings, but my favorite is the wedding of Agnes and Bert, my Grandma and Granddad Rogers. They talked about it so often, I almost felt as if I had been there.

Chapter 11
Eloping Family Style

1922

"If you get married now, you won't be eligible to go to Atlantic City!" Helen exclaimed, making her exasperation at her sister clear. "You have a real chance of being chosen."

"I don't care about Atlantic City. I just want to marry Bert." Agnes glared back at her sister. "I only entered that pageant because they asked me to at work."

"But you won Miss Photogenic! They asked you to pose for that magazine advertisement. And you have to admit you looked really fabulous in those photos."

"You have just as much chance of being chosen for Atlantic City as I do. Probably more. You won Best Smile, and besides, you've always been prettier than me."

The two young women sat on their beds in the back bedroom they shared in the little one-story bungalow. The window looked out over a small backyard where some guava bushes, a couple of orange trees, and their mother's vegetable garden dotted the coarse St. Augustine grass—so different from the soft bluegrass they had grown up with in Missouri. In fact, everything about the house was different than Missouri. In St. Louis they'd lived in a tall, brick row house with a tiny plot of grass in front. Here the family home was a Spanish-style stucco bungalow, painted white with dark green shutters, surrounded by a fair-sized yard. Mama now had enough room to grow tomatoes and a few other vegetables.

Agnes pushed her hair off her face. Even with a breeze it felt muggy, and she was sweating. It was late April and already hotter than hell. She wouldn't say "hell" out loud, certainly not where Mama could hear, but that was just how hot it was.

She wished she were at the beach right now. It was always cooler there. Of course, unlike Helen, Mary, and their brother Leon, she had never learned to swim. Of all the family she'd been the most excited to move to Miami. And she did love it. Now.

But it had taken a while to settle in. Miami hadn't been anything like they'd expected, and while Leon and Mary seemed to make friends easily at school, she and Helen had taken longer to feel like Miami was home.

The town was small. Well, not as small as Advance where they had grown up, but after several years in St. Louis, with its streetcars, brick-paved streets, and more than 700,000 people, Miami was the backwoods. Most of the streets were dirt, which turned to mud when it rained—and that was every day from May until November. There were very few stores—and the fashion! Or to be more specific, the lack of fashion.

In St. Louis the women were wearing their skirts short, well above the ankle, and the men were wearing wide-legged pants. In Miami most of the women who weren't tourists still wore longer dresses, and the men wore their pants pegged.

Helen had spent most nights crying herself to sleep for the first few months. Then, slowly, the two young women had begun to make friends. They were helped along by Bert Rogers, who'd taken a shine to Agnes almost from the day they arrived. And Bert had several brothers and sisters so they suddenly had a group of friends.

Agnes had begun to love Miami—except for the heat—as much as she had expected to. And she certainly loved Bert. She never would have met him if they hadn't moved here. They often went dancing at the Million Dollar Pier on Miami Beach and the other open-air bandstands where they only had to pay a dime to dance all night.

Her only remaining gripe was that everyone she met seemed to want to swim all the time. Bert was a great swimmer; in fact, he was the one who had taught Leon. Bert took Leon along with his nephew Herbert when they went to the pool at the Royal Palm Hotel sometimes. She loved watching Bert cut through the water. But she couldn't stand the feel of water splashing in her face. It always made her think of drowning. She was content to sit on the sand or by the pool or wade in up to her knees to cool off.

Her dislike of swimming made it even more ironic that she had won a trophy in the Miss Miami Pageant held on the beach a few months ago. Agnes had represented *The Miami Metropolis*, where she worked as a receptionist. The other women in her department had insisted she enter because she was the youngest unmarried woman there. They had fashioned her a "bathing suit" out of strips of newsprint attached to her own suit, and she had won a prize for her "daring paper swim fashion." The men judging it had loved the way the paper swirled around when she moved, giving glimpses of her legs beneath. That was what Mama said. Dad just held his hand over his eyes during the whole thing. He'd supported his two oldest daughters by showing up, but that didn't mean he was really comfortable with seeing them parade in front of people in their bathing suits. Bert loved it, though, and he gave her a congratulatory kiss at the end.

The pageant had been fun. She'd enjoyed spending time with all the girls but posing for the photographs on the beach had been hot, sandy, and boring. Her black wool bathing suit had a white belt and white stripes around the legs and came to the middle of her thighs—the latest fashion. It would have been scandalous to wear back in St. Louis; they might even have arrested her! After she'd added a polka-dotted head scarf, she felt like she would be the most stylish girl in the pageant. But then the ladies at the *Metropolis* decided she had to add swim boots. They were flat, with rubber soles, and made of canvas that laced halfway to her knees. As soon as they got wet, they stuck to her calves while sand seeped in at every opening, chafing her legs. But they were the latest fashion.

Now, unlike Helen, she was ready to grow up, move on, and marry Bert. Helen loved the attention from many men the event had brought.

"I'm going to marry a rich man someday, and this has given me the opportunity to meet wealthy tourists at speakeasys," she said.

"You'd better be careful how you act or no decent man will want to marry you," Agnes warned.

Helen just laughed. "I'm not looking for decent; I'm looking for exciting. Maybe I'll get chosen to go to the Miss America pageant in Atlantic City. Then think of the excitement I'll have."

"Oh, Helen, you are never happy with what you have; you are always wanting something more."

"Just because you're ready to settle down doesn't mean I have to. Anyway, I'm two years younger than you. I've got plenty of time to find a man."

Agnes rolled her eyes. Her sister was so stubborn. If she got it in her head to do something, she would do it. Like that time back when they were ten and twelve years old and still lived in Advance. One of the boys bet Helen she wouldn't stick her head on the railroad track when the train was coming. Of course, she did it. And then she did it again the next day because not all the kids in town had seen her do it the first time.

Agnes thought her sister should have learned about consequences that day. An engineer who'd spotted her had headed right down to Dad's barbershop and told him. Helen had her hide tanned but good. And she hadn't been allowed to play after school for two weeks.

But it seemed to Agnes that the only lesson Helen had learned was don't do something when you might get caught. Now twenty-one, she snuck out to speakeasys—not just the dance stands but the clubs where they served liquor—every chance she got. Agnes always knew and didn't tell. Because that's what sisters did for each other. But she worried about Helen's headstrong ways.

"So when are you and Bert getting married?" Helen took the conversation back to where it had started.

"As soon as the church in St. Louis mails me my baptismal certificate. Father McLaughlin says he can't list the banns until he sees my certificate. Then three weeks for the banns so sometime in late May," Agnes explained. "I just wish that certificate would get here from St. Louis. Why can't the mail come any faster?"

~~~

A week later Agnes came home from work to find her youngest sister, Mary, standing on the porch excitedly waving an envelope.

"I've been waiting for you all afternoon!" Mary cried. "Your letter is here—the one from St. Louis."

Agnes ran up the steps and snatched the precious envelope from her sister's hand.

"Let me see, let me see!" Mary said excitedly. "I've never seen a baptismal certificate before. What does it look like?"

"Silly girl," Agnes said fondly. "It's just a piece of paper that says where I was baptized and when."

"Then why is it so important? You and Mama and Dad have done nothing but talk about it for weeks."

"Because Father McLaughlin says I can't marry Bert until he sees it."

Just then Mama came out of the kitchen wiping her hands on a dishtowel. "Agnes, I'm so glad you're home. I've had a time keeping Mary from opening that envelope, and frankly, I was half tempted to do it myself. Now open it, quick. Then tomorrow you and Bert can make an appointment with Father, and we can finally set a wedding date."

Agnes tore open the envelope and pulled out the one typed page. She glanced at it, turned it over, looked in the envelope again, then read the letter out loud.

"Dear Miss Sawieja," she began, "I regret to inform you that the church office burned to the ground last year. All the documents recording previous marriages, deaths, and baptisms were lost in the fire. We cannot send you a certificate of your baptism because we no longer have a record of it. I hope that the priest at your church will understand . . ."

When her voice trailed off, her mother snatched the letter from her hand.

"That can't be," Mama said, reading the paper over to herself as if she could make the typed letters on the page say something different.

"Mama, what are we going to do?" Agnes began to cry. "How am I ever going to get married if I don't have a baptismal certificate?"

"Don't worry, sweetheart," Mama said, putting her arm arounds Agnes's shoulders and walking her toward the kitchen where she sat her down at the table. "Let me get you a Coca-Cola. It's going to be fine. You take Father McLaughlin this letter, and show it to him. I'm sure he'll understand, just like the note says."

"I don't know, Mama," Agnes replied. "He's such a stickler for the rules."

"She's right, Mama," said Mary. "Father always says that we have to obey the rules because it's what God wants us to do."

"Don't you worry, Agnes. We won't let a little piece of paper stop you from getting married," her mother vowed.

Agnes really hoped her mother meant that. She knew Mama had her heart set on all her children having church weddings, and as the oldest, it was up to her to lead the way.

~~~

A few evenings later Agnes sat with Bert, his sister Anna Mae, and his two youngest brothers in their backyard talking about the meeting they'd had with Father McLaughlin.

"I can't believe he's being so stubborn," Agnes said for at least the tenth time in the last hour.

Bert rubbed her shoulders comfortingly. "I know, sweetheart, but we'll figure something out."

At that moment Bert's father returned from his daily run driving the train down to Key West and back. Bert's mom had died a few years before, and ever since then Anna Mae had run the household.

"What's going on?" Herb asked. His hair had gone gray in the last few years, and his expression held a sadness that had not been there before his beloved Mary had died.

"Still talking about Father McLaughlin and how he wants Agnes to get baptized before they get married," Anna Mae answered. "Come on, Dad, I'll get you some supper."

She got up from her chair and headed into the kitchen. The rest of the family trooped after her, and they settled at the long kitchen table, which could hold all seven of the siblings and a few more friends besides.

"So why don't you just get rebaptized?" Herb asked his future daughter-in-law when he had his supper in front of him.

"Because my dad says I've already been baptized, and the catechism says you only get baptized once. He doesn't want me to do it."

"Sounds like he's being just as stubborn as the priest," Herb responded.

"Oh, he is. So is my mother, who says she wants me to be married in the Catholic church, no matter what."

"So we're stuck, Dad," Bert said. "Mrs. Sawieja wants us to have a Catholic wedding. Mr. Sawieja doesn't want Agnes to get baptized a second time, and the priest won't marry us unless she does. Got any ideas how to get out of this mess?"

"You could always just live in sin," his brother Toby laughed. Toby was always the one in the family to make a joke, whether it was appropriate or not.

Anna Mae swatted him on the shoulder. "Toby!"

Harold, who was only nineteen and the quietest, suddenly spoke up. "You can always elope."

"What!"

"How does that help?"

"We can't do that."

"Mama would never forgive me."

As everyone talked at once, Harold looked as if he regretted saying anything.

"No, wait a minute." Their father broke into the babble of conversation. "This could work. Father McLaughlin isn't the only priest in south Florida. There is a church in Fort Lauderdale and one up in West Palm Beach. The priest in Fort Lauderdale isn't a Jesuit either. Maybe he would be more reasonable."

"That's an awfully long way," said Agnes. "And what does it have to do with eloping?"

"Well, we'll call it a family elopement," Herb said. "Next weekend all the family—us, as many of your other brothers and sisters who can make it, Bert, and all of Agnes's family—will get in a couple of cars, and we'll drive up the coast, stopping at all the Catholic churches to see if someone will marry you with just the documentation we have."

The cacophony of voices reached new heights as everyone put in their suggestions for pulling off this "family elopement." After another half hour or so, Bert and Agnes left to explain it to her parents.

"If it looks like there is even a small possibility that we can be married by a priest, I think my mother and father will agree," Agnes said hopefully.

"And if we try our best and no priest will marry us, we will just find a justice of the peace," Bert vowed. "Your parents can't object once they see there is no other way."

~~~

At six a.m. on Saturday morning, May 9, two cars pulled up in front of the Sawieja home on S.W. 13 Avenue. Bert jumped out of the passenger side of the Model A that he and Toby had purchased together. Harold got out of the back seat while Anna Mae, his oldest sister Stella, and her husband Stan, along with Bert's dad, got out of the second vehicle.

Mary was already standing on the porch and turned to yell through the open door, "They're here, everyone! They're here!"

"Mary, hush, you'll wake the whole neighborhood," Agnes's mother scolded, still tying a scarf over her wide-brimmed straw hat to hold it on her head.

Bert ran up the steps as Agnes came out. She was wearing her best dress of pale blue cotton, with a long-waisted blouson bodice and pleated skirt. Bert complimented the dress whenever she wore it, and since there had been no time for her to get a new dress, she'd decided this would be her wedding outfit, along with a matching blue cloche hat. He kissed her and handed her a small bouquet of purple bougainvillea and bright red powder puff flowers from his family's garden.

"Are you ready?" he asked. "I picked these this morning. I know it wasn't what you thought you'd have. I know this wedding isn't what you thought it was going to be." He hesitated, searching her face.

"They are beautiful. It doesn't matter that it isn't the wedding I'd dreamed of. I just want to marry you. What else do we need besides our families and someone to marry us?"

Clearly nervous, Bert answered in a very literal fashion. "The letter from the church? You have it, don't you? And your birth certificate? I've got my stuff right here." He patted his suit pocket where he'd placed not only his papers but Agnes's wedding ring as well.

"Yes, I've got my letter and my birth certificate. We'll see how much good it does us," Agnes said as they walked down the steps.

"Remember, we are getting married today by someone, I promise you," Bert responded.

Toby opened the car door with a flourish. "You're wedding chariot awaits," he joked as she and Bert hopped in the back seat.

The Dixie Highway, which wound from Miami up the coast, wasn't really much of a highway but more a series of interconnected roads, some paved, some sand, and many in poor repair. It would take several hours to drive the fifty-some odd miles from Miami to Palm Beach. There weren't a lot of places to eat in between so Agnes's mother Mollie, along with Anna Mae and Stella, had filled several picnic baskets to feed the small horde that was coming on this elopement.

After the picnic baskets were stowed, Agnes's parents and Mary and Leon piled into the old family Buick. Helen was at the wheel since their dad, Sigmund, had never gotten comfortable driving a car, even after the lessons he'd received on their trip down to Florida.

When everyone was settled the three-car procession started out. It took over an hour to drive the thirty-five miles from Miami to Fort Lauderdale. They arrived a little after eight a.m., and Bert, Agnes, and the three parents got out while the rest of the sisters and brothers waited anxiously in the cars as they knocked at the rectory of St. Anthony Church. The priest himself, Father Plunckett, opened the door.

A short time later the front door opened, and they all walked back out.

"I don't think it's good," said Harold, standing next to the Sawieja car.

"Yeah, that's not a good look on my mom's face," Leon agreed.

"Well, no luck here," Herb said. "It looks like we are heading to Palm Beach."

Everyone groaned.

Anna Mae ran over to give both Bert and Agnes hugs. "We are going to get you married today, no matter what. I need another sister to help me keep all these men in line." She gestured to her father and brothers.

"Hey, what about me?" Stella said, climbing out of the third car where she had been sitting with her husband, Stan.

Anna Mae laughed and added Stella to the group hug. "You're too busy keeping your husband in line."

"Well, kids, time is wasting so let's head off to Palm Beach," Agnes's dad called out.

Herb walked over to the Sawieja car. "Leon, why don't you ride with Agnes and Bert for a while so I can talk with your mom and dad on the drive?"

"Yes, sir," Leon said, then scrambled out to sit next to Harold in the Model A.

"I wonder what Dad wants to talk about with Agnes's parents?" Harold questioned once Toby had started the car. It was at least two more hours to go the forty-five miles up the coast to Palm Beach, the next town with a Catholic church. That was a lot of talking.

"He wants to make sure the Sawiejas are on board with going to a justice of the peace if the priest at St. Ann's won't marry them," Toby explained.

"Are you sure you're okay with that, Agnes?" Bert asked her.

"I'm fine with it. I wanted to get married in the church, but if the priests won't let us, then what else can we do? We are getting married today, just like you said!" Agnes leaned over and kissed Bert as their younger brothers groaned.

It was almost lunchtime when they finally reached Palm Beach. Agnes, Bert, and their parents got out of the cars and rang the doorbell at the rectory. They were inside for almost an hour. The siblings were by that time sitting rather impatiently in the shade of a large live oak.

"I'm starving," Mary said.

"So am I," put in Leon.

"We have to wait for everyone," Helen told them. "It's taking such a long time. Maybe they have convinced the priest to let them get married—or the priest has convinced Dad to let him baptize Agnes."

The group continued to idly speculate on what was taking so long until finally the door opened. It was instantly obvious from the dejected expressions that the answer had been no. Bert and Agnes were not getting married at this church. They had driven all this way for nothing.

"Well, I think the first thing we need to do is find a place by the side of the road and eat," Herb announced. "Then, once our bellies are full, we can figure out a new plan."

Mollie rolled her eyes. "Men! All you think of is your stomachs."

"I want to eat, Mama, and I'm a girl," said Mary.

Mollie laughed and gave her a hug. "All right, we'll find a place to eat and then plan the next maneuver in this campaign."

They stopped close to the ocean a few miles south of Palm Beach. After pulling out blankets, baskets of food, and bottles of beer and Coca-Cola, they got comfortable before anyone broached the subject on everyone's minds.

"So exactly what did the priest say?" Anna Mae finally asked.

"Same old thing," replied Agnes. "I can't get married in the church without a baptismal certificate."

"What about another type of church?" asked Helen. "If you just want to get married in a church, there's Baptists and Methodists and all sorts of religions."

Everyone looked at her as if she had suddenly sprouted two heads.

"What?" Helen said with surprise. "What did I say that was so terrible? Mama, you and Dad have always said all religions are good. And we used to have the Baptist minister and the Jewish rabbi and the Catholic priest over to Sunday dinner all at the same time when we lived in Missouri. You said they liked it because it was the only place they could all talk religion without anyone thinking they were heretics."

Sigmund tapped his pipe and looked over at Herb. They'd eaten at each other's houses. They had mourned with Herb when his wife died. They had all gone to the same church every Sunday but had really never talked about how each of them felt about their religion. It had always been taken for granted. They were Catholic. They had always been Catholic. They would always be Catholic. And now here they sat on the side of the road, their children about to start a new life together. That would make them all family. If this wasn't handled well, it could lead to a rift that would eventually tear Agnes and Bert apart.

Sigmund took a deep breath. "You are right, Helen. I've always been proud that I accept every religion, but I've also just accepted what my Catholic faith taught me. Now I'm part of the reason Agnes and Bert are in this position. My view doesn't seem to line up with what these priests are saying. It just seems to me that the priests are too concerned with the letter of the law and not enough with the spirit. But this is Agnes and Bert's marriage. Not mine. Not your mother's. And not any of the rest of yours. It's Bert and Agnes who must decide what they are going to do. I know I'll stand by them no matter what their decision."

Bert took hold of Agnes's hand. "I think I know how you feel," he said. "We've already talked about it."

Agnes nodded so Bert continued.

"Dad, I know Mama wouldn't have liked it. But we've tried everything we could think of to get married in a Catholic church, and it just hasn't worked out."

"I know, son. I agree. You've done the best you could, and I think your mom is looking down and understands. So what do you two want to do now?"

Bert looked at Agnes again. "We are going to find a justice of the peace and get married today."

Everyone—from Stella and Stan, the oldest siblings there, to little Mary—shouted in excitement. "Hooray!"

"Then let's pack up and head to Fort Lauderdale," Mollie said as she began putting the leftover food and dirty plates back in the baskets.

"You really don't mind, Mama?" Agnes asked, bringing some dishes over to the basket.

Mollie kissed her daughter on the cheek. "No, Bert said it all. You—we have all—tried as hard as we could. Now it is time for you to get married."

Two hours later they arrived back in Fort Lauderdale. The courthouse, of course, was closed on a Saturday afternoon. But Herb had a plan.

"I kind of thought this might happen so I phoned the

justice of the peace the other day and arranged for us to meet him at his house."

A short time later the three cars pulled up at a little white bungalow a few blocks from the beach. Agnes clutched her now-bedraggled bouquet as her father walked her from the porch into the living room where Bert waited with Toby, acting as his best man. His beautiful blue eyes were damp as he watched his bride walk toward him.

A few minutes later he was kissing her as both families clapped and whistled. After signing the marriage license, they crowded into the three cars for one final trip home. Agnes laid her head on Bert's shoulder as Toby started the car.

"I can't believe we're really married," she told him. "I think it was the most beautiful wedding anyone could ever have."

Chapter 12
Hurricane Rules

If you live in Florida, hurricanes are just a part of life. Maybe that is why we name them. It is said that to know something's name is to have power over it. Is there some superstitious part of us that thinks calling a storm "Camille" or "Andrew" or "Katrina" or "Betsy" will help us to tame it? To make it less destructive?

Hurricane Donna in 1960 was my first hurricane. I was four years old, and I have just one vivid memory of it. My mother and grandfather are outside making the house safe, closing the shutters and picking up anything in the yard that might fly off in the wind. I'm in the living room playing with a toy town and placing the trees on the street, then turning them over and saying, "The hurricane blew all the trees down."

It's not much of a memory. In fact, all my memories of hurricanes are similar: just snapshots, moments in time, whether I'm age four or fourteen or in my forties. I'm standing in the carport with Granddad catching a glimpse of the storm from a safe place. I'm helping to gather as many mangoes as possible from the backyard tree before they become two-pound missiles flying around the neighborhood. I'm crouched down at the sliding glass doors placing towels to stop the water from leaking in and ruining the rug. I'm helping to tape windows with duct tape to prevent them from breaking. (That's a practice that has proven to be wrong. Taping the windows just turns them into large, taped-together pieces of flying glass, rather than small pieces of flying glass.)

It is always hot and still in my memories of preparing for hurricanes. The air is so close and humid you can hardly breathe. Granddad always called it "hurricane weather." You could tell the storm was really coming, he would say, when everything got perfectly still and the sky was the deepest, most beautiful blue you have ever seen. It was as if nature wanted to make up for what was to come by giving everyone a perfect day right before the storm.

And then the wind would begin to pick up. I remember our little dachshund running happily around the yard, enjoying the feel of the breeze on his ears as the wind blew them behind him.

The gusts would grow stronger and stronger till the first bands of rain lashed down. Until that finally happened everyone always hoped against hope that somehow the hurricane would turn and head back out to sea. It did happen. Occasionally.

I've seen hurricanes in Florida, the Carolinas, and Puerto Rico, and Superstorm Sandy in New Jersey. I've been very lucky. I've never been in real danger, or if I was, we had time to run. And I've never been in a home that sustained major damage. My family followed the hurricane rules, which were helpfully printed on the handout the *Miami Herald* published at the beginning of each hurricane season, along with a storm tracker map so that you could mark down the coordinates each time the National Weather Service updated them.

Rule number one: Plan an evacuation route.
Rule number two: Cover all the windows if possible, or at least the large ones.
Rule number three: Get your food and gasoline supplies early.
Rule number four: Move all possible flying objects indoors.
Rule number five: Gather lots of batteries and flashlights.
Rule number six: Clean and fill the bathtubs in case the water becomes unsafe to drink.
And the most important rule of all: Never go out in the eye of the storm because you don't know how long it will last.

Do you know what the eye of the storm is? It's that's calm window in the center of the hurricane. The sun comes out, the winds die down, and the sky becomes so clear that you can see all the way to the blue, cloudless heavens. It's very deceptive and has killed thousands of people over the years because once the eye passes over, the back side of the storm hits, which is often worse than the first half.

Along with taping windows, other "hurricane rules" have proved to be wrong such as opening a window on the leeward side of the house to equalize the pressure and keep it from imploding. Considering how much breeze leaked through the old-fashioned jalousie windows popular in the 1950s and '60s, it's a wonder anyone thought they needed to let in more air. I have never heard of a house imploding from a hurricane, and I don't think it is because we all cracked a window during the storm.

But no matter how silly the rule, my family followed them all. The rules were certainly drilled into my sister, Cheryl, and me. "This is what you do to stay safe during a hurricane." We heard it over and over again.

"Why do all the Aunts and Uncles always come to our house during a storm?" we would ask my mother and grandparents.

"Because we have the safest house," we were told.

"Why do we never go to a storm shelter?" They looked like fun to me; everyone camped out in school gymnasiums like a giant sleepover.

"Our house is safer than a storm shelter," the grown-ups said.

Some part of me must have had some suspicions, though, because I know I asked the questions before every single storm. And there were a lot of them when I was a child—until my grandfather and the Uncles made heavy plywood shutters. They turned out to be a lucky charm. We had had a storm every year for five or six years, but once the shutters were made, we didn't have a hurricane for at least another ten.

By the time another storm hit, my grandfather had died. I was home from college and helping Mama and Cheryl drag the incredibly heavy shutters down from the upper storage level of the carport while balancing on a rather rickety old wooden ladder. They were made from three-quarter-inch plywood and secured to the house with two-by-fours that were held in place with screws about four or five inches long. They had to be that long to go through the two-by-four, the plywood, and far enough into the concrete to ensure that they wouldn't come loose in a sixty-mile-per-hour wind. Each shutter was marked with red paint to show which window or door it went on. We had four large, sliding doors and one picture window so most of the shutters were the size of a full sheet of plywood.

We huffed and puffed in the stifling heat as we forced those boards out of the small hatch and juggled them down the ladder to the ground. "How did Granddad get them up there anyway?" we grumbled. "And why didn't he put them on the bottom level where they'd be easier to get to?"

Then the three of us set about putting them up. We carried each of them to their assigned window or door, then went back to the closet to look for the screws.

We looked. And looked. And looked. And we couldn't find anything that fit those shutters. Granddad had been a very organized man—he should have had them in the same place as the shutters. But we couldn't find them anywhere. Finally, we called Uncle Stanley, who had helped to build the shutters, and asked him if he remembered.

"Of course," he said. "Your grandfather painted them all with red paint, just like the markings on the shutters, so you'd always know they went together. Then he put them in a Mason jar. They should be on the shelf in the storage closet."

Yes, that was exactly where they had been, Mama remembered. When Granddad died and she cleaned out the closet, she found a jar of screws with red paint all over them. "These are a mess. I wonder why he kept them," she said as she threw them in the trash.

By now we had only twenty-four hours before the hurricane. Stores were closing, and supplies were low at the ones that were still open. We scrounged as many fasteners as we could from the hardware store, and then ran around the neighborhood borrowing any four-inch-long screws that anyone had lying around. It's not a common size. And the neighbors who had screws that size were already using most of them to secure their own shutters.

We finally found enough to hold everything in place. Not every hole was filled, but at least each shutter was secure enough not to blow off during the storm.

And when that storm passed my mother called a hurricane shutter company and paid the money to have new, aluminum ones installed. They were the accordion kind that stayed permanently affixed to the windows and slid across whenever there was a storm. Easy-peasy and you're safe from storms in just ten minutes.

~~~

When we became adults, Cheryl and I realized that our family's strict adherence to the hurricane rules was more talk than reality. The Aunts and Uncles came to our house for hurricanes not because it was safer but because, Mama finally admitted, Granddad was worried about our house flooding and wanted to be there to take care of things if it did.

That meant all his brothers and sisters came to our less secure house and supported him rather than staying in their own home, safely behind its metal shutters. And storm shelters? Well, Mama was in her seventies when she bought a condo on Biscayne Bay. When the first storm came through, she assured us it was safe to stay in a first-floor apartment just fifty feet from a large body of water, even though it was clearly listed as being in an evacuation zone. She finally confessed that she just didn't like the idea of having to sleep on a cot surrounded by a bunch of strangers.

And then there is the "don't go out in the eye rule." It turns out my family had a history of ignoring that rule, too.

Chapter 13
What Not to Do in a Hurricane

Saturday, September 17, 1926

It was late when the telephone rang, almost eleven p.m. Agnes, always a night owl, ran to the kitchen in the house on S.W. 13 Avenue. She picked up the receiver quickly, hoping her husband, parents, brother, and sister wouldn't wake up before she got to it.

"Hello?" she asked warily. It could only be bad news if someone was calling this long after bedtime.

"Agnes?" She heard her father-in-law's voice. "I wanted y'all to know the Weather Bureau just upgraded to a hurricane warning. I got the word from the station. No trains will be going out tomorrow."

"What do you want us to do? Should I wake Bert?"

"I'll call the rest of the family. If you have any plywood, try to board up the windows as fast as y'all can. This could be a big one, not like that little storm back in July that barely counted as a hurricane. Made all these newcomers think these storms ain't nothing to worry about."

Herb hung up abruptly, presumably to get in touch with the rest of his sons and daughters.

Agnes ran to the bedroom she shared with Bert. As real estate prices had soared, they had found it impossible to rent a place of their own and were living with her folks and younger brother and sister. Her sister Helen had moved out a few months ago when she married Godfrey Smith, who had a room over the drugstore where he worked on West Flagler Street. While it was only a few blocks away, it seemed strange to Agnes not to see Helen every day. But since no one in the family was really thrilled with Godfrey, her sister tended to keep her distance.

"Bert! Wake up!" she called out, shaking her husband awake.

"What's going on?" he asked sleepily.

"Your dad just called. They've upgraded to a hurricane

warning, and he said to tell you to board up all the windows as fast as you can."

"Okay, you wake up your parents. I'll get Leon," he said, then hastily pulled on a shirt and pants.

Sigmund and Bert headed to the small garage at the back of the lot and started to pull out the plywood stored there. Leon ran to the neighbors' houses to spread the warning, and soon lights were on all over the street as people made preparations.

Agnes and her little sister Mary brought in the chairs off the porch of the Spanish-style bungalow and checked around the yard for anything that could blow away, then helped with boarding the windows. It only took a couple of hours to get everything as buttoned up as possible, and by that time it had already started to rain.

They came inside where Mollie had eggs and coffee made on the brand-new electric stove. "We might not have anything hot to eat tomorrow if this thing gets bad," she told them. "You'd better enjoy it now."

They savored their late-night breakfast, then all headed back to bed.

"I guess I don't have to get up early in the morning," Mary said. "We aren't going to church."

"That's right, no one's going to church in the morning so just sleep in," Sigmund answered. "Goodnight, everyone."

Back in their own room Bert turned off the lights, kissed his wife, then turned over and quickly fell back to sleep. But Agnes couldn't settle down. She tossed and turned, listening to the wind pick up and begin to howl even louder than the sound of the rain slashing down in torrents.

It was a little after six a.m. when she heard the wind and the rain begin to slow. She shook Bert awake again.

"Sweetheart, what is it? Can't you sleep?" he asked drowsily.

"No, Bert, it's almost morning. Wake up."

Bert cracked one eye open. "It's still dark out. It's not morning."

"I know it's dark. It's a hurricane. Remember, silly? And the windows are boarded up."

"Then why are you waking me up? Didn't we all agree we could sleep in today? No one's going to be working in this weather."

"But that's just it, Bert. I think the storm is almost over."

"What time is it?" Bert asked.

"It's 6:15."

"It can't be over this soon. This thing is huge. Even before they upgraded to a hurricane warning, the Weather Bureau was saying that. We must be near the eye." Bert sat up and finally paid attention to his wife. "You know what I've told you. It will look like everything is over, but it's not. Don't be fooled."

"Well, how will we know if it's the eye or the end of the storm?"

"We wait, honey; we just have to sit tight and wait." Bert settled back down in bed and tried to pull Agnes down with him, clearly content to snuggle in bed with his wife.

Unfortunately, Agnes had other ideas.

"I'm going to just step out on the porch and see how things are in the neighborhood. I won't get off the porch, I promise."

Bert sighed and sat back up. He pushed back the covers and began to get dressed.

"You don't have to come with me. Stay there."

"Of course, I'm coming out with you. I'm not letting you go out in a hurricane by yourself."

"I'm not going out in the hurricane, just to the porch."

Bert gave her a look that said he knew her well enough not to believe she wouldn't get curious about something out in the yard or the street. His pants and shirt were a little damp from their earlier preparations, but before this was over, he suspected he'd be a lot wetter, and probably filthy, too. No point in getting another set dirty.

Sigmund and Mollie were already up and in the kitchen. With plywood on the windows, only a small amount of light leaked inside. The electricity had obviously gone out during the night because a kerosene hurricane lamp flickered on the table.

"Oh, I'm so glad you two are awake," said Mollie. "I was just telling Dad that with the rain slowing down we need to go over and check on Helen."

"Mama, Bert says it's the eye of the storm and we need to stay put."

"She's right, Mom." Bert had called his in-laws "Mom" and "Dad" since getting married. "We'll know in an hour or so that it's over. We should wait until then."

"Listen to the boy, Mollie. He's the only one here who's been through more than one hurricane, and that one in July was a small one from all I've heard," Sigmund told her.

"But the electricity is out," Mollie insisted. "The phones are down. We don't know anything. It's only a five-minute walk, and I'm worried to death about Helen. I don't trust Godfrey to have the sense he was born with."

Bert and Sigmund looked at each other with resignation. They knew when they were beaten. When Mollie got something into her head, it was best to just go with it. "Agnes is going to be just like her mother when she gets older," Sigmund had warned his son-in-law several times.

~~~

The pharmacy was only a few blocks away, but it took several more minutes than usual to get there because of all the debris strewn around the streets. Trees were blocking the road, and electric lines were sparking as they hung off their poles and dragged in the water, which was ankle-deep in some areas. As they got closer to the pharmacy, things got worse.

"I'm really getting worried about Helen," Sigmund said. "I don't like this at all."

"Well, the good news is it's getting lighter out, and the rain is letting up. Whether it's the eye or not, that's a good thing for us right now," Bert said as they pushed past several cars that had blown onto the sidewalk, some of them on their sides or upside down. Other people were now joining them, some wandering around looking stunned as they stared at the mess their city had become, others already purposefully clearing away the wreckage.

As they turned onto Flagler Street, at first glance the damage didn't seem as bad. Because it was all storefronts with apartments on the upper floors, there were no lawns or trees. But as they walked toward the drugstore they saw that many windows were broken, signs lay on the ground, or hung twisting in the wind, ready to fall on an unsuspecting person. The cars that had lined the street were now scattered around like a child's wooden blocks. As they got to the store the rain stopped and the clouds suddenly cleared away. They could see the sun just starting to lighten the sky overhead. The front of the store was blocked by a couple of cars, pieces of signs, portions of walls and roofs, and other trash.

"Helen!" Sigmund called out, standing below the window he knew belonged to her and Godfrey.

A moment later the sash was raised, and Helen put her head out. "Dad? Is that you? And Bert! We are so glad to see you!"

"Are you hurt?" Sigmund asked.

"No, our room is fine, but as you can see, we are kind of stuck in here."

Godfrey came to the window. "Hi, Mr. Sawieja, Bert. Can you help us clear enough stuff away from the door to get out of here?"

"Godfrey, I'm not sure how much time we have," called Bert. "This is probably the eye. The storm could start again in a few minutes."

Godfrey had been born in Kentucky, but he'd lived in Florida for quite a few years now.

"Then you'd better start clearing a path to get in because you won't have time to get back to your place," he replied.

Bert ground his teeth. It definitely made sense, which was rather irritating coming from Godfrey. He would rather run back to Agnes than stay here helping her sister, but the eye could last anywhere from a few minutes to a couple of hours, and it had already been fifteen since the sun had come out. In his opinion, Helen was a little selfish. But family was family, and Helen was now a part of his. He set to work pushing the first car out of the way so they could get close enough to the building to get a door or window open. It took them only a few minutes to get to the door.

"Godfrey? Do you have a key?" Bert yelled.

Godfrey and Helen had come downstairs and were standing rather helplessly watching from just inside the store.

"I tried it earlier. You can see something big hit the door. The knob and lock are pushed in and bent on the wooden door that pulls shut over the glass one. I can't get through it."

Godfrey was right, damn him. The door to the pharmacy was designed to keep burglars from breaking in easily. It would take too long to get in that way. Bert pulled his watch out of his pocket. It was 6:55, almost thirty minutes since the rain stopped. And it wasn't getting any lighter as it would if the hurricane was really over.

Just as he thought this, the wind began to pick up again.

"Okay, Dad, we need to get inside quick. Let's break the window." Bert pointed to the large window next to the door where various first aid items were on display.

He looked around and found a two-by-four still with several nails and pieces of lathe attached to it. It had obviously been a part of someone's wall.

"Stand well back," he called to Helen and Godfrey as he swung it like a baseball bat at the window. It cracked, and he swung again. This time pieces of glass flew everywhere, some inside the window but also out toward him.

"Damn it!" he said again. A large chunk of glass had hit his upper arm as it flew past, and blood was already staining his sleeve. But the wind was growing stronger, and a new flash of lightning was followed almost instantly by the roll of thunder. He didn't have time to worry about a little cut.

"Let's get in there, son," Sigmund said. He had picked up several large boards and was tossing them through the opening. "These will help us close up the window from the inside, maybe keep a little of the storm from getting in down here on the first floor," he added.

Bert followed suit and threw in the two-by-four he had used to break the window. Then they helped each other pick their way carefully through the broken glass and into the store.

They were immediately enveloped in a big hug by Helen. "Oh, thank God, I was so scared here all alone," she said.

Godfrey gave her a startled look but recovered quickly.

"We need to get this window boarded up as best we can. I'll look in the back room for a hammer and nails."

He came back a few minutes later with a few carpentry tools, and they went to work covering the opening as securely as possible.

"Well, at least we have first aid supplies for Bert," Godfrey said cheerfully as they finished boarding up. He took some bandages, a small bottle of mercurochrome, and some adhesive tape from the display. "Let's go upstairs. We should board the window up there, too."

They trooped upstairs, Sigmund carrying the last piece of plywood that he had rescued from the street.

"Why didn't you close the window?" Godfrey asked Helen as he ran to shut it.

"I didn't think about it. Why didn't you?" she shot back.

Bert and Sigmund glanced at each other and looked away. This was no time to worry about the state of Helen and Godfrey's marriage. Helen lit a kerosene hurricane lamp as Sigmund and Godfrey boarded the window. It was almost pitch-black inside now.

"Sit down, Bert," Sigmund said. "Let's take a look at your arm. I think you'll need stitches, but for now we'll just close it up as best we can."

After Bert's arm was bandaged, Helen got some bread and leftover beef from the icebox and they ate, listening to the sound of the wind outside. "I think it is worse out there now," she said. "I wonder how everyone is back at the house."

No one answered. Bert didn't want to say what he was thinking, which was that if Godfrey had shown some gumption, not to mention a little common sense, Bert would be back at the house with Agnes right now. At least they were dry. The roof on the building was holding so far, and Godfrey had found clean, dry shirts for them.

Still, they could hear thumps and thuds against the walls outside as flying pieces of wood, roof tiles, and who knew what else hit the building. It seemed as if they sat for hours in the dark, just waiting for the storm to end and praying that their loved ones were all still safe, too.

~~~

Back at the house Leon and Mary had wanted to go outside and explore the damage, but Mollie insisted they stay in.

"Your father and Bert only went out to make sure Helen is all right. Other than that we follow the rules and stay inside until we are sure the storm is over," she told them. As if to prove her point, a few minutes later the winds picked up again.

Agnes went to the door a few hundred times, hoping to see Bert, her father, Helen, and Godfrey walking down the road. Finally, her mother made her stop.

"If they aren't here by now, they aren't coming. They've found someplace else to shelter. We just need to pray that they got to Helen's and are all safe at her place. Now sit down. You can't do anything to help them by wearing a path to the door."

Much like the electricity, the telephone was no longer working. They had a radio, but with no electricity, it, too, was useless. The storm was growing in intensity. They had no barometer, but they could tell from the sounds they heard outside that once again the wind and the rain were steadily picking up.

"It's louder this time than before," Mary remarked. "Does that mean it is worse out there?"

"I think so," said Leon.

Just at that moment a loud crack was heard, as if something had hit the wall of the house. Mary screamed.

"It's all right. We are going to be fine," Mollie told her, giving the girl a hug. They continued to sit in the kitchen, drinking cold leftover coffee. Just as they all settled down again, there was another loud, ripping noise, and the kitchen suddenly became a little bit brighter.

"The roof is coming off!" said Leon, pointing at holes where the tarpaper had blown away. The flat bungalow roof was made with wide planks that only had a tar paper covering to keep the rain out. As more and more of it peeled away, rain came pouring into the room.

"Get under the ceiling planks. Don't stay in between the boards!" shouted Mollie above the wind, which was now much louder without the protection of the roof.

All four of them attempted to huddle beneath one of the

planks, scrunching their shoulders in to keep them from sticking out in a useless attempt to stay a little bit dry as the water poured in.

"Should we open the door and let the water back out?" Agnes asked, shouting to be heard.

The water had begun to inch up the furniture legs and over their shoes.

"No!" Leon shouted back. "That will only let the wind in, and the house will tear apart from the inside. We just need to hold on here until it is over. There's nothing else we can do."

So hold on they did, clinging to each other as they stood in the kitchen with several inches of water on the floor and more rushing in through the ceiling every minute. They finally crawled up on the dining table and huddled there for another two hours, soaked to the skin, until the rain and wind began to subside.

Leon got down off the table first. "I'll go look around the house and make sure everything is safe," he said, trying hard to protect his mother and sisters, just as he knew his dad would want.

"How bad is it?" Mollie asked when he returned a few minutes later.

"There's water everywhere. I don't think there is anything that isn't wet, but the door is still on, even if the roof isn't. I guess we're safe from burglars," he said with a grin. It was hard to keep Leon serious for long. "Y'all might as well get off the table now. You can't get much wetter down here than you are up there."

Although the wind was still blowing, they could see patches of blue sky behind the dark clouds when they stepped cautiously onto the front porch. They waved to other neighbors who were also slowly emerging from their homes to survey the storm's aftermath.

Only one of the houses on the block still had a roof and four walls intact. All the other homes were missing their roofs, walls, or both. The street was flooded with about a foot of water, trees were uprooted, and cars were scattered haphazardly on lawns.

"Hey!" Leon shouted as he opened the door to the small garage at the back of the lot. "Bert's car is fine. Looks like we should have stayed in here instead of the house. Everything is dry."

"Yes, but where can we drive?" asked Mary. "If all the streets are like ours, it's going to be days before anyone can go anywhere."

Agnes couldn't stay in the yard, or even in the neighborhood, for one more second. She felt an urgent need to go check on everyone she loved. Bert would take care of Helen and her dad so she would check on his family for him.

"I'm going to walk over to Stella and Stanley's and find out how they made out," she announced to her mother.

"Agnes, you should stay here. Look at this street. You don't know what you will find," Mollie told her. "It could be even worse."

"Bert would want me to see how everyone is and help out if I can. Just tell him where I am as soon as he gets back," she said with more bravado than she actually felt.

It frightened her that Bert wasn't there. Doing something would keep her from worrying. She went inside and grabbed her pocketbook, which was as soggy as everything else, then headed off in the direction of her sister-in-law's house a few blocks away.

Of course, it took a lot longer than the fifteen minutes it usually did to walk there. She had to detour around downed electric lines and flooded streets. The devastation was unbelievable. She passed blocks where no house was left standing. In other areas the water had flooded everything to waist high. And every time she thought she was getting close to her sister-in-law's house, she had to detour another block or two out of the way. In some areas people were out clearing debris and starting to make repairs. On other blocks no one was to be seen. Had the people evacuated before the storm? Or were they inside the buildings, hurt and unable to get help? Agnes couldn't stop to find out. If she did she'd never get to Stella's house.

She breathed a sigh of relief when the house came into sight. It was intact. The walls, windows, and roof were all in good shape, and although the two palm trees on either side of the yard were now on the ground, they'd somehow managed to miss the house when they fell. The clean-up would be messy, but it was not nearly as bad as her own family's home. She knocked on the door, and no one answered. After knocking several more times, she walked around the house and found Stella and Stanley's car was gone. *They must have gone to check on some of the others.*

After sitting down on the front step, she thought about what to do next. Bert's brother Eddie lived just a few more streets over. She might try there; that was probably where Stella and Stan had gone. But what if no one was home there either? She would be that much farther away from her own home and still have to walk back.

Her feet hurt, she was hot and thirsty. Wishing for a glass of water, she sighed and got up. There was nothing for it but to head home and hope Bert had gotten there ahead of her. The more she saw of the hurricane damage, the more worried she became. What if her father and Bert had been caught outside when the second half of the storm hit? What if the building where Helen and Godfrey lived had been destroyed? They all could be drowned.

As she walked back as quickly as she could, the sun came out in full force. It seemed as if the hurricane had left Miami as quickly as it arrived.

She was threading her way through the mess of palms fronds, tree branches, and portions of walls, windows, and roofs when suddenly a jitney appeared, driving slowly as it wove its way through the trash-filled street. It stopped next to her, and the driver popped his head out of the car window.

"Hey, lady, y'all want a ride?"

"Oh, my lord, yes!" Agnes said as she picked her way over.

She got in and gave him her address. Then she sank back in the seat, exhausted, and closed her eyes. She didn't need to see any more of the destruction right now. She just wanted to make it home and find Bert there, safe and sound.

A short time later they pulled up at the house. As she

paid the man, she noticed that someone had already pried the wood off all the house windows. That was a good sign. She didn't think Leon could have done all of them by himself. She jumped out, ran up the porch steps, and pulled open the front door. Everyone was inside, sorting through soggy belongings to see what could be saved, but she only had eyes for Bert as she ran into his arms.

"Thank God you are all right," he said as he hugged her tightly. "What in the world did you think you were doing going out in all this? You could have been killed." He sounded angry, but she knew he had just been afraid for her, the same as she had been for him.

"I wanted to see if your family was okay. I went to Stella and Stanley's house, but no one was there. The house is fine, and their car was gone. I just don't know where they are."

"It's okay. We'll go find out where everyone is later, or they will make their way over here. It's going to be fine now that you are home."

"Wait!" she said, as she pulled back and looked at him. "Your arm. What happened?

"I got cut on some glass, but it's not too bad. Your dad bandaged me up."

Sigmund, who'd been waiting for Agnes and Bert to finish so he, too, could hug his daughter, came over. "Bert was a big help in getting to Helen and Godfrey. They were trapped in their building."

After seeing her sister, Agnes headed over to give her a big hug, too. "I'm so glad you are okay," she said.

"Me, too. I think it was the scariest thing I've been through since the time I stuck my head on the railroad track," she said, making Agnes laugh despite her shock.

The joke broke the tension. They all laughed at the old family story, then went back to work trying to find enough dry bedding to sleep on.

~~~

The neighborhood banded together. The first night everyone crowded into the one house that had a roof, sharing any dry bedding and clothing between them. The Sawiejas owned a portable kerosene stove, which they set up in their garage. The ten or so families took turns cooking, once again sharing whatever food they had.

By the next day Bert had managed to get in touch with all his family, even his brother Leo. His oldest brother and his wife, Sadie, seemed to be settling down a bit, maybe even drinking less in the last year. He hoped so, now that they had a son, Herbert, named for his grandfather.

The brothers banded together and went to each of the homes to repair the damage as best they could. The Sawieja home had fared the worst. Not a scrap of tar paper was left on the roof, and some of the roof joists were gone as well. Inside most everything had to be thrown away as it began to mold almost immediately in the heat and humidity. Mollie mourned the loss of the family photos; the pictures of their life in Missouri were mostly gone. Only the few Helen had taken with her were left.

It was over a week before they got electrical power back and could once again cook on a real stove. They were so busy dealing with their own hurricane damage it took a few days to realize just how bad things were. Because of looting, martial law was declared in Miami, and three hundred extra police officers had been sworn in.

When they finally had a chance to sit down and read the newspapers, they learned why the storm had become such a catastrophic event. It formed quickly and had stayed outside the usual shipping lanes so there were very few sightings by ships—meaning it was very close to the Florida coast before the National Weather Service realized it was a threat.

Even then the Weather Bureau had authorized only a "storm warning," for winds from 55 to 63 miles per hour. People assumed the hurricane would be small, similar to the one that had passed over the area that June when they didn't bother to board up or leave danger areas.

It was only when the director of the weather service field office in Miami, Richard Gray, noticed that the barometer in his office had begun to fall drastically that he issued a hurricane warning. But by that time the storm was already upon them. Top wind speeds were clocked at 149 miles per hour, almost 100 miles an hour higher than originally predicted.

The stories the family read in the *Miami Daily News* pointed out that in the rush to build hotels and houses on Miami Beach, Carl Fisher, the "father of Miami Beach," and other developers had destroyed most of the mangrove swamps. This had a major effect on the island's ability to withstand the storm surge or act as a barrier for the mainland. The low-lying mangrove trees, rooted in the water, would have helped to absorb and slow the surge both on Miami Beach and in Miami.

"That's what I've been saying," Herb said. "We need the swamps. They are there for a reason. They are draining too many of them."

On top of that, the newspapers reported, the lack of general safety awareness among Florida's population also contributed to the death toll. "We didn't know that all windows should be covered," the wife of the mayor of Boca Raton was quoted as saying.

When Herb heard that he fumed again. This time about "the damned Northerners coming down here knowing nothing about how to live in the tropics and still trying to run things."

None of his children had the courage to point out that he had once been one of those "damned Northerners," one who had tried to outrun a hurricane on the Seven Mile Bridge.

When the streets were finally cleared enough to travel, the family was able to get out and see the devastation themselves.

Thousands of homes and buildings had been destroyed. The beautiful Royal Palm Hotel built by Mr. Flagler would never open again. The Million Dollar Pier, where Agnes and Bert had danced so often under the stars, was gone as well. Almost four hundred people died in Miami alone, and more than one thousand were injured. A large number of the casualties had died when they went out in the eye, thinking the storm was over. When Agnes realized how dangerous it had been to be outside, she felt incredibly lucky her husband and father had not been killed. She and her mother both felt a little guilty, too, that they had forced the men to go.

~~~

"Bill and Doris Nexson are thinking of leaving," Bert told Agnes one evening a few months after the storm. They were in their room where they could have a little privacy.

Bert was sitting on the bed, leaning on the headboard, and now he beckoned Agnes over. He was tired; he and his brother-in-law had worked all week repairing and rehanging a sign on the top of the five-story Burdine's department store on Flagler Street. In the aftermath of the storm, jobs were hard to come by. Bert had left his job at the railroad shortly after they were married, after he lost part of his thumb when two baggage carts slammed together. He'd seen too many accidents at the station, he told Agnes, and preferred to keep all his limbs intact. At the time, with real estate booming, construction jobs were easy to come by, and he'd made a good living. Now, though, he and everyone else he knew scrambled every day to find work.

"Oh no, not another one! Everyone seems to be leaving Miami. Even Leon is talking about going back to Missouri. He can stay with Aunt Jenny's family in Cape Girardeau and find work there, Mama says. Doris was my first friend when I moved here. She can't leave, too."

"I know, honey, but Bill has relatives in Athens, Georgia, who can get him steady work. They don't want to leave, but they may have to."

"You're not thinking of leaving, are you?" Agnes asked hesitantly.

"No, of course not. Where would we go? This is our home."

"I know, but it's Doris and Bill's home, too. Doris was born here. A lot of people are saying Miami will never recover. That it will never be the same again."

"Do you want to leave?" Bert asked her. "If you want we could probably go to Missouri, too. It might be easier there than it is here right now, and besides, I've never seen snow. It might be fun."

Agnes thought for a few moments. Did she want to go back? She hadn't been happy the first few months she was here, but that seemed like a lifetime ago now. She had a life, friends, and Bert's family as well as most of her own here in Miami. She didn't want to ask Bert to leave his folks. She gave an imaginary shiver. "You wouldn't like it. It's very cold."

"But I'd have you to keep me warm." He put his arm around her and hugged her close.

"No, I don't want to leave Miami. Home is where you are, and this is your home."

"All right, we stay. It's going to be tough for a while, but we'll make it through. Maybe we can even start a family sometime soon," Bert replied.

"How about right now?" Agnes gave him a long kiss, and no more words were needed between them.

Chapter 14
Depression Baby

1928

Verna Jean Rogers came into the world at nine p.m. on Wednesday, January 4, 1928. Bert was ecstatic. Agnes was exhausted. It had been a long and difficult birth. But when they put the little girl—well, she was ten pounds, not really that little—into her arms, Agnes melted a little.

"Look what we did," Bert said proudly, hovering over them both.

Agnes wasn't quite ready to let him get away with that.

"We?" she said. "I didn't see you in here doing the work."

Bert just laughed and kissed her. Everyone had warned him that right after giving birth a woman was likely not to be feeling "quite herself." Agnes had required a lot of stitches and was sore. "I'll leave you alone to sleep," he told her, gently taking the baby from her arms.

Agnes was sound asleep before he even got to the door.

Most of the family had managed to crowd into the tiny apartment the pair had finally been able to afford to rent a few doors down from her parents on S.W. 13 Avenue. Dr. James had just left, and Mollie, who had been with her daughter through the birth, had gone out to the kitchen to see him off. Bert's father, father-in-law, and Agnes's sister Mary, along with Anna Mae, Stella, and Stanley, were all there, too.

Toby and Harold were out with the dogs—literally. Toby, Stella, and Stanley had gone into business together raising greyhounds to run at the Hialeah Park Dog Track. Greyhound racing was a new sport; it had only become popular about twenty years before. Harold did most of the care of the animals, Toby handled the business end, and the dogs lived at Stella's house. Everyone else in the family pitched in as needed.

Gambling wasn't strictly legal in Miami, but almost everyone in town did gamble. Although Bert himself had been known to stop at the bootleggers, he never bet. He worked too hard for his money, he said, to take a chance on it. The rest of the family, though, including Agnes, enjoyed an afternoon at a betting parlor or a night watching the dogs or horses run. Still, they never bet on races the family dogs were running in; that could get you into a lot of hot water with the wrong people.

His thoughts were quickly brought back to the present as everyone crowded around to see the baby. She had a mop of dark hair and was sleeping soundly. "

For now," Mollie said with amusement. "Just you wait until three o'clock in the morning."

"And on that note we should all get out of here and let the new parents sleep," his dad said.

The group started to head for the door.

"No, wait! You aren't leaving us alone with her!" Bert said in a panic. "What if something happens?"

"Don't worry. I'll stay the night," Mollie put in. She expertly lifted the infant from Bert's arms and cradled her in her own. "We'll do just fine, won't we?" she said to the baby as she automatically began to sway back and forth.

~~~

It was several weeks before Agnes felt well enough to take care of little Verna by herself. Thankfully, it was rare for a day to go by without some member of her or Bert's family stopping in. Even Toby and Harold spent many an afternoon playing with the child, or just sitting and talking with Agnes. Handling the dogs meant they worked mostly at night.

The Hurricane of '26 had been the final nail in the coffin of the great 1920s Florida Land Boom. It was the first of many "boom and bust" cycles that the state would see over the next century. For Miami it ushered in the Great Depression three years early. Land that sold for sixty thousand dollars in 1925 was "marked down" to six hundred dollars after the storm.

The rest of the country followed Florida into the Great Depression on Black Tuesday, October 29, 1929. Herb still worked for the Florida East Coast Railway as an engineer, but in 1932 another big hurricane came through. This one struck directly at the Florida Keys and took down many bridges, including the Seven Mile Bridge. It was the end of Flagler's

Folly. The Overseas Railroad was remade as the Overseas Highway, although that didn't open until 1938. The immediate result in the Rogers family was that Herb had less work and his salary was cut.

The rest of the family felt the effects of the Depression, too. Sigmund often had to take items in trade rather than cash for a haircut. Leon had headed back to Missouri, ostensibly for a job, but Agnes knew it was really because he wanted to see if his childhood sweetheart, Catherine, was still interested. They had been seeing each other regularly for about a year now, and Agnes hoped they would get married one day.

By the time Verna was four years old, the entire family had established a routine to get them through the months, then years, of hard times.

Every morning Bert, who had managed to keep his Model A Ford, picked up his brother-in-law Stanley at his and Stella's house a few blocks away. Then the two of them drove downtown and joined the large groups of men who stood on the street corners looking for work. If one of them got a job, the other called Agnes to let her know.

Agnes would get Verna ready for the day, then she and Verna walked the five blocks over to Stanley and Stella's house, where the three single siblings, Anna Mae, Harold, and Toby, also lived. She would let her sisters-in-law know if either of the men had work and how much money they could expect, and the three would set about making sure there was enough for everyone to eat dinner. They shared their income and ate together almost every night, sometimes at Stella and Stan's house, sometimes at Bert and Agnes's home. There were weeks when it was only cabbage and bread, while other times they had enough for meat and potatoes, too.

Toby and Harold had begun to travel the country with their dogs and were generally only home during the winter months when the Hialeah track was open.

"I can't figure out how people with no money for food still have enough money to gamble," Bert often grumbled.

"I don't know," was Toby's usual response. "But as long as they do, they keep Harold, me, and the dogs working and fed."

It was true. The money from racing helped keep the family going. When the pair were out of town they sent money back to Anna Mae. Some weeks it was a struggle just to get enough money to fill Bert's car with gas—which they needed for the advantage it gave them in getting jobs.

One week they had a job delivering telephone books throughout the city. They loaded as many books as they could into the back of the vehicle, then drove around town dropping them off at any house that had a telephone. Not every house, of course, or even most, had a phone so they did a lot of driving. But still, they made enough money to bring home a very good paycheck for several days, a real windfall for the Rogers clan. Other weeks they picked whatever crop was in season down in the South Dade farmlands—mangoes, oranges, tomatoes, bell peppers—even though those jobs were some of the lowest paid. When they could get it, they worked construction, which usually paid better. And then there were weeks when they found nothing.

They were poor—poorer than any of them ever remembered being before—but they all had enough to eat every day and a roof over their heads. A lot of people did not.

"We're poor," Agnes joked one day, "but Verna isn't."

And it was true. If Verna needed something someone in the family made sure she got it. At Christmas and her birthday there were always toys and a new dress, too. Stella sewed exquisitely—she did sewing, mending, and embroidery as another way to bring in income—and she made sure her little niece always had beautiful clothes.

Verna, Agnes acknowledged, was "just a little bit spoiled." She was an only child with a dozen doting relatives. Like many only children, she knew exactly how to play with adults but very little about children her own age, and that made her very shy.

She also had a temper. "But what can you expect?" her grandfathers both said fondly as they let her get away with a lot more than Bert or Agnes ever did. The two men thought Verna could do no wrong. Even the day she kicked her grandfather Sigmund, or "Bawpaw" as she called him, in the shins. Agnes spanked her, even though Sigmund said not to.

"We have to teach her what is right and wrong," Agnes told her father.

"I know, but don't spank her too hard. She didn't mean anything by it."

Yes, it was sometimes difficult for Agnes when everyone else took the child's side. Of course, if she was really naughty, Verna heard the traditional threat of all mothers: "Wait until Daddy gets home." Verna was definitely a daddy's girl, which meant he was the one person who could be counted on to make sure she behaved. Despite her mother's fears, the spoiled toddler became a little girl who adored and respected everyone in her family.

On the whole life was pretty good for the Rogers and Sawiejas despite the Great Depression. And as things began to improve throughout the country, it got easier for them. By the late 1930s, Bert got his plumbing license and started helping the owner of a company, Stolpman Plumbing, run the business. The Stolpman family went up to Tennessee every summer to escape the heat, and they would ask Bert to live in an apartment over their shop on Miami Beach during those months so he could open and close the store. That meant that for several years Verna got to spend the three summer months living within walking distance of the ocean.

Agnes still hadn't learned to swim and was afraid of the water. Verna couldn't swim either. "I hate the way it feels when water splashes on my face," she'd tell her father whenever he tried to teach her. But unlike her mother, Verna loved the beach. She spent hours every day building sandcastles, playing with the tourist children, and generally enjoying life.

Soon they were able to rent a bigger house with a separate bedroom for Verna, and there were even a few weddings in the works.

Chapter 15
Searching for Happily Ever After

It's a shock when you realize your relatives weren't always middle-aged. They weren't born with wrinkles and gray hair. They were children, teens, young men and women with lives and careers, and romances and broken hearts long before they became Mom and Dad and Grandma and Auntie. I remember seeing pictures of Mama and my other relatives and thinking, "Wow, they were really young. I wish I could remember them that way."

The photos showed my grandparents laughing as they played on the beach in those ridiculous 1920s bathing suits, my parents passionately kissing, a teenage Uncle Harold playing with some dogs, a large family group sitting under the shade of a palm tree, my Aunt Helen dressed in a beaded gown and mink stole.

My Aunt Helen was always different from the rest of the family. It wasn't just that she was my grandmother's sister, and all the rest of the Aunts and Uncles were from my grandfather's side of the family. She dressed in a more sophisticated way; she walked as if she owned the world. She wasn't in town as much, and when she was, she often had other things to do—parties, dinners, golf and bridge at the country club— so her visits were more of an occasion, more special. We wore our play clothes when we visited "the folks" house, the home where the five of my grandfather's brothers and sisters lived together. We wore our best dresses when we went to see Aunt Helen.

The two houses even smelled different. The Aunts and Uncles lived a few blocks away from us, in Miami Shores. Their house always smelled of red rice and beans, sweat, and the dozen kinds of flowers Uncle Stanley grew in the yard. Inside, the house was always dark, its large front and back porches and metal awnings kept the sunlight to a minimum. The mismatched sofas and chairs were large and comfortable, the back and arms of all of the furniture were covered with hand-crocheted doilies made by Aunt Stella and Aunt Anna Mae. When I got my first apartment at age twenty, my mother went around to all of the relatives and asked them to clean out their drawers and closets and donate anything they didn't need that they thought I could use. I laughed out loud when I opened one box and found a complete set of doilies.

Aunt Helen lived over on the beach, in Bal Harbour, one of the very best addresses in the entire county. The rooms were painted cream, the furniture was white and yellow French provincial, everything matched and the rooms always looked as if a *Better Homes and Gardens* photographer was coming to take a magazine cover shot at any moment. There was always a breeze from the ocean a few blocks east so that the house smelled of salt air and Aunt Helen's make-up and perfumes. Every now and then I'll catch a hint of someone wearing the perfume or make-up she used and I am immediately transported back to her house.

Going there was always special. The tall, mahogany grandfather clock with its Westminster chimes sounded every quarter hour. I would run to stand in front of it each time it rang. The ivory sofa cushions were filled with down, and Cheryl and I were small and light enough that if we sat down slowly and carefully, we would softly sink into the cushions. It was the one place I ever sat down "like a lady," as my mother, grandmother, and Aunt Helen always wanted. You turn your back to the chair, carefully run your hand over the back of your skirt to smooth it so it doesn't wrinkle when you sit, and then sink gracefully into the seat. I couldn't usually manage it. I didn't sink, I plopped. The women in the family despaired of my ever managing to become a lady.

In some ways, the two sides of the family were rather like the two halves of the county. Miami and Miami Beach, two cities totally different, separate yet totally intwined. There was the Miami side, west of Biscayne Bay, where the average people lived. They crossed back and forth on the various causeways to work or to swim, but they rarely lived there. Then there was glamourous side, the island of Miami Beach, where movie stars stayed in high rise hotels and gangsters lived in swank mansions, trying to become respectable by mixing in with the Northern society ladies, and playing bridge and golf at the local country clubs.

Aunt Helen always wanted to be a part of that society. I've never been sure why she married Godfrey, who certainly wouldn't have fit in with the wealthy and famous on Miami Beach, and certainly never made enough money to even try. She wouldn't talk about it much, got upset when anyone even mentioned his name. The marriage only lasted a year. "It was a stormy year," she said once, referring not only to the Hurricane of 1926, which had changed Miami for all time, but to her marriage that same year. But it did not take Helen long to realize that Godfrey was not her true love, her Prince Charming come to take her away to a castle in the air—or a mansion on Miami Beach.

She got a divorce, moved back home, changed her name back from Smith to Sawieja, and started all over again.

Chapter 16
Two Weddings

1934

"What is wrong with my sisters?"

Verna's mother put her cup down on the table so hard the coffee sloshed into the saucer. Verna's eyes got big. What was Mama upset about?

"We've been over it and over it, Agnes. You know you can't change either one of their minds. It's a little late for Mary now, anyway." her dad said, picking up his toast and calmly spreading fig preserves on it.

Verna's head swiveled back and forth between her parents, trying to figure out exactly what they were talking about.

"Why would she want to elope?" Mama asked.

"Well, we did," Dad said with a smile. "Maybe she just wanted to be like her big sister. She's always looked up to you."

"That was different, and you know it. We took the whole family with us. We didn't sneak around behind anyone's back. Not to mention that they're both barely eighteen."

"What's a lope, Mama?" put in Verna.

"It's ee-lope, and it means when you run away to get married, honey," Mama answered.

"Did you and Daddy ee-lope—run away to get married?"

"No, not really. It was different. Your daddy always called it an elopement, but we took the whole family with us. Right, Bert?"

"Right. Your mama and I took all your grandparents and the Aunts and Uncles with us when we got married."

"And everyone approved of it," emphasized Mama.

"Did Aunt Mary run away? When is she coming back? Did she pack her clothes in a handkerchief on a stick like in the cartoon at the theater?"

"No, honey, she didn't really run away. She just didn't tell anyone that she and Herndon were going down to the courthouse yesterday. Your Mamaw and Bawpaw didn't know."

"Why not?"

"Because they don't approve of Herndon," Dad said dryly.

"Bert! Don't tell her that. She'll just repeat it."

"Verna, honey, don't tell anyone what Daddy just said, okay?" Her father turned to her with a smile. "We don't want to hurt Aunt Mary's feelings."

"Okay, Daddy. Can I tell Ann?" Ann Raywood was her best friend and lived just across the street.

"Yes, you can tell Ann, but no one else," Mama said.

"That's because you are heading right over there after breakfast to talk it over with Ann's mother," Dad chuckled.

Agnes got up and began clearing the table. "Well, I have to talk to Marie because you aren't being sympathetic."

"I'm as worried about Mary as you are. I just hope either Herndon turns out better than Godfrey, or Mary comes to her senses as fast as Helen did and divorces him."

"And that's another thing. You would think Helen would have learned. This time she wants to marry an old man."

"Come on, Agnes, that's not fair. Ed Jones is not an old man and—"

"He's thirteen years older than she is!" Agnes turned on the water at the sink and began scrubbing the frying pan with a vengeance. "He's over forty! He's even bald."

"I like Mr. Jones. Is he gonna be my uncle when he marries Aunt Helen?" Verna interrupted again.

"Yes, honey, and remember, you don't repeat anything your mama says here at the table to anyone," Daddy said.

Verna nodded solemnly. "No one but Ann. It's a secret. I know. But why? Everyone can see Mr. Jones is bald."

Mama put her hand over her face. Her shoulders started to shake.

"Mama, are you crying?"

Worried, Verna got up to comfort her mother. But when Mama turned around, there were no tears on her face. She had started to laugh. Bert got up, too, and put his arms around them both, and they all laughed. Verna was glad. She didn't understand why Mama had been upset.

"Oh, honey, Mama's being a silly. I'm sorry if I worried you," she said. "Bring me your plate if you're done with breakfast and then go outside and play. Maybe Ann is ready to play, too. But don't bother Mrs. Raywood if she is cleaning house. Play outside."

"Right!" Dad chuckled. "You want to save the pleasure of interrupting her work for yourself."

~~~

When Verna was safely out of earshot, Bert and Agnes continued the conversation.

"Don't worry about Helen," Bert said. "She's a lot more careful now. She's thirty, after all. Not eighteen, like Mary."

"I know, but I always worry about them. I'm the big sister. I'm supposed to take care of everyone. Even Leon, and he's back in Missouri."

"And perfectly happy there, from all I hear. You don't have to worry about him. I know you feel responsible for them. I feel responsible for my brothers and sisters, too—but there comes a time when we have to let them make their own mistakes. Come on, sit down and have another cup of coffee with me." He led her to the table and refilled their cups. "I've talked a lot with Ed. He's a good guy, even if he is a little older."

"But his background is so different than ours. He's just not like us."

"Just because he has money doesn't mean he's that different. He seems responsible, and he appreciates Helen's family. He's always nice to Verna."

"I know, but what if they have children? He could die before they are even grown. Then where would Helen be?"

"Sweetheart, any of us could get run over by a bus tomorrow. And forty-two is not all that old. He's younger than either of our fathers. They've managed to stick around long enough to see us grow up."

"He's only ten years younger than Mama, Bert."

"Well, he acts a lot younger. He plays golf and goes out dancing and—"

"And races speedboats! His boat could crash, and he could drown. It's happened, you know. I read about an accident last year—"

"You are borrowing trouble."

"He's been divorced."

Bert started to laugh. "So has Helen! Agnes, please, try not to get all balled up about things you can't change. It won't help anything. I'm going to go out and cut the grass. Why don't you head on over to the Raywoods, talk to Marie, and get some of this out of your system?"

He stood up, gave Agnes a quick kiss, and headed out the back door.

~~~

Children are good at being both unseen and unheard when they want to find out more about grown-up business, and Verna was no exception. As an only child she was probably better at it than most.

A few days later Aunt Helen picked her and her mother up after school, and they all went to her grandparents' house. Sigmund and Mollie had moved to N.W. 24 Avenue a few years before. It was a coral rock home with cheerful red and white striped canvas awnings over the doors and windows.

Mama sat with Aunt Helen and Mamaw in the kitchen, drinking Coca-Colas and enjoying the late-afternoon sunshine. Verna was playing house under the kitchen table.

"When will Mary be home?" she heard Aunt Helen ask.

"I'm not sure. She just started her job at McCrory's and doesn't have a set schedule yet," said Mamaw.

"Why she had to go to work at a dime store I'll never know," her aunt complained. "If she has to be a cashier, at least she could have applied at Burdine's. It has so much more class."

"She took the first job she could find. Don't give her grief for that, too," said Mama.

"You don't suppose she's pregnant, do you?" asked Aunt Helen.

"Lord, I hope not," said Mamaw. "She says they never—"

All three adults suddenly got quiet.

"Verna, why don't you go play outside?" Mama picked up the edge of the checkered tablecloth and leaned under the table to look at her.

"I'm playing house, Mama. This is my kitchen," Verna pointed to one corner of the table. "And this is my living room." She pointed to the other side.

"I know, honey, but I think you can find a nice house to play in outside, don't you? It will be cooler there than under the table."

Verna knew that her mother wasn't really asking—she was telling. She reluctantly crawled out from under the table and headed out the door. The new "house" she found was just under the ixora bushes by the front door. She took a few minutes to sip the nectar from the little red ixora flowers, then, just as she got settled, Aunt Mary walked up.

"I see you, Verna," her aunt called.

"Hi, Aunt Mary. Mama sent me outside to play."

"She did, did she? I see from the car that Helen is here, too. They are having a real hen party, aren't they?"

"What's a hen party?"

"It's when a bunch of ladies get together to talk about another lady," Aunt Mary said. "Come on in with me, Verna. You're going to be filthy playing under the bushes like that. Maybe the rest of the hens will let us join their party."

She held out her hand, and Verna walked with her back into the house. Mary was her favorite aunt. She was a lot younger than all the others, having just graduated from high school a few weeks before, and always made time for Verna.

"So I hear y'all are having quite the confab," Mary said as she and Verna walked into the kitchen. "Verna, do you want a Coca-Cola?" she asked, pulling a bottle from the refrigerator for herself.

"Can I, Mama?" she pleaded.

"Honey, we were just about to go."

"Oh no, Agnes, please stay. I wouldn't want to inhibit the conversation," Mary said sarcastically.

Verna watched as her mother squirmed a little bit.

"Really, Mary, I have to get Agnes and Verna home so I can meet Ed for dinner," Helen said.

"You spend so much time at Ed's you just ought to move in there now and not wait for the wedding," Aunt Mary said.

"Mary! You apologize to your sister right now," said

Mamaw.

"I apologize." Aunt Mary rolled her eyes, took a long drink from her bottle of Coke, and tried to change the subject. "I hope Herndon gets here soon. I want to know how his job interview went."

"Well, I hope he gets one quickly. You found a job right away. If he's really trying he shouldn't have too much trouble." Even Verna heard the disapproval dripping from Aunt Helen's voice. "Things have gotten a lot better than they were a few years ago."

Verna didn't yet know the term "catfight" but was about to witness one.

"Well, at least I didn't have to marry someone ancient to keep from being an old maid," Aunt Mary said.

"You just wanted to make sure you got married ahead of me. You couldn't wait a few weeks, could you?"

"You're not satisfied with all the articles about you on the society page? You have to be married first, too?"

"That's just mean. I'm not marrying Ed because of his position. He's the most kind, the most—"

"Rich," put in Aunt Mary.

"I'm not marrying him because he is rich. I love him."

"That's enough, girls. I want you both to apologize to each other. I understand that everyone's tense right now. We've had Mary's news and then have so much to do for Helen's wedding."

"I know, Mama. I'm sorry. I'm sorry, Helen," Aunt Mary said sincerely. "I didn't mean any of it. Ed's a really nice guy."

"Oh, come here, little sister. You know I love you, and I didn't mean it either," said Aunt Helen, giving Aunt Mary a hug before grabbing her purse. "But Mama, we really do need to get going now. I'll be back late tonight. Don't wait up."

Agnes stood up, too. "Come on, Verna, we need to get home and see your dad."

Verna gave her grandmother and aunt a kiss goodbye and headed out the back door.

"Wait, Verna, you can't go out that door!" called Mamaw. "You know you have to go out the door you came in or you'll never come back."

"Mamaw, Daddy says—"

"Come on, Verna, let's hurry home." Her mom practically pushed her toward the front of the house and outside. "This is not the afternoon to discuss Mamaw's many superstitions or what your dad thinks about them," she said. "He hasn't had any competition for favorite son-in-law until now. I don't want him to lose his place in the very first week."

When Aunt Helen and Mama laughed as they got in the car, Verna knew all was right with the world again.

~~~

Lucky for Mary, no one in the family had time to focus on her new marriage to Herndon. They were all quickly swept up in Helen's upcoming nuptials. The wedding was a quiet family affair "emphasized by simplicity," or so reported the *Miami Daily News* in a large write-up on the society page, including a large, full-length picture of Helen in her wedding gown. It was held at Ed's house on Palm Island. Among the most exclusive addresses in the county, Palm, Hibiscus, and Star Islands had been created in the middle of Biscayne Bay by Carl Fisher, who built Miami Beach. Part of their exclusivity came from the fact that the islands were only accessible by driving to the middle of the Venetian Causeway, then going over a small bridge with a guard at the end of it.

Ed Jones's two-story Spanish colonial home was decorated for the wedding with white flowers and potted palms throughout the entire first floor. The ceremony was held fashionably late at nine-thirty p.m. in the living room, a beautiful space with a slanted, wood-beamed ceiling and a view of Biscayne Bay just at the edge of the terrace. Agnes, Verna, and Bert arrived early along with Mollie and Sigmund.

"Leon!" Agnes squealed when she saw her brother. "We weren't sure you were coming."

"I wanted to surprise y'all," he said, hugging her. "I can only stay a couple of days, then I have to get back to work."

"Well, I've got to get upstairs and help Helen. Verna, you stay here with Daddy and Uncle Leon," she said. "I'll see y'all after the ceremony. Then, Leon, we're going to have a long talk."

She headed up to the main bedroom, where her mother Mollie, Mary, and Helen's bridesmaid, Ila Lovelady, were helping her fix her hair and makeup. Outside was a view of the pool and patio.

"You look beautiful," Agnes said to her sister, who was wearing a simple, column-style dress of lace with wide sleeves that narrowed at the elbow.

"There, you're ready to go," their mother said, setting Helen's matching lace hat carefully on her head.

"I'm so nervous, Mama." Helen held out a shaking hand.

"Of course you are. Everyone is nervous on their wedding day," Mollie assured her.

"I know I was," put in Mary.

Agnes, Helen, and their mother carefully met each other's eyes and refrained from saying anything.

"Let's not keep your bridegroom waiting. Let's get downstairs," said Agnes.

Sigmund waited for his daughter in the front hall. As the rest of the family slipped into the living room, he kissed her tenderly on the cheek. "You look beautiful, Helen. You are making Ed a very lucky man."

Billy Greene, the guitarist and a friend of Ed's who performed at the clubs on the Beach, began to play, and Ila, carrying pink roses to match her pink organdy lace dress, walked in ahead of them.

Ed and Helen only had eyes for each other as the minister pronounced them man and wife. Their love for each other was evident to everyone. It was a lovely ceremony, just long enough, and then they all headed into the dining room for the reception, which spilled onto the patio.

It was a small event, only thirty guests. All of Helen's family, with the exception of Herndon who'd found a job and couldn't make it, were there. Ed's mother had come in from Nebraska. *She is a lovely woman*, Agnes thought. She didn't put on airs, as Agnes had been afraid she would. She and Mollie sat in a corner and launched into a wonderful conversation on the advantages and disadvantages of living in the Midwest versus Florida.

"Yes, sometimes I do miss the snow. There's nothing like a pretty snow at Christmas," she heard her mother say. "But I don't miss the blizzards or slipping and sliding on ice—and the cold." Mollie gave an exaggerated shiver.

However, she refrained, Agnes noticed, from suggesting that Mrs. Jones move down to Miami to be closer to her son. Helen and Ed didn't need that kind of interference.

The rest of the guests were, well, rather eclectic. Everyone from entertainers to real estate developers to society ladies.

"That's Saul Cohen," Agnes whispered to Bert, trying to discreetly point to one of the guests. "He was in the papers all last year for that murder at his house."

"He didn't do it. They never convicted anyone in that case," Bert whispered back.

"You mean they never figured out who did it. How do you know it wasn't him?" Agnes still loved reading murder mysteries, and she'd avidly followed the trial in the newspapers. Now she was torn between horror at being so close to a murder suspect and a desire to go up and introduce herself.

The best man was Fleetwood Stoltz, whose father had developed the Fleetwood Hotel on Miami Beach in the 1920s. It hadn't survived the storm of '26, but the family had continued to develop real estate in the area so Agnes assumed if he was here at the wedding he was doing well. "The man actually had an entire hotel named after him!" Agnes whispered, half impressed, half scandalized.

"Well, they could hardly have named half the hotel for him," Bert teased.

As she watched Helen talk and laugh comfortably with everyone there, Agnes became more and more uncomfortable. "They're all so rich. They have to know we are just the poor relations," she said.

"Hey, speak for yourself," Bert continued to tease his wife. "This isn't the only house on Palm Island that I've been invited to."

Mary, who had joined them, giggled. "Just because you've been called to fix the plumbing in Al Capone's house doesn't mean you've visited!"

Agnes also couldn't help laughing. The notorious Al Capone lived just down the street at the other end of the tiny island. "What if he'd been invited to the wedding!"

They all laughed harder at the thought.

"It's what your sister has always wanted," Bert reminded them. "She's talked about wanting to marry a rich man since I've known her. That's just one of the reasons I never understood what she was doing with Godfrey."

"Shh! Don't mention him here!"

"Remember how Helen always said, 'I want luxury,' when she was a little girl?" Mary giggled again. "I guess she's found it."

"Let's go, Bert, Verna is asleep on her feet," Agnes put in.

Bert scooped the child up and put her on his shoulder, where she immediately closed her eyes. They made their way over to Helen and Ed, who stood in a group of their friends.

"We have to go, Verna's already out," Bert said. "It was a lovely wedding. Ed, welcome to the family." He shook his new brother-in-law's hand.

"I hope you'll help me fit in," Ed said.

Bert laughed. "It's easy. Just do what the women say."

"Will we see you at the party tomorrow night?" Helen asked.

"I don't think so. We'd have to find a babysitter, and I really want to spend a little time with Leon before he heads back. You won't even miss us," said Agnes.

The wedding might have been small, but Ila was hosting a party for four hundred people at the Deauville Hotel and Casino on the north end of Miami Beach. Then the couple was heading off for a ten-week honeymoon so Ed could introduce his new wife to his friends in the North, and maybe sell a few yachts while there. They planned to stop in Colorado, Nebraska, Michigan, and New York City. And Helen would get to travel in the sleeping cars on the train. She hadn't admitted it to anyone but Agnes how that was the part that excited her the most.

When Agnes, Verna, and Bert arrived home, he picked up the sleeping child in the back seat and carried her to the house as Agnes unlocked the door. She took a deep breath, finally feeling relaxed now that she was back in her own home. She looked around the small living room of the two-bedroom house.

"This is just perfect. I don't need a fancy house on Palm Island, or a ten-week honeymoon. I just need the two of you."

Chapter 17
And a Baby

1936

It had taken two tries for Helen to find her happily ever after. Although the rules of society were always much looser in Miami than in a lot of other cities, the age and wealth differences between the pair raised many more eyebrows than just her family's. But soon it became clear they were a perfect love match. Helen enjoyed everything about their life together, from summers on the Great Lakes at their cottage in Saugatuck, Michigan, to the trip to Europe they took on the *Queen Mary*. And she loved Ed, not just for the life he gave her, but for himself. It was obvious to everyone.

They moved from the house on Palm Island to Bal Harbour. The community was just being built when they bought their lot. Ed told her it was a good investment. "It's going to be an even better address than Coral Gables," was how Helen put it to her sisters.

Mary was also convinced that she'd met her Prince Charming. She'd known Herndon ever since she was a child and had first moved to Miami, after all. "Just like Agnes and Bert," she told her mother. "I'm not like Helen. I'm more like Agnes. I just want to settle down with a nice, responsible man in a little house and have children."

Mollie managed to bite her tongue and not say Herndon's uncle was one of the best-known bootleggers in the county. From everything she'd seen over the years, Herndon's upbringing had been anything but responsible. It wasn't the bootlegging connection that worried Mollie. The whole family was unreliable; they were always looking for the quick and easy way to make a buck.

~~~

Mary and Herndon felt the push and pull from both of their families, and moved out of the Sawieja home and into a small apartment as quickly as they could.

"It's the only way," Mary told Agnes, "for us to avoid all the pressure from both sides of our family."

A year and a half later she was thrilled to find out she was pregnant. In early 1936 she gave birth to a son, Milton.

By that time Miami could boast its own hospital, named after the town's first doctor, Dr. James Jackson. Mary and her baby spent three days there before coming home to their apartment. That night when little Milton cried, she asked Herndon to change his diaper. Herndon got up, walked out the door, and never came back.

Mary and Baby Milton moved back in with her parents, and she got a divorce from Herndon. She didn't bother to change her name back to Sawieja, like Helen had. "I've had a baby; I can't pretend I wasn't married," she said.

A year or two later she fell in love with a man named Terry Turragano, who wanted to marry her and adopt Milton. It looked like Mary was going to follow in Helen's footsteps after all. She'd learned her lesson in her first, disastrous marriage, but she was choosing better the second time around. Everyone in the family loved Terry. He was smart, steady, and adored both Mary and Milton.

But happily ever afters don't happen for everyone, and things did not work out well for the couple. Soon after Terry proposed her doctor discovered a lump in Mary's breast. It was cancerous. She told Terry that she wouldn't get married until she was healthy. She had surgery and began radiation therapy. At that time the treatment for cancer was even more devastating and less effective than today.

Agnes came every day to her parents' house to help Mollie take care of both Mary and Milton. Verna arrived after school each day and played with the little boy. And Terry also came every day. Mary was sick for months before she died in 1940. She was twenty-four years old.

Terry did get married several years later and had a daughter. He remained friends with the Sawiejas, and they were thrilled he found new happiness. He returned to school to follow his dream of becoming a licensed pilot. He died at age thirty-nine in a plane crash ferrying a plane from Miami to Lima, Peru.

Chapter 18
The Family That Watches *Lawrence Welk* Together…

Throughout my childhood Saturday nights belonged to Mama's family, which consisted of her parents and the Aunts and Uncles. That's how we collectively referred to them. Most of them were Granddad's brothers and sisters. Grandma's sister Helen and Helen's husband, Ed, along with a few stray cousins sometimes thrown in.

In Mama's world, being "family" wasn't just a matter of birth. It took a lot more than that. It had to do with stepping up and taking care of each other. It was difficult to get kicked out of the family, but it did happen.

My grandfather Bert, or Granddad Rogers as we called him, may have been the most judgmental when it came to claiming family. Aunt Helen, his sister-in-law, sometimes passed the family test, and sometimes she did not. While Grandma and Aunt Helen's youngest sister, Mary, died when she was only age twenty-four, thirty years later Granddad still brought up that when Mary had cancer Grandma went over to help out every day, but Aunt Helen only went once a week, when she was in town, and she was gone half the year vacationing. He never really forgave her for that.

Her husband, Uncle Ed, however, was family, even though he was different from the rest of us. He came from "old money" back in Nebraska and had even been to college. He raced speedboats, took Aunt Helen on trips to Europe, played golf at country clubs, and worked at trading stocks and selling yachts. But what made Uncle Ed family was that he insisted my mama should go to college and even gave Grandma and Grandad the first hundred dollars to send her to Florida State University. And he somehow managed to do it without offending his very proud brother-in-law. Now that is family.

Granddad's oldest brother, Uncle Leo, and his wife, Sadie, had been big drinkers, and Leo was stricken from the family roles for repeatedly pawning their mother's gold watch. After years scraping together the money to redeem the watch, finally Granddad kept it.

The core group of "family" were Aunt Stella, her husband, Uncle Stanley, and Grandad's three unmarried siblings: Aunt Anna Mae, Uncle Toby, and Uncle Harold.

All five of them lived together in a house in Miami Shores. This was just another example of the family sticking together. Back in the Depression no one could afford a house by themselves so the five of them all moved in together to make ends meet and then just kept on that way for the rest of their lives.

Aunt Stella was granddad's oldest sister. She was married to Uncle Stanley. At 5' 8" Aunt Stella was the tallest woman in the family until I passed her at age twelve—and then kept on growing. She liked to swear and would always say, "Well, pardon my French. Now you girls know not to say what your Aunt Stella does, don't you?"

Aunt Anna Mae was a few years younger than Stella. She was short and looked softer than her sister, but she wasn't. She ruled the rest of her siblings with an iron fist. Then there was Uncle Harold, the baby of the family who had worked with the greyhounds for a while but then got a plumbing license, just like his brother Bert. Uncle Harold was the quiet one who never said much. But when he did talk, the family listened.

And finally, whenever he was in town, there was Uncle Toby, the black sheep of the family. He worked as the handicapper for the horse racetracks and followed the season. He worked summers at Churchill Downs and Saratoga, winters in Miami at Hialeah and Tropical Park. While you might think working for the tracks was what made him a black sheep, it wasn't. Everyone in the family enjoyed gambling and racing—both horses and dogs. What made Uncle Toby the black sheep was he was known to go to bars. The family approved of a drink or two before dinner, you see, but after their experiences with their oldest brother Leo, they were very much against going out to bars and getting drunk. And even though Uncle Toby was not an alcoholic, everyone remembered Leo and the problems he had caused.

~~~

When I was about three, we moved to a house in a new neighborhood about ten blocks from the Aunts and Uncles. Like most of Miami, the area had been a swamp before land developers decided to make something of it and built the Biscayne Canal. But the contractor who built our block made a mistake when grading the lots. Instead of everything running downhill to the drainage canal, it was graded so that when it rained all the water ran to the very middle of the block. And that was where our house sat. Right in the middle.

Luckily, it was a typical Miami-style building with a high crawl space so the house itself only flooded if there was a hurricane. Your typical bad summer thunderstorm just dumped water in the street and in the yard, turning the back fifteen feet or so of our lot, and a few of the neighbors', into a minor lake. The street in front became a river with lovely waves whenever cars drove by. The neighborhood boys would take short pieces of plywood and make wake boards to surf the street. If their fathers were really adventurous, they were allowed to tie a rope onto the family car and get towed as if they were water skiing. I always wanted to try it, but Mama and Grandma wouldn't let me. They said it was too dangerous. And while I wasn't above attempting to get away with things—and often did—I knew this time they meant it. If I'd ever been caught surfing the street, first my hide would have been tanned, then I'd have been restricted to my room for the rest of my life. And I spent a lot of afternoons there already.

I was pretty content just catching tadpoles in the backyard until the water receded. I could wander around and play by myself, just making up stories in my head. Once the water was gone, though, the neighborhood was permeated with a swampy, mildewy smell, and the grass was slimy with algae until it grew long enough to cut. The plants my mother kept trying to grow in the backyard would also be dead. Again. But she kept trying. That was Mama. If something didn't work the first time, she tried and tried again until she forced it to work. She planted oranges and guava and mangoes and roses over and over. You know what they say about doing the same thing over again and expecting a different result? Well, in this case, maybe it wasn't quite so crazy.

My grandfather and the Uncles spent a lot of Saturdays spreading sand and dirt until the yard drained properly and Mama eventually got to have her garden.

When the shutters needed to be repaired at the Aunts and Uncles' house we all headed over there. When it was time to decorate for Christmas, Uncle Stanley spent days making sure our house had the most elaborate outdoor display in the area. If there was a plumbing problem or an electrical problem or someone wanted to paint a room, the entire family gathered to take care of it. The older women made the food, and the men did the work, helped out by my mother and the two of us girls.

~~~

Our new house on N.E. 115 Street was painted pink with a white tile roof. It had four bedrooms, big enough for my grandparents, my mother, my sister, and me. My sister and I shared a bedroom painted blue that had blue and white eyelet bedspreads. Mama even painted our dressers blue and white to match. When friends came over they always said we were rich because our house was larger than most of the ones in the neighborhood. The other homes on the block all had two or three bedrooms.

That was one of the many things that embarrassed me when trying to explain my family to other kids. Why don't you have a father? Why do your grandparents live with you? Why do you have such a big house? I would tell them we had a big house because we all lived together. That was how my mother and grandparents put it: "We live together." We didn't "live with" my grandparents. They didn't "live with" us. We all lived together.

It was a distinction that was important to them. It was about family sticking together—no matter what. Our family ship might not be fancy. It might be battered and torn. But if we all stuck together, we'd come out all right in the end.

No matter what was happening in the family, the Aunts and Uncles were a part of it. They came to every school event and dance recital. They were at our house for every holiday. They even came to church to watch us make our First Communions, even though none of them, especially not my grandparents, ever went to church at any other time. And they came over every Saturday night.

How many families spent every Saturday night in the 1960s watching *Lawrence Welk* and then *Perry Mason*? At our house that was just one part of the unvarying ritual. The Aunts and Uncles came over about five p.m. Before dinner there were drinks: whiskey and water for the men, whiskey and ginger ale for the ladies. Whether they attended church or not, the Rogers were the Catholic side of my family. They believed in drinking, playing cards, and gambling.

After drinks and time for gossip, Grandma and Mama served dinner, although I don't remember it as anything particular or special. The Aunts and Uncles were family so whatever we were having that night was fine with them. It might be meatloaf or pot roast or even just eggs and bacon. Never cabbage, though. Granddad would not eat cabbage. He said he'd eaten enough cabbage during the Depression and was never going to eat it again. When Grandma made corned beef and boiled potatoes, she put cabbage in, just like her mother, Mollie, had taught her, but she made sure not a leaf was on Granddad's plate.

When dinner was over we gathered in the Florida room (that's what family rooms were called in Florida in the 1960s) to watch *Lawrence Welk* and *Perry Mason*. Sometimes my sister and I put on plays we had written or we "auctioned off" things we had made, such as painted seashells and incredibly bad-smelling miniature bottles filled with colored water and a few drops of each of my grandmother's and mother's perfumes mixed together so they stunk to high heaven. The Aunts and Uncles would graciously give up their pennies and take home our handcrafted "treasures."

We were always a little afraid of Uncle Harold and Uncle Toby—they were men, and we were afraid of most men. But no one could be afraid of Uncle Stanley. He could fix any broken toy, grow any beautiful flower, and make two timid, fearful little girls feel comfortable. I don't think we ever talked to any of the Aunts and Uncles much. We just listened and let the flow of warm family love and talk wash over us. It had always been that way, Mama told us. Saturdays. *Lawrence Welk*. The Aunts and Uncles. We would stick together no matter what happened, and our family ship would make it through the storms.

Chapter 19
Legal Technicalities

I was in high school when the latest Paul Newman and Robert Redford movie, *The Sting*, came out. Mama, Cheryl, and I headed to see it one Saturday afternoon. We were late as usual since Mama was a chronic over scheduler and always left late for everything. My sister and I had long learned that to see the first ten minutes of a movie we would have to sit through the beginning of the next show. Luckily, in those days, theaters had one screen running one movie and didn't waste a lot of time between viewings. Usually there was just enough time to run out and get another box of popcorn and a drink before the show started again.

That day we arrived just as Robert Redford's friend was killed—an important part of the plot. So, of course, we were a little behind in following the plot, but hey, we were used to that.

My sister and I enjoyed the movie, and my mother was utterly charmed. She told us it reminded her of her own childhood, which seemed a little strange given she grew up in Miami and the movie is set in Chicago. And I knew none of my relatives had been con men. Well, except maybe my father. And apparently, he hadn't been very good at it.

The family's relationship to gambling, however, was always a little, shall we say, loose.

Maybe it was a Miami thing. Miami was founded on illegal gambling, after all. Yes, Julia Tuttle's oranges had a lot to do with convincing Henry Flagler to build his railroad, but a new stop also meant he could build another hotel with another casino attached. It isn't often mentioned in the Florida history books, but all of Flagler's hotels came with a casino, even though until 2004 gambling was illegal in the state of Florida. The law in the town, and in the state, just looked the other way.

When the family started racing dogs, the track at Hialeah was illegal. Or at least gambling at the track was illegal, which meant that basically, they were involved in an illegal industry. But they never looked at it that way. For them gambling on dogs was illegal. Racing dogs was not.

And just like my family, the city once again carefully looked the other way when these little legal technicalities came up. The results of the races were even published in the daily newspaper—at least until the *Miami Herald* decided a crusade against gambling was a good way to sell more newspapers, but that was a couple of decades later.

The society pages had no problem in 1934 writing that the fancy dance for four hundred given in honor of Aunt Helen and Uncle Ed after their wedding was held at the Deauville Hotel and Casino. Yes, the official name of the hotel included the word "casino," and no one seemed to care.

But the casinos and the tracks brought their own set of problems. Or rather, just a new kind of technicality for the city fathers to ignore. Miami has always had a love affair with mobsters, from Al Capone and Meyer Lansky to the "Big Five" New York crime families who considered South Florida a "home away from home." In the 1980s the TV show *Miami Vice* glamorized the city's mob connections and made the town popular again when it was going through another "bust" cycle.

Let me be clear. The Rogers' closest connection to the mobsters was my grandfather fixing Capone's plumbing. And my Uncle Ed might have sold a yacht or two to someone "connected." And when Uncle Toby worked as a handicapper for the horse tracks, he always knew which horses weren't running well. That was his job, to know which horse had the best chance of winning and to handicap the race so the track had the best opportunity to make money. But he never, never, talked about his information. And racetrack gambling was legal by that time, of course, as long as the bets were only placed inside the tracks and not at outside parlors.

Maybe the family attitude toward gambling was a Miami thing, or maybe it was a Catholic thing. The pope said drinking and gambling were fine as long as they were not done in excess. Although their relationship with the Catholic church had become strained, the Rogers apparently felt that if the pope said it okay, then it was okay. It was evidently their own interpretation of "Render unto Caeser that which is Caeser's and to God, that which is God's."

They certainly had no problem buying bootleg liquor, and I was always told that Uncle Stanley made "the best bathtub beer around." He could have made a fortune if he had sold it, the Aunts and Uncles declared, but instead he just gave it away. Again, it seemed to be one of those legal technicalities in the family's mind. Making illegal booze wasn't wrong if you gave it away; it was only wrong if you sold it. Or possibly it was more about the fear of being arrested than some high moral ground. I'm not really sure.

In the 1960s when my grandmother and the Aunts wanted to go to the horse races, they would take my sister and me along, and one of them would stand with us outside the fence where we could watch the horses' legs race by. I found it both exciting and boring at the same time. Even though we never went inside, it still felt a little bit illicit. No one was supposed to watch from outside, which was why we had to push our way through the tall hedge where we couldn't easily be seen.

There was a lot of standing in the hot sun, and I did my share of whining. But each time the horses' legs galloped past us, so close we could have reached out and touched them if our hands had fit through the holes in the chain-link fence, it was thrilling. The pounding of the hoofs was so loud, and the dust cloud that followed them was so close we coughed each time they ran past.

And then Aunt Anna Mae or Aunt Stella or Grandma would come out with some candy or a Coca-Cola in a paper cup, and trade places with the adult watching us so she could go inside the track. We would give them a dime or two to place bets for us. They picked the horses since we were too young to be able to read the program. I couldn't wait to be old enough to actually go inside the track and watch from the seats.

But back to *The Sting*. My mother loved the movie so much that instead of just watching the first ten minutes of the next show to see what we had missed, we stayed to watch the entire movie a second time through. When she got home she told Grandma and Granddad they just had to go see the movie the next weekend.

I think Grandma may have enjoyed it a little more than her husband did. For both of them it brought back memories.

Chapter 20
Afternoon at the Races

1938

 The city bus pulled up to the curb, and Verna, her mother, and the Raywoods, Marie and her daughter Ann, stepped off onto the sidewalk. It was a warm and sunny Friday afternoon in early spring, and Verna and Ann were skipping with excitement. They loved these excursions. About once a month, as soon as the two girls arrived home from school, they all got on the bus to go to town.

 Verna was in the green and red plaid dress she had worn to school, a matching headband holding back her long, black curls. Ann went to Gesu Catholic School and still had on her uniform of a dark skirt and a loose, white sailor blouse with a long tie.

 Verna breathed in the smell of the exhaust from the buses and cars. She listened to the noise of the newsboys hawking their papers: "Read all about it. Austria Joyful as German Pact Signed, European Panic Grows. Read all about it in the *Miami News*."

 "Why is Europe in a panic?" Ann asked her mother.

 "I'm not really sure, dear. Some fight between Austria and Germany. It's got nothing to do with us," replied Mrs. Raywood.

 "Bert's worried about it," said Verna's mother. "He's afraid the problems will spread over here."

 "I don't see how it can. What do we care about what the Germans do?" answered Mrs. Raywood. "Who do you think will win?"

 "We won't make it in time for the first, but Lady Bessie looks good in the second," said Mama, switching from world news to something much more important: which horses they would bet on today. "Ethel gave me money to put on Ethel's Choice in the third race—even though he is a long shot." Mama referred to another neighbor, Ethel Merrell, who hadn't been able to come with them that day. "Hold our hands, girls, we have to cross the street."

"Mama, I'm ten years old, I know how to cross the street by myself," said Verna.

"Well, I'm thirty-five, and I need help so hold my hand," her mother said with a grin at Mrs. Raywood.

"Oh Mama!" Verna said in that voice that children have used throughout time to express how silly and old-fashioned their parents are. But she took her mother's hand as they hurried across the street.

A few doors down they arrived at their destination, the Turf Club, a well-known betting parlor.

"All right, girls, you both sit down right here under the window and don't get in anyone's way," said Mrs. Raywood.

"Be good," added Mama, then both women gave their children a kiss and headed inside.

"You brought the jacks, right?" Verna asked.

"Of course, I did!" said Ann indignantly.

They weren't first timers at this, after all. The monthly excursions were part of their routine.

After they sat cross-legged and spread their skirts over their knees, Ann pulled the leather pouch out of her pocket and tossed the jacks and ball on the ground between them. "Eenie, meenie, mynie, moe…" she began, pointing back and forth from herself to Verna to decide who would go first. "Oh darn! You always win if you get the first turn," she complained when her finger pointed at Verna last.

After about thirty minutes Verna had finished fivesies, and Ann was still working on picking up three at a time.

"I'm bored. Let's go look in the windows and see what's going on," Ann suggested.

Verna grinned. "You just don't want me to beat you again." But she good-naturedly helped Ann scoop up the jacks and ball and place them in their pouch.

Looking in the windows was part of the ritual for these afternoons. They enjoyed seeing the men and women playing cards near the front of the room. Many of them wore tuxedos or evening gowns in the middle of the day. Either they had never changed since the night before or were ready to go out to a nightclub after the betting parlor closed. They could see their mothers sitting at the back. They, of course, were dressed very differently, in the dresses they had worn to work and ladylike hats. They were listening to the radio, which was broadcasting the horse race running at Tropical Park.

Suddenly, both women stood up and cheered. Verna and Ann grinned at each other. It looked like they had a winner.

Next they headed over to the door, but they weren't waiting for their mothers. Sometimes one of the men coming out of the parlor would give them a couple of nickels or dimes, and they were allowed to use it to buy some penny candy.

Today was apparently just as lucky for Verna and Ann as it was for their mothers. They had just taken up their stations when an older man came out, saw them, grinned, reached into his pocket, and tossed a dime in the air. Verna caught it quickly.

"Thank you very much," Ann said. Verna always let her say the thank-yous. She was shy and didn't really like to talk to strangers, even though her mother constantly told her it was only the polite thing to do.

They headed next door and picked out their sweets.

"I like the black cows best," said Verna. They were chewy caramel "slo-pokes" with a chocolate covering that could be made to last a very long time as long as you didn't give into temptation and chew them.

Ann chose the Boston Baked Beans, peanuts with a red candy coating.

Munching and sucking, they headed back to the betting parlor door, where they didn't have to wait long before their mothers emerged. Verna knew her mother had promised Daddy she wouldn't bet on more than three races. He didn't like gambling, and he *really* didn't like the betting parlor. He worried one day the police would decide to raid it just as Mama and Mrs. Raywood arrived.

They often had words about it. But in the end, Mama always promised she'd be careful, and Daddy just said, "I know you have good sense. You won't do anything foolish—will you?"

Verna didn't like it when her parents argued—or "bickered," as they called it. "We aren't really arguing, we are just bickering. You'll understand when you are married as long as your father and I have been," Mama always told her.

Verna couldn't imagine being married twelve years. But this afternoon she had something else on her mind.

"It seems so boring just listening to the races on the radio, Mama," said Verna. "Why don't you go to the track like Aunt Anna Mae and Aunt Stella?"

"It takes a lot longer to get over to Tropical Park; I would get there too late. And besides, I don't have any place to leave you," her mother said as the bus stopped in front of them, and they got on for the ride home.

"Well, when will you take me to the races?"

This was another thing Daddy often mentioned when they talked about gambling. He didn't like the fact that the Miami fathers winked and turned their backs at the many types of gambling in the city, from the Cuban *bolito* or the lottery games or the casinos that drew the wealthy to the hotels along Collins Avenue, but drew the line at children entering a casino, betting parlor, or racetrack. "It seems hypocritical," he would say. "It's not that I think that children should be in a gambling establishment, it's just they ignore the gambling then arrest people if they have their children inside."

Her mother never disagreed, but Verna knew that Mama didn't have quite the same attitude. Now, as they sat on the bus, her mother answered Verna's question the way she always did. "When you are as tall as Aunt Stella."

At 5' 8" Stella was the tallest woman in a family of tall people.

"I might never get to be that tall!" Verna whined.

"Well, then you'll just have to wait until you are twenty-one."

"But that's forever. It's eleven years!"

Mama and Mrs. Raywood laughed. "It will be here before you know it," Mrs. Raywood assured her in that patronizing way that grown-ups always made that statement.

Maybe, thought Verna, *I should start asking the Aunts, not my mother.*

~~~

It took a few more years, but not quite the eleven that Verna had feared it would take. When she turned age thirteen, the Aunts deemed that Verna was old enough for them to sneak into the racetrack.

"She's almost as tall as I am," Aunt Stella said, standing back-to-back with Verna so that her sister and sister-in-law could judge their comparative heights.

They were at the Aunts' house on N.W. 34 Street.

"She's just about an inch shorter," Aunt Anna Mae declared. "A little taller than I am. That's tall enough, don't you think, Agnes?"

Verna's mother put her face in her hands. "What is Bert going to say? You know how he is about gambling. He doesn't mind me going but—"

"He's our brother, just let me handle him," said Aunt Anna Mae with great confidence.

"But what if we get caught? We'll all get a fine and then we won't just hear it from Bert, we'll hear it from all of them," her mother said, referring to the collective group of Uncles. "Toby will be merciless!"

"Oh, Agnes, don't worry so much. It's time to show the child the horses," Aunt Stella said. She made it sound as if they were going out for pony rides, rather than taking their underage niece to the horse track. "Here, let's see what I have in my closet that will fit her."

As Verna stood in the middle of the room, the three women tossed through all of Stella's clothes. They found a very grown-up-looking beige shirtwaist dress, then pulled out sheer hose—Verna had never been allowed to wear hose before.

"Hose, Stella! Really," said Mama.

"If she's going to look like a lady and not a little girl, yes. Here, honey, try these shoes. I think we wear about the same size."

Verna kicked off her black-and-white saddle shoes and slipped into the brown spectator pumps with three-inch heels. She stood and admired the shoes like Judy Garland looking at the ruby slippers in *The Wizard of Oz*.

"Perfect," said Stella.

"She still looks thirteen," pointed out Mama, who had obviously been completely overwhelmed by her sisters-in-law. She knew she was beaten. Now she could only stand back and hope they could pull this off.

"A hat," said Aunt Anna Mae. "I have just the thing." She hurried out and came back a minute later with a wide-brimmed straw hat. She put it on Verna's head. "Now keep it low, like this, to cover your face."

"And she'll need some makeup," said Aunt Stella.

"Makeup! I get to wear makeup!" Verna squeaked.

Mama just shrugged.

~~~

The next day was a school holiday so they left the house before lunch and took the bus to Aunt Stella's where Verna was given her makeover.

"You look very grown-up," Aunt Anna Mae assured her.

"If I can only walk in these shoes without tripping," she said, as she practiced walking back and forth in the living room, stumbling only a little.

Soon they headed out to catch the bus to Hialeah. Verna alternated between trying to act like a grown-up and bouncing up and down like a six-year-old. "Will the flamingoes be out? Are they always there?" she asked.

Considered the most beautiful racetrack in the world, Hialeah was known for its flamingoes, which had been imported from Cuba and lived in the infield pond. The beautiful pink birds often took flight around the track, as if they knew they were an important part of the entertainment.

"Yes," Aunt Stella said. "The flamingoes are always there. We'll take you as close as we can so you can get a good look, and we'll stop by the stalls, too, to see the horses. Now let's take a look at the racing form and decide who you want to bet on. You need to figure it out now and give your mother your money. We can't let anyone see you betting. It will be easier if we get caught if we can honestly say you've just been watching."

Verna knew there was something illogical about that, but she gave up worrying about it and just enjoyed the day. She loved everything, from watching the flamingoes to cheering in the stands for her horses. She had beginner's luck and picked two winners, Violante in the first race and Highscope in the third.

"I'll give you your winnings when we get home. We can't have anyone seeing you take any money," Mama said.

"Oh my God!"

They both turned at the exclamation from Aunt Stella.

"Hi, ladies, what are y'all doing here today? I thought you were going shopping?" asked Uncle Toby, walking up to them.

"T-Toby. What are you doing here?" stuttered Aunt Anna Mae.

"I work here, didn't you know?" he teased.

"We thought you had the day off," she replied.

"Mark got sick, and I'm filling in. I usually stay up in my office but decided to head down to the restaurant for lunch today. And—" He stopped. "Verna?" He tried to peer behind her mother, where Verna was desperately trying to hide.

"Now, Toby, it's not what you think," said Stella.

"Of course, it's exactly what I think. Verna's been begging to go the track for years, and you finally decided she was old enough to smuggle her in."

Toby sounded angry and was beginning to get red in the face. Verna had never in her life seen her Uncle Toby angry. He was the best natured of all her relatives.

"What kind of trouble do you think I could get in if someone finds my niece here? I'm the secretary of the track, for God's sake. I can't be seen breaking the rules. That new county commissioner is threatening to crack down on gambling. He's just looking for an excuse."

"I think we'd better go," Aunt Stella said, mustering up as much dignity as she could manage before they gathered their things.

"You don't think he'll tell Daddy, do you?" asked Verna when they got out of the park and were waiting at the bus stop.

"Of course he'll tell your father," said Mama. "I didn't even bother to ask him not to. That would have meant he'd make sure he got on the telephone even faster. This way, if he gets busy, at least we may have a chance to tell him before Toby does."

"Mama, do we have to?"

"Yes, baby, we have to. And don't you worry. You are not in trouble. You are a child; you didn't do anything I didn't let you do."

"Well, at least the only person who caught us was Toby, not the track officials or the police," Aunt Anna Mae said brightly.

Verna, Mama, and Aunt Stella all turned and glared at her.

Once home Verna wasted no time taking off her borrowed outfit and changing into a pair of dungarees.

"Go scrub your face again, honey, you've still got lipstick on," Mama said when she came out to the kitchen.

She was still in the bathroom when she heard her dad come in. She decided to linger in the hallway and listen before going in.

"Hi, honey, did you have a good day?" she heard her mother ask.

"Yes, a very good day. But not as interesting a day as I hear you had."

Verna sank to the floor. What was her father going to do?

She could hear the hesitation in her mother's voice as she said, "So you talked to Toby?"

"I think he must have run all the way to the nearest phone as soon as you all had left the park. Agnes, what were you thinking? And don't tell me it was Stella's idea. I know it had to be. I just expected you to have more sense."

"Oh, Daddy, don't be mad at Mama." Verna ran into the kitchen. She really hated it when her parents were angry or upset.

"I'm really not mad at Mama, and I'm not mad at you either, Verna," he said, sitting down at the table so he was closer to her level. "I just expected your Mama not to get carried away with my sisters' silly ideas."

"It wasn't a silly idea. I had a really wonderful time, and I even won two dollars."

Dad put his head in his hands. "Agnes, you let her bet?" He sounded shocked.

"No, Bert, of course not. We let her pick her horses before we went, and I put the money down. Verna never got near the betting. Now come sit down at the table, Verna, dinner's on."

Daddy shook his head at Mama's very illogical logic but didn't say anything else as Mama began serving up liver and onions—Daddy's favorite.

Nothing more was said about the trip to the racetrack. At least not in Dad's hearing. Uncle Toby teased all of them about it whenever he could—he was just smart enough not to do it when his big brother was around.

And Verna always wondered how her mother, who really didn't like to cook, had managed to come home and get liver and onions on the stove and ready to eat in such a short time. When she asked her mother later, she said, "Well, of course I got it ready to go just before we left. There's no better way to distract a man than with his favorite dinner."

Verna guessed she'd never understand her parents. They seemed to bicker a lot over little things. "It's their way of showing they love each other," Aunt Stella explained to her one day. "It's a little noisy and hard on the rest of us sometimes, but they rarely are actually angry at each other."

When Verna talked to her mother about it, she just said, "Someday you'll have been married as long as your dad and I have, and you'll understand."

Verna couldn't see herself ever getting married, let alone staying married for fifteen years.

Chapter 21
Wheels

I rode my tricycle down the sidewalk on a bright and hot spring afternoon. Only the moms and preschoolers were out at this time of day. It was my first taste of independence. I was finally trusted enough to go three houses away from home, to where the sidewalk ended, as long as I stayed on my trusty three-wheeled steed.

At the last house on the block a girl with long blond hair was playing in the grass. I stopped my trike and stared for a while. I was shy and my social skills were not exactly well developed—staring was the only way I knew to make friends. Thank goodness she was slightly more outgoing. After a short time of watching each other, she came over and asked my name. Her name was Denise. A few days later her mom came down and met my family, and we were allowed to take off on our trikes together, back and forth from her house to mine. Three houses up, three houses down. It cemented our lifelong friendship.

Eventually, we graduated to two wheels and a little more distance from home. We were allowed to cross the street so we could go to a friend's house one block over. It was on the corner so my grandmother could stand at the window and keep an eye on us as we rode there, knocked on the door, and went inside. Then, once everyone was sure we had mastered the art of crossing the street and avoiding cars, we were allowed to ride our bikes to school and back. That was exciting.

I had a turquoise American-style bike with a heavy frame and foot brakes. Cheryl and Denise each had English racers, three-speed bikes with a light frame and hand brakes. In the mornings Denise would stop at our house, and the three of us would ride the ten blocks to school. The only problem was I had to get up earlier if we were riding our bikes, and I was never a morning person. Denise would get mad at me if she was late for school.

What was really fun was riding back home. Our school, St. Rose of Lima, was at the top of a slight incline that passed for a hill in Miami. I think the change in elevation was no more than thirty feet between the school and home, but it did mean we really did walk or ride our bikes uphill on the way there. But we got to coast downhill all the way home, and it was easy to go really, really fast. After you crossed the block by the school, you pedaled as fast as you could for about two blocks, then started to coast. The person who coasted the farthest without having to pedal was the winner. I spent a lot of my childhood with skinned elbows and knees.

What was really bad was if I messed the bike up, too. I remember walking the last five blocks one day with skinned elbows, skinned knees, and a bike whose frame was bent so that the front wheel would only point to the right. That was a long five blocks. Luckily, Granddad could fix almost anything, and that weekend he straightened the bike and fixed it as good as new.

Once we had mastered the trip to school and back, we wanted to go farther afield. The Miami Shores Library was just a few blocks beyond St. Rose, and the tiny three- or four-block downtown shopping area of Miami Shores was just a few streets south of that. A lot of kids did their homework at the library. Cheryl, Denise, and I wanted to do that, too. We decided to make the very reasonable argument that we just couldn't do research for our school projects at home. This was back in the day when encyclopedias were multi-book references that could not be checked out.

Of course, Mama had purchased *Compton's Pictured Encyclopedia* on a payment plan from a door-to-door salesman as soon as my sister started school. It took up a good two feet of space on the built-in corner shelf in the Florida room. Denise's family also had a set of encyclopedias. Who did we think we were fooling with our claim of needing the library?

Luckily, our parents were all for independence and let us go. And it didn't take long to convince them we were capable of riding those few more short blocks to the Miami Shores Five and Ten, where you could buy kites for ten cents, fifteen cents, or really splurge and get the twenty-five-cent plastic ones. Not to mention candy, presents for birthdays and Christmas, packets of Valentine cards, and anything else a ten-year-old might need.

Bicycles remained important even after we were old enough to take the bus to the 163rd Street Shopping Center. It took over an hour each way so that usually left us only an hour to examine all the delights of Burdines, Jordan Marsh, and all the little stores in between. We usually saved our trips to the shopping center for when our parents could take us.

My first date involved bicycles, too. He picked me up in his parents' station wagon, loaded both our bikes in the back, and we headed "down south" (as we called anything south of Coral Gables) to Mattheson Hammock to ride through the park. This did not make a lot of sense because Mattheson Hammock was a good twenty miles from my house, and we could have certainly found some very nice parks a lot closer in which to ride. But it did ensure privacy so we could try out kissing.

Then I passed my driving license—just in time for the great 1970s gas crisis. It began in late 1973, and I got my driver's license in the spring of 1974. My family was ecstatic; they had a new person they could send to wait in the gas lines. Hey, at least I was out by myself in a car, even if all I got to do was drive ten blocks to the gas station, wait an hour, fill up, and come home.

There were days when no station had gas. There were stations that sold to people only on odd or even days, depending on the last number of their license plate. Some stations put out flags to let you know if they had gas or not.

But somehow if my sister or I wanted to go somewhere, Mama and Grandma and Granddad always found a way.

I could talk endlessly about the adventures my high school friends and I got into once we had the independence of the automobile. There was a late-night trip to Coconut Grove with my friend Diane, which was one of the most foolish things I ever did since Coconut Grove was considered a very dangerous place in those years. There were the drives in our friend's old VW microbus—the most iconic vehicle of the 1970s—where we piled a ridiculous number of people into it. The most coveted seat was on the motor in the middle. And my safety conscious mother didn't say a word. It was the '70s; no one worried about getting fried in a car accident.

When Mama told me about one particular journey she made at thirteen on a bicycle, I exclaimed, "You would never have let Cheryl or me do that!"

Chapter 22
December Morning

1941

It was late morning on a sunny December Sunday. The sky was a cloudless blue, and the temperature was about 75 degrees. At the Rogers house Verna's mom, Agnes, was sitting at the kitchen table doing the crossword puzzle. Daddy sat next to her reading the front section of the *Miami Herald*, as he always did on weekend mornings. Bawpaw Rogers, who lived with them now that he had retired from driving trains for the railroad, was drinking a cup of coffee and looking over the sports section.

"They are expecting two million tourists here this winter," Dad said conversationally.

"Where are they going to put them all? The traffic is going to be terrible," Mama answered.

"We can sure use another good tourist season, though," Dad said. "Things seem to get a little better each year. I just hope it keeps up."

The Great Depression had ended slowly in Miami. Although the economy had not returned to the frenetic pace of the 1920s, it had improved significantly. Bert and Agnes had finally been able to buy their own home. They purchased a two-bedroom house on N.W. 46 Street and turned the sunroom at the back into a bedroom for Bert's dad.

Sundays were a day to relax in the Rogers household. Everyone pretty much got to do as they pleased. Mama usually made a big meal on Saturdays so they just had leftovers or maybe went out to a restaurant. Bawpaw read the newspaper and dozed in his chair in the living room, and Daddy did a little work in the yard, stopping often to visit with any neighbors who happened to walk by. He always came in with all the latest neighborhood gossip.

"I'm going out to trim the croton hedge," he said now.

"Didn't you just do that last week? They can't need it again already," Mama said.

"If they are going to stay looking good, they have to be trimmed regularly," Dad replied.

"Soon they'll look like little old sticks," Mama laughed. "But you go ahead and trim them again if it makes you happy."

Dad gave her a kiss as he went out the back door. A short time later they heard the *snip, snip, snip* of the hedge clippers through the open window.

Mama and Bawpaw looked at each other, shook their heads, and laughed. Dad was famous in the family for his meticulously kept yard. He and Uncle Stanley had a friendly competition going as to who had the best-kept lawn. Verna was often called in to help. Her regular chore was to weed all the beds. It was boring work, but Dad usually rewarded her with a trip to the ice cream parlor.

Now they heard a lawn mower start next door, and the smell of newly mown grass wafted in through the open jalousie windows. It was a typical, quiet weekend morning. For Verna, though, the Sunday routine her parents and grandfather found so relaxing could be a little boring. Most of her friends went to church, and even once they got home, their parents often didn't allow them to come out and play. All her homework was done; she had finished reading all her library books and had nothing much to do. She decided she really needed to just get out of the house.

"Mama, can I ride my bike down to the burger stand and get a hotdog for lunch?" she asked. At age thirteen, she had recently been allowed to cross N.W. 6 Avenue, one of the busier streets in the area, and riding her bike to get a hotdog made her feel very grown-up.

"That sounds fine, Verna," her mother said, looking up briefly from her puzzle. "Just be careful crossing the street."

Verna got on the chrome and green Schwinn she had received last Christmas and headed down the street. She waved to her dad and Mr. Merrell, who had both quit working on their lawns and were now standing between their two houses talking.

She pedaled at a leisurely pace the ten blocks to the burger shop. She wore dungarees, rolled at the cuffs, and a striped, short-sleeved shirt. Her long, curly black hair was held back out of her face with a red ribbon. According to her mother, her scuffed saddle shoes needed to be polished, but Verna was resisting—it wasn't fashionable to have freshly polished shoes. They were supposed to look worn. If they were too clean and shiny, she might be teased. Verna had a horror of being teased.

She crossed the avenue at the stoplight, then rode on the sidewalk past several small shops, almost all of which were closed on Sunday. As she neared the shop, she heard a newsboy calling out the latest headlines. At first she couldn't make out the words, but she could see that several people were starting to gather, and he was selling newspapers as fast as he could. She was still a half a block away when the man's words became clear: "Japan Wars on U.S.—Planes Drop Bombs on Pearl Harbor!" he shouted.

Verna pulled her bike over to the edge of the grass, set the kickstand, and pushed through the group of people.

"What's happening? What is it?" she asked.

"The Japs have bombed us. They've bombed the Navy at Pearl Harbor," one man told her as he scanned the newspaper in his hand.

"Where's Pearl Harbor?" she asked.

"It's in Hawaii." The man looked up and focused on her for the first time. "Little girl, you'd better get on home. This is a war. It's going to change everything."

Verna started to bristle at being called "little girl," then looked at the man again. He and everyone else around him were upset and distracted. She pulled out the change she had stuffed in her pocket to buy her hotdog. She wasn't hungry now. She got in line and bought a paper. Her parents and grandfather needed to know this news right away. They never turned on the radio on Sunday afternoon. They might not hear about this for hours if she didn't tell them.

She folded the paper and tucked it under her arm; she didn't want it to fly out of the basket on the front of the bike so kept it there as she took off at full speed, heading back home.

Her father was still out in the yard talking to Mr. Merrell.

"Dad, Daddy," she shouted, waving the newspaper as she hopped off her bike and dropped it to the ground without putting down the kickstand—something she would usually get in trouble for skipping. This time she knew no one would care once they heard her news.

"Daddy, the Japs have bombed Pearl Harbor!" she called, out of breath from her mad dash.

"What! What are you talking about?"

She waved the newspaper in front of his face. "Daddy, see, it's right here."

Her took the paper from her and read the headline, "'Planes Drop Bombs on Pearl Harbor.' Powell, you'd better come on in with us; we'll turn on the radio."

"I'll get my wife and be right over." Mr. Merrell ran toward his house.

Dad ran in, waving the newspaper just as Verna had done a few minutes before. "Agnes! Dad! Turn on the radio."

And for the rest of the afternoon, they sat with the neighbors and listened as reports came in one after another. Two and possibly three battleships had sunk...scores of smaller vessels had also been destroyed...between one hundred and three hundred warplanes had been bombed...and finally, the Japanese had declared war on the United States.

The next day at school, the bombing of Pearl Harbor was all anyone could talk about. The teachers were tense and worried. The students were, too. Right after lunch the entire school was brought into the auditorium to hear the president's speech to a joint session of Congress.

President Roosevelt's voice came on. "Yesterday, December 7, 1941—a date which will live in infamy—the United States of America was suddenly and deliberately attacked by naval and air forces of the Empire of Japan...."

Verna listened to everything and tried to understand just what it would mean. She thought about what the man at the newsstand had said: "It's going to change everything." She didn't yet know how things would change, but she knew he was right.

Chapter 23
The Big Leagues

I moved up to the Big Leagues—North Miami Junior High—in the fall of 1970. Junior High wasn't bad, but I didn't really come into my own until I got to high school. I found my place with the artsy kids, the ones who wore slightly outrageous clothes. Luckily, Goth hadn't yet come into style, or we would all have been wearing black with heavy eye makeup. I don't like black, and I still hate wearing makeup, probably because my mother loved makeup. Try dressing like a hippie when you live with a mom who thinks that 1945 was the height of fashion and wants to give you a Toni home permanent when everyone else is ironing their hair. My bell-bottom jeans were always creased!

I found the artsy group by way of the Creative Writing class, which I took as an elective. The spring before I noticed from my sister's yearbook that the senior high had a creative writing magazine. "I'm going to be the editor of that magazine when I'm a senior," I said to myself.

And I was.

We never like to think we are like our parents, certainly not when we are teenagers. My mother was one of those kids who was the leader of everything, even if she didn't know it. If you look through the yearbook for Miami-Edison Senior High School, class of 1945, you will find her on almost every page. She was a member of the Edison Cadettes, the flag-twirling group that was considered very elite. She starred as "Jo" in *Little Women*. She even dated the drum major, Perry Watson. She and Perry loved to dance. A musician who picked up money on the weekends performing wherever he could, he knew a lot of the people who played in the nightclubs on the beach. Sometimes he and my mother were able to sneak into the clubs. On Saturdays they often went to the beach and tried to spot German ships out at sea.

No, there was no way I, with my group of artsy misfits in scruffy hip-hugger bell-bottoms and white peasant blouses (well, everyone's bell-bottoms were scruffy except mine), was anything

154 Karen Hodges Miller

like my mother. And then one summer we visited her friend Judy Drewry, who lived in Washington, D.C.

"It was our freshman year of high school," Judy told me, "and we were walking down the hall to get to the next class, and Verna saw a blue-and-yellow ribbon on the floor. She picked it up and handed it to me and said, 'When we are seniors we are going to be wearing these.' I asked her what it was, and she told me it was for the National Honor Society; she was going to be president of it when she was a senior. And she was. She pulled me along with her and made me study harder so that I got in, too."

Yes, I suppose the apple didn't fall far from the tree.

~~~

High school is supposed to be about education and getting into a good college. But what we all remember best are the friends, the clubs, the football games, the fun. If we are lucky we keep our grades up and manage that college dream, too.

I don't have a suspenseful or humorous story about Verna's high school years. She had a lot of friends and a boyfriend; she was popular. The other kids in school probably thought she had it all. Verna's only problems were her shyness and insecurity, which had her always judging and finding herself wanting. It was a problem that plagued her all her life.

It was wartime, though, and that changed things. Gas was rationed. That meant the band and flag-twirling Cadettes didn't get to go to other counties to perform when the football team played in central Florida or down in the Keys. The annual Cadette trip to Washington, D.C., to march in a parade never happened.

For Verna the war meant paper drives and aluminum can drives. Her mother tried, rather unsuccessfully, to plant a victory garden, although her grandmother Mollie did start raising turkeys. Boys in her high school were quitting school and enlisting as soon as they turned eighteen. Uncle Harold went off to war.

But for the most part, the war was just something happening "over there." High school was great, and Verna gave very little thought to what was to come after.

Chapter 24
Uncle Ed's Surprise

1945

It was January of Verna's senior year at high school. She and her boyfriend Perry had been at the school all afternoon for a special combined band and Cadette practice. The Cadettes were the elite flag-twirling team at the high school. There would be a parade in downtown Miami in a few weeks, and the band would perform, along with the flag twirlers. Verna was one of the color guard. She wished she was a twirler but, as one of the tallest girls, she'd been assigned to color guard duty and the task of carrying the American flag.

After Perry pulled up in front of her house, she gave him a quick kiss goodbye and hopped out of the car, surprised when she noticed Uncle Ed's tiny Crosley convertible parked in front. Leave it to Uncle Ed to not only buy a car no one had heard of, but one that turned heads because of its different shape and petite size.

Verna wondered what her aunt and uncle were doing here this afternoon. Mama would have mentioned a family dinner. She headed into the house and greeted everyone with hugs and kisses.

"I need to go change before I sit down," she told them. "I'm all hot and sweaty after practice. We were on the field all afternoon."

"Go on, but come back quick. Your uncle has something he wants to ask you," her father told her.

Verna looked at everyone in surprise. What was going on? If Dad had said Aunt Helen wanted to ask her something, she would have assumed there was some special event her aunt wanted her to attend; she sometimes asked her to go to ladies' events at La Gorce Country Club or the Surf Club. Verna really enjoyed those, unlike her mother who always felt uncomfortable at her sister's parties. Verna liked to get dressed up in her best dress, hat, and gloves, and eat the delicious food.

Now she hurried out of the room, quickly washed her

face, took her hair out of the ponytail it had been in during practice, and brushed it out as quickly as she could. Then she changed from her dungarees and old shirt into a gray skirt and lightweight navy pullover. After pulling on her white bobby socks and loafers, she was back in the living room in five minutes.

"Come sit down, Verna," Uncle Ed said.

Aunt Helen sat next to him.

She perched on the arm of her mother's chair, sticking close to her parents for moral support.

"Have you thought about going to college?" Uncle Ed asked.

She hadn't known what she expected him to say, but of all the things in the world she might have thought of, that hadn't been on her list.

She turned and looked at her mother and then her father. "Noooo," she said slowly, drawing the word out. "Some of my friends are going but—" She left the sentence hang. No one in the family except Uncle Ed had ever been to college. It was expensive. It had never occurred to her that she would do anything after high school except look for a job.

"Your uncle has a proposition for you," Dad told her now, smiling encouragingly, and she turned back to where Uncle Ed and Aunt Helen sat.

"You're a smart girl, Verna. You get excellent grades. If you go to college, you could be a teacher or a nurse."

"A teacher," Verna replied instantly. "I don't like blood."

Aunt Helen chuckled as her husband said, "Okay, a teacher; you could go to FSCW."

There were only three state colleges in Florida. The University of Florida in Gainesville was for men. Florida State College for Women and Florida A&M for black students were both in Tallahassee.

"You want me to go North for college?"

"Well, it's still Florida; it doesn't even snow there," Uncle Ed said with a smile.

"But it's...it's—"

"An all-day bus ride," her mother put in.

Verna turned to look at her. Mama was trying hard not to cry. "Mama, don't you want me to go?"

"Of course, I do, honey. It's a great opportunity, and your uncle is so nice to offer it to you. I'll miss you, but if this is what you want, of course I want you to go."

Verna jumped up and hugged her uncle and then her aunt. "Wow, thank you so much. I'd really like to go to college. I never even thought I could. But Maude is going, and Peggy, and—and I'd really like to be a teacher."

"Well, before you get too excited, you need to listen to your uncle's conditions," Dad put in.

Verna sat back down by her mother, ready to listen.

"I'm going to give you one hundred dollars to start you on your way," Uncle Ed explained. "That ought to take care of your first year's tuition and books. Your parents are going to take care of your room and board. Now we all expect you to do well, keep up your grades. There are lots of temptations when you go away to school—I ought to know."

"Oh, I'll study all the time."

"Well," he chuckled again, "you don't have to study all the time; you are allowed to have some fun with your friends. We just want you to know that we expect you to keep up with your work, too."

"We know you'll make us proud, Verna," Aunt Helen added.

"I'm going to college. I'm really going to college! I need to go call Maude right away." Verna jumped up and ran to the kitchen to immediately begin calling all her friends.

"Well, I think that went pretty well," Ed said to his sister-in-law. "And Agnes, don't worry, she'll be fine."

Agnes sniffled. "I know she will. I'm just crying because I'm so proud of her."

~~~

That last semester of high school seemed to fly by. There was the prom, then graduation, and, of course, parties to attend. Verna hardly had time to study but knew she had to keep her grades up. They were more important than ever, now that she was going to go to college.

She and Maude made plans to room together in the Freshman dorm. Perry, who was going to study to be a music teacher, would only be 150 miles away at the University of Florida.

"I'll come see you every weekend," he promised. "The guys tell me there is always someone with a car driving up to see his girlfriend. And there's always the bus."

Verna could see the future. She would go to Tallahassee, have a wonderful time, come home to Miami, and then marry Perry. They would both teach school until it was time to start a family.

The future looked rosy, and on May 8, a few weeks before her graduation, Germany surrendered. Everyone said Japan would also soon surrender and the war would be over. Yes, everything was going Verna's way. But history is personal, not just national, and sometimes the most insignificant events turn out to change a family's history forever.

Chapter 25
The Picnic

I

Dinner that night was just as usual. Meatloaf maybe? Spaghetti? I don't really remember. Granddad sat at the head of the table, Grandma at the foot closest to the kitchen; funny, Grandma hated to cook but was always in charge of dinner. My mother and I sat together on one side of the table. We always had to sit next to each other because we were the only two "lefties" and those privileged right-handed people complained that we bumped their arms. Cheryl sat across from us.

There was the usual talk.

"How was your day?"

"Is your homework finished?"

"There was a traffic accident on the expressway near 79th Street."

And then the phone rang.

Granddad got up to answer it. It was in the days before spam callers and cellphones and caller ID. If the phone rang at the dinner hour, you knew it was something important.

A few minutes later he came back into the dining room. We knew before he said a word that something was wrong. He looked sad, serious. "Catherine died," he said.

We were all shocked. But for different reasons.

"Oh my god, what happened?" asked Grandma.

"A heart attack apparently," he said.

"Who is Catherine?" Cheryl and I asked simultaneously.

"Your great-aunt," my mother told us.

My sister and I looked at each other across the table. We never remembered hearing of an Aunt Catherine.

~~~

Not every story is a happy story; they don't all end well. My earliest memory is lying on a bed knowing that my father had left and was not coming back. I was two. I don't know if it is a real memory, or bits and pieces of other memories, or just a feeling that I attached a "memory picture" to.

Some stories come down through newspaper clippings, photographs, or letters. The letters my great-great-grandmother in Poland wrote to her son, Sigmund, are full of the pain of missing a child she knows she will never see again and the grandchildren she will never meet. They drip with Mom Guilt. "Thank you for the letter; you don't write often . . ." How much more would that pain be if a child had died?

And then there is the picnic. It is a story that changed my family in big ways and small. The consequences of that day could never have been foreseen when it started out.

II

1945

"Come on, get a move on. The day is wasting," Leon called playfully to his wife.

Catherine was still in bed at nine in the morning, and Leon was ready to go. He'd woken up early and fed Mary Lou, their seven-year-old daughter. Then he'd helped her get dressed in her swimsuit and got her involved in playing with her dolls while he got everything ready.

He'd fixed the sandwiches—some ham and cheese, some bologna, some peanut butter with the homemade guava jelly his mom, Mollie, always made—and packed bananas and fresh oranges and Animal Crackers for Mary Lou. He'd filled an oilcloth bag with towels, as well as a shovel and pail for Mary Lou and a pair of goggles for himself. He remembered to add the bottle of Coppertone lotion for Catherine—it was all the latest rage, and Catherine always wanted the latest, the newest, the best. Leon didn't understand that; he thought she was beautiful just as she was. She didn't need some fancy new "tanning lotion" to make her any prettier.

Now it was time to go, and Catherine still wasn't out of bed.

"Do we have to spend the day with your family?" she whined when he went in to wake her. She hid her head under the pillow, trying to ignore him.

"Yes, we do. I promised we'd be there. You'll have fun. You love the beach."

"Why do we have to go down to the Keys? It's a two-hour ride down there, and we pass plenty of beaches before we get to Bahia Honda."

Leon gritted his teeth. Catherine didn't like his family, even though she and Agnes had been good friends growing up in Missouri. She didn't like Miami; she wanted to go back to Missouri. She didn't like his job. She didn't like saving money. They'd come back to Miami a year ago because, with the war, there were jobs again. He now had a good job as an electrician at the Naval shipyard, but it was never enough for her.

He counted to ten and took a deep breath. He reminded himself she was trying. She had agreed to give their marriage one more chance. He didn't want to lose her, and he certainly didn't want to lose Mary Lou. She was his darling. The light of his life.

"Please, Catherine, you promised. It's Father's Day, and now that Germany has surrendered, the gas rationing is easing up. We haven't been able to have a trip like this in a long time, and I want to spend today with my father. And besides, Mary Lou will really love the beach, and she'll get to play with her cousin Milton. She doesn't get to spend much time with other kids."

"I wish Helen and Ed would be there. Why do they always spend the summer in Michigan? Like Miami isn't good enough for them."

"You just want to flirt with my brother-in-law."

"Well, Ed is certainly more fun than Bert. He's so damn self-righteous all the time."

"Well, you're in luck. Agnes just phoned. Bert was called out on a job, so she's driving over to pick up Mom and Dad and Milton and then she'll meet us here, and we'll all drive together. You'd better hurry up; they'll be here soon."

Catherine finally got out of bed and gave Mary Lou a big kiss and hug when she ran in to watch her mother put on her makeup. She always had time for Mary Lou. Catherine was a good mother. If only they could recapture what they used to have.

"You look fabulous," Leon said, giving her a kiss as she got dressed.

She wore bright green, wide-legged trousers and a red-and-green print shirt. She tied a green scarf around her brown, permed curls and declared herself ready just as Agnes pulled up.

"Let's go, what are we waiting for?" she asked Agnes with a bright smile as she put Mary Lou on her lap in the back seat. "It's a beautiful day, I can't wait to get to the beach!"

Catherine's sudden enthusiasm sounded forced to Leon, and apparently to Agnes, too. He watched his sister give a big smile—it looked strained to him, too, and he hoped Catherine didn't notice. But neither she nor Agnes said anything so he ignored it.

He leaned in the window, gave his mom a quick kiss, then rounded the car and climbed in the back seat of Bert and Agnes's new 1945 Chevrolet next to his wife. On the other side of Catherine, Milton was looking at some books he had brought along. *Milton is a good kid,* Leon thought, watching as the boy helped Mary Lou decipher the words on the page. At eight he'd already had a hard life. His deadbeat of a father had run out on Mary almost as soon as Milton was born. Leon had tried to tell his sister the guy was no good when she first started dating him, but Mary wouldn't listen. And then Mary had gotten cancer and died a few years ago, leaving Milton to be raised by their mom and dad.

Mary's dying had been tough on all of them. While she was sick Agnes had spent almost every day at his parents' house, and her daughter Verna had come there after school to entertain Milton. And Bert had never once complained. *Yeah,* he thought, *Bert can be annoying sometimes and, just like Catherine says, maybe a little self-righteous, but he is a good egg and always puts family first—not just his own family, but ours, too.*

The chatter around him brought him out of his thoughts.

"Where's Verna?" he asked Agnes.

"She wanted to go the beach with her friends instead of coming with us," Agnes replied.

"Well, I can't say I blame her," Catherine put in. "She's in high school. Of course, she'd rather spend the day with kids her own age and not a bunch of old people and little kids."

"I just hope they are careful around the water," Agnes replied.

"All these years in Miami and you still can't swim. Why

don't you let me teach you today?" Leon asked.

"I can enjoy the ocean just fine while watching it from the beach," Agnes retorted.

Leon laughed. Of the four siblings Agnes had been the most excited about seeing the ocean when they first moved to Miami. And she'd won second place in a beauty contest before she was married. Photographs of her in a bathing suit had been all over the newspapers; one of them, with her holding a trident and staring longingly at the ocean, had been used in some tourist ads promoting the town. *It's ironic,* he thought. But she'd never mastered swimming. He suspected she was afraid of the water, but she'd never admit it—at least not to her little brother.

It wasn't too long until they had crossed the Bahia Honda bridge and decided to turn back and head north to look for a picnic spot on the Atlantic side of the highway. By the time they found a likely spot on Upper Matecumbe Key, it was past noon.

"We want to go in the water," Milton said as soon as they got out of the car.

"Look after your cousin, she's younger than you are," Catherine called as the children headed off.

The water was shallow, and the pair jumped happily up and down in the waves until they were called back for lunch. Then they came in for sandwiches and a rest.

III

Agnes spread the blanket and helped her mother pull out the sandwiches, fruit, and cookies they had packed for lunch. She looked over at Catherine slathering her arms with fancy lotion and getting ready to lie back on the sand. Agnes rolled her eyes. Catherine had changed so much since moving to Miami. The friend she remembered was nothing like this person who never had anything good to say about her brother, his family, or even Miami. She remembered how hard a time she and Helen had had when they moved here and tried to be sympathetic. But Miami was not the tiny backwater town it had been in the 1920s. It was a thriving city with stores and restaurants, and nightclubs on the beach. They had known nobody when they arrived. Catherine at least had her to do things with—if she wanted to—but she never seemed to want to do anything anymore.

Mama touched her arm and shook her head. "She's trying. Be nice for Leon's sake," she whispered.

Agnes took a deep breath and picked up the metal thermos of iced tea. She and Catherine had been friends once. Maybe they could be again.

"Would you like some, Catherine? Or would you rather have a Coke?" she asked, holding out the thermos.

"Tea, please; you always make it just right," Catherine said.

Mama gave her a look that said, *See, she's trying. Be nice.*

Everyone knew that Leon and Catherine had been having problems. They had made no secret of it; their battles were loud, long, and frequent. They had just bought their own home four weeks ago, and Leon had confided to Mama they were giving it one last try. Agnes wished Bert were here. Or Verna. Anyone so the burden of conversation didn't fall on her.

What was it with her brother and sisters? Why had they had so much trouble finding the right wife or husband? Of course, the second time around Helen had gotten a gem. Godfrey had been a lazy bastard, but Ed was the best. He was even giving Verna a hundred dollars to start her college education.

Yes, she admitted she sometimes felt jealous of Catherine. The woman managed to look elegant no matter what the situation. Today, her shirt and trousers and scarf all matched flawlessly.

Agnes looked down at her own outfit. Somehow the trousers and blouse she thought were so stylish this morning now seemed to make her look plump and frumpy compared to her younger, thinner sister-in-law. If Bert were here he'd make her feel beautiful, but someone's toilet was stopped up. On Father's Day. Of course, Bert would go instead of sending an employee in. That's just how he was.

"How's your job going?" Catherine asked.

"It's fine. I really enjoy working as a secretary at the Navy base, but I'm pretty sure I'll be laid off as soon as the war is over," she replied.

"But you really don't have to work. Leon says Bert is

making good money at the plumbing company."

"He runs everything for Mr. Stolpman," Agnes said with pride. "But I like working and, with Verna going to college next year, I'll have time on my hands."

"You just don't want to start cooking again," Leon teased, coming over. "Bert told me about the deal you made—the days you work you don't cook."

"Well then, how do you eat?" asked Catherine.

Leon laughed. "They go to a restaurant five nights a week. Mama, what about you? You could go get a job and make Dad take you out to dinner every night!"

"Ha! That will be the day. He likes my cooking too much," their mother replied. "Go call the children in now; lunch is ready."

~~~

Agnes and Catherine cleaned up the lunch trash while the children took a half-hour rest, then Milton and Mary Lou headed back to the water as the grown-ups relaxed and smoked—well, everyone but Mama, who said it wasn't ladylike. Mama had been shocked when Agnes and Helen had taken up cigarettes, but everyone did it, from the movie stars on down to her next-door neighbor. Mama didn't like it but finally quit saying anything.

Catherine leaned back against Leon as he put his arm around her. *Maybe things would work out there, after all*, Agnes thought. She really hoped so. Leon reminded her so much of Dad, not just in looks but in the way he tried to take care of everyone, particularly Catherine and Mary Lou. She wanted him to have the same happiness she did. As they relaxed Leon and Dad talked about the barbershop. Business was good. There were enough soldiers and sailors in Miami so he was always busy.

Suddenly, Catherine screamed. Agnes looked over, startled. She was pointing at the water.

The children had disappeared.

Leon and Dad had already sprung up and were racing to the beach. Still in their clothes and shoes, they waded into the waves.

What had happened? The water was shallow here. The kids had been jumping up and down. It was never deeper than their waists.

Catherine kept on screaming, and Agnes realized she had joined her. Maybe someone would hear them and come help. Their mother stood in silent shock. Agnes watched as Dad reached Mary Lou and began to swim back toward them.

Then he was gone. And where was Leon?

Catherine ran toward the waves, heading in after her family. Agnes followed. Catherine couldn't swim any better than she could, but Agnes didn't even think about her fear of the water. She just knew she had to help.

Suddenly, Catherine disappeared in a hole right in front of her. Agnes reached down and pulled her out, and they struggled back toward the sand.

Milton had managed to make it to shore and now was heading back in to help his grandfather and uncle and cousin. Agnes grabbed him and held him tight, even though he struggled against her, crying.

"I have to help them! I have to help them!" the boy kept saying over and over.

There were people all around now. Two men and two women were there pulling bodies out of the ocean. Bodies.

And Mama stood in shock—as still as her husband who lay on the sand.

IV

Milt Sosin grabbed the bottle of rum from the bottom desk drawer and took a healthy swig. This might be a three- or four-drink story before he got through with it. He shook his head, running through the events of the afternoon, crafting the story in his head before his fingers ever touched the keys.

He'd only been at the *Daily News* for a year. That was why he had been in the newsroom on a Sunday afternoon—and Father's Day at that. But it was okay. He had no family to celebrate with and, besides, now that he'd finally landed his dream job, he wasn't going to grouse about opportunities that came his way. It was supposed to have been a slow day. That was why they'd left things to the rookie reporter.

Sosin turned to his typewriter, stacked three sheets of

paper separated by two thin sheets of carbon paper, and rolled them into the machine.

A gay family picnic ended in tragedy....

The words began to flow smoothly from his fingers onto the page.

After lunch while the adults sat on the rocky bank smoking and talking, the children were wading in the shallow water a little distance away and the people on the bank suddenly became aware that the children were floundering in the water and screaming.

They had stepped off a shelf into water about 15 feet deep.

Mary Lou's father, Leon, and grandfather, Sigmund, fully dressed, started running into the water. Leon tried to send his father back but the elderly man persisted and had reached a point where Mary Lou had by this time disappeared when suddenly he too went down.

A moment later Leon lost his footing also as he went off the edge of the underground rocky shelf.

Mary Lou's mother went plunging in, screaming, followed by her sister-in-law Mrs. Rogers. Mrs. Sawieja went into another hole, not as deep, but over her head, and was saved only because Mrs. Rogers was near and grabbed her and pulled her to safety.

Their screams had by this time attracted Pvt. Hubert Brougton, 21, and Dixon Green, 17, who were visiting a friend at a fishing cabin in the neighborhood along with Dixon's sister, Barbara Jane Grosse, 19, and Betty Ross Hall, 19.

Broughton recently arrived home after seven months in a German prison camp. He holds a Boy Scout award for saving the life of a boy in Guantanamo Bay four years ago.

Both youths plunged into the water and reached the vicinity of the hole. Hubert found the younger Sawieja floating just below the surface of the water and dragged him out, and Dixon found the grandfather and child together, the elderly man's arm around Mary Lou. He pulled them out.

In the meantime, Milton had swum to safety and had actually started back in again to help his grandfather when he heeded the pleas of Mrs. Rogers and came out of the water.

While the women ministered to Mary Lou, the boys started artificial respiration on the men. Dixon was relieved by his sister, got into the Sawieja car, and drove about a half-mile to the Caribee Yacht Club at Islamorada, where Mrs. E.W. Fowler telephoned Tavernier. From Tavernier, the recipient of the message drove two miles to the summer home of Dr. M.H. Tallman, a Miami physician at Plantation Key. There is no phone in the Tallman summer residence.

The doctor had pronounced the two men dead at the scene, but he was able to bring the little girl around. He had driven back to his home with the mom, Catherine following with Mary Lou lying next to her on the front seat of the family car. He'd treated the girl some more, then told Catherine to take the child to Jackson Memorial Hospital—the first hospital north of the Keys and at least another half hour's drive away.

...Mrs. Sawieja started for the hospital and a few miles from the doctor's home, a tire went flat.

She jumped out of the car and flagged down the first approaching car. It was driven by Mrs. Ethel Fox who was returning from the Keys. Mrs. Fox took the mother and daughter into her car and drove to Jackson Memorial hospital at 60 miles an hour. Part of the time the girl was conscious and told her mother, "Don't let them hurt me."

Sosin looked up from his typewriter. It had long since grown dark, it must be close to midnight. The phone on his desk rang.

"Yes, this is he." He listened for a few minutes. "Thanks for letting me know."

He hung up the phone, took another long pull of his rum, and returned to work.

Mary Lou was given other injections and placed under an oxygen tent. She was given a fighting chance but during the night she lost consciousness again and died.

He finished the story with all the basic facts—funeral arrangements and a list of surviving family members. He thought of their faces as he had last seen them when he left the hospital. The older woman so silent in her grief; she'd just lost her husband, son, and granddaughter. The young boy looking lost. A teenage girl with wild, black hair who had obviously come straight to the hospital from some other beach picnic. The little boy had clung to her—his cousin, Sosin learned—and cried when she arrived. The brother-in-law got there and tried to comfort his wife, but you could see his own guilt. "If I'd been there I could have helped. I'm the best swimmer," he heard the man say.

The little girl's mother, now a widow, sat all alone, a part of the family but still separate. What was the story there?

Sosin pulled the last page from his typewriter and walked it over to his editor.

"A tough one, huh?" the man said.

"The toughest." Sosin shook his head.

"Don't say that. If you stay in this job you'll see worse—but you'll see better, too. Your job is just to tell their story. You going home now?"

"No, I'll wait for you to read it and let me know if you have any edits."

Damn, Sosin thought, turning to go back to his desk. *How can I be hoping for a byline and good position for my story when that family was just devastated? That father, he was just thirty-seven, only a couple of years older than me.*

He put away his guilt and sat tensely in his chair, waiting for his editor's approval.

V

1960s

Cousin Milton was always excused from funerals and hospital visits. I never understood why. He was an adult; I was a child. Why did he get excused when I didn't? I complained.

"He has been through enough," was the only answer I got.

Neither my mother nor my grandmother were ever comfortable with the water. My mother made sure, however, that Cheryl and I learned to swim, and swim well. She never let on she was afraid. I know Grandma was a nervous wreck whenever we went to the beach.

"Grandma's father, brother, and niece drowned on the same day." That was all anyone ever said. And I never asked for more information. Sometimes we let people know not to ask by just not saying anything.

The newspaper clipping was in the box of family photos and papers. Whenever we looked at the photos, the article was always picked up quickly and put down in the stack. No one said, "Don't read that one," but again, that subtle message was delivered as clearly as if it had been shouted. *No one wants to think about it. No one wants to remember.*

When I finally picked up the clipping and read it, I looked at it with the eye of the newspaper reporter I had become. The story made the top lefthand corner, above the fold on the front page of the first section—the most important position back in the days when newspapers were really made out of paper. I noticed it was a byline story—unusual for an article on a family tragedy, even in the small city that Miami had been back in 1945. The reporter's name was Milt Sosin.

Then I read the article, and I was struck by his writing. It was a marvelous piece, filled with tiny details that made it come alive even while written in the stark "just the facts" style of old school journalism. Milt Sosin was obviously a talented reporter. Had he written anything else? Or had he quickly moved on to a better paying career? I was intrigued. I googled him.

Milt Sosin's story was just as interesting as his writing style. He'd been working less than a year when he'd covered my family's tragedy, but he'd moved up quickly from the police beat and soon made a name for himself. Over the years he interviewed everyone from Fidel Castro to famed Miami-based gangster Meyer Lansky who'd been involved in the Watergate scandal. He'd outlasted and outlived many an editor, and one story about him was repeated in several articles reporting his death.

As times had changed, a new editor banned alcohol from

the newsroom. Sosin threatened to quit if his bottle of rum was removed. He must have been considered a valuable asset because the threat worked. The ban didn't last long. His bottle was allowed to remain in his desk and Sosin continued to write—although no other reporter was permitted to have a bottle of alcohol at work. He died at age ninety-two and filed his last story only two days before his death. No family was mentioned in any of the articles. He had no one, it seemed.

~~~

Grandma almost never mentioned her brother Leon, not even when talking about their childhood days in Missouri. She spoke about her father, and she spoke about her sister Mary, but I think she couldn't bear to think about her younger brother and her little niece who had died so tragically. She helped her mother raise Milton, and he always had a special place in his heart for "Aunts," as he called her, and his Uncle Bert. He lived with his grandmother, Mollie, until she died in his teens, then moved in with Agnes and Bert. My grandparents were the mom and dad he never had. When his first child was born, he named her Mary for his mom and his cousin.

After the incident Catherine "just drifted away" from the family, my mother told me. They tried to include her, but it was too painful for everyone. She began drinking but finally found "a new man," Mama said. I hope he made her happy.

I felt sad as I looked through the photos. There were so many of Agnes and Helen, fewer of Mary, but then she had died in her twenties so there wouldn't be as many of her. And maybe they had been given to her son Milton. But where was Leon?

Finally, I found an envelope with Leon's name on it and spilled out the photos. There was a formal picture of Leon and Catherine, maybe an engagement photo. They looked happy. There were several grainy photos of Leon as a boy on their road trip to Miami, but you couldn't tell much about him from those. Then I found an old, formal photo taken when he was about seven. I stared at it in surprise. It was the image of my sister's seven-year-old granddaughter. Yes, it was a boy dressed in knickers and a jacket, his short brown hair very different from our little girl's long, straight, black hair. But the shape of the face and eyes were just the same. And even more striking than that was his expression: just a little belligerent, ready to take on the world. One foot was forward, and his shoulders hunched. He almost looked like he was ready to swing at the cameraman. It was his great-great niece to a T. We've all seen her in just that pose so many times—ready to take on the world.

No, no one is every truly forgotten. From the tilt of a chin to a look in the eyes, our loved ones remain with us if we only know where to look.

Chapter 26
Valentine's Day

1976

I shivered as I followed Academic Walk back toward the dormitories with a crowd of other kids coming from the chapel. Saturday night Mass was usually a very crowded event, as students liked to take care of their weekend obligation so they could sleep late in the morning after heading over to the bars on Pittsburgh's Forbes Avenue. Tonight, however, the annual Valentine's Ball was being held in the Student Union so not as many people had attended.

As I walked with my friend Armeda, we could see the party going on inside. Girls in brightly colored floor-length formals, guys in suits and tuxes. It was 1976 so some of those suits and tuxes were more flamboyant than the dresses. There were guys in plaid leisure suits or tuxes rented to match their ladies' gowns, whether powder-blue or maroon or a deep green. My roommate, Sue, had been invited and had borrowed a black floor-length crepe dress from me. It had a square neck trimmed in cream-colored lace and looked a lot better on her. Armeda's roommate had been asked to go, too.

Armeda sighed. "I could have gone, you know. I turned down two different guys."

Several of our male acquaintances referred to Armeda as "No-Man's Woman" because she was so picky about her dates. They never said it to her face, of course, but she had a reputation of playing way too hard to get.

"I know. But at least you got asked. He never asked me. See, he's up there walking with his friends."

I pointed to my persistent crush, Matthew. We'd been dancing around each other for a year and half. Both too shy to actually ask each other out, we contrived to run into each other anywhere we could: in the dining hall, at the grotto behind Old Main on warm evenings, at the library, and a half dozen other places several times a week. We talked, we walked, we ignored the other people making out at the grotto, and then did it all over again the next day, but never going any further.

Armeda and I sighed again and continued to trudge up the hill. Duquesne University was all hills. Built on top of a bluff overlooking the Allegheny River, it was an isolated and quiet oasis in the middle of downtown Pittsburgh, a real ivory tower. As we walked I shivered again. I'd wanted to go to college in the north—the real north, not just North Florida. I had wanted to see snow, and I had wanted to get so far away from my mother and sister no one would ever say, "You're Verna's daughter," or "You're Cheryl's sister." And I'd managed it. On this tiny campus of about five thousand students, I'd met only one other person from Florida. We were the only two people strange enough to want to leave the Sunshine State for the snowy gray skies of Pittsburgh, Pennsylvania.

I make impulsive decisions. A friend of mine tells me that I "follow the signs and listen to my instincts." I became editor of the creative writing magazine after seeing information about it in my sister's high school yearbook, and my decision to go to Duquesne University was made almost the same way.

Me going to college was essentially a done deal.

"You can skip college as long as you come up with a viable alternative," my mother told me right up front. The trick was she had to approve of the alternative, and the only other alternative she would consider, she said, was going into the military. "And they won't take you because your vision is too bad."

In other words, I was going to college. No other choice.

My sister was considering making a transfer during her sophomore year and had about as many school catalogues sitting around the house as I did. One afternoon I picked one up and thumbed through it. It was from Duquesne University.

"I'm going to go to Duquesne University and major in journalism," I told everyone that night at the dining table. And I did. The oddest thing about this decision may be that throughout high school I'd never taken a journalism class or written for the school newspaper. The newspaper kids and creative writing kids were from different social circles. If you were active in one, you weren't active in the other. It was just one of those unwritten high school rules.

Now, a year and half later, I was in the middle of my sophomore year at Duquesne, loving the school and hating the weather. I had a good imagination but never dreamed that it was possible to be so cold.

"Do you want to meet me at Frank and Wally's in a bit?" Armeda asked. Frank and Wally's was the largest of the bars in walking distance and a favorite student hangout.

"No, not tonight. I went out drinking every weekend in January. I'm taking February off."

She laughed at me. It was well known that I would only have one drink a night when I went out. It wasn't a moral thing; without a boyfriend, I was buying my own and was too cheap to buy more than one.

We reached the dormitory and went our separate ways. My room was on the tenth floor of Towers, a coed dorm. Each floor had three wings in the righthand tower for men, three wings in the lefthand tower for women. The center wing held a study room and a TV room with a door connecting the building's two halves. It was locked at midnight on weekdays so that no one could stay overnight on the wrong side of the building, but the doors did stay open all night on weekends. Given this was a small, Catholic college in the 1970s, this was considered an extremely liberal policy. You can imagine my shock when I visited a friend attending West Virginia University and found that there "coed" meant boys and girls all on the same floor—even sharing bathrooms.

I got to my room, shed my coat, and put on the "school uniform" of jeans, a plaid flannel shirt, and, since I was a girl, a bandana over my hair, tied behind my head. It was not an official uniform, of course; it was just what everyone wore. Freshman year I'd had no flannel shirts, certainly not a plaid one. It would have gotten me laughed off the streets in Miami. But here it was fashionable, and I'd asked for one from my mother that Christmas. I can't imagine how much trouble it was for her to find a plaid flannel shirt in Burdine's or Jordan Marsh but find it she did.

I headed over to the television room and got comfortable. There were only a couple of guys there tonight, no girls. That Valentine's Dance again. I knew two of them, Frank and Rick, but there was a third guy there I'd seen before yet never actually met. He was tall, with black hair that curled a little at his collar— long enough to be fashionable but not too long. He already had a white streak in front, which I thought was kind of sexy. He wore his sideburns long and had a mustache. Of course, he wore jeans and a plaid flannel shirt. And yes, platform loafers. It was the '70s.

We began to talk. He was a great listener. Pretty soon I was telling him my life story along with my guiding principle for life: "All men are bastards; never trust them." Apparently, he took it as a challenge.

His name was Sam. We kept on talking. I remember Frank and Rick watching us with amusement since they couldn't get a word in edgewise. They knew what was going on, even if we didn't.

The partygoers from the Valentine's Dance trickled in, and still we talked. A couple of pizzas were ordered. We talked. *Saturday Night Live* came on, and we talked through it. We talked until Sam headed to bed because he had to get up early to drive to work on Sunday morning; in pharmacy school, he needed a certain amount of internship hours every semester.

On Sunday afternoon I carried my portable typewriter into the study lounge to write some articles for my Reporting 102 class. At about five o'clock I looked up when I heard someone sit down beside me. It was Sam, my new friend from last night.

"Here," he said, holding out one red rose. "I got it at the drugstore. It kind of sat in my car all day so it's not in the best of shape. Maybe you can make it bloom."

Then he headed out of the study lounge.

I looked at it. He was right; it did look like it need some TLC. I found a vase and filled it with water, sliced the tip off the stem as my mother had taught me to do years ago, and found a little sugar to add to the water. I set the vase on my dresser and studied the rose.

"I'm going to marry that man," I told myself.

Chapter 27
Blind Date

1947

John Hodges straightened the collar of his sport shirt in the mirror of the boarding house where he and his friend Jay had rented a room for their weekend in Tallahassee.

He'd agreed to accompany him up from Miami so that Jay could see his best girl, Nita Nord, since Jay was just too tired to make the all-night drive up to Tallahassee by himself. It had been a month since he'd seen Nita, and he'd promised her he'd take her to some sorority dance. He'd even gotten Nita to find John a date, too.

"Why don't you just take the train or the bus?" John had asked. It was a good twelve-hour drive from Miami to the northwest corner of the state, near where the panhandle curved below Alabama.

"Because I won't make either one tonight, and if I wait until tomorrow, I'll miss all day Saturday with her, then just have to turn around and head home Sunday morning after the dance. Come on, John, be a good buddy."

"Okay, okay, I guess I'll play cupid for y'all this weekend and keep you from driving off the road in your sleep. I haven't been in that part of Florida in a couple of years; it's sort of close to where I was born. Maybe I'll make a detour to Odum and see if it's changed."

"Oh no you don't. Nita's got a nice girl set up for you, too. She went to Edison High with Nita. Verna was a couple of years younger than we are, but I met her a few times."

"Verna, Latin for 'spring.' That's a nice name."

"Only you would know that, buddy. Y'all always know the strangest facts. I thought you were an engineering major, not poetry."

"Hey, selling electronics may be my bread and butter, but I still have the soul of a poet."

Jay laughed. "Whatever you say. I'll drive up to Pompano

and meet you at your parents' place. That way you'll have time to pack a bag and change."

John headed home early to get his bag packed. He'd finally been released from the army in early 1946 and now, about a year later, was still living with his parents at the rooming house his mother ran near the railroad tracks. It was bustling most nights, and he worried she was working too hard. But since his dad had retired, Mama worried they would starve to death if she didn't bring in any income. She didn't want to rely on their savings.

"We've got some long-lived people in both our families, Johnnie," she said. "You never know how much money we'll need. I don't want to be a burden to you in my old age."

"Frugal" was his mother's middle name.

"You and Daddy ain't ever going to be a burden to me," he told her.

"I tell her that all the time, Snooks," his father said, referring to him by the childhood nickname he still insisted on using. "But she won't listen to me. She can squeeze a dime until it thinks it's a dollar."

He and Daddy laughed at his mother, who just ignored them and went about cleaning the kitchen. Sometimes it was hard to still live with his parents, especially after the freedom he'd had as a soldier in England during the war. But it made his parents happy to see him every day after worrying so much about him while he was overseas. They didn't understand that he liked to go out and have a good time, to eat meals at fancy restaurants, to go to shows and movies. But still, he stayed with his parents. He knew a lot of guys who were still doing the same—except for the ones who had already gotten married.

John had hoped that would be him; he'd had a girlfriend, Lillian, before the war. But it hadn't taken her long to dump him once he was gone. He'd only been on a few dates since he got back.

"Hey, you done primping?" Jay asked. "I want to go meet the girls."

They'd gotten in at four in the morning and had slept until almost noon. Now they were meeting Nita and her friend for a picnic lunch.

"I'm ready," John said, hoping this Verna would be interesting. It was going to be a really long weekend if she wasn't. He figured she would be into athletics like Nita. John enjoyed throwing a football around the yard for an afternoon, but that was about all. If Verna was that into sports, John was probably in trouble. He could talk University of Florida versus University of Miami football, but that was about as far as his sporting interests went.

The two men headed over to the Alpha Xi Delta sorority house. Nita was the president there this year. Verna was her sorority little sister.

"So Verna dated a guy named Perry Watson all through high school," Jay explained. "But apparently she was more serious about him than he was about her. Right after they both got up here to college last year—him at Gainesville and her here in Tally, of course—he dumped her for some other girl. Not even a college girl, mind you. Someone from the town. Verna was really broken up about it, and she's hardly dated since, Nita says. She's been trying to get her to go out for a while, but this is the first time she's agreed to it."

"Oh good," John joked, "I'm a rebound date."

"It's been a year, and she has had other dates."

"That's okay, I ain't looking to get serious right now. I've got to make a name for myself with Shaw-Hardy first. It takes all my time."

John had spent two years studying engineering at the University of Florida before enlisting. But once he got out, he just hadn't wanted to go back to school. At twenty-six, he felt like he'd be an old man among all the fresh-out-of-high-school eighteen-year-old boys. When the sales position at a good Miami firm had come up, he had jumped on it.

The pair drove up to the sorority house, jumped out of the car, and headed up the front walk. Inside they were greeted by the housemother, who everyone called Aunt Ruth, and a few minutes later Nita and Verna came down.

"How do you do?" Verna said politely, then held out her hand.

John had a hard time answering. He was stunned. He'd expected someone like the athletic Nita, who was dressed in a tennis outfit for their picnic, obviously ready to play that or any other game. Verna, with her long black curls and trim figure, wore a bright blue broomstick skirt and a peasant blouse that showed off beautiful shoulders.

The day was starting to look brighter.

After a few minutes of conversation, the girls got the picnic basket they'd prepared, and then they were off. Jay had already negotiated that John would drive so he could sit in the back with Nita.

John took directions to a local park from Verna, and when they arrived, he helped her set out a blanket the girls had brought. Jay and Nita immediately took off for a walk in the wooded area nearby.

"Well, I guess they aren't hungry just yet. How about you?" Verna asked shyly.

John had already noticed that she was a bit timid. He didn't have a shy bone in his body and set about making her comfortable, taking time to find out just what her interests were. He soon discovered she was majoring in English and hoped to become a drama teacher.

"I saw *Brigadoon* the last time I was in New York," he told her.

"You've been to New York? Do you go there often?" she asked with interest.

"Only twice so far, but I reckon I'll be getting there more often. My boss promises me there'll be more trips if I do well— and I plan to be the best salesman on the east coast of Florida."

"You think a lot of yourself." Verna laughed. "When Nita said you were an old friend of Jay's, I pictured someone just like him. He's a great guy, don't get me wrong, but he can only talk football and baseball. That is unless he and Nita start talking chemistry, and then I'm really lost."

John laughed, too. "That's what I thought about you. That you were gonna be one of Nita's tennis buddies."

"No, I can barely throw a ball," Verna confessed, obviously becoming more comfortable. "Tell me more about yourself. Nita said you are from Pompano Beach. How did you meet Jay?"

"We met at Gainesville before the war. I was a year ahead of him then."

"Oh, I didn't realize you were over there. My uncle was in Europe. But he's so old."

"Well, I reckon I am a mite older than Jay, but I'm only twenty-six. I'm not that ancient," John teased.

Verna blushed. "I'm so sorry. I didn't mean to call you old. It's just the only soldier I know personally is my uncle."

She turned her head, obviously embarrassed.

"Don't worry. I thought it was cute."

Verna tried to find a safer topic. "I know you live in Florida now, but you sound more like Georgia to me."

"Y'all caught me! Yeah, I'm originally from a little town called Odum, Georgia, only a couple hours from here. My daddy owned a grocery store there, but he lost it in the Depression. We moved down to Pompano Beach when I was in junior high, and he got a job as a butcher. He's retired now."

The pair spent a lovely afternoon talking about everything from their favorite books and movies to the changes that had taken place when Verna's college in Tallahassee went coed at the beginning of the year.

"I know a lot of the boys want to go to college on the GI Bill, and they need to make space for them. But I enrolled in the Florida State College for Women—not Florida State University. It's like they've taken our whole identity away," Verna said.

"Well, y'all will soon have your own football team to watch—what are they calling it? The Seminoles?"

"I do like football, but I don't think that makes up for taking our college name away."

"You still have your friends and your sorority. And I bet some of the girls like having boys in their classes instead of waiting to have them drive up from Gainesville each weekend," John teased her.

"My roommate, Maude, has already found a boyfriend who's going to school here."

"What about you? No boy has caught your eye?" John

asked and was surprised at how anxious he suddenly felt to hear her answer.

"No, no one."

"I'm very glad to hear that," he replied.

Verna blushed.

The pair barely noticed when Jay and Nita rejoined them. Finally, it was time to drop the girls at the sorority house and head back to their boarding house so they could all get ready for the dance and meet up again.

"So you and Verna, huh? Y'all looked pretty cozy there for a first date," Jay said as they changed into suits and ties.

"She's a great girl."

"But you're not interested in seeing anyone permanently," Jay teased.

"Did I say that?"

"Just this morning."

"Well, a guy can change his mind, can't he? Come on, let's go take these ladies to a dance."

They had a wonderful evening. Verna was an excellent dancer, better even than John who considered himself no slouch on the dance floor.

"Well, it's one thing I picked up from dating a musician for three years," she said when he complimented her.

He noticed that she deflected any praise or compliments. It was yet another thing he found charming.

By the end of the night Verna and John had arranged to meet in Gainesville in two weeks to watch the University of Florida play the University of Miami. The sorority was renting a bus for the game because so many of the girls wanted to go.

"Jay will already be up in Gainesville," Verna mentioned. His friend had just gotten readmitted to the university and planned to finish his degree in two years' time. "I'm sure he doesn't plan to miss the football game so maybe you could stay with him in the dormitory."

"Who are you rooting for?" John asked.

"Well, I was going to root for Miami, but now since I'm going with you, I'll have to be for the Gators."

"That's my girl," he said, then gave her a quick kiss.

"Maybe someday soon Florida will play FSU now that they have a football team. We'll have to divide up and root against each other then."

Verna blushed again.

~~~

"Do I need to warn you about breaking my friend's heart?" Jay asked later as they returned to the boarding house. "Or should I warn her about breaking yours?"

It was past midnight, and they wanted to get a few hours' sleep before getting on the road again.

"What do you mean?"

"I saw that kiss, and it was only the first date."

"Second," John said smugly. "The picnic was our first date."

"I've never seen you move this fast before."

"And you never will again. Jay, I've already decided. I'm going to marry that girl."

Chapter 28
Sundays With Miss Leotti and Miss Leotha

Sunday heat was the worst kind of heat. Sundays meant getting up even earlier than usual and dressing up in go-to-church clothes. Dressing up meant crinolines. What is a crinoline? Girls born after about 1965 have been spared these particular objects of torture. A crinoline is an underskirt with a wide, elastic waistband into which someone has sewn row after row of itchy, scratchy ruffles designed to make your dress stand so far out from your waist that you look like you are wearing an open umbrella. Thank the Lord crinolines went out of fashion. Skirts went from wide to a slim A-line, and my mama declared that just a nylon slip was enough to make us decent for church.

But back to Sunday dressing. First came the cotton panties, then the nylon slip. Over the slip went the crinoline. The slip was supposed to keep the net from scratching my legs and bottom, at least that was what Mama always told me. It never seemed to work, however, and the hotter it got, the more the nylon stuck to all the wrong places and the more the net scratched in all the wrong places. And, of course, young ladies were NEVER supposed to scratch THERE!

Over the crinoline went a dress. Then the white ankle socks and dress shoes—black patent leather Mary Janes from September to Easter, white patent leather Mary Janes from Easter to September. The final touch was the hat, usually straw, and always secured to the head with an elastic band around the chin that was so tight it made a crease across the neck. That was one more thing I wasn't supposed to fidget with.

Mama always told us it had to hurt to be beautiful. My sister Cheryl Anne bought into it. I decided I didn't care. Beauty wasn't worth it.

Once Mama had tugged and pulled my sister and me into our Sunday best, she hurriedly put on the adult version herself, only she didn't have to wear the crinoline. But what got substituted seemed even more torturous. A bra stuffed with foam rubber pads. A girdle, another medieval torture device that encased her waist and flattened her stomach with elastic. It had metal clips attached to additional short pieces of hanging elastic. Stockings attached to the clips. Finally, there were high-heeled, pointy-toed pumps, clip-on earrings, and a matching chunky necklace to complete the outfit.

Then Mama put on her makeup. She rubbed beige cream called foundation all over her face then patted it down with powder. Next, she rubbed red liquid rouge over her cheeks with a little, rubber-tipped stick. Finally, bright red lipstick went on her lips.

She looked beautiful.

As a last touch, we all grabbed our purses with envelopes for the church collection tucked in, and white cotton gloves (usually just carried, not actually worn—the one concession from the dictates of the North we were allowed in the tropical heat of pre-air-conditioned Miami).

I liked church. My sister had made her First Communion and was expected to kneel reverently at the appropriate times, but I was still young enough that I could just crouch down and play house on the kneeler, as long as I was quiet.

Every Sunday after church Daddy picked us up. Grandpa always rode with him. Sometimes we would go back to Pompano Beach where Daddy lived with Grandma and Grandpa. Other times all three of them would pick us up and we would go to the cafeteria and then out visiting. Visiting meant I had to stay dressed up, but going to the cafeteria was almost worth it.

I loved eating at the cafeteria. There were a lot of them around Miami back in the 1960s. The one I liked best was the Shores Cafeteria, just a few miles down the road from our house. When we went to a restaurant, I had to sit still for a long time and pay attention while somebody read the menu to me, but at the cafeteria I got to walk through the line, look at all the food, and pick out exactly what I wanted. The ladies behind the counter put whatever I asked for on my tray, and there was always lemon meringue pie. At the end of the line tall black men waited to take the trays, balancing them high on their shoulders as they picked their way through the tables of diners. It was fascinating how they could walk with those big old trays, one on each shoulder, and never spill anything. I wanted to work in a cafeteria when I grew up. It looked like fun. My father laughed when I told him that. Only black people work in cafeterias, he said.

After we were done eating, we'd go visiting. That meant going to see Grandma and Grandpa's friends, Miss Leotti and Miss Leotha. One of them was the mother and one of them was the daughter, but I could never tell which was which. They both just looked old.

Grandma and Grandpa liked to talk to Miss Leotti and Miss Leotha because they understood each other. You see, they were all exiles. Born in Southeastern Georgia, they all now lived in South Florida. While Northerners might think Florida is the South, Southerners know it isn't and never will be. There were way too many Yankees living in South Florida for it to ever be truly Southern. So even though they'd all lived there a very long time—much longer than the six years I'd been alive—South Florida would never be home.

Miss Leotti and Miss Leotha's last name was Odum. They came from Odum, Georgia, where my daddy had been born. In fact, the town had been named for their great-great-great-great granddaddy. I was never sure how many greats it was.

Although we had to stay dressed up, going to Miss Leotti and Miss Leotha's wasn't too bad. The house was dark and always cool, even though it wasn't air-conditioned. It was an old-style Florida house with a wide overhanging roof meant to keep the sun out and lots of shade-giving palm trees surrounding it. The Venetian blinds were always closed. Cheryl and I quietly fought over who got the best seat on top of the old-fashioned floor fan. It was round and about two feet high with a cushion on top. I loved the way the cool air felt on the back of my knees. Miss Leotti and Miss Leotha gave us peppermints to cool our mouths, and we brought coloring books or picture books. I'd pretend to look at the books or color so that the grown-ups wouldn't notice me, but mostly I'd listen to their stories.

There were always stories about my relatives in Georgia, news and gossip about weddings, births, funerals, and who was stepping out on whom. These were sometimes interesting, sometimes not. The stories I liked best were about the old times. Hearing the stories, I felt as if I knew these people well, even though I'd never been to Georgia, and they never came to visit Grandma and Grandpa, even though they were family.

They had interesting names—old-fashioned country names, I realize now, although at the time they seemed exotic: Maxie and Florrie, Jimps, Coy and Floy, Clarice, and Deena. Yes, the names were odd and old-fashioned, and the stories were often funny. My favorite story was about Daddy and his friend Clarice.

Chapter 29
Johnnie and the Holy Rollers

1934

Johnnie was ten years old. He lived in Odum, Georgia. His daddy was the grocer and had a store down on Main Street. The store wasn't very large, but then neither was Odum, Georgia. It was only four blocks long and consisted of a couple of stores, a dozen or so houses, and three churches: one for the Baptists, one for the Methodists, and one for the Holy Rollers.

Everybody in town went to one. Mama was a Baptist. Daddy was a Methodist. Johnnie knew that was kind of scandalous. And it was also kind of scandalous that none of them went to church very often. It was a very bad thing. He was sure of that because Aunt Florrie told his Mama so whenever she came for Sunday dinner. Aunt Florrie was Daddy's youngest sister.

"But you'd think the way she acted," said Mama after each of those dinners, "that she was the head of the whole family. Well, she's not the head of me!"

Aunt Florrie was a Methodist. When Johnnie, Mama, and Daddy did go to church, they went to the Baptist Church, which was a scandal again.

It seemed like his family was always just a little scandalous. Mama's sister Aunt Neta and her husband, Uncle Doug Thomas, who lived in Odum, too, just down the street from Johnnie's house, were scandalous, too. Aunt Neta had something called epilepsy and she had fits. Johnnie saw it once. She fell down and started shaking, and Mama shoved a spoon in her mouth to make her stop.

The house Johnnie lived in actually belonged to Uncle Doug, who was a county judge and had lots of money. Mama always mentioned that to Daddy—that they had to live in her sister Neta's house because the grocery store never made any money.

"How can we ever have any money when you give it away to every Tom, Dick, and Harry who comes into the store?"

she asked.

"Now, hon, I couldn't charge Miz Jones. She has three babies to feed. I couldn't let them go hungry. What if it was you and Snooks here needing food?" Daddy answered her using the nickname he always called Johnnie. "I'd want someone to help you out so I have to help others."

It was pretty much the same story every Saturday night when Mama went over Daddy's store accounts. Johnnie tried to make sure he wasn't around. He usually tried to be next door at Clarice's house on Saturday evenings. And that's how it all began.

Most of the other boys would laugh if he said it out loud, but he guessed Clarice was just about his best friend. Clarice understood things that the boys didn't. She liked to read books and play imagination games. The boys in town just liked to play baseball. Johnnie liked baseball, but he'd rather spend his time reading a book or making up a story.

Daddy didn't understand that either. But then everyone in town said Johnnie wasn't much like his daddy. Sometimes that got whispered about, too. Johnnie was tall for his age, with olive skin and bright blue eyes. Daddy was, well, round. He was short and stout with a little round face. He did have blue eyes, though. Mama always pointed that out when anyone said anything about Johnnie not looking like his daddy.

Johnnie sometimes talked to Clarice about it, but she just said, "Don't you waste your time with that. Those old gossips ain't got nothing better to think about. That's what my mama says."

On Saturday evenings Johnnie and Clarice escaped their houses as fast as they could after supper and wandered down the road. What usually drew them was the Holy Rollers church. There was a field in back, and they'd head down there on warm evenings to lie in the tall grass and relax. Holy Rollers wasn't its official name, of course. "The Fellowship of God" was what was painted on the sign out front, but everyone in town just called it the Holy Rollers. Johnnie and Clarice spent a lot of time talking about what happened in the Holy Rollers church.

Odum was a quiet place most of the time. But not on

Saturday nights. Cars and wagons pulled up from miles around. There must have been twenty or thirty vehicles parked outside the little white building on Saturday evenings, each one packed with Holy Rollers come to worship.

That in itself was rather scandalous, said Clarice, that they didn't know any better than to pray on Saturday night rather than Sunday morning. But on top of the scandal was the mystery. Because at seven o'clock, when the doors were shut, and all the windows were covered, and the Holy Rollers began to pray, the church started to hum. It was a low buzz, like a giant bee that filled not just the field where Johnnie and Clarice watched, but the whole town. No matter where you walked in Odum, Georgia, on Saturday night you could hear the hum of the Holy Rollers praying.

Tommy Jones, who was a year younger than Johnnie, was a Holy Roller, and so one day at recess Johnnie finally got up the courage to ask him just what they did at his church. What made that hum? The Baptist and Methodist Church didn't make that much noise when their people were worshipping.

"Oh, we speak in tongues," answered Tommy matter-of-factly.

"Of course you speak with your tongue. How else you gonna talk? But why do y'all make all that racket?"

"We speak *in* tongues," he insisted. "The Holy Ghost comes down on us just like he came down on the Apostles in Jerusalem, and we speak in all the tongues of the world."

"Everybody at once?"

"Well, no. Just the ones the Holy Ghost calls. Some of us, like my sister Sally, get called every Saturday night. She screams and yells, and pretty soon she just falls down like she's dead," he explained enthusiastically. "We do other stuff, too, but I can't tell you because you're not a believer."

"I am a believer. I believe in Jesus."

"You don't go to my church so I can't tell you."

Johnnie was irritated. No matter how he pushed, Tommy wouldn't tell him anything else about the mysteries of his church. When the teacher rang the bell for recess to end, Johnnie came up with a plan. The more he thought about it, the more excited he got. He could hardly wait until school was over to tell Clarice.

When they were sitting on her Mama's back porch eating cookies, Johnnie looked around carefully to make sure Miz Sarah wasn't around.

"I know how to find out what they do at the Holy Rollers church," he said.

"Really!" said Clarice. "What are you going to do?"

"*We* are going to go there and find out."

"You know my mama ain't gonna let me go to another church, and your mama ain't either."

"Of course not, but we ain't gonna tell them."

"Well, they'll be sure to find out. Someone will tell them they saw us there."

"No one's going to see us there. We're going to be sitting under the pews. Not in them."

There it was. The idea just sort of sprang up and sat between the two of them. They stared at it for a while, just stared at the floor as if they could see that idea sitting right there in front of them as solid as a table or chair.

"We can't get in," whispered Clarice.

"We *can* get in if we go early. Someone always comes early to open up the church. I see a car by the back door every Saturday afternoon," said Johnnie.

"We can't. It's not right. It's a church," said Clarice.

But Johnnie could tell, even as she shook her head no, that she really meant yes.

Now that the idea was there, they wouldn't rest until they got in that church to see for themselves. It was only Monday afternoon. That meant five whole days until they could carry out their plan. Five days to think, to anticipate, to gather their courage—or lose it.

As soon as Saturday supper was over, Johnnie knocked at Clarice's back door. It was late afternoon; the sun was just beginning to set, cooling the early June heat from "hotter than Hades" to "almost tolerable," at least according to his daddy.

"Can Clarice come out and play?" he asked Miz Sarah politely when she answered.

"Of course, Johnnie."

But then God must have come down and whispered in her ear before he settled over at the Holy Rollers because Miz Sarah looked at him and said something she'd never said before. "Y'all don't go getting into any trouble now, ya hear?"

"Oh no, ma'am," said Johnnie solemnly as Clarice ran down the steps.

Together, they ran all the way down to the field behind the church and fell into the grass laughing hysterically.

"Did you tell your mama?" Johnnie demanded. "Did you say something to her?"

"No, Johnnie, I swear I didn't say a word. She don't know a thing."

"Well, maybe we shouldn't do it," he said, having second thoughts.

"You're a chicken, Johnnie Hodges! You are just trying to chicken out of this."

"Take that back! I am not a chicken!"

"All right then, let's go see if the door is open," said Clarice.

They crawled through the tall grass to the edge of the field and took a peek at the back door. Sure enough, a car had already pulled up, and a couple of men were walking into the church carrying a large, covered box.

"What's in the box?" Johnnie whispered.

"I don't know. Maybe the cookies for after church."

"It sure looks heavy for cookies," he said.

Then he shrugged and crept quietly up to the door, which opened into a small kitchen.

They could hear the men talking inside. When their voices retreated, Clarice and Johnnie slipped in and quickly crawled underneath a worktable just as the men's voices got louder again. One of them was Tommy's father, Johnnie saw, peeking out from under the table. The men walked back out toward the car and Johnnie and Clarice quickly scrambled out from under the table and headed through the door and down the hall until they were in the main room of the church.

"Under there," said Johnnie, and they slid under the very front pew.

It was just after six. Almost an hour to wait, scrunched on their hands and knees on the wooden floor. It was hot under that pew. The air didn't move, and the dust under the pew smelled of the sweat that ran down Johnnie's forehead and dripped on the floor.

As the congregation began to saunter in, Johnnie and Clarice tried to make themselves smaller and smaller. Clarice's head touched the floor as she curled herself into the tiniest ball possible. Johnnie nudged her.

"Don't you go to sleep. How you gonna see that way?"

"I'm not sleeping," she whispered back. "Wait! They're starting."

Johnnie peered out from between the legs of the man who had sat down above him. He could just see the altar at the front of the church. The box the men had been carrying sat in the middle of it.

That's strange, he thought to himself. *Why would they put the cookies up there?* Then he settled in to listen as the preacher stood up to talk.

At first the congregation sat silent, but as the preacher continued, an occasional "Amen" or "Hallelujah" was shouted from the pews. The crowd got more excited as the preaching continued, and more shouts and cries rang out.

"'In my name shall they cast out devils; they shall speak with new tongues,' says the Lord," cried the preacher.

As if it was a signal, the congregation grew very still.

"Do you believe?" he shouted. "Who has the courage to share their beliefs?"

As three or four men walked up to the front, the preacher began to open the box.

Clarice nudged Johnnie. "What's he doing?" she whispered.

"Shut up," he said.

In his effort to see his head was nearly all the way out from under the church pew. If anyone had looked they would have been caught. But no one did. The entire congregation was focused on that box.

"They shall take up serpents, and if they drink any deadly

thing, it shall not hurt them; they shall lay hands on the sick, and they shall recover!" shouted the minister. And reaching both hands into the box he pulled out two large rattlesnakes.

A scream erupted in Johnnie's ear, nearly deafening him, and he was pulled from the pew—not by one of the members of the church, but by Clarice. She had grabbed hold of Johnnie and started to run for the window. He had no choice but to follow. As fast as they could they climbed over the wide, wooden sill, and jumped out. After landing in the bushes they rolled to their feet and started to run. Johnnie looked back to see faces staring at them through the windows, but neither he nor Clarice stopped running until they landed on her front porch.

Gasping for breath they started to laugh. "Do you think they saw who we were? They couldn't have, could they?" Clarice asked anxiously. "It was too dark."

"There's no way they could have seen us," Johnnie said. "We were too fast. But I better get on home now. I'll see you tomorrow."

He hurried home and headed to his bedroom before his mama and daddy could ask where he'd been. But when a knock sounded at the front door a short time later, he knew who it had to be.

"John Wesley Hodges!" his mama called in a sharp voice. Slowly he came out to the living room. He recognized the two men; he'd seen them both just an hour before. One was the minister, the other was Johnnie's father.

Later his daddy took him outside, unstrapped his belt, and prepared to mete out Johnnie's punishment.

"I've got to punish you, Snooks," Daddy said with just a hint of regret. "Your mama expects it. And I expect you to sit down real tenderly when you come into breakfast next morning. But you know, I've always wondered just exactly what they did in that church, too."

Chapter 30
Summer in Odum, Georgia

1967

"I wasn't in love with your grandpa when I married him."

Wow, I thought, my eyes popping wide in surprise.

That was quite an opening line to give an eleven-year-old girl—one who thought her grandpa hung the moon.

I stood at the open kitchen window, trying to catch a few breaths of the hot, humid air that passed for a breeze on an August afternoon in Southeast Georgia as I helped Grandma Hodges wash the supper dishes and put them away.

Grandpa, Grandma, and Daddy had moved back to Odum from Pompano Beach a few years before. The house had only a few window air conditioners, and the one in the breakfast room at the end of the kitchen never seemed to throw air from the tiny eating area into the long, skinny galley kitchen. Another was in Aunt Neta's bedroom at the other end of the house. Her suite stayed closed off so no one could use it, even when she wasn't there. It was her house, you see, and she only let Grandma and Grandpa Hodges and Daddy live there out of the goodness of her heart.

I loved the house in Odum, and Grandpa did, too. It did not look like it had been built but more had grown, topsy-turvy, over many decades. As different families needed a room, they just tacked one on the end, usually without even a hallway in between. The result was a rambling, white, one-story building that reminded me of a dollhouse because you could have opened it up in the back and seen all the rooms inside.

Grandma continued her story. "I was only sixteen, you see, and in love with another man."

"What happened?" I ventured to ask. Curious now, I was willing to stay in the hot kitchen rather than head out onto the porch with Grandpa.

"My father wanted me to marry your grandpa. He thought Mr. Hodges"—she always called her husband Mr. Hodges, in the old-fashioned, formal way—"had better prospects than my other beau." She laughed a little bitterly.

I understood. My grandpa, while the nicest, kindest of men, had never been good at business. I'd heard that many times from many people—my grandmother, my father, my great aunts and uncles who were his half brothers and sisters. They all agreed. J.W. Hodges had never been able to make money.

"I was in love with David," Grandma continued. "He was tall and dark with brown hair and blue eyes."

My eyebrows rose. Even at eleven, I knew what she was implying. I'd been raised watching soap operas with my other Grandma, Grandma Rogers that is, and soap operas were a great place to learn all about where babies came from—particularly when they came from someone other than a woman's husband. My grandparents were both short. At only eleven, I was already taller than Grandma, who had blue eyes and red hair. It came out of a bottle, but she had a lock of curls she had cut one time to prove it had always been red. I didn't know it just then, but I was soon to hear the story of that cut-off lock of hair.

My grandfather wasn't much taller than Grandma. He was short, and round and fair, and his hair, although it was now gray, had been a sandy blond. And then there was my father: six feet tall and olive-skinned, dark haired, with bright blue eyes. The one person he didn't look like was his father.

"I was so in love with David, but then your grandfather came around," she told me. "He was older, twenty-seven, and he already owned a grocery store, so my daddy said I should marry him. My Mama had died and I'd been taking care of your Aunt Neta and my other brothers and sisters for a long time. I was just sixteen, and David wasn't ready to get married . . ."

Chapter 31
Wedding Day

November 1912

Alma was excited. She was dressed in her best dress—baby blue with a ruffled lace collar and cuffs. She and her sister Neta had redesigned it so it looked more like the dress a bride would wear. They had copied it from the cover of a 1910 *Vogue* magazine—only two years out of date—that they had borrowed from Mrs. Oliver around the corner. It was the most up-to-date book on fashion in Tattnall County, Georgia.

She and Neta had carefully taken out the stitching to raise the waistline and lower the hemline until it almost touched the tops of her shoes. Then they'd found a lovely brown velvet ribbon in the "plunder box" of fabric scraps and turned it into a belt. Alma was sure that she now looked every bit the married woman rather than the sixteen-year-old schoolgirl she had been just yesterday. As a final touch Neta had helped her do up her hair in the latest fashion, one they'd seen when they went into Claxton last week. Her long, dark red hair had been curled into ringlets, a satin ribbon tied to each curl.

Alma took a deep breath to calm her nerves as she came down the stairs to see her new husband standing in the front room waiting for her.

"You look lovely, hon," he told her.

"Thank you, Mr. Hodges." Alma blushed.

They'd been married just a few hours, and until now he had only ever called her "Miss Hilton." "Hon" felt almost too familiar coming from this man she barely knew, and there was no way she could call him "J.W.," or even the slightly more formal "Mr. J.W.," the way many women in the area referred to their husbands.

"My family is going to love you," he told her, taking her left hand, which now wore his wedding band along with the engagement ring he'd given her the week before when he asked her daddy for her hand. It had a round ruby stone surrounded by tiny diamond chips.

"I do hope so," she said nervously.

Just then a knock at the door interrupted them, and Alma hurried over to open it.

"David!" she said in surprise. "What are you doing here?"

She hadn't expected to see him for a month when he returned home from Georgia College in Milledgeville for Christmas.

David held his hat in his hand. "My sister sent me a telegram. She told me—I couldn't believe it—so I had to come," he stuttered.

Alma looked over her shoulder. Neta had come into the front room just in time to distract J.W. "Let's go out on the porch," she said, guiding him out the door.

"This can't be true," David said, running his fingers through his hair. He grabbed her left hand and stared at the wedding ring. "I thought you loved me. I thought you were going to wait for me."

"I do love you, David. I didn't want to do this. My father made me. He says Mr. Hodges has better prospects than a boy still in school. He doesn't really believe you'll learn anything useful in college."

"I'm going to be a doctor," David said indignantly.

"I know, but Daddy doesn't trust doctors. They've never been able to do much for Neta's epilepsy. Mr. Hodges owns a grocery."

Just then Neta stuck her head out. "Alma, hurry up. I can't hold him much longer."

"You've got to go, David. I'm sorry. I don't love him, but it's what's best for my family."

David walked away, and Alma watched him go with tears in her eyes. Then she pulled a lace handkerchief out of her pocket and wiped the tears away. She was torn. Yes, she loved David. But here she was, sixteen, the first of her friends to be a married woman. It was scary. It was exciting.

"Are you ready to go?" J.W. asked, coming out to the porch. "Your bags are already on the back of the buggy." He held out her crocheted shawl and wrapped it around her shoulders; the air was crisp on this fine November day.

"Yes, I'm ready."

He held out his arm, and she placed her hand in the crook of his elbow.

It took a little over an hour for the horse to make the nine-mile trip to Manassas. The silence was broken only by the shush of leather and the clop of the horse's hoofs. Every now and then they would pass another buggy, and Mr. Hodges would slow and introduce her as his wife.

"This is my bride, Miz Alma," he would say proudly.

"Mighty pretty bride you've got there," they'd say in return.

He seemed to know everyone in two counties.

"Why don't you call me by my first name?" he asked finally.

"It just seems too familiar. I don't really know you yet, and my mama always called Daddy 'Mr. Hilton.' I guess it's just our way." She put her head down, afraid to look at him.

"We have the rest of our lives to get to know each other," he said, and pulled her closer. Alma enjoyed it. It felt good to have this man look at her as if she was pretty as a peach.

"Tell me about your family," she said. It would be good to know who she was going to meet when she arrived.

"Well, there's my daddy and my stepmother. She's, well, she's still fighting the War," he explained with a chuckle.

Alma smiled. She'd met old people like that before, stuck in a past where everyone lived as if they were in high cotton, and no one ever worried about money.

"Then my younger half-brothers, Jimps and Wright, are still at home. And my half-sisters Maxie and Bessie and Florrie, too."

"Don't you have any whole brothers or sisters?" Alma asked, getting another chuckle out of J.W.

"Just Hardie. He's a year older than me. I'm number two in the family. My mama died shortly after I was born, and Daddy married Miz Eliza. I have thirteen brothers and sisters altogether."

"You call her Miz Eliza, not Mama?" asked Alma.

"That's how she's always wanted it," J.W. said with a shrug.

"And your daddy?"

"He does what Miz Eliza says. I guess we all do—well, or what Florrie, my sister, says. Miz Eliza and Florrie pretty much rule the roost around home."

Alma took a deep breath and wondered what they would think of her. She was no one special, just a girl from the country.

"Don't you worry. We don't have to stay there very long. Just a couple of days, then we'll go over to Odum. I've just got a room right now, but we can rent a house before long."

Alma nodded. She couldn't decide if she was more excited about the prospect of having her own home or terrified at the thought of meeting Miz Eliza and Miss Florrie.

It seemed like no time at all before they pulled up at the Hodges home in Manassas. It was a large white colonial home with tall, round columns supporting a second floor sleeping porch. Even though the paint was peeling and the steps sagged a bit, it was in better shape than many of the old homes in Georgia these days. In fact, it was the grandest house Alma had ever seen.

"Welcome to my parents' house," he said.

Alma noted that he did not call it home.

"Is anyone home?" he called as they entered the front hall.

Two women, obviously mother and daughter, hurried down the stairs to greet them as an older gentleman came from the back of the house.

"Everyone," J.W. said proudly, "this is Alma, my wife."

They all crowded around her, talking over each other.

"It's good to meet you, Alma."

"I'm so happy J.W. has found someone."

A few more young men and women entered the room, and J.W. began to make so many introductions that Alma couldn't keep up: Jimps, Nan, Lester, Joe. Finally, one of the girls took pity on her.

"Alma, bless your heart, you look all done in," she said. "I'm Florrie, J.W.'s half-sister. Let me take you upstairs and help you clean up before supper."

Alma allowed herself to be dragged away, looking back

at J.W. He had felt like a stranger this morning before they were married, but now he was the only person in this house—this town—that she knew.

"Come on, come on, I'll take care of you," said Florrie. "I know y'all have come from over Claxton way, practically out in the sticks, but we'll get you fixed up in no time."

Alma grinned, remembering what J.W. had said about his stepmother and sister being a bit snobby. Claxton wasn't that much smaller than Manassas; neither town could claim more than a hundred souls living there. Alma allowed herself to be towed into a bedroom and settled on the bed as Florrie went to the oak dresser and took a comb, brush, and scissors from a drawer.

"Now we just can't have you looking like this," she said as she started to pull the ribbons from Alma's hair. "I know you're young, and you don't know a lot, so I'll help you out. First thing, married women just don't wear ribbons in their hair."

"Ow," Alma said as Florrie tugged the brush through her curls.

"Is your hair naturally wavy? That just makes it harder to get it to lay properly." She went out and came back with a small basin of water, using it to wet Alma's hair and pull it into a tight bun at the back of her head. Then she cut a few of the longer curls off.

With tears in her eyes, Alma quietly picked up one of the curls Florrie had cut and pushed it into her pocket, hoping the older girl didn't notice.

"You're not crying now, are you? A married women crying over hair! I don't know what J.W. was thinking, marrying a child from out in the country like he has. How are you going to keep up the family reputation? What are people going to think?"

Florrie finished with the hairstyle and turned Alma to look in the mirror. The beloved curls that had framed her face so becomingly were now slicked back tight. She tried to smile politely.

"It looks very nice," she said softly.

"Good, now if you have any questions about how things are done properly you just come to me. I'll let you know what to do. We'll head down to dinner now."

Chapter 32
Off the Porch

Where do you draw the line between eccentric and crazy? Between crazy and dysfunctional? Between dysfunctional and mentally ill? I think it must be when the family takes the cocktail out of the crazy relative's hand, ushers the person off the porch, and hides them up in the attic.

Aunt Neta, Grandma Hodges's younger sister, absolutely belonged on the porch. In fact, that is how I remember her, sitting in a rocking chair on the porch of my grandmother's rooming house in Pompano Beach. She wore Bermuda shorts, an old T-shirt, and always smoked a cigarette and drank a Coca-Cola—the Baptist equivalent of a cocktail, I suppose. Aunt Neta had epilepsy, which at the time when she was born in backwoods Georgia meant some people thought she was cursed, and others thought she just wasn't mentally right. That she had gotten married at all was considered a wonder in my father's family. And that she had married a wealthy, well-respected judge? Well, that was a downright miracle. After Uncle Doug Thomas died, she took turns living with his sister, Miss Elizabeth Thomas, and with my grandmother.

Everyone said Aunt Neta was spoiled, first by her parents, then by my grandmother, and finally by her husband. He must have been a very nice man because Aunt Neta was kind of a pain. My mother said Daddy didn't like her because his mama paid too much attention to her and not enough to him when she was around. I agreed with him. When Aunt Neta was around, Grandma didn't have much time for my sister and me either. And we were used to having Grandma at our beck and call.

Aunt Neta certainly fit in the "eccentric heading toward crazy" category. I don't remember too much about her, even though we saw her quite often. I think she didn't like children very much. But the good thing was, when he died, Uncle Doug left her a big house in Odum, Georgia. It wasn't too many years before Grandma and Grandpa needed that house.

~~~

The year I was eight, my father moved off the proverbial porch and into the attic. Before that my mother had explained to us that he "had problems," which was why they were divorced. And yes, I knew all about the gambling. He had taken the money my mother had been saving to buy me a "big girl bed" and lost it, and that was why I had to stay in a crib until I was past three.

My mother had gotten a "church-sanctioned divorce." Not an annulment, which my mother always felt would have been cheating on her faith, but permission from the Catholic Church to divorce.

In 1960.

No Catholic got divorced in 1960.

But somehow my mother managed it. Things must have been bad.

It didn't seem strange to me that after the divorce my father lived with his parents at the rooming house my grandmother ran in Pompano Beach. After all, my mother, sister, and I lived with her parents. I just figured that's what divorced people did—a reasonable assumption since I knew no one else whose parents were divorced. My father did have a job. He worked in sales for an electronics company.

The rooming house was a big, old, square wooden building. In South Florida good buildings were made of stucco. It's called CBS for "concrete block stucco." When you're in Florida, if you hear someone talking about CBS, they are probably not discussing a TV station. Cheap buildings at the time were made of wood and were more likely to catch fire or blow down in a hurricane. Grandma's rooming house had a giant screened porch across the front with a "haint blue" ceiling. Haint blue is a pale blue color almost all Georgia and South Carolina porches are painted. It is said painting your porch ceiling the color of the sky will confuse the ghosts and keep them from haunting your house, thus the name.

The rooming house porch was lined with about a dozen rocking chairs, each with a standing ashtray or spittoon next to it so the roomers—all men—could sit on the porch and relax in the evening.

There was a center hall with about six bedrooms on each

side. The downstairs and the second floor each had a shared bathroom. Upstairs four of the front bedrooms had been turned into an apartment for my grandparents. Their bedroom connected to the big kitchen, which had a dining table in one corner, but to get to the living room, which had originally been an upper porch, you had to either go out into the public hallway and through another door or climb through a window in their bedroom. Cheryl and I, of course, preferred the window route. My father had the first bedroom on the left, next to the stairs. It wasn't connected to the rest of the apartment.

Since there was only the one shared bathroom upstairs, at night my grandmother insisted we use the chamber pot in the bedroom. She didn't want us wandering the hall where the gentlemen lived. The bathroom had two stalls, four pedestal sinks, and a clawfoot tub—all chipped from decades of use. Pedestal sinks and clawfoot tubs may be considered quaint and even fashionable again, but to me they are still creepy.

The rooming house was just a block from the railroad tracks, and when my grandparents first moved there in the late 1940s it was a bustling place filled with traveling salesmen and the occasional tourist. But by the 1960s the railroad was no longer the preferred method of travel, and the more upscale salesmen stayed at the motels along U.S. 1.

An air of shabbiness permeated the place. Grass struggled to grow in soil that was mostly beach sand, and a fine layer of that sand coated the wooden floors and furniture no matter how often my grandmother swept and dusted. Termites had invaded decades before, and if you pushed too hard against a wall it might peel away like paper. In the back of the house my grandfather grew trees from scratch in two-pound metal coffee cans—tiny palms he planted from seeds, and oranges and lemons and loquats and guava all grafted onto other plants.

And then there were the cats. At least a dozen feral cats called the backyard home. Grandpa, always a soft touch, fed them every day, and my grandmother fussed that they would leave if he would only stop feeding them. But if he wasn't able to get out and feed them some mornings, there was my grandmother with three or four plates of scraps, standing at the top of the outdoor stairway calling, "Here, kitty, kitty, kitty." And the animals came running for their breakfast.

When the city decided to expand the street, the rooming house was scheduled to be torn down, and Daddy bought a house on Biscayne Canal in North Miami. It was exciting! We no longer had to go down the hall to the bathroom. And I could spend hours throwing stones into the canal, as long as I didn't get too close to the water.

The house only lasted for about a year. Then Daddy fell off the sanity wagon for the first time in my memory. He ended up in the hospital, and we heard whispers about things called electroshock and schizophrenia. We learned that they were hooking cords to his brain and shooting him with electricity to "fix" him. My mother explained that schizophrenia meant "not knowing fantasy from reality." Not a bad explanation to give to a young child.

When he got out he had lost his job and the house, and he and my grandparents moved to an apartment that was smaller, and in not as good a neighborhood, although it was closer to us, over on West Dixie Highway. It had a pool so we got to swim when we visited. He found another job, not as good, and we thought things were going to return to normal.

That was the year I learned to be afraid of the telephone. Any time things settled down, the telephone would ring, my mother or grandparents would answer, and I would know instantly from the change in their voices that my father had done something, again.

Then there would be hours of whispered conversations. Late-night explanations about what Daddy had done this time. Hours in hospital or nursing home waiting rooms wearing Sunday dresses. Why did we have to wear our best dresses to the hospital? The patients certainly weren't dressed up! I hated those walks through long hospital hallways where people sat in wheelchairs, drooling.

And then things would get better, and Daddy would be back, maybe not quite like before but back.

One day the phone rang, and after we listened from the hallway to the long, confusing conversation, my mother took us into the bedroom and explained that my father had really lost it this time. Well, she didn't say it exactly like that. She always tried to be nice about Daddy. Nice but truthful. A difficult combination under the circumstances.

This time Daddy had run off to Atlanta with some woman before trying to kill himself and, of course, ended up in the hospital—again—in Georgia. And since there was now no money for my grandparents to live in the apartment, they were going to have to move back to Odum, Georgia, and live in Aunt Neta's house.

I was devastated. I would only see my grandparents one week every August instead of every weekend.

A few months after they moved, we visited them there for the first time. Odum hadn't changed much since my grandparents and Daddy had lived there thirty years earlier. The Holy Rollers church was still on the corner, and you could hear the hum of the worshipers on Saturday nights. Everyone knew everyone, together with all their business. So while no one ever talked out loud about why they had moved there or why Daddy didn't have a job, everyone in town knew—and whispered.

I didn't really care, though, because these weren't my friends. And when kids back at home asked why I didn't have a dad, I could just say he lived in Georgia. It was so much better than the long explanations I used to have to make for why he didn't show up for school events, or why I never went to a father/daughter dance. I guess, in my own way, when he moved to Georgia, I moved him off the porch and into the attic.

In the end I came to have a real fondness for the house in Odum, with its giant porch and its yard filled with scrub pines. And I finally met the people I'd heard stories about for years. Miss Clarice still lived in town, and Uncle Jimps often came for Sunday visits.

I'd always loved the story of Uncle Wright and Aunt Esther. They were among the few of my grandfather's relatives that my grandmother actually liked. Now I got to meet them and hear their love story right from Aunt Esther.

Chapter 33
The Carpetbagger's Granddaughter

1932

Esther carefully pushed back the lace curtains and peered out the window—again. There were a dozen cars at the Hodges house next door, and more were joining them every minute. A brand-new, shiny black 1932 Ford coupe pulled up. She knew who owned that car; it was Jimps. Not the person she was looking for—hoping for. Another, older car came next, and a couple got out with a young boy—J.W. and Alma, with their son Johnnie.

Esther sighed, let the curtain fall, and walked away, shaking her head indecisively. She should just get the banana nut bread she had baked and take it on over. It was the neighborly thing to do. After all, she'd lived next door to these people her entire life. If she didn't go, she would be considered rude. There would be gossip.

But if she did go, they'd all stare. They'd whisper behind their hands. Would anyone even speak to her? It had been almost twenty years since she had stepped foot in that house. It had been hot that day, too, just like today, with no breeze to stir the curtains. She'd been only seventeen, and she'd been damp with sweat just walking the short distance over from her house.

Well, maybe it hadn't been the heat so much as her nerves that day. Even with Wright beside her, encouraging her, her stomach had been in knots.

~~~

1914

"Don't worry, everything will be fine," Wright said reassuringly, holding on to her hand and guiding her up the steps.

"Your mama has never liked me; you know that," Esther said nervously.

"That's history. She's being ridiculous."

"You don't understand. I get it everywhere I go in town. Everyone looks down on me. They'll look down on you now, too, if we do this."

"I don't care. I love you, Esther."

Wright stopped on the front porch and turned her to face him, kissing her tenderly. She flushed a bright red just as the door swung open and Wright's older brother Jimps came out.

"Hey, brother, what's up?" he asked. He fumbled in his pocket for something imaginary, obviously trying to pretend he hadn't just seen the two of them kissing right out in front of God and everyone in Tattnall County. "Do you two want to ride over to Jesup with me? I'm going to look at that hardware store over there. Old Man Sawyer says if I come up with the money, he'll let me buy in as a partner."

Jimps was five years older than Wright and at twenty-seven he had declared he was done with farming and was looking for an easier way to make a living.

Wright rolled his eyes. "Like Daddy's gonna give you money," he said.

"Well J.W. owns a grocery store. Why can't I own a hardware store?"

"Because J.W. earned all the money himself, that's why. You know Mama would never let Daddy give J.W. money."

"Yeah, but I'm not J.W. If Daddy won't give it to me, Mama will," Jimps said with a grin. "You know I'm her favorite."

Standing behind Wright, Esther snorted—a not very ladylike noise.

"What were you two doing standing at the door? Besides kissing, I mean," Jimps said, changing the subject.

"We need to talk to Mama and Daddy."

Jimps gave them a knowing look. "So, you're really going to do it?" he asked.

"Yes," Wright said defiantly. "I've loved Esther since we were kids. I'm going to marry her no matter what anyone says."

"Brother, you think I have nerve asking Daddy for money to buy a share in a hardware store. You want to marry the town scandal." Jimps put one hand over his mouth as if he could push the words back in. Then he said, "Jesus, I'm sorry, Esther. You know I don't think that. It's just that's what Mama will say I'm sorry. You know I love you like a sister."

Esther had never seen Jimps, always self-assured, even

cocky, so flustered. She quickly put a hand on his arm. "Don't worry, Jimps. I know what everyone says about my family. It's been almost forty years. You'd think everyone would have forgotten by now."

"Esther's a Southerner now, just like the rest of us. It doesn't matter where her grandfather came from."

"Well, it doesn't matter to me, that's for sure. I couldn't care less. But it matters to Mama, y'all know that. She's all, 'Her Granddaddy was a Yankee.'" Jimps made his voice high, perfectly imitating their mother's intonation. "'He fought against us in the War. And worse than that, he was a Carpetbagger. He came down here just to steal our land and crops when we were down and out. His people wouldn't have any money now if he hadn't stolen it from us in our time of desperation.'"

Esther put her hand over her mouth to hide her giggles. She really shouldn't laugh about her future mother-in-law.

Wright, however, had no such problem. He chuckled and slapped Jimps on the back. "Don't let her hear you if you want that hardware store," he said.

Then he turned to Esther. "Are you ready?"

She took a deep breath, straightened her shoulders. "Yes, let's get it over with."

Inside the front parlor was slightly cooler. Two black ceiling fans rotated slowly, stirring a very slight breeze as long as you stood directly under one of them. The parlor was dark and filled with furniture that had been new back when the War Between the States had been fought; everything looked just a little bit worn.

"You wait here," Wright told Esther, leading her to the black leather wingback chair Esther knew was considered a "company" chair, one that only guests were allowed to sit in.

"Are you sure?" Esther said. "We don't want to make your mama mad right off."

"I'm sure. You are my honored guest, and you'll be treated that way."

"All right," she said uncertainly, and took a seat on its edge.

"I'll be right back. I'm going to go tell Mama and Daddy

you are here and bring us some iced tea."

Esther waited with her ankles crossed and her hands folded, trying to look patient even if she didn't feel that way. She took slow, deep breaths to calm her jitters. She could hear voices coming from upstairs—Wright, his mother, his father.

"Well, I don't know why we have to come down and sit in the parlor like the girl is special company, just because her family has more money than we do. You know where they got it from—" Wright's mama's voice faded off.

"Let's go down and be polite. You can do that much for your son," she heard his daddy say.

Then there was the clatter of several people heading down the stairs, and Wright ushered in his mama, daddy, and sister Florrie.

Esther mentally rolled her eyes. Not Florrie. She had too many opinions about everything and was never reluctant to share them.

Wright came over and perched on the arm of her chair as his parents and sister sat opposite them on the sofa.

"Well, what is this all about, son?" asked his father.

Esther heard Wright draw in a deep breath. He grabbed her hand. "Esther and I are going to be married," he said defiantly.

Esther held her breath, and it seemed as if for at least a minute everyone else in the room did, too. No one made a sound. The silence went on long enough that she began to hope. They couldn't really be surprised. Everyone in town knew how she and Wright felt about each other. His mama was going to accept their marriage. She began to breathe again and apparently Wright's mama did, too, because suddenly the silence was over.

"Y'all are what? Are you out of your mind, Wright?" His mama hissed the words as if afraid the whole town might hear.

That seemed to open the floodgate, and everyone began to speak at once. The commotion attracted Wright's sister Bessie and she entered into the discussion. Throughout it all Esther kept her hands folded in her lap. After a lifetime living next door to the Hodges clan, she knew that when they "discussed things" outsiders had better not get in the way lest they wanted to get their heads bitten off.

Finally, she had had enough. Even Wright didn't seem to notice when she got up and tiptoed quietly toward the front door. She was wrong, though. Just before she closed the door behind her, he stepped onto the front porch.

He held her tenderly. "I know they're a mess, but you'll see. They'll come around. After all the yelling is done, Mama will give in to Daddy and everything will be fine."

"I don't know, Wright. I'm not sure it will work out that way this time."

He kissed her gently on the forehead. "You go on home. I'll come over tomorrow and tell you all about it."

"Don't come until everything is decided. I don't think I can bear too much more of this back and forth. It's our lives, Wright."

"I know it is. I know. I'll make Mama understand. I promise."

Esther headed home through the dusk and opened the door to find her own mama waiting for her. She gave her a big hug.

"Well, how did it go with Miz Eliza?" Mama asked. "Can I start planning the wedding yet?" She took Esther's chin in her hand and looked her in the eyes.

"I don't know, Mama. I don't know if Wright can stand up to all of them. It's not just Miz Eliza, you know. It's all the damn women in that family!"

"Esther! Don't you swear."

"They drive me to swearing sometimes."

"Then are you sure this is what you want? Even if you and Wright move down to Odum, near J.W. and his wife, you'll still have to see all of them every holiday, wedding, and funeral. And given all those children, they could have a wedding every week for a year and not be done."

Esther laughed. "Wright only has thirteen brothers and sisters, and three of them are already married. It wouldn't take a whole year!"

"Well, there now, I got you to laugh." Esther's mother put her arm around her shoulders and pulled her toward the kitchen.

"Let's go get dinner on the table. Your father should be home soon."

~~~

It was three days before Wright knocked on the door. Esther spent the time staring out her window at the front porch of the neighboring house. She saw everyone come and go. Jimps, Florrie, Miz Eliza, Wright's father.

Where was Wright?

They couldn't have locked a twenty-two-year-old man up in his room. Could they?

Finally, on the third night, there was a knock.

"Who the hell is that at this hour?" grumbled her father. He got up from the sofa where he had been reading the newspaper, shoes off, top button of his shirt undone.

Esther's heart was beating so fast she thought it would fly out of her chest. There was only one person who would come calling at nine p.m. at night.

"I'm sorry it's so late," she heard Wright say.

She started to get up, but her mother stopped her.

"You don't go to the door chasing a young man at this time of night," she said severely.

Esther strained her ears to hear the conversation happening in the hallway.

"I shouldn't let you in, boy. It's much too late to come calling on a young lady."

"I know, I know, sir. But I have to see her."

Her father grumbled a bit more, and then finally there was Wright in the doorway.

"We'll leave y'all alone for a few minutes," her mother said.

Her father sputtered, "We will not—"

"Yes, we will." Her mother took her father's arm and led him into the kitchen.

"I had to see you—" Wright began, coming straight over.

Esther immediately noticed the strain on his face.

"Your mother has put her foot down, hasn't she?"

His mouth thinned into a grim line. "She has."

"And what did you tell her?"

Wright said nothing.

"You know my parents approve of the marriage. They'll help you get a start. My father would love to have help in the store—"

Wright turned away. "I can't do that. I can't defy my mother and then stay here and work in your dad's store and see her every time she comes to town. Besides, what would it do to your father's business? My mother would bad-mouth your family to the entire county. He'd lose money because of me."

"Eliza Hodges isn't as all-powerful as she thinks she is," Esther said. "You'll see. There are plenty of people in this county who don't dance to her tune."

"No. I just can't do that to you—or to her. Esther, I'm going away."

For the first time Esther noticed that he was wearing his best suit. She stepped toward the front hall. A suitcase stood by the door.

"Wright! No! Where will you go?"

"I've always wanted to see the world. I'm going to join the Merchant Marine."

"Wright, that's the most ridiculous thing I've ever heard."

Wright drew himself up stiffly. "I'm sorry you feel that way," he said. Suddenly, his voice no longer held the softness it always had when he talked to her. "My mind is made up. I'm leaving. You need to forget about me and find someone else. There are plenty of men in the county who would love to marry you."

"But I don't want to marry them! I want to marry you."

"You're young. You'll find someone. I'm leaving tonight. Jimps is going to drive me to the station. Esther, I won't be back. I want you to have a good life."

Before she could say anything more, he grabbed his suitcase and was gone.

~~~

1932

Esther marched into the kitchen, picked up her homemade banana bread, put it on a glass plate, and walked toward the front door. She stopped for a moment and checked her hair in the front hall mirror. A strong woman looked back. *And not a bad-looking one either*, she thought to herself. There was no gray in her hair and only a few laugh lines around her eyes.

"Let's get this over with," she said to herself.

After opening the door Esther headed down the steps. Just as she reached the bottom, another car pulled up. There were so many cars at the Hodges home that this one had to park in front of her house. She didn't mind; it was only neighborly. But as she continued down the sidewalk, she kept half an eye on the car to see who it was.

Its door swung open, and a man stepped out. He was tall and wore a dark blue suit. As he turned back to the car and pulled out his hat, a white sailor's cap, she realized it wasn't a suit but a uniform. Esther stopped short, and the banana bread slipped from her hand, the plate shattering as it hit the stones.

The man turned around. "Esther—"

"Wright?"

He walked over and stopped in front of her.

"Wha...what are you doing here?"

"I've come for Mama's funeral."

"Well, yes. Of course. I know that. But I thought you wouldn't come. It's so late." She gestured to the crowd of cars already parked next door. "I didn't know if you'd get away, if you were at sea—"

Why can't I put a simple sentence together, she thought, frustrated at herself. It was just Wright Hodges. A man she hadn't seen in twenty years. A man who hadn't come home for his sisters' and brothers' weddings, or even for his daddy's funeral. Why was he here now?

"Are you coming to the service?" His eyes seemed to search her face, looking for something. What, she wondered?

"No, I—"

"I understand. As soon as I can get away from everyone I want to come and see you. Will you be here?"

Esther knew he wasn't asking if she would be at home, but rather if she would open the door to him. "Yes," she said.

"Good. I'll see you soon."

It was late afternoon by the time there was a knock. She watched Wright closely as he stood in the hall, hat in hand, much like he had the last time he had stood in this spot.

He wasted no time in coming straight to the point. "Esther, can you forgive me?"

Esther's breath caught in her throat. She wouldn't pretend she didn't know what he was talking about.

"You were young. We both were," she said. "Your mother put a lot of pressure on you. Yes, I was angry at first, but that was a long time ago."

"I was a coward."

"You were young," she repeated. Her voice softened. "And she was a hard woman to stand up to. I knew that. Even that day we went to see her, I knew how difficult it would be for you."

"You're very forgiving," he said. "You're right. I couldn't stand up to her. I could only run away. I'm sorry."

"Wright, why are you here now? Is it only to ask me to forgive you? To catch up on old times? What is it you want from me?"

"I want you to marry me."

"What?" Esther caught a look at herself in the hall mirror, the shock on her face was obvious. Yes, she'd hoped to get a glimpse of Wright, the man she still foolishly loved after twenty years. And yes, she'd hoped to have a chance to talk to him. But marriage? It had never occurred to her that he would ask her to marry him now.

"I have no right to ask. No right to expect you still have feelings for me after the way I left. But Esther, I've never stopped thinking about you. I know what it looks like, my coming back now—now that my mother has died—like I'm a coward who could never stand up to his mama. But I'd have been here now, even if she were still alive." He looked down at his hat, turning it nervously in his hands.

"I liked my life at sea. I saw the world. I learned so much more than I ever could if I'd stayed at home—with you. And somehow the months and then the years slipped by. I never forgot you but just figured you'd found someone else and got married and had a houseful of kids by now—"

He looked up at her finally. "I never got married. There was never anyone else I wanted to marry," Esther replied. "I've had a good life. I've run the store since Daddy died—"

"I know. Bessie told me when I was in Savannah. She's living there now, you know."

Esther nodded.

"She told me you never married. And, well, I got my hopes up. I couldn't come then. My ship was only in port for a day. But that's when I put in my papers to leave."

Wright got down on one knee. Esther gasped and put her hand to her mouth as he pulled a small ring box from his pocket.

"Esther, will you marry me? Marry me as soon as possible. I don't want to waste any more time."

"Yes," she said, going down on her knees next to him. "Yes, I'll marry you. You're the only man I've ever loved."

And there, in the spot where he'd left her so many years ago, they kissed.

Chapter 34
Savannah

1967

"I've never liked your great aunt Florrie," Grandma said.

We were back in her kitchen a few afternoons later, cleaning up after dinner. Grandma and Grandpa never ate lunch. They ate dinner every day at noon—a hot meal with meat, potatoes, vegetables, dessert, and iced tea, then supper—the cold leftovers from earlier, about six o'clock in the evening.

As she continued to tell me more about my relatives, she scrubbed the china plate so fiercely I feared for its life.

"But you have to be nice to her when you go to see her tomorrow."

"I'll be polite, don't worry."

"Well, that's enough about Florrie." She handed me the plate. "You know where this goes."

I carefully put the plate in the stack on the shelf.

"And you remember, when I die Cheryl Anne gets my china, and you get my silver."

I grinned. "I remember."

It may seem like a strange thing, even a morbid thing, to tell an eleven-year-old child, but you have to understand that if there is one thing a Southern woman values more than even her family, it is her china and silver. And I'd been a lot younger than eleven when the decisions about who got Grandma's china and who got her silver were made.

I must have been about five years old when Cheryl and I sat in the kitchen of Grandma's rooming house in Pompano, watching her make dinner.

"Someday, girls, Grandma's gonna die. I won't be here anymore, but one of you is going to get my silver and the other my china. Do you know which one of you wants what?"

I spoke up immediately. "I don't mind eating off paper plates, but I really hate using plastic forks and knives."

"That's fine," said my seven-year-old sister. "I love the ivy on your china. I think it is beautiful."

And so it was decided. It wasn't something we thought about, we just knew it. Cheryl Anne would get the china, and Karen Lee would get the silver because she didn't like to use plastic forks.

~~~

Daddy was having a good summer. Mama had only called us into the bedroom once during our weeklong visit to talk about what behavior we were to look out for. She'd even agreed to all three of us spending an overnight with him in Savannah, without my grandparents to run interference. She never said it that way, you understand. We just knew it—learned it by osmosis or something.

The next morning we were up early, dressed in our best summer dresses. We were going to visit Aunt Florrie and then we were going to see *Gone With the Wind* in the movie theater. It hadn't been in theaters for over twenty years, and I'm not sure who was more excited, my mama or my daddy. I do know Mama wasn't all that happy about the stop at Aunt Florrie's house, but not only was it family, it was going to involve a history lesson, and that meant she couldn't really object. Family and history were two of the most important things to Mama.

"Aunt Florrie lives in the family homestead," Daddy explained as we drove to Tattnall County. "She'll tell you all about it. Uncle Wright and Aunt Esther live next door in what was Aunt Esther's family home."

The ride seemed to take forever, even though I suspect it was less than an hour. I never could sit still for very long. We arrived at the two-story white colonial with large columns supporting a second-floor sleeping porch. It had been painted recently; although the porch steps sagged, it was in fairly good shape for a house that was more than a hundred years old.

We stood behind Daddy as he knocked and a trim woman with blue-gray hair opened the door. She wore a dress and earrings and necklace; you could tell she had dressed for company.

"Oh, come in, Johnnie, it's so good to see you. And these are your babies?"

"Yes, Aunt Florrie," Daddy said deferentially. "This is Cheryl Anne, and this is Karen Lee." He brought us forward. "And you remember Verna."

"Of course," Florrie said rather coldly, looking down her nose. A divorced woman, particularly one who had divorced a Hodges, just wasn't worth her notice.

"We wanted to see the family homestead and hear a little bit about the history," Daddy said as Aunt Florrie ushered us into a sitting room stuffed with old-fashioned sofas and chairs that looked like they had been there since at least the Civil War. A large curio cabinet was filled with figurines, tea sets, dishes, and various mementos, the good dishes crowded next to the palm tree salt and pepper shakers and neon seashells from various tourist destinations.

My sister and I packed ourselves in together in a large, black leather wingback chair. We sat with our hands folded, a little bored and a lot too warm. I noticed that as my mother sipped her coffee, she had the same bored-but-trying-not-to-show-it expression on her face.

"How are your parents, Johnnie? It's a shame they couldn't be bothered to come out and see me," Florrie said.

And then I spotted that same, strained expression on my father's face, too. I guess he really wasn't enjoying this visit as much as I had thought he was. His look was more, "I'm going to be polite if it kills me." He wanted his daughters to know about the family history. It was one of the few things he felt he had left to give us at that point, knowledge that his family used to be "somebodies." Of course, two pre-teen girls didn't care a hoot about that. He couldn't give us what we really wanted from him.

"Daddy hasn't been doing so well this summer," he responded to Aunt Florrie.

"Well, bless his heart, that's just a shame. I suppose I'll have to try and make it over to see him," she said.

"I'm sure Mama would love to see you." Daddy quickly changed the subject. "Aunt Florrie, I wanted the girls to hear some of the history of this house."

And then Florrie really came alive. She brought us into the dining room and sat us down where we could look at large sheets of paper with names and lines running from one person to the next. They were genealogy sheets, she explained, showing the whole history of the family right up to the birth of Richard Hodges in 1700. She showed us our place and informed us that we were eligible to apply to the Daughters of the Revolution and the Daughters of the Confederacy. Daddy looked proud. Mama rolled her eyes.

The house had been built well before my grandfather or even my great-grandfather was born. "We owned slaves before The War," Florrie said proudly.

Cheryl and I looked at each other in horror. Wasn't owning slaves a bad thing? And you could tell by the way Aunt Florrie pronounced "The War" that in her mind it had happened just yesterday. The Spanish-American War, World War I, and World War II—in which my daddy had fought and probably gotten PTSD, although they didn't call it that yet—did not count in her eyes.

Next she took us on a tour of the house.

"Now this front room," she pointed out, taking us back to the entryway, "is the part of the house Sherman didn't manage to burn during his March to the Sea." She took us over to the china closet. "This is the silver that my great-grandmother buried in the backyard when Sherman came through."

There were other "highlights." I don't remember them all. I came away with an impression of a family that had once been grand and wealthy but had fallen on hard times because the Damn Yankees had stuck their noses into Southern business and messed up a lovely way of life.

It was certainly a fitting introduction to watching *Gone With the Wind*. I identified with the Southerners. I wanted to be a Rebel soldier and go off and fight, not Scarlett O'Hara, she was too much of a girly girl. I got up to leave at the intermission, feeling satisfied with the two-hour movie. Then my mother explained it was only the intermission. There were another two hours to go. I whined until Daddy got us some more popcorn, then managed to sit reasonably still through the movie's last half. It was much more boring than the first. At least the first part had included some good battles. Cheryl thought the part where Rhett carries Scarlett up the stairs was *the most romantic*. I just thought it was stupid.

I'm making the trip sound like I didn't enjoy it. I did. Despite Aunt Florrie, and despite a really, really long movie. The next day we visited the home of Juliette Gordon Low, founder of the Girl Scouts, and ate at The Pirate House restaurant. It was one of the oldest buildings in Savannah and had tunnels where the shanghaied men were smuggled out and put on ships to serve as sailors until they either died or escaped. What was best was spending two days pretending that we were a normal family with a mother *and* a father. It is my only memory of just the four of us together.

As much fun as spending time in Savannah was, what I really loved most was returning to Odum where Grandpa Hodges waited for us, rocking in his porch chair.

~~~

Grandpa spent most every day sitting in his rocker, smoking a cigar and waving to the people who walked or drove by. Odum was a small town, a one-stop-sign town, and he knew everyone. The conversation was always the same. The person would slow, roll down the car window, and wave. "Hey, Mr. J.W."

"How are you? This is my grandbaby."

"Mighty big baby," they'd say, and drive on.

At first I was offended at being called a baby—and a little offended at being called big, too. I was always tall for my age, but did everyone have to mention it? Grandpa explained they were just commenting on the fact I would always be his baby, even though at eleven I was obviously very grown-up.

That summer Grandpa had gotten a slingshot so he could shoot at the groundhogs tearing up the garden. Of course, I wanted to learn. And, of course, Mama wasn't thrilled with the idea. I'm not sure if she didn't think it ladylike for me to shoot a slingshot, if she didn't trust me with it (probably a smart idea on her part), or if she didn't trust my grandfather (also a smart idea). Or maybe it was all of the above. Anyway, after Grandpa and I wore her down, she finally agreed, and I had a wonderful time learning.

We would sit together for hours as Grandpa told me to shoot at a particular tree or bush in the empty lot across the street. When we'd used up all the stones, I was sent out to the driveway to find more smooth, flat rocks, and then we'd start all over again. I couldn't think of a better way to pass the time.

One afternoon Grandpa took me for a walk down the road, putting his hand in mine.

"You know, sugar," he said when we were about halfway, "I've had a good life. I've got your grandma and your daddy and you and your sister. That's all I've ever wanted. But, sugar, I'm an old man, and my time is coming. I want you to know when I die you shouldn't cry for me. I'm ready to go."

I protested. I didn't want to hear it. I didn't want to think about it. But maybe Grandpa, the man everyone dismissed, the man who wasn't good with money, the man who had courted a woman who hadn't wanted him but loved her dearly for more than fifty years, was the wisest one of all.

"No," he told me. "It's the way of the world. I just want you to understand I won't be sad, and you shouldn't be either. I want you to remember that when the time comes."

I didn't understand. But I did remember.

Chapter 35
The Funeral

1968

The table in the dining room was covered in a lace tablecloth and loaded with food—ham, macaroni casserole, deviled eggs, green bean casserole, salads, desserts. Two glass pitchers of iced tea, sweet and unsweet, sweated on the side table, drops of water sparkling as they ran down the sides. Grandma had brought out the best silver, china, and crystal. The napkins were cloth. It was a typical Southern funeral. I'd been to many, just none here in Georgia, and none where someone I'd really loved was the person who had died. And not one where I knew next to no one either. Because while these were my relatives, I'd never met most of them.

My sister sat in one of the big leather chairs in the living room while I perched next to her on the arm, stifling in my best dress. Oh, why had I wanted that dress for Easter? It was a heavy cotton damask, white with tiny blue flowers in a striped pattern down the length of the fabric. A blue velvet ribbon divided the puffed upper sleeve from the tight lower sleeve that pinched my elbows when I tried to bend my arms. A velvet bow adorned the high-necked collar. And at age twelve, I'd finally been deemed old enough to wear stockings. White lace stockings were all the rage, and I'd been so excited when my mother bought them for me. But how I regretted them now. It's one thing to wear long sleeves, high collars, and stockings for an hour in an air-conditioned church. Quite another to wear it all day long in the un-air-conditioned heat of late May in Georgia. My sister looked just as uncomfortable, even though her dress was a much more sensible cotton—pink and white with a round neck and cap sleeves.

We sat with frozen smiles as my father proudly introduced us to relative after relative. Aunt Bessie, Aunt Maxie, her husband, Floy, and her son Coy, my seventh cousin once removed Deena, Aunt Esther and Uncle Wright. Thank God they were nice and sat and talked to us about Grandpa, or "J.W." as they called him. My father was in hog heaven acting as master of the house. He always wanted to be the center of attention, and now, as the grieving son, he was.

It was eleven a.m., and things were just warming up for what was going to be an excruciatingly long day. My Georgia relatives were all Baptists and Methodists so there was no whiskey or rum on the table. When I heard the voice of Uncle Jimps (yes, that was his Baptismal name, not a nickname) raised above the others, I realized some of them were drinking more than sweet tea.

"Laura, you can't talk to me that way," he was saying to his wife. Uncle Jimps was one of the few among my grandfather's thirteen brothers and sisters to be considered successful. He owned a hardware store in the "big town" of Jesup, ten miles east of Odum.

"You've had enough to drink, Jimps," his wife said. "You don't want to make a fool of yourself in front of everyone here."

"I never make a fool of myself," he argued loudly, waving his flask around. "Just ask J.W. Oh wait, we can't ask him, can we?"

"Daddy, come on inside and sit down and I'll get you something to eat," his son said, taking him by the arm. Uncle Jimps pulled away just as Aunt Florrie came out on the porch.

"Jimps, settle down and quit making a scene," she hissed.

"Yes, Florrie," he said obediently, and Laura and his son led him over to one of the porch rocking chairs where he continued to drink sullenly.

My attention turned back inside when my grandmother motioned for my mother to come into her bedroom.

Over the years the relationship between Grandma and Mama had gotten much more cordial. I know they didn't love each other, maybe didn't even really like each other, but they did respect each other. Mama, in her less charitable moments, said that Grandma liked her because when she divorced Daddy, Grandma "got her baby back." But in reality, it had to do with their mutual understanding that Mama took care of us, the grandbabies, while Grandma took care of Daddy. They needed each other to take care of everyone they loved. And Mama did still love Daddy—maybe not in the way she had when they first met, but it was love nonetheless. You could tell sometimes. She just wished she didn't.

At any rate I was bored with the goings-on of the grown-ups in the living room so I headed in to see what was up with Grandma. At least I could sprawl on her bed and be more comfortable.

"Do you think it's all right if I wear these tan shoes, Verna?" Grandma was saying, holding out the comfortable orthopedic sandals she usually wore. "My black dress shoes hurt my feet. You don't think anyone would think I was terrible or that I wasn't being respectful to Mr. Hodges?"

"Of course not. You wear the shoes that don't hurt your feet. It's going to be a long enough day as it is without your feet hurting," Mama told her.

Grandma put on the shoes just as Daddy came in and started to hurry everyone out to the cars.

"Mama, are you really going to wear those shoes?" he asked.

"John, your mother's feet hurt. She's going to wear what is comfortable," Mama said in her schoolteacher voice.

"Of course, of course," he said. Just like his daughters, he knew not to mess with his ex-wife when she used that voice. "Mama, come on. We need to get to the church on time."

He hurried everyone out with my mother mumbling something about why were we hurrying; the funeral wasn't going to start without the widow.

We were ushered into the big, black limousine for the ride around the corner to the little Methodist Church. Once there my father herded us up the steps and to the front of the church where the coffin was displayed. I didn't really want to look. I'd already learned that people in coffins just don't look like themselves. But somehow Daddy had hold of me and my sister, and we were parading past the casket. No, Grandpa didn't look like Grandpa. His expression was wrong. It just wasn't Grandpa. I tried to remember what he'd told me the summer before, that he was happy to be going to heaven. It didn't help.

My sister cried. I didn't. I'd mastered the art of not crying in front of people. Ever.

Luckily, we were allowed to head to the pew where paper fans printed with funeral home advertisements waited. Grandma grabbed one and fanned herself. The church was beyond hot. It didn't even have ceiling fans. What was it about backwoods Georgia? Hadn't they heard of that newfangled invention the air conditioner? It had only been around for about fifty years. I picked up my fan and followed Grandma's example. Once again I cursed my choice of Easter dress, which must have been the hottest dress in the history of dresses. And it was going to be my "good dress" from now until Christmas.

The minister, in a black suit and tie, droned on and on. We sang songs. We waved our fans back and forth. Finally, it was over, and we processed out to the black limousine. That was when the funeral director apologized. The car's air conditioner had quit working. The trip from the house to the church had been so quick that I hadn't noticed.

"Do you want to take your own car?" he asked Daddy.

"No, no. This is fine. We'd rather ride in the limo," he replied.

"But John—" my mother started to say, but it was his turn to put his foot down.

He gave her a look that hushed her up. That didn't happen very often, let me tell you. But I understood what it was all about. Daddy had this fantasy of how the day should go, and it included riding in a fancy limousine, even if the air conditioner wasn't working.

"It is thirty miles to the cemetery," the funeral director reminded him apologetically.

But Daddy waved him off. We were traveling in that limo even if we all died of heatstroke. And I was beginning to think it was a possibility. It was 1968. Those nice little water bottles hadn't been invented yet, and no one ever ate or drank in a car anyway. It was going to be a long, hot trip.

My sister and I got in the car and watched through the open window. Grandma was still on the sidewalk talking and hugging the many people who were coming up to her. And there was Aunt Florrie, sailing in like the Queen of England. No one could miss her.

"Alma, why are you wearing those shoes?" were the first words out of her mouth. "It's disgraceful wearing tan shoes at your husband's funeral. Don't you own black shoes?"

And then my grandmother let loose.

"Florrie, you have been telling me what to do and how I should look and what I should wear since the day I came home married to Mr. Hodges. You pulled all the curls out of my hair. And I've put up with you for my husband's sake, although why he ever cared what you thought I will never know. But he is gone now, and I don't have to put up with you anymore. My daughter-in-law says it is all right to wear my tan shoes to his funeral because my feet hurt, and she comes from Miami and knows a lot more about these things than some old lady from backwoods Georgia. You and your relatives have been putting me and Mr. Hodges down our whole lives, and you just aren't going to do it anymore."

There was silence around the churchyard. Everyone had heard. Uncle Jimps was quietly chuckling. Aunt Bessie had her hand over her mouth. My sister and I were grinning like Cheshire cats. My mother was trying hard to keep her expression serene. Aunt Florrie's mouth was open. She looked like a startled fish.

And my poor father had turned bright red and looked like he hoped the sidewalk would open up and swallow him whole. This was not the way the funeral was supposed to go. It was supposed to be quiet, dignified. It was supposed to show the Hodges relatives that his branch of the family weren't the black sheeps, with Daddy himself as the biggest black sheep of all.

"Mama" he kept saying while her tirade had gone on. "Mama." But it had no effect. When she finally stopped, he grabbed her by the arm. "Mama, why don't you get in the car." He talked as he pulled her after him. "Aunt Florrie, I'm sorry. Mama is just so upset."

"Well, I never!" Aunt Florrie huffed and turned away.

Everyone slowly came to life and shuffled into their cars

as the long, hot, thirty-mile ride to the cemetery began.

I'm not sure Aunt Florrie and Grandma ever saw each other again. I only saw her one other time. She was there at Grandma's funeral several years later. She was dressed perfectly in black, from her hat to her shoes. Even at the funeral of a woman she had never liked, Aunt Florrie would dress the part of the perfect Southern lady.

Chapter 36
Love Letters

Tuesday Morning
Verna Darling, [and I don't call EVERYBODY darling.]
Just a short note, which you may not even get, but you'll know I
had good intentions. I love you and am counting the hours until
Thursday morning.

I love you now and forever
John

~~~

My mother saved my father's letters. She said it was in case we ever wanted to look at them, but for a long time I didn't want to read them. They sat in one of her boxes, mixed in with old photos, birth certificates, school report cards, and other sentimental things.

It was only after her death when I'd appointed myself the family member in charge of organizing a hundred years' worth of mementos that had been stored in hot attics and damp storage containers for decades. Miami weather is hard on paper. Some of the photographs were mildewed, too damaged to save. Some of the letters and documents were so yellowed and fragile they fell apart as I tried to open them.

I wanted to throw away my father's letters without looking at them. But somehow I couldn't. *I'm past sixty years old,* I told myself. *Isn't it time to get over my daddy issues?* When I finally got up my courage, I saw that most were from 1948. My mother had saved her love letters for over seventy-five years, even though she'd been divorced for more than sixty of those.

She never said much good about my father, even though when we were children she tried hard not to bad-mouth him either. It was a difficult line for her to walk, telling the truth to children without making them hate their father.

I would have thought she'd have made a bonfire out of the letters. I would have in her place. But maybe she was less vengeful than I am. What did this say about her true feelings that she had kept these for so many decades?

230 Karen Hodges Miller

The letters I looked at now showed me a very different person than the daddy I remember. My mother always told me I got my storytelling ability from him, which I took as her saying I knew how to lie well—I did. But my father's letters showed me she'd meant something more complimentary. He was an excellent writer and expressed his feelings beautifully. When he uses the word "swoon," he sounds like a man in love, not a wimp. In some of the letters he is a witty, fun-loving young man who thinks he is going to conquer the world and get the princess (Verna) as his reward. In others he is an exhausted businessman who has traveled up and down the state of Florida in less than a week. And in still more he is just a lovesick guy who misses his girl and wishes he could see her more than once a month.

There are hints of the trouble to come. Not all of Verna's friends like John, particularly her oldest friend and roommate, Maude. John is often "blue" or "in the dumps." He borrows money from her and doesn't pay it back for several weeks.

That was an eye-opener for me. The mother I knew would have dumped a man who even asked to borrow money. The guy would never have gotten another date. But at the time she was very much in love, and so was he.

~~~

Oct. 10, 1948
Sunday night

My very dearest Verna,

Here I am back in Pompano again. We got back about 10:30 last night, but several things delayed us—no car trouble though.

Jay came on home with me. We were almost to Lake City when we decided we hadn't nearly talked long enough, so we didn't even go by G'ville. I took him down to Nord's this morning and he went back on the 2 o'clock bus.

Verna darling, the trip to Tally all seems like a dream. In one way you are right about it being worse to see you for a short time, and then leave. How I envy boys like Wayne and Scott who can be there every day; or even Charley Steel, who can go over every weekend. But then I think about J.'s situation and I feel better.

Jay and I have been friends a long time, but I think we are closer friends now than ever before. He certainly made the trip home a lot easier. [Interruption—right now on the "Stop the Music Show" they are playing "Every Day I Love You Just a Little Bit More." It fits me like a glove. Best you think of me when you hear it.]

Now back to Jay. He certainly thinks you are tops next to Nita. I think he's more happy about us than any of our friends. He cautions me, though, to come down out of the clouds a bit because he thinks I may get hurt. You know how I worry about little things. It took him two hours to talk me out of the dumps after that. Guess that's friendship though. Everyone except he and Nita have said, "John Hodges, don't you dare hurt Verna." Jay and Nita are the only ones who have thought of me being hurt. I suppose they are the only ones who really know me inside the shell I try to live in . . .

Honey, I called your mother and dad from Nord's. One night next week I'm going out and spend the evening with them. I know you know I love them very much. I hope you will love mine when you meet them.

Verna darling, I'm so glad you are sensible enough for us both. I'm certainly crazy enough for us both...I have so many things to do. Although I don't think you expect it, I want to give you the world.

Verna, I am so sorry I am the cause of you and Maude not being such good friends anymore. I know how much friendship means, and even though you don't admit it, I'm afraid it hurts you. I love all your friends because they are your friends. It makes me very happy to think most of them like me and approve of me.

Darling, I have one aid to this missing business for you. If you still miss me as you say you did, just stop and think for a minute, no matter what the hour, day or night, no matter where, Miami, Pompano, New York, or Timbuktu, I'll be thinking of you every minute of every day and always dreaming that someday I can be with you for always.

Yours always and always
John

Oct. 11, 1948
Monday night

Verna dearest,

Hope I didn't upset you too much by writing you again tonight after the epistle last night. When I was writing that I planned to write every day. I could hear you say, "Yeah, Every day!" But as you see, I mean every word of it.

I know you aren't interested in my business activities, but I must tell you I got three whopping big orders today. I went around and told all the boys to work up everything they could for me to take to New York with me.

Got the schedule of the Bundry Convention today. I will be free after 6 p.m. Friday. Also got a note from Fred telling me to get prepared not to sleep any for four days at least. Do you think I can hold out?

Honey, how long does it take my letters to get to you? I want to know so I'll know what day to mail a special delivery so you will get it on Sunday. Or do you want one?

Darling, I hope my letter last night wasn't too blue. At least I hope it didn't make you blue. God forbid that I ever do anything to make you the least bit unhappy.

Guess you know the Hurricanes took a drubbing Saturday night...Maybe the Gators will beat Miami after all.

Page 5 again and time to say, Verna, I love you. Those words I can never say enough.

Verna darling, please take care of yourself and get rid of that cold. It worried me a lot more than I let you know. Please start thinking about Verna and taking care of yourself.

Hey baby, it's only 39 more long days 'til Homecoming. That's five weeks and four days. Bet my willpower goes to hell and I call you. In fact, I almost did today. You at least have some pals around, and so far as I am concerned, South Florida is deserted. Wish I had just one somebody to talk to, and most of all, I wish that somebody was you.

Forever and ever
Your John

Oct. 17, 1948
Sunday Night

Hi Honey,

Guess you are back in Tallahassee by now. I'm just back from Miami myself. Had to work a couple of hours this afternoon. The 4018 Parade began at 6 on Lincoln Road. Wore my uniform to the Reunion last night. Believe it or not I can still squeeze in it. If I had breathed real hard though, I would have popped some blouse buttons. And also believe it or not it felt good to wear it again. Wish you could have seen it. Along about 3 this morning we were really strutting down Flagler singing "Lilly Marline!" What a night!

Remember me and remember always that I love you more than anything. Good night darling.

Forever your
John

Oct. 25, 1948
Monday Night

Verna darling,

Here I am back in Pompano at long last. What a week. I'll try to give you a detailed account as I go along.

The first night I was in New York, Fred Wright and his wife Joon picked me up at took me to dinner at Toot Shors, then to see Mr. Roberts, and then to the Copacabana for a <u>couple</u> of drinks. Lena Horne was singing at the Copa.

When I got back to the hotel, the Burndy Suite was going strong. Naturally I couldn't go to bed and let those boys drink all the scotch by themselves. So to bed at last at 6. Up at 8:30 in order to make the first conference at 9. Conference from 9 until 9. Then down to Greenwich Village with Fred, Chester Davis from Houston, Bill Nodder from San Francisco, and Paul Nebleth from Los Angeles. What a night. To bed at 6:30. Up at 7:30...

Darling, I love you, Very, very much I love you. I don't have to tell you that 'cause you know it already, don't you? And darling, I didn't forget you in New York, whatever you think.

Re: Jay and Nita. That's none of our business. Best we keep our opinions to ourselves.

> *Good night, darling*
> *Forever and ever,*
> *John*

Jan. 12, 1949

Verna Darling,
Will dash off a short note. The mail hasn't come in yet this morning, so I don't know if I get a letter today or not. I'm hoping—

So far I have kept my resolution. The only drink I've had since New Year's night was the one the night before you left. I'm also keeping my other resolution, too. I haven't been anyplace; not even to a show. And, as you might imagine, I'm becoming a very dull boy.

My schedule is such a mess. I don't know anything until I hear from Porter. But will definitely not go to Key West until he comes down. Will probably go up to the Lake (Clewiston and Moore Haven), Vero Beach, Ft. Pierce, West Palm, and Lake Worth next week. The work I did before Christmas is beginning to show up definitely in numerous LARGE orders. I feel very good. Burndy upped my quota quite a bit for '49. What do they think I am—don't answer that—I know.

I love you and miss you. In case I never told you, I think you are a good influence on me. Sometimes, that is.

> *So much for now.*
> *Always & Forever*
> *John*

Feb. 7, 1949
Monday night

Verna darling,
The trip was rather uneventful unless you can call a week of hard work eventful. I stayed in Sarasota Monday night, Tampa Tuesday and Wednesday, and Orlando Thursday. I have really stuck to my resolution. I didn't take a drink on the trip. Talked to Agnes this afternoon. She says you are in the doghouse at home

because you haven't written. She also said to tell you that if she didn't have a letter by Wednesday, there would be no food money or allowance mailed. SO...

Good night, Baby. I love you.
Forever and ever
Yours
John

The most poignant of his letters was the one written a week or so before Verna's college graduation. It is a glimpse of the future, and it isn't bright.

May 31, 1949

Verna darling,

You will no doubt be interested in learning that I have visited the doctor again. I swear, I do believe I'm becoming a neurotic. Anyhow, the 'condition' I had in Gainesville persisted all during last week. Diagnosis: Nerves. I told him I wasn't nervous, but he said I was nervous inside, and that I didn't realize it. Isn't that a hell of a note. But his medicine is working, and I am going to take a vacation this summer. I have to take some foul-tasting liquid stuff before I eat, and a shot of B1 every other day. That goes on for another week, then I'm supposed to be as good as new. There is nothing wrong with my heart at all. The nervous condition was making my heart react. I know that sounds sissy as hell, but I also thought you might like to know.

Forever and ever
Your
John

Chapter 37
Hibiscus Strong

The Southern matriarch is a stereotype for a reason. Southern matriarchs are the glue that hold a family together. They pick up the pieces in times of tragedy. They have expectations of how every member of their family is supposed to behave—and God forbid someone doesn't live up to those expectations.

I come from a long line of strong Southern matriarchs, women who kept the family together in good times and bad. They also held down jobs at a time when they were supposed to stay home cooking and cleaning while wearing pearls, a fancy dress, and high heels like June Cleaver in the iconic 1950s TV show *Leave It to Beaver*. No, none of the women in my family did that. They wore their pearls (usually plastic, but the effect was the same) to work.

The ladies in my family weren't going to let anyone tell them what to do or how to do it. I call them Hibiscus Strong, the South Florida version of the Steel Magnolia. Magnolias are fragile flowers, a bland pale white. Hibiscuses come in vibrant colors— orange, yellow, red, hot pink—just like the women in my family. They were, and are, sassy, strong, self-reliant, and with an extra dose of the Florida quirkiness that comes from knowing every time you take your garbage out—whether it is real or metaphorical—you just might encounter an alligator in your backyard.

My Great-Aunt Helen was Hibiscus Strong. Her first marriage only lasted a year, during which she quickly found out what she didn't want in a husband—someone who was going to expect her to be the breadwinner. The second time around she knew what she wanted, and she went out and got it. I'm not saying she didn't love her second husband, Ed Jones. She adored him. She just had learned it would be easier to love a rich man than a poor man and made sure she found a rich one for her second go.

My Aunt Anna Mae Rogers was a more traditional type of matriarch. She never married. Some of her brothers suggested it was because she couldn't have run their lives as effectively as she did if she had a husband. Of course, they never said it to her face. When Anna Mae said, "Jump," her five brothers, her brother-in-law, and all the nieces and nephews asked, "How high?"

Of course, those brothers had been trained by their mother, Mary Rogers, my great-grandmother. Imagine moving to a place that is little more than a collection of huts in a swamp and raising seven children. And while I've never heard that she "worked outside the home," don't tell me raising five boys and two girls wasn't a 24/7 job. And when she first arrived, they didn't even have electricity.

The original Strong Hibiscus had to be my great-grandmother, Mollie Sawieja. She learned strength long before she moved to Florida. She ran her millinery shop in Advance, Missouri. A big-city girl, she was viewed with some suspicion when she arrived in town with three small children in tow, telling everyone her husband would be joining her shortly from St. Louis. It didn't help she was there to claim a piece of property that had long been the source of mysterious rumors. Mollie showing up and chasing off intruders with a shotgun would certainly have put a damper on the locals' favorite pastime—digging for treasure.

Her daughter, my grandmother Agnes, worked throughout the Depression and World War II. That wasn't unique; there was the whole Rosie the Riveter thing at that time. I don't think the ad man who came up with Rosie thought about her not feeling like cooking at the end of the day. Neither did most of their husbands. So the women worked, then came home and cooked and cleaned. Not my grandma. She believed in sharing the burden of housework and in equality of the sexes decades before anyone coined that phrase.

And then there was my mother, Verna, Hibiscus Strong for sure. When life handed Verna lemons, she just made Whiskey Sours. After growing up with Agnes, all Verna wanted was to be the opposite of her mom—of course. She wanted to be a traditional 1950s housewife and mom. She wanted to play bridge two afternoons a week, join the garden club, become president of the PTA, and make dinner every night for the family. But she married my father, and things didn't turn out quite that way.

Chapter 38
Doubts

"I was very much in love with your father when I married him."

That's what my mother said whenever we asked why she and my father had ever gotten married in the first place. But often the truth is a little more complicated.

~~~

1949

"You don't have to get a job this year, you know," Agnes told Verna one morning in early summer. She had just unpacked all her college books, clothes, and other things and was settling back into their home in Miami.

"No, of course I'll go look for a job. Maude already has one at an elementary school," she said.

But somehow the days passed, and there was always so much to do that she didn't find time to go job hunting. Her resumes were ready; she just needed to call and make a few appointments with some high school principals. But she was shy and insecure. What if the principals didn't like her and no one offered her a job? What if she got a job and couldn't teach? How was she going to control a classroom of high school kids when she was only a few years older than they?

None of us are born strong. We are forged by events that often are out of our control. Verna's path from timid college girl to Hibiscus Strong took many years, and it was not a straight road but a winding one. It was easier to try out the role of society debutante; she had Aunt Helen's help, after all.

"I'm going out with John tonight," she called to her mother, hanging up the phone "We're meeting some of his clients and having dinner. We're going to Joe's Stone Crab," she added excitedly.

The restaurant was well-known and expensive. The type of place her Aunt Helen and Uncle Ed went to, but never her mother and father. They were more likely to eat at Wolfie's or Pickin' Chicken.

John picked her up wearing a lightweight summer suit of grey, white shirt, and narrow grey tie. He looked the quintessential successful salesman, and Verna was very proud of him. She was introduced to the three businessmen John was hosting. *All of them were older, in their 30s and 40s*, Verna thought. They were nice, polite, but the conversation revolved around electronics sales, and she was happy to play the quiet fiancée.

"Let's order the pompano, in honor of my hometown," John said after they had had a few drinks.

It was one of the most expensive dishes on the menu. They all laughed, but the other three men declined and chose salmon and trout instead while Verna ordered shrimp.

"Have you ever had pompano?" one of the salesmen asked with a sly smile at the others.

I wonder what that is about, Verna thought. She didn't have long to find out. The pompano arrived, served in traditional fashion, head on and unscaled.

John might have spent many years in Florida, he might often travel to New York City these days, but at heart he was still Johnnie, that boy from Odum, Georgia, just trying to fit in. Verna could see the three salesmen were waiting to see how this young upstart would handle things. They sat back and pretended to enjoy their dinner while covertly watching John with grins on their faces.

He took a deep breath, picked up the sharp knife his waiter had handed him, and proceeded to skin and filet the fish. "My father was a butcher," he grinned at the men. "I did learn a little something from him, and fish is a lot easier to work with than a slab of ribs."

The men laughed with John this time, and they left with promises of orders in the next few months.

"Why did you order something when you didn't know what it was?" Verna asked on the drive home.

"How do y'all know I didn't?" He glanced over at her from the driver's seat, a grin on his face, still high from the success of the night and the alcohol he'd consumed.

"It was pretty obvious when the waiter put that fish in front of you. You should have seen your face."

"But I pulled it off, didn't I?"

"Yes, you did."

But John had been showing off, pretending to be someone much more sophisticated than he was, and it made her uncomfortable.

~~~

When she wasn't with John, she was busy not only planning her own wedding but acting as a bridesmaid for all her friends. Maude and her boyfriend Scott were getting married soon, and Verna would be the maid of honor. Nita had gotten a job in the chemistry laboratory at Eastman-Kodak in Rochester, New York. Her parents had insisted that she and Jay wait until he graduated to get married, and he had received his degree the same semester Verna did. Now Jay had also found a job at Eastman-Kodak. John acted as the best man at their summer wedding while Verna was in charge of the guestbook, an important role in a time when wedding receptions were both simpler and more formal than today. The keeper of the guestbook and the person who cut the cake were always mentioned in the newspaper write-ups.

Verna was active in her sorority alumni group. She was elected recording secretary and helped plan events for the "ladies," as the *Miami Daily News* society reporter referred to them when the bridge parties, afternoon teas, and formal dances were mentioned. She joined the brand-new Dade County alumni club for Florida State University. And between those activities—and the showers and parties for the half dozen friends who were getting married, and the ones her friends were planning for her—she didn't have time for a job. Verna and John were to get married on June 25, 1950.

"We need to push her a little more," Bert told Agnes many times.

"I'm just so happy to have her here, and she doesn't have to get a job right away. I'm just glad to have her home."

"You think not getting a job is going to help her get over John?" Bert asked doubtfully. "I think she needs to get out and meet some more men, see what she is missing."

Yes, both her parents had doubts about John, but what were they going to do? They felt he spent too much money, and Bert, in particular, believed he drank too much. The drinking reminded him of his brother Leo. Agnes just said, "I can tell something isn't right, I just can't put my finger on it." There were too many times his stories didn't add up.

"If we talk too much against him, she's just going to defend him even more," Bert said whenever they talked about it—and Agnes brought it up whenever Verna and John went out on a date.

"What is it with my family?" Agnes asked once again. "Although Helen did get it right the second time."

"See, you were wrong about Ed. You thought he'd be a terrible husband for Helen when she first met him. Maybe we are wrong about John," Bert tried to comfort her.

"But you were right about Ed, and you don't feel good about John," Agnes reminded him.

The logic didn't necessarily make sense, but Bert understood what she was trying to say.

When asked they found out Ed agreed with Bert and Agnes about John, although he admitted the young man did seem to be a smart, savvy salesman. But he just didn't like what he saw in John. He bragged too much and made too many plans.

"But," Ed quietly asked Bert, "where are the results?"

Helen was a different story. She was caught up in helping her only niece plan a brilliant wedding, and so Verna found herself spending a lot more time with her aunt that year. In March Helen hosted a dinner party at her home for "the bride-elect," which was reported in the society pages.

Then Verna made a drastic decision a few weeks before her June wedding. She was going to cut her hair.

"A new hairstyle for a new decade and my new life as a married, working woman," she told Maude when she called and asked her for moral support.

"Are you sure?" questioned Maude. "Your hair is beautiful, and I know John loves it."

"I'm sure about it. I have to go to my job interview at Miami-Jackson High this week, and I want to look professional. This long hairstyle looks like a schoolgirl."

She made an appointment for the next day, and they headed down to the beauty salon. Cliff, who had been trimming her hair for several years, couldn't wait to get his hands on her.

"You're going to look fabulous. I'm giving you the latest style," he said as he started to cut.

An hour or so later, when Cliff spun her around to look at herself, obviously in love with the new look he'd given her, she started to cry.

"I-I've never seen my hair this short. Not since I was a little kid and my mother made me get a Buster Brown haircut," she sobbed.

"Oh, Verna, it looks wonderful," Maude told her. Maude had cut her own hair several months before. "You're going to love how easy it is to take care of."

Cliff felt terrible. "You're just not used to it," he told her, hope in his voice. "I know you'll love it by the time your wedding rolls around."

That night she wore a scarf on her head when John came to the door.

"Darling, let's see. Maude told me you weren't happy, but it's just hair, you know, it will grow." He gently pulled her scarf off and did the only thing a man can do in that situation.

"It looks beautiful. You are beautiful," he said, kissing her.

She always wondered if he really thought that or just had a great deal of tact. It was one of the things she loved about him, though. He always managed to make her feel beautiful. And when he did things like that, she forgot her doubts and just remembered how much she loved him.

Despite all the excitement leading up to the wedding, more and more doubts kept creeping in. Verna kept ignoring them. Mr. and Mrs. Hodges—she always called her in-laws that even after she was married for several years—came to see her a week before the wedding. John had borrowed money from them, they told her, and never paid it back.

"He's done it more than once. We aren't asking y'all for anything. We aren't expecting y'all to pay us back. We just thought it was something you should know before your marriage," Mrs. Hodges said.

Verna was young, naïve, and very much in love—and it was only a week before the wedding. She couldn't change her mind now. She told herself she could change John. She promised herself things would be different. Once they were married and she was with him every day, he would no longer have his "blue" moods. He would be home every night with her so he wouldn't need to drink. She would show him that he was everything she wanted. He'd learn he didn't have to give her fancy things to make her feel special. He was already drinking less. That's what he told her, and she was sure he wouldn't lie.

Their wedding was a mix of everyone involved. John and Helen both wanted everything to be as fashionable as possible while Agnes was practical and frugal, and Verna had her own sense of style. It was held at St. Mary's Church, the most fashionable Catholic church in the county at the time. Meanwhile, Agnes's good friend and next-door neighbor, Thelma Merrell, made Verna a beautiful ivory satin wedding dress with a yoke of nylon and seed pearls, a full skirt, and long sleeves that ended in medieval style points at her wrists. She wore orange blossoms in her hair and carried white orchids.

Her five bridesmaids included her old friend Ann Raywood, from their days of playing jacks outside the betting parlor, as well as Maude, who acted as the matron of honor. Maude wore peacock-blue taffeta and carried pink roses. The bridesmaids wore "Mamie pink" gowns and carried carnations dyed peacock blue. They wore matching elbow-length gloves and picture hats.

John wore a white summer suit with a white tie and white shoes. In 1950 it was considered the only appropriate attire a Southern gentleman could wear to get married. He looked incredibly handsome, if just a little scared.

The groom's mother, Alma, wore a coral-colored dress and cried throughout the ceremony.

"You would think she was burying her son, not seeing him get married," Agnes whispered to Bert.

While backyard receptions were quite fashionable, one thing Agnes was willing to splurge on was a reception at the Miami Shores Country Club because Agnes still did not cook— at least not willingly.

They spent a few nights honeymooning at a hotel on Collins Avenue, then settled down in a little rental house on Miami Beach.

Chapter 39
Forging a Hibiscus

Verna got her first job that September, teaching English and drama at Miami-Jackson High School. They were able to buy her a tiny Ford Anglia to drive, and pretty soon they'd saved money to buy a house in a new subdivision out on 119th Street and N.W. 12th Avenue.

Little things continued to bother Verna, however. Things that just didn't add up. She tried to ignore them. Between the two of them they made a good living, but there never seemed to be any money.

John was charming. He'd do anything for a friend, and he had many of them. If they went out with his buddies or he entertained clients, he always had to be the big man and pay for everything. Verna didn't particularly enjoy these nights. She much preferred when they went out by themselves or with her parents for pizza and then to the Jackson or Edison High football games.

And then in the summer of 1954 their little girl Cheryl Anne was born. She had been expected to quit work while she was pregnant. Being pregnant, even when married, wasn't acceptable for a teacher at that time. Luckily, a sympathetic principal understood that she needed the money and allowed her to finish out the school year.

She had hoped she'd be able to stay home and take care of her baby, but there just wasn't enough money. With an August baby, she was ready to return to school at the beginning of the fall. She dropped Cheryl Anne off with her mom each morning.

John adored his daughter. He was a man of his time, and so, of course, he somehow managed to miss much of the diapering, although he would pitch in and change his little girl if he needed to. Certainly, he'd heard the story of Mary and Herndon, who'd left when asked to diaper baby Milton. If he wanted to stay on the good side of his mother-in-law, Agnes, he knew better than to refuse to diaper his child. John played with the baby, gave her lots of attention, and showed her off proudly to everyone he knew.

Still, Verna had to acknowledge that despite his obvious love for her and the baby, things were getting worse. John was depressed all the time. Late in 1954 he went into the VA hospital to be treated for his depression. When he got out he swore to her, his parents, and his in-laws that he was better. The depression was why he drank and overspent. The medication was helping him. He wouldn't need to drink or spend a lot of money to feel good anymore.

A few months after that Verna was pregnant again. Why is it that couples in trouble always seem to think that another baby will fix everything when things are difficult enough with one? On May 8, 1956, I arrived. And I had health problems. They didn't get me home from the hospital for six weeks.

Agnes and Bert and Verna decided it would be best if her parents moved in to help take care of the babies. But Agnes was a bit afraid to take care of an infant with health issues as well as an active two-year-old. So I was sent to Pompano to live with Grandma and Grandpa Hodges for a couple of months. Of course, I'm too young to remember, but I know I was absolutely showered with affection and attention.

Verna was distraught not seeing me every day. She was working again, and her time was limited. She could only see me once a week, and it was killing her. I was older and healthier by that time—Mama was actually afraid I was getting too fat under the care of my loving grandparents—so they brought me back from Pompano when I was six months old. Somehow they made it work: two small children, two parents, and two grandparents in a three-bedroom, one-bath house.

~~~

"Daddy," Verna said to her father one day after opening the mail. "I was turned down for a credit card at Jordan Marsh. I just don't understand it."

"You're going to have to find out why," he told her.

It was the beginning of the end. Bert knew it, even if his daughter didn't. He started looking for a lawyer.

A month or so after that John came home one afternoon, quite agitated. He owed someone money, and if he didn't pay it by that afternoon, the man was threatening to throw him in jail.

"We have to cash Karen Lee's savings bond," he told Verna.

The fifty-dollar bond, which the Aunts and Uncles had given them when I was born, was only worth $37.50 if cashed early.

"It doesn't make sense to cash it now," Verna argued, but John insisted she go down to the bank with him.

"You don't have to cash this bond," the bank teller told her, obviously sensing that something was wrong. "It's only listed in your name and your child's name. Your husband can't make you cash it."

Verna hesitated. The woman could tell she was upset.

"You really don't have to do this, Mrs. Hodges," she said again. By that time Verna was incredibly embarrassed. Since she couldn't open up a hole in the floor and disappear through it, she just wanted the quickest way out of there. She cashed the bond.

"Do not ever let this happen again," she hissed at John as they left the bank. "If you do I will divorce you."

"Darling, I promise. This is the last time."

He seemed to get better after that. He'd taken her words to heart, he told her. Things seemed to be going so well that Agnes and Bert began to talk about moving back to their own home.

And then came the phone call.

"This is Acme Loan Company. I'd like to know when you are going to start paying back your loan," the man's voice said.

"What loan?" Verna asked with a sinking feeling.

"Come on, Mrs. Hodges, you know what loan. You signed for it. It's a loan for six hundred dollars."

"I'm serious. I don't know what loan you are talking about. I've never signed for any loan with you or anyone else."

The man on the other end of the line also became serious. Maybe he suddenly understood his company was never going to see this money again. He explained there was a piece of paper with her signature on it. She would need to come down to his office and verify that it was not hers.

Bert by this time had found a lawyer, Earl Barber, for his daughter. "He's a very nice man with a daughter about Cheryl's age. They go to St. Rose of Lima."

Bert might have given up on the church a long time before, but his daughter had not. He knew her well enough to realize she was going to be even more of a stickler for church rules than someone who had been raised Catholic. Finding a Catholic lawyer meant the man would understand Verna's doubts about what Bert now saw as inevitable. Mr. Barber investigated and quickly found out that there were four more loans outstanding. John had forged her name on all of them.

"If you don't divorce him, you will always be liable for any loans he takes out," Mr. Barber told her.

He arranged to go with her to see her priest and explain the situation. And somehow, out of that conversation, Verna ended up with a church-sanctioned divorce, not a civil divorce and a church annulment as common a decade or so later. The priest gave her one condition, and she followed it strictly for the rest of her life, even after John had died: She was never allowed to marry again or she would no longer be able to take communion.

If you aren't Catholic this means nothing to you. If you are you will immediately understand how rare the decision to grant a church-sanctioned divorce was. If you aren't Catholic you will not understand how seriously Verna took the ruling to never marry again. Church laws and norms changed in the decades that followed, and church annulments became more easily available and accepted. But my mother never talked to any priest about it.

"This was the condition they put on me for my divorce, and I was just so grateful I got it that I never wanted to question it. Besides, I didn't want to get married to anyone ever again," she often said. She wouldn't trust a man with herself or with her daughters.

~~~

After that things moved quickly. Bert made sure John moved out. He stayed with his parents for a few weeks, then went back into the VA hospital for continued treatment of his so far undiagnosed psychiatric disorder.

Bert was cynical. "You notice," he would say, "that whenever things get bad for John, he goes back into the hospital where no one can touch him."

In those days divorces were only granted "for cause" so a hearing had to be held. Luckily, John did not attend since he was still in the hospital. Verna and her father were the only ones there, and they both testified. The charges were ugly, and the judge quickly granted the divorce.

It was 1958. Verna's marriage had lasted a little less than nine years. She had two children, no credit rating, and a lot of debt. She threw herself into raising two "strong, independent girls who knew how to take care of themselves." That was how she always described it to us. She didn't blame her parents; they had raised her well but always expected her to have a responsible husband—like Bert himself—who would take care of her. You might think that given the family history they would have been a little less short-sighted, but sometimes it is hard to see the big picture when you are standing in the middle of it.

Verna threw herself into becoming the best teacher she could be. She got her master's degree in education from Barry College, which was just down the block, then set about climbing the Dade County School Board ladder. She became a guidance counselor at Miami-Jackson, then moved to Ponce de Leon Junior High as Assistant Principal for Guidance. Her boss there told her that she'd never make principal at the junior-high or high-school level. He wasn't being deliberately unkind, just truthful. The school board only approved women as principals for the elementary schools—and not too many of them either.

So she moved to Miami Park Elementary and then Miami Gardens Elementary as assistant principal. But then she learned the hard truth about politics in the school system. She was never going to be a principal. She just didn't know the right people.

Bert died in 1976, when I was in college, and a few years after that Agnes's vision was so bad she no longer could drive, and we forbade her to ever touch the stove. She couldn't see well enough not to burn herself. She hated not seeing well, but having an excuse to give up cooking was not a burden for her. The Aunts and Uncles were getting older. None of them had children; they all needed Verna's help. She retired from teaching after twenty-five years and opened her own business selling vitamins and nutrition products. It gave her the time to be a caretaker and still work without running herself into the ground.

Each little challenge she overcame or found a way around helped to make her a little stronger. And somewhere along the way, that timid, insecure young girl became Hibiscus Strong.

Chapter 40
The War Within

I heard my father called many things over the years: alcoholic, gambler, liar, bastard. I used a few of those words myself. He was labeled paranoid schizophrenic. But he was also a veteran, and that was something many people tried to ignore.

Over the years I have read a lot about mental illness and PTSD; I had a special interest, after all. Let me emphasize I am a layperson in this field, not an expert. Everything I write here I learned by reading books and articles on the subject.

One way to explain PTSD in as simple a way possible is that when our bodies are subjected to stress, we experience a "fight or flight" response. This is a chemical response to help us cope. If that reaction is needed for a long period of time, however, it can affect the body for months or years afterward.

For the soldiers coming home from war in the late 1940s, PTSD—or "Combat Stress Reaction," as it was called at the time—was not well known. It was talked about as "Battle Fatigue" or "Shell Shock" in World War I. But because of the national euphoria created by our victory in the war, the fact that some soldiers came home with wounds that could not be seen and could not be healed became almost a dirty little secret after the Second World War.

An article on post-traumatic stress disorder published by the National World War II Museum describes it this way:

There's an old saying in the army: 'Stay Alert, Stay Alive!'

Wise words indeed. But how long can a soldier remain in a constant state of alertness before damage is caused to their mental state? How long before this damage becomes permanent?

It's difficult to say because the results of long-term exposure to combat varies among individuals.

During World War II, it was determined by the US Army that the breaking point for a soldier on the front line was somewhere between 60 and 240 days, depending on the intensity and frequency of combat.

It is not surprising that people at the U.S. War Department

in World War II and earlier believed Combat Stress Reaction affected only those who were mentally weak or had a preexisting mental condition. This was the prevailing attitude toward mental illness by almost everyone at the time. People were expected "to just get over it" if they were depressed or had other symptoms of mental illness. The War Department tested young men and rejected them if they had a perceived "weak constitution or mental deficiency." General George Patton famously did not believe Combat Stress Reaction was real. He thought soldiers who suffered from it were just weak or cowardly.

It took the Guadalcanal campaign in 1943 to begin to change military medical personnel's views of Combat Stress Reaction. It took a lot longer for the rest of the military, and the rest of the public, to begin to understand. The horrific battle at Guadalcanal lasted over five months. Within a few years more than 500 Marines who had fought there started to suffer significant psychiatric problems, including tremors, sensitivity to loud noises, and periods of amnesia.

Along with the more obvious symptoms of anger, rage, or depression, another symptom of PTSD is an unwillingness to talk about it. It is not uncommon to hear someone who had a parent in the military—no matter what war—say that their father or mother would never talk about their experiences. Ironically, the one thing that might help alleviate some of the stress is the one thing a person suffering from PTSD least wants to do.

My father was typical of the men of his generation; he was proud of his service but wouldn't talk about it—particularly not with his daughters. And I was always cautioned never to believe anything he said without making sure it was true. I still have a fourteen-page letter he wrote to a friend of the family, Miss Elizabeth, his Aunt Neta's sister-in-law, a spinster schoolteacher who shared the burden of caring for Aunt Neta with my grandmother after Neta's husband died. She was always close to my grandmother. He wrote the letter on January 30, 1945, from "somewhere in Belgium," as he headed it. The letter has the careful cut marks of the censors so that the dates and some exact locations could not give anything away to the enemy if a bag of mail went astray. The back of several of the pages are scribbled with additional messages from family members in the States. Paper was rationed, and the precious letter was obviously passed around until it came to my grandmother, who kept it as a treasured memento.

The letter tells John's personal experiences of the war from the time he registered for the draft at age twenty-one in February 1942 to receiving a letter that *"my friends and neighbors had selected me to represent them at the induction station at Camp Blanding"* on July 6, 1942.

At some time in 1944, John, who had been assigned to the XVIII Air Corp, was in England training as a gliderist, who were *"the boys who, in an airborne operation, ride behind enemy lines and land. We get a 50% increase in base pay, and wear all the airborne paraphernalia, plus paratrooper boots, and think we are 'hot stuff.'"*

He must have known his mother would eventually read the letter because, while he talks with a young man's enthusiasm about his cool uniform, he doesn't mention that the motorless gliders were towed into the air by another aircraft, then cut loose to sail to the ground silently. Extraction was only possible if an aircraft was able to fly over the landing area, "snag" the glider, and tow it back to safety. Being sent on a mission meant there was a good chance you weren't coming home.

"Things were going along very peacefully" in England, he continued in the letter that gives wonderful descriptions of the English countryside and tourist excursions to London. *"Until the breakthrough came, when as you have probably read in the paper, the part of us in England with our units there plus what we had on the continent were flown in and here, as the papers say, we stopped the German drive. We are very proud of ourselves, even prouder and boast more than the airborne has ever done before."*

The "breakthrough" was the beginning of the Battle of the Bulge on December 17, 1944. The five-week battle was one of the most significant of World War II and the deadliest with 19,000 Americans killed and 75,000 total casualties. It had only officially been over for five days when he wrote the letter.

From where we landed in France, five of us came on to

the front in a jeep. We stayed overnight near Namur, Belgium, in a 200-room chateau that belongs to a Belgian Baron. It was somewhat damaged but enough remained to show us it must have been magnificent at one time. (This was probably Chateau Miranda in the Namur area of Belgium.) *The next day we came on to the front, several miles behind where we are now. I can say I passed through Liege.*

The first few days were very exciting. No one knew where anyone was, and everyone was tense, what with German troopers landing behind the lines, buzz bombs, etc. I am fast approaching censorable ground, if I haven't already trespassed, and had better stop. The weather here is something. I wouldn't attempt to say how much snow is on the ground, and it snows more almost every day. You can imagine how I like that after so many years in South Florida.

One question everyone seems to be curious about is whether or not a person gets scared up here. I have had several bad minutes and I think everyone has them sooner or later.

Miss Elizabeth, I have written far more than I should have but I think I know you well enough to know you will be interested in it all. At least I hope so, anyhow.

So long for now.
The same except a little older and wiser,
Johnnie

~~~

At the same time the army psychologists began to record the problems with the soldiers from Guadalcanal, they also noted a soldier's readiness for battle diminished after thirty days in combat. After forty-five days they "were in a near vegetative state." During World War II more than half a million men suffered "some sort of psychiatric collapse due to combat," according to the National World War II Museum article.

When my father wrote that letter, he was twenty-three and had spent over a month in continuous combat. There is only one other thing I know about his war experiences. He was in a jeep accident that resulted in scar tissue on his brain. He fought for years to have his disability declared "service related." In 1968, twenty-four years after his service and fifteen years before his death, it was finally designated "a hundred percent service related." Would he have been diagnosed with PTSD if he had been in a later conflict? How would his life had been different if it had been recognized and treated sooner?

Because PTSD was not recognized as a psychological disorder during World War II or for quite some time after it, experts have found it difficult to estimate just how many soldiers suffered from it. A study of hospital records from the time shows that about forty-three out of every one hundred soldiers were hospitalized for psychological trauma. But how many more did not ask for help? The way in which we still stigmatize emotional disorders makes it easy to believe the true number was much higher. And those who did not seek help were even more likely to continue to suffer.

The disorder does not just affect soldiers but anyone who has experienced a trauma, including children. There is no "cure" for PTSD. However, symptoms can be treated by psychotherapy and medication. Luckily, treatments have come a long way from my father's time.

~~~

The last time I saw my father was at my grandmother's funeral in 1972. I was fifteen. Without his mother's steadying influence, he soon left Odum. In true dramatic Southern fashion, he took a good portion of the family china and silver with him. This was, of course, the china and silver Grandma Hodges had "left" to us back when my sister and I were five and seven years old.

He wandered around the country for several years. We would occasionally get a phone call from him, sometimes on holidays or our birthdays. He had an uncanny knack of calling when something important was happening he could have no way of knowing, like my sister's engagement party or the day of my high school graduation. As we got older we also got calls from creditors to whom he had given my sister's or my name. He became kind of a boogie man in our lives. We never knew when he would pop up and scare us again.

The last year or two of his life he settled down at a VA hospital in South Dakota. I think he finally found some peace.

Still a good salesman, the last year of his life he received an award from the American Legion for signing up the most new members in his area. He was very proud of it. He told us about it during a phone call.

He died at the VA hospital in South Dakota in 1983 and is buried in a military cemetery there. He was only fifty-seven.

Chapter 41
The Ecuadorean Emerald

2022

"Here you go, Mia," my sister, Cheryl, said to her youngest grandchild after handing her a gaudy green brooch. "You can have this one."

"No!" I snatched it out of her hand. "Not that one!"

We were gathered in my mother's bedroom, all of us females in the family from my sister Cheryl, the oldest, to her daughter Catheryn, to her three of her granddaughters—ages nine, seven, and five. In a family where most of us don't have the same interests, we were all solidified in that moment by a mutual love: jewelry.

"Mamaw's" jewelry was legendary in the family. And now that she had died, it was time to decide who got what.

This was not a covetous meeting. It wasn't a scene from a soap opera where the family members haggle and fight. Most of Mama's five drawers of jewelry—yes, count 'em, five—were the typical beads and baubles that one buys at Macy's to go with a particular outfit. Each of us had a special interest in claiming one or the other for sentimental reasons. My sister wanted to keep the mother of pearl earrings she had given Mama one Christmas. I wanted to make sure I got the little silver bracelet with roses that reminded me of a special day Mama and I had spent at the Coconut Grove art festival when I was in high school. Catheryn wanted the purple and white beads her Mamaw had lent her a few times because she loves purple.

But then there was the "good stuff." The family pieces. The jewelry my mother saved to wear on special occasions, and sometimes let us borrow. Of course, my mother had never separated out the "good stuff" from the costume jewelry. It was all mixed together: rings, necklaces, earrings, bracelets, brooches, in a hoard worthy of a dragon. Periodically she would lose a piece, and everyone would have to scramble through the collection to find it for her.

"I'm missing my brooch, you know the one Aunt Stella gave me," she would say. Or "I can't find my mother's ring. The one she gave me when I was sixteen." And when we questioned how we were supposed to remember which ring was from her mother, or which of her many brooches had been given to her by an aunt only two of us were old enough to have met, her reply was always, "Well, I've shown it to you before. You should remember it." She would then describe it in more detail, and we would search the drawers until we found it.

On this day, the day before my mother's funeral, we had been going through the hoard quite equitably for a couple of hours. The three little girls each held a plastic grocery bag and had been allowed to have all the junk jewelry their hearts desired, so when I suddenly snatched a particularly large and gaudy brooch from the hands of a five-year-old, everyone in the room stopped and stared at me.

"Not that one," I repeated. "Mama told me it might be worth money."

"I never remember seeing it before," Cheryl said.

"Neither do I," added Catheryn.

The brooch was a dull green square, about an inch in size, bearing a carved head. Its setting consisted of a sort of double pagoda arrangement, one on the top and one on the bottom, made of bright red and clear stones. The brooch wasn't graceful or beautiful. The carved green square was had no shine or shimmer; it looked rather lifeless to me, and the whole setting was just awkward and well, unattractive.

"Mama said it belonged to Pauline," I told them.

My sister nodded. "Oh."

The girls looked at me questioningly.

Pauline had been one of my mother's vast collection of people. You see, my mother loved people. And she collected friends as easily as she collected jewelry. Yes, she had been shy when she was younger but had become a schoolteacher, a single mother, a businesswoman. She was Hibiscus Strong. The Mama I remember most never met a stranger. When she went to a restaurant, she asked the server's name, their background, how many children they had. And she genuinely listened to the answers. Even when she was in the hospital, if someone came in the room, she would learn about them. When an orderly came to take her away for a test, she would return and tell me, "That's Raul. He came here from Paraguay five years ago to live with his aunt. He's studying at the community college right now to become a nurse." And what was always even more astonishing to me was that when that person came back to her room two days later, my mother, at age ninety-four, would remember him and ask about his family and how his classes were going.

I never understood it. By nature I don't strike up conversations easily with strangers, despite my original career as a newspaper reporter. Mama's propensity to talk to everyone embarrassed me from the time I was a child until the day she died.

Cashiers and waitresses were just the tip of her friend bucket. She had met Marjory Stoneman Douglas, the "Guardian of the Everglades," who is unfortunately now more famous for the 2018 mass shooting that occurred at the high school named in her honor than as a pioneering conservationist. She knew Janet Reno, another Miamian, who became famous as President Bill Clinton's attorney general. When she became a grandmother, she took me and my son down to meet one of her old high school teachers, who she had kept in touch with for forty years. She was still good friends with several of her former students.

Then there was her collection of people she decided to take on as a crusade. This included Cosmo, a lovely Jamaican man in his nineties who walked to Mass every morning. My mother, who was only in her eighties at the time and was still driving (much to her children's horror), stopped and offered him a ride home. Eventually, she would come to pick him up and drop him off at daily Mass, and she learned all about his family, his life in Jamaica, and why he had moved to the States. She was invited to his 100th birthday party and he and his daughter attended her 90th. Her collection also included Maria, who had issues with depression. I don't know how they met, but somehow my mother offered her a job and ended up babysitting her son whenever the woman couldn't handle life.

And then there was Pauline. She had lived in the Shores Condominiums, where Mama had moved when she decided she no longer wanted to live by herself in a four-bedroom house with a large yard.

Pauline's husband was dead, and she had no children. She and Mama bonded over their mutual love of the theatre and often went to see plays together. When Pauline developed cancer, it was my mother she turned to. Pauline gave Mama her medical power of attorney and made her executor of her will. Pauline had money, and most of her estate went to charity. My mother took care of everything and made sure that her wishes were carried out, and as a gift before she died, Pauline gave Mama this incredibly ugly brooch and told it was "worth something."

Mama never wore it. It was just mixed in with the other pieces in the jumbled hoard. I would never have looked twice at it, but when we moved Mama in with me, and I helped her straighten out her drawers, she told me about the brooch.

"Now don't just going throwing this one away, it might be worth something," she said, explaining who had given it to her. It was so distinctively ugly it couldn't be forgotten.

And now here it was. What were we going to do with it? And what were we going to do with all the other maybe good, maybe junk baubles, bangles, and beads?

"I'm getting everything we think might be good appraised," I told my sister. "We've been sitting around with this stuff for decades, never knowing whether or not it is worth anything. And a lot of it no one wants."

My sister agreed. We bagged up about a dozen pieces for me to take to a jeweler, including the "dinner ring" my mother had had made from her wedding and engagement rings. It was bad luck, Cheryl and I had decided long ago. We didn't want it, and we didn't want anyone in the family to take a chance on "catching" that bad luck from the ring.

~~~

A few weeks later I sat in a jeweler's back room and pulled each piece, one at a time, out of a canvas tote. The large "gold" cross my mother had loved turned out to be worthless while the opal ring and the 1950s pearl necklace were deemed "pretty good." There were several diamond rings—which sounds extraordinary until you consider that they were engagement rings or wedding bands that had been passed to my mother, basically the last surviving female, from her mother and her grandmothers as well as the Aunts. These, the appraiser Rebecca told me, varied from "really nice old cut diamonds" to cubic zirconia, or in other words, a fancy piece of glass.

When I came to the brooch, I was rather apologetic. "This may be junk," I said. "But my mother always said it was worth something. What do you think?"

Rebecca took the piece carefully. "I love it!" she exclaimed as she placed it under her microscope. "It's very unusual."

After a few moments her excitement grew.

"This is a carved emerald. It's a Medusa head. It's very interesting. The setting is odd, though. It's awkward. Obviously, this stone was set in something else before it was put in this. Even though this setting is old, I think the emerald is much older."

"Oh." I nodded stupidly.

"These are small diamond and ruby chips," she continued to explain, pointing to the two "pagodas" on the top and bottom of the brooch. "They aren't particularly valuable. But this…" She paused and placed it under the microscope again. "I just don't know. I don't have enough expertise for these. I need to send it to the man I send all my emeralds to."

I was laughing by this time, enamored by the phrase "the man I send all my emeralds to." Every woman should have an "emerald man" in their list of contacts!

"This may be an Ecuadoran emerald, which would be nice. But it may be a Colombian emerald and then …well, then it's a seven or eight on scale of ten."

Rebecca suggested I pay to have it insured and sent to her "emerald man," and I agreed. It wasn't going to cost that much, and by this time I was intrigued and wanted to know as much as I could about the ugly brooch.

It took several weeks to hear back, and the suspense was killing me by the time Rebecca called. We went over all the pieces the family had decided to sell, and finally she came to the emerald brooch. "Well, the carving on the emerald is finer than the stone itself," she told me. "That's to be expected. The best stones have always been kept for faceting."

The final verdict was that the emerald was from Ecuador, not Colombia, and was "good but not great." She had decided she would take it out of its setting and redesign it to make it more saleable. She offered me five hundred dollars. I said yes. The whole point of taking the jewelry to Rebecca had been to make some money from the items no one in the family wanted.

But there are still so many questions. How old was the gem? How had Pauline come by it? Had it really been in another setting before it had been turned into an ugly brooch? The carving was a Medusa head. I can imagine all sorts of fascinating tales about the emerald. A cursed object, stolen from a famous necklace, set in the brooch to disguise its origins....

~~~

All families have stories they tell at every gathering, from Sunday dinners to funerals to afternoon picnics. I've only told a few of my family stories here. There is still the story of the Chupacabra Hunt, and the story of a little girl sitting on a concrete stoop with all her possessions in grocery bags around her. But these tales are not mine to tell. They will have to wait for their owners to decide if they will be shared.

But the Ecuadorian Emerald is right now a mystery. Maybe that is the next story I need to tell. I'll have to start my research.

Afterthoughts
Facts and Fiction

Someone asked me recently when I decided to write *Hibiscus Strong,* and I replied without really thinking about it, "when I was eight years old." As I heard what I had just said, I realized it was true. It will sound strange to people who are not writers, I suppose. I had just finished *Little Women,* and the character of Jo was my hero. "When I grow up, I'm going to be a writer like Louisa May Alcott," I said to myself and even wrote it in my diary.

I didn't know what that meant; I didn't know what "becoming a writer" would look like. Maybe it was one more of my impulsive decisions like making up my mind to be the editor of the high school creative writing magazine or choosing a college. I do know it has looked nothing like my eight-year-old self imagined it might. All I thought at the time was that at some point I wanted to write a book about my family.

I started writing these stories decades ago. The first one was actually "The Funeral," which I did as an assignment for a Radio and TV class in high school. It was actually performed as a radio play by the class. A version of "The Hurricane" was written for a college course. I worked on a few others here and there throughout the years whenever I felt inspired. I didn't get serious about the stories until the members of my writers' group challenged me to quit playing it safe and write something new and different, something that would require me to be vulnerable, to use my senses and my emotions.

This book is a blend of fact and fiction. I've tried to make it as truthful as possible, both in what I know of the characters and motivations of the people in the stories as well as the stories I tell. Obviously, I wasn't present to tell you exactly what each character said and thought. I know a lot of details about some of the incidents; for others I started with only the basic facts. Sometimes I needed to create a minor character or give a fictional name to a real person to make the stories work. I began to research the people and the places that I was writing about to make the stories as authentic as possible.

Thank goodness I come from a family of sentimental hoarders. I have boxes of old photographs and documents that date back more than a hundred years just stuffed into various closets around my home. That was where I began my search. These items included a list my mother made of the addresses of all the houses the Sawieja family lived in. I've backed that up with information from City Directories; Verna had a very good memory. There were photos taken in front of some of the homes, and I used Google Maps to try and look at others. Some are still there.

The coral rock house on 24th Avenue is still standing; the only differences are the awnings have been removed and it has been whitewashed. The house at S.W. 13 Avenue where they weathered the Hurricane of 1926 is now a vacant lot, but there are several original homes in the neighborhood that give a good idea of what it would have looked like.

I googled "betting parlors in Miami in the 1930s" and came up with three or four names for "An Afternoon at the Races." Although I can't be sure which parlor my grandmother and her friend frequented, The Turf Club on N.W. 70th Street seemed like the best bet because it was the closest one to their home at the time. Of course, there were probably a few dozen other parlors around whose names have been forgotten.

I do know the address of Uncle Ed's house on Palm Island, although they had moved to Bal Harbour by the time I can remember visiting them. I looked up the home on Zillow and was amazed that I could see several photos of the interior. Whoever lives there now has a feeling for the history of the home. Unlike so many buildings in South Florida, it has been carefully preserved. The beautiful wood beamed ceilings are still there along with many other original Spanish Colonial architectural features.

I'm sorry to say history hasn't been so kind to Al Capone's home, which was just down the block from my aunt and uncle's place. The 100-year-old Mediterranean-style villa where Capone died in 1947 was razed on August 27, 2023. The home and guesthouse had nine bedrooms, and at one time the swimming pool was the largest in the city. Capone supposedly planned the St. Valentine's Day Massacre there. The current owners fought for the permit to demolish it for several years and were able to get it when the Republican state administration enacted a law stripping municipalities of their ability to prevent the demolition of historic properties. They began the destruction within weeks of the bill being passed.

As far as what else is real and what is not, I'll give you a little background on some of the minor characters who are mentioned in the book and what happened to them. Clarise, Johnnie's friend in "Johnnie and the Holy Rollers," was his very real next-door neighbor. I met her many years later when the family moved back to Odum, Georgia. I called her "Miss Clarise," of course, and still had a hard time not adding that "Miss" in front of her name even while writing about her as a child. It's a Southern thing. I did create their other friend, "Tommy," because I needed another character to give Johnnie and Clarise just enough information about the church to pique their curiosity.

In "Wedding Day," the story about Alma and J.W. Hodges' wedding, I cannot remember the name of the man my grandmother told me she wanted to marry. I was only eleven years old, after all. But the rest of the story of the wedding, my grandmother's first meeting with her sister-in-law Florrie Hodges, and, of course, their confrontation at Grandpa Hodges' funeral is as true as I could make it. I still have a picture of myself in that awful white and blue dress I wore to Grandpa's funeral.

I could not find a date for the marriage of Uncle Wright and Aunt Esther Hodges, the Carpetbagger's Granddaughter, despite doing quite a bit of research on Ancestry.com. Again, the dates may be off, but the story is how it was told to me many times by several family members including Aunt Esther. Hodges Hardware, which Uncle Jimps owned, was a fixture in Jesup, Georgia, for many years. You can find a few photos and references to it on the internet. I'm not sure exactly when he opened it or if he purchased it from someone or was the first owner.

The story of the Miami Christmas fire is well-documented, including by my great-grandfather Herbert Rogers. He was interviewed about his life in the *Miami Herald* in 1934. My family, of course, kept several clippings. I used many of his own words and descriptions in the story. In the article he talks about his conductor, Ed Steinhauser, and mentions their staying at Captain Vail's Floating Hotel. He tells about waking up, seeing the fire, and the alerting the captain. In the article he describes Captain Vail as having "a heart bigger than that Royal Palm Hotel." I borrowed this phrase for my story, along with his very specific and rather unflattering first impressions of "The Magic City." Ed Davies, another railroad worker who in my story Herbert talks to during the fire, is also mentioned in the newspaper article. The article states that Davies and his family lost their home in the conflagration.

Herbert did not mention, or the reporter did not write about it if he did, his "going backward" on the Seven Mile Bridge during a hurricane. Either he knew how fantastic it sounded and kept the story for family ears only, or the reporter (it was not a byline article) decided it just didn't sound credible. And by the way, Herbert's train was the last one to arrive back at the Miami station from Key West ahead of the Hurricane of 1932, the storm in which the Seven Mile Bridge was destroyed.

Along with the many papers and photographs my mother saved, she had the foresight to sit down and tape her mother and aunt discussing their childhood memories of Missouri and Florida. The cassettes contained a treasure trove of information for me. Listening to my grandmother's voice after more than thirty years was a priceless gift. Her accent was much more "Southern" than I ever noticed before. I guess we all sounded that way at the time.

Agnes and Helen talked about their memories of moving to Advance (don't forget, it's pronounced ADD-vance), staying in a tent, and the treasure hunters who kept digging holes on the property. Their mother, Mollie, really did chase some people away with a shotgun. My grandmother's clearest memory of that time was touching the canvas tent in the rain when she had specifically been told not to touch it.

Again, the story of the Sawieja family's move to Miami

is as true as I could make it. Agnes and Helen discussed it on those tapes. Their father did have a camera—quite a luxury at the time, I would imagine—and there are some rather fuzzy photos from the journey. They had no memory of the name of the man who drove them from East St. Louis down to Miami. To the two young girls he was obviously not important so I used a fictional name. And I'm not sure exactly when Agnes met Bert. I know it was quite soon after they moved to Miami; I just thought it was a nice way to tie things together for them to meet at the station when she arrived.

The story of Agnes and Bert's family elopement is one they loved to tell. I heard it so often as a child it almost wrote itself. The website for Gesu Catholic Church did supply me with the names of all the pastors for the parish and the years they had served. So Father McLaughlin would have been the priest who refused to marry them without a Baptismal certificate.

Then there is the Hurricane of 1926. The more I researched it, the more fascinated I became. The Hurricane of 1932, which took down the Overseas Highway, is the storm I have always heard the most about, but this one may have been even more horrific. And yes, my grandfather and great-grandfather went out in the eye of the storm to check on Helen. On the tapes Helen mentions Bert cutting his arm.

Richard Gray really was the head of the weather service in Miami, and he is the person who finally put out the hurricane warning. His detailed report of the storm can be found on the National Weather Service website.

My family's love of saving things came into play again in the story of Aunt Helen's wedding. She did not save nearly as many photos as Agnes and Verna, and many had to be thrown away because they had mildewed. But she did keep the little wedding program, which had a place for guests to sign their names in the back. And once again I fell down a research black hole. I used Newspapers.com to look up all the people who signed their names. There was quite a lot about Saul Cohen and his wife and the murder trial. The murder occurred on Halloween night 1931 while the Cohens were hosting a bridge game at their home. Sigmund L. Baar, the president of the Seaboard Soap

Company and the Miami Manufacturers Association, was shot and killed as he apparently ran out to assist his wife when two people attempted to steal her car. The story was quite confusing, to say the least, and a coroner's trial came to no conclusion as to who committed the murders.

I found little information about Ila Lovelady other than society notes, the same for Fleetwood Stoltz, the best man who had a hotel named for him. The Fleetwood Hotel is a long-forgotten resort that must have been quite elegant in its day.

The story of the family picnic in which Sigmund, Leon, and Mary Lou died was very difficult for me to write. In it, I wrote about Milt Sosin, the newspaper reporter who filed the article about the drowning. But there were a few other minor characters who fascinated me.

Private Hubert Broughton was just twenty-one when the incident occurred, but he had already lived a fascinating life. When he was only age fifteen, he received a Boy Scout award for saving someone from drowning in Guantanamo Bay in Cuba. (Imagine being able to have a Boy Scout camping weekend to Cuba!) He graduated from Miami High School in 1943 and almost immediately enlisted in the army. He was captured by the Nazis and held prisoner for nine months. He had just been released for a little over a month when he attempted the rescue of my family on Matecumbe Key. He was with Barbara Jane Grosse, her brother Dixon, and a friend, Betty Rose Hall. Hubert married Barbara the next year in a garden ceremony on Christmas Eve, soon after she received a Bachelor's degree from Colorado State University. Her brother Dixon and friend Betty seem to have lived much quieter lives; I found very little about them.

In the story of John and Verna's first date I talk a lot about Nita Nord and Jay Little. Mr. Little's name was John, and my father referred to him as "John" in his letters. It was too confusing to have two of the four characters in the story with the same name so I shortened it to "Jay."

I remember meeting some of the Nord family as a child, and though I remember the names Nita and John, I don't think I actually met that part of the family because they were living in Rochester, New York, at that time. Nita retired from her chemistry job at Eastman-Kodak when they started a family. Later in life she moved back to Vero Beach, and at some point she and John divorced.

My mother's lawyer, Earl Barber, was a real person. My sister and his daughter were in the same class at St. Rose of Lima. My mother thought he was wonderful because he got her out of her marriage with as few financial consequences as possible, and she used him as her lawyer until he retired.

~~~

I also need to talk a little about the photos I've referred to in this book, along with the photo on the cover and some that I have used on my website, www.HibiscusStrong.com. My grandmother had about a dozen photos of herself and her sister Helen in the 1923 beauty pageant. They were both proud of them—with the exception of the photo of Agnes with the fishing fork. For some reason that photo, the most beautiful of them all, embarrassed her.

Neither Agnes or Helen remembered exactly when they received the photos, or where they had come from. The family tried for many years to find out more about them. In high school I went to the downtown branch of the Miami Public Library to search old microfiche versions of the *Miami Herald,* the *Miami Daily News,* and *The Miami Metropolis*, but found nothing. I continued to search off and on for the photos as more and more information became available on the internet. But it wasn't until I asked Lori Hager, my wonderful copyright expert, to help me out that I finally found the information I was looking for. Lori's intern, Serafima Morrow, finally found one of the photos from the pageant on the State Library and Archives of Florida website at https://www.floridamemory.com/.

The photo there is credited to William Arthur Fishbaugh, a well-known photographer who lived in Tampa and Miami in the first half of the 20th century. While he preferred to take architectural photos, saying that buildings didn't move or complain, he apparently supplemented his income taking photos for the local newspapers. His wonderful photos of the 1923 beauty pageant evoke the hope, the excess, and the new freedom many women were gaining in those years.

Acknowledgments

First, I thank my writers' group, Janice Detrie, Sherrie A. Lynn, and Wendy Wyatt. They were the ones who told me to get out of my writing comfort zone, use my senses, and try something new. It turned out the something new was something old, a project I'd had in my heart and head for many years. Without them, I never would have gotten back to writing *Hibiscus Strong*.

Thanks to all my developmental editors and beta readers, Andrea Robinson, Jacquelyn Pillsbury, Noelle Stary, Nicole Loughan, Steve Procko and, of course, my "babies" Catheryn Levine, and Paul Miller. Each of you gave me great advice.

I also thank Steve for his help with photos, as well as for our long discussions on Florida history. My friend and copyright expert, attorney Lori Hager, along with her intern Seraphima Morrow, helped me immensely by finally locating the name of the photographer who took the 1922 beauty pageant photos. My family had been searching for decades for information on those photos with no results. Ed Taylor turned the cassette tapes of my grandmother and aunt into computer versions I could listen to. Without his help, I wouldn't have known about several of the stories of their life in Missouri.

And, of course, thanks to my husband, Sam Miller, for listening to me talk, worry, and overanalyze each chapter as well as for patiently scanning and improving the many, many family photos that we have.

Here are some great resources I used in doing research on old Miami:

- Jane Feehan of Jane's History Nook
  https://janeshistorynook.blogspot.com/
- The Florida Archives
  https://dos.fl.gov/library-archives/archives/
- Miami History Blog
  https://miami-history.com/
- Newspapers.com for articles from the *Miami Herald*, *Miami News*, and *The Miami Metropolis*
- Ancestry.com for details and confirmation on historical as well as family members and family friends

About the Author

"I've spent half my life in the tropics, and the other half trying to get back there," says Karen Hodges Miller, a proud third-generation Miamian. She planned to only leave Miami long enough to see snow so chose Duquesne University in Pittsburgh, PA, for her college education. What was supposed to be a quick four years away from Miami turned out to be a lifetime of living around the country in several states and in Puerto Rico. Family brought her to the Raleigh, NC, area, where she currently lives with her husband, Sam, her two cats, Felix and Olive, and is very close to her son and daughter-in-law.

In addition to writing her own fiction and nonfiction, Karen is a publishing consultant who helps authors navigate the world of self-publishing. While *Hibiscus Strong* is her seventh book, it is her first about Miami's history. You can find more information about her at HibiscusStrong.com where you will also find a kit for book clubs, complete with recipes, questions, and more.

HibsicusStrong.com

and on LinkedIn, Instagram, and

OpenDoorPublications.com

Facebook.

www.ingramcontent.com/pod-product-compliance
Lightning Source LLC
Chambersburg PA
CBHW070812180626
46818CB00001B/222